LYRIA

ROBERT NORTHAM

World Castle Publishing, LLC
Pensacola, Florida
Copyright © Robert Northam 2020
Paperback ISBN: 9781953271389
eBook ISBN: 9781953271396
First Edition World Castle Publishing, LLC, December 7, 2020
http://www.worldcastlepublishing.com
Licensing Notes
Cover: Karen Fuller
Editor: Maxine Bringenberg

CHAPTER ONE

She would only remember the darkness.

She was surrounded by brightness, so stark it hurt her eyes. Her memory of the meeting was sketchy, the usual greetings to start. But she knew something was amiss right away. Was it his tone? No, it was his eyes — she could always tell from the eyes. She remembered that the brightness in the room had become apparent as soon as she saw his eyes. It was an antiseptic environment, this room. But she was thinking, couldn't they change the color? Do something to make it less bleak? She was surrounded by shiny, clean equipment and a small counter with a bunch of bandages, gauze, and stuff. And one of those chairs that would tilt back and rise and fall upon command. It was covered by clean, sterile paper. The room was probably used a hundred times a day. Was she the only one bothered by the brightness?

He started speaking, but she didn't need to listen. She knew what he was going to say. At first, he directed his comments to him. Did he know she wouldn't hear him? She would catch certain words or phrases. "...acute." "...affects mature and immature cells." "...repeat the CBC, just to be sure."

She heard someone wailing, then realized it was her. Both men looked at her. The first man stopped talking, the second man wrapped his arm around her. She became aware that the first man was wearing a white coat. Really, that didn't help with how coldly impersonal the meeting felt. White coat started speaking again, though the wailing continued, and she could barely hear him. Did it really matter?

She looked up and realized the other man had tears running down his face, but he was trying his best to remain rational. Suddenly, she hated him with all her heart. She pushed his arm away, but he didn't look at her. He just continued with his calm-sounding rational questions. She thought she knew him, but how could he be such a heartless bastard?

"Assuming the blood count still shows the high level of white cells, we'd like to do another test just to confirm," said white coat. She thought she knew his name but couldn't come up with it or didn't care enough to try.

"Like what kind of test?" asked the father of her child.

White coat hesitated, looking at her.

She couldn't make out his features, squinting through the brightness of the room and her cascade of tears. She heard herself say, "Go ahead. Tell us, you son-of-a-bitch."

If her retort bothered him, he didn't show it. At least not that she could see through her blurry vision.

He cleared his throat. "Well, we'd like to do a needle biopsy and aspiration of marrow from a pelvic bone. We'll be looking for abnormal cells, DNA markers, and chromosome changes in the bone marrow."

There was a moment when nobody moved. It seemed nobody was even breathing. She didn't look at the other man. Her attention, her fury, was honed in on this apparition in white.

"A needle? A biopsy? Fr...from his hip bone?" she stammered.

Before she could stop herself, she projected herself at the white coat, swearing, screaming, swinging fists at his face. The other man tried to stop her, but she turned on him as well. Her last memory was the two of them holding her down on the floor, with her looking up into the sterile white lights. She felt a pinch on her arm and realized that white coat had just injected something into her. She remembered saying, "You fucking bastard." Then the brightness turned to dark.

She would only remember the darkness.

CHAPTER TWO

"Who puts this crap together?" asked Boof Parsons. "'What does your typical Saturday night look like?' Shit, if it was any good, do they think I'd be on here?"

Don't ask me how it happened, but I found myself in the truly unenviable position of "staying after school" to help Boof fill out his questionnaire on a dating site. Now, when I say "school," I really mean work. It was after hours on a Friday night, and I had a non-work-related reason to want to stay. More on that later.

Conner David here. Boston resident, rich kid, financial analyst, and wooer of the undead. Boof and I both work at Beacon Hill Associates, a cleverly named firm located...well, on Beacon Hill. BHA is an investment banking firm, and I know that sounds impressive, but the employees — or *associates,* as we've come to be known — range from money-grubbing genius quintillionaires to calculator-tapping analytical peons working their lives away, trying to make sure the former group never has to layoff their domestic help. In case you haven't guessed, Boof and I are firmly implanted in the latter group. Our main goal in life is to evaluate business entities, mostly companies, to recommend to our superiors and determine whether any would be a good candidate to be bought out or otherwise ravaged financially. If that seems like a cold-hearted way to make a living, it is, but, as the saying goes, it beats a kick in the pants.

I had finished my work a while ago but needed to find an excuse to hang around. Considering what I ended up doing to kill the time, you know it must have been important.

My compadres and I work in what is commonly referred to as a "cube farm." The nickname speaks to the modular and impersonal nature of our workspaces. The other members of my department are lined up along an aisle. My cube abuts theirs but is set off by itself. The arrangement was no accident. Shortly after I came on board, it became clear that our boss, one Darren Dobson, the director formerly known as Shrek, had for reasons unknown at the time taken an instant disliking to me. So when the company realigned the cubes, as they frequently do, it was decided I was "radioactive" and should be set out by myself. As the junior member of the group, I didn't have too much to say about it. But anyone who thinks there's no such thing as guilt by association has never worked in the corporate world. My coworkers didn't want to be near me when Shrek went off. Can't really say I blame them.

That evening, I cruised down the aisle, nosing around to see what everyone was up to.

"Conner, c'mere," said Boof.

He was sitting at his desk, staring at his computer monitor with a look of consternation. At least I think it was consternation, but with Boof, it's hard to say. Could have been gas.

Edwin Parsons came to be known as Boof because it was his favorite utterance when his ongoing search for sexual conquests had been successful the previous evening. Boof claimed to be five foot five, but we were all pretty sure he was sneaking in an inch or two. He had a pudgy build, thick glasses, and an out-of-control mop of curly brown hair.

Ah, "thy prince hath cometh," huh?

Despite having a sharp analytical mind and good business instincts, Boof expended most of his personal resources, thinking and worrying about sex. As Vicky Temerlin, the only female in the financial analysis group puts it, Boof is "undersized and oversexed." Everyone knows the human body is about sixty percent water, but we're all guessing that somewhere along the line, Boof's water was changed out for testosterone. His specialties in life are profit and loss statements and perversion.

"What's going on over there, Boof?" I asked, entering his cube. "You look pretty tense. HR coming down on cruising porn sites at work again?"

He made a "pssh" sound. "No...well, yeah, but that's not it. You need to help me with this questionnaire. Never seen such a load in my life. 'What do you spend way too much money on?' Think I should put 'live cam girls' in there? What do you think that'll turn up?"

"Whoa. What exactly are you doing?"

"Well, things have been a little dry lately, if you know what I mean. I figured I'd try one of these websites, you know? Supposedly hooks you up with your perfect match? Sounded like it was worth a try. So I paid for a year in advance. Unbelievable. Cost more than my first car. I better get something out of the honey tree for that. Anyway, I have to fill out this questionnaire. A hundred and fifty questions, can you believe it? Shit, what girl's gonna want to go out with me once she *knows* me that well?"

I had no answer for that, so I pulled up a chair next to his desk. "Well, I don't think you should mention the cam girls. Why don't you just say something innocuous? Like rent. You pay a lot for that place in Winthrop, don't you?"

"Damn straight. Just 'cause it's near the water. Shit, you don't even see that many bikinis out there. Hey, good idea on the rent. I figured you'd be as clueless as me on this stuff. Okay, next question. 'List three sex turn-ons and three turn-offs.' Only three? What, do they think I live in a convent?"

I was beginning to see the error of my ways in sitting down.

"But turn-offs?" said Boof. "Hmmm." He looked off into space. "I don't know. Bestiality, maybe?"

"Maybe? Uh, look, Boof, I gotta get going...."

"Oh, yeah, okay. Hey, think about that over the weekend, will ya? I have to come up with answers that aren't too scary, but don't make me sound like I'm in love with my mother or something."

"Sure," I said. "Top priority." With that, I bolted for the exit and nearly ran into Vicky, who looked like she was packing it in for the night.

"Oh, sorry, Conner," she said. "You in a hurry? You guys solving the world's problems in there?"

She gave me a look that said she was totally aware that my meeting with Boof was not even close to being business-related. Sound carries, and there are damn few secrets in a cube farm.

I stuttered my response. "Uh, yeah, we're almost there. Anyway, who has the duty tonight?"

Vicky performed a minor eye roll. "Razor," she said.

Vicky Temerlin was good at her job, and she thrived in an environment that had been a male bastion not all that long ago. She was an attractive woman—pretty face, blonde hair, slender figure, the works. She was career-oriented and kept most of her personal details close to the vest. I got the feeling she thought of her five male colleagues as immature, sophomoric, emotionally stunted nerds, all of which was essentially true. Yet she managed to fit in well. The guys came to think of her as their "work sister," and even Boof had cleaned up his act around her.

Vicky and I moseyed over to Razor's cube. We passed by Larry Berman, who was in a close conversation with his "twin" Chauncy Stillwell. We called them the twins because they were inseparable, and they walked alike and talked alike. They even looked a little alike these days, which was kind of scary. Berman had dark hair and a dark complexion. Stillwell was blond and fair skinned, but otherwise, they both had plain faces, medium builds, and the requisite thick-lensed glasses.

Razor's real name was Fernando Rojas. He got his nickname because he always looked like he needed a shave. Unlike the other analysts in the group, Razor had grown up on the street. But he had an eidetic memory for things like tax rates and interest charges, and he was our go-to guy whenever we were trying to build a historical perspective on a company we were studying. Razor was burly, dark-skinned, and hairy. He had a five-o-clock shadow at about 9 a.m.

Razor was pounding away on his keyboard when we walked in. The financial analysis group usually had a heavy workload. Our analyses and recommendations could make or break the company's decisions to move forward on a deal.

"Yo, Razor, look sharp," I said. He looked up from his work and sported a bemused smile. Razor was the most stoic member of the group, often hiding his true thoughts behind a practiced facial expression. "Vick's ready to go."

"Oh, hey, if you're too busy, I can manage on my own tonight," said Vicky.

Razor looked around at the carnage on his desk. "No, I guess this stuff isn't going anywhere. And I wouldn't want you to get stuck with Boof two nights in a row."

"I heard that," said Boof from his cube, and we all laughed.

Vicky had been taking mass transit to the office from her apartment in the Back Bay area of Boston. But with the late nights we were all pulling, getting on the train by herself was getting a little sketchy. So she had splurged and bought a car, which she was parking in a garage down the street from the office. That was all well and good until there were reports of a man sexually assaulting women walking by themselves on the streets nearby. When that started happening, we began taking turns escorting Vicky to her car.

Who says chivalry is dead?

"I feel like I'm being a burden," said Vicky. "Seriously, I'm sure I'll be okay. I have my mace and everything."

"No, no, it's no problem," said Razor. "You're doing me a favor. My eyes were getting blurry, looking at all these numbers."

"Hey, maybe we can all hit The Hill for a pop." Boof had materialized next to us. "I mean, it is Friday night, you know. Here, I'll put it in terms you guys can relate to. My stochastic process resulted in this group needing to have some fun before rigor sets in permanently. There, you see? An invitation tailored to financial analysis geeks."

"Ah, I don't think so, Boof," said Vicky. "The last time I went for 'a pop' at The Hill, all I can remember was trying to perfect my Macarena dance moves in my living room that night."

We all laughed, then Razor and I made our apologies to Boof as well.

"All right. Well, hell, might as well get back to that damned questionnaire," he said. "Goes against my better judgment, though. You know, I count on girls not knowing enough about me to make an informed decision. That and alcohol—yeah, alcohol usually helps...."

With that pearl of wisdom, Razor and Vicky made their way out. I looked at the exterior windows and realized it was almost time for me to go as well. It was a July evening, and the sun was setting late. But it was twilight, and that was my cue.

So, if you're wondering what it was I had been waiting for, it's really pretty simple.

I was waiting for it to get dark.

CHAPTER THREE

The Shade knew where to find what he was looking for.

Let the losers troll downtown and the really lowlife areas like Cambridge. Yuck. Even if a Grade A prime babe around there asked him in for a drink, he probably wouldn't go—no telling what you could catch in a place like that.

He knew where the best selection could be found. You had to go to the upper crust neighborhoods, where women thought nothing about leaving their expensive homes and strolling down to the corner for a latte. Or walking one of their little rat dogs so it wouldn't whiz all over their expensive oriental carpet. The Shade didn't usually visit with anyone walking a dog, no matter how little and useless it looked. Fact was, they could still yip up a storm, and he didn't want to trouble himself with having to break its useless little neck. But he would make a mental note of the location if the target looked like she was worth it. She would have to appear without the miserable little fleabag at some point, right?

The Shade was all about stealth. His "clients" would never see him coming. They would never even know he was there. And, if all went according to plan, they wouldn't be able to describe him afterward either. That's why he'd given himself his nickname. His given name just didn't do him justice. Mason Williams—what were his parents smoking when they came up with that one? A "mason" was someone who worked with rocks for a living. The Shade was far too high on the evolutionary scale to be tossed in with manual laborers. He was The Shade. He came out of nowhere and disappeared after he was finished. Just like real shade.

He made sure his looks would allow him to blend in no matter where he went. Nobody would notice him—average height and weight, plain clothing, no notable physical characteristics that someone might remember later. Move at a normal pace. Not too slow, even when he was scoping out a neighborhood. Not too fast either, and never run. People always notice someone running, even in a city.

Women had been ignoring The Shade his whole life. He had the kind of looks that blended in with the scenery, as they say. But not when he was operating. That was when he had the power. He lived to see the fear in their eyes. Most of the time, the fear changed to acceptance when they realized what was going to happen and that they were powerless to stop it. Afterward, he always left them with a message. "That's what you get for walking in the shade," he would say.

The Shade was in his element, cruising the Beacon Hill area shortly after dusk on a beautiful summer evening. Upscale everything. Expensive brownstone buildings, a hilly terrain, and close enough to downtown that he could vanish down some side street never to be seen again. On such a day around dark, there was enough foot traffic that a stranger wouldn't be noticed, but still a sufficient number of potential targets out walking by themselves. Okay, it had been a slow evening so far, but The Shade was a patient man. He knew he could wait until the situation was just right.

He was strolling east on Revere Street when he saw her. She was perfect—a tall, beautiful brunette walking west on the other side of the street. Wow, what a looker—long brown hair sashaying with each step. A classically gorgeous movie-star face with high cheekbones and smooth skin. And the body. She was wearing a yellow flowery dress that accented her amazing curves. She was moving with remarkable grace, almost like there was no friction between her shoes and the sidewalk. The Shade made all these mental notes at a mere glance without slowing his pace—no way a woman like that would ever take notice of him.

The only problem was Ms. Perfect was on a busy street. So, after she went by him, he swung around, very casually, of course, and maneuvered behind her at a safe distance. He would mark his time and see if she would be so kind as to present him an opportunity to come "say hello."

***

And then, it happened. Ms. Perfect turned right on Garden Street. He knew Garden was a tony residential neighborhood with lots of alleys. Even better, he could double back up Irving Street, quicken his pace, and be in position long enough to be sure the setting was right for he and Ms. Perfect to become "friends."

He hustled up Irving—no running, of course—crossed over on Cambridge Street, and backtracked down Garden, where he found himself a perfect dark alley with lots of shade from the street lamps and scanned the area. *It's remarkable how the other half lives*, he thought. *Even their alleys are clean*. The street was quiet, not a soul in sight. It couldn't have worked out much better. The only way this setup could go wrong was if Ms. Perfect entered one of the brownstones before reaching him.

He waited, his breath coming harder now, anticipating.

There she was, "gliding" on his side of the street. She appeared to be admiring the scenery, completely oblivious. His heart was pounding. He had rarely seen such an incredible beauty, nevermind had the chance to "meet" one.

He would have to establish control quickly. Even though people in urban areas tended to mind their own business, there were a lot of residences around. He would have to be sure Ms. Perfect didn't make any noise before their "meeting" started.

She passed by his alley, and he soundlessly emerged. He came up behind her and wrapped his forearm around her neck. The Shade knew just the right amount of pressure to establish control and cut off her airflow without her being able to make any noise. He sported his blade for her to see. He was used to a slight gurgle sound at this point and the initiation of a struggle. Ms. Perfect hardly resisted, and he easily pulled her back into the alley.

"Now you listen," he hissed in her ear. "I won't hurt you as long as you don't make any noise. Understand? If you understand, nod your head."

She nodded.

"Very good."

He quickly shifted his hand around her neck, turned her around facing him, and pressed her to the ground. It bothered The Shade that she wasn't resisting as much as normal. And her eyes. The look of terror he craved was not there. Her skin felt cool as he pressed on her windpipe while straddling her body.

He came up close to her face and whispered. "Ah, this is special. I don't get to meet many beauties like you in my line of work. And cool too. Not scared at all, eh? Well, we'll see what we can do to take care of that."

He kept the pressure on as he shifted the knife to his right hand and pushed it against her throat. Still no fear? This was where they would normally start begging him not to kill them. It made them very susceptible to what would come next—it was all okay as long as they got to live.

"You're a rare one. I'll give you that," he said. "Let's see what we've got here."

He reached down to the bottom of her dress with his left hand and started to lift it up.

"Okay, that'll be about enough," she said.

His head nearly exploded with rage. "You don't talk," he hissed. "We haven't even gotten started, *Ms. Perfect*. The Shade will say when we've had enough."

She reached up and grabbed the knife hand before he could react. He felt pressure crushing his hand and was cognizant of the knife clattering to the ground. He reached up with his left and tried to pry her hand away, but it was no use.

Suddenly they were upright, and she was pressing him against the cold brick wall. How had she gotten up? His full weight had been on top of her.

She kept squeezing his knife hand, grabbing him by the throat with her free hand. Now it was The Shade with fear in his eyes. How was this possible? She was close to his face, her eyes showing a different emotion than he'd ever seen before. It was almost like...hunger.

He tried to protest, but she pressed on his windpipe, and no words came out.

She actually had a hint of a smile. This was impossible. This was insane.

Then, the she-creature spoke.

"Did you get that, Conner?" she said.

***

The Shade heard a male voice say, "Got it. Kept your face out of it and everything. I'm getting pretty good at this."

A tall skinny guy with glasses emerged from around the corner of the building, holding a phone out in front of him. The Shade had been followed! Impossible. This couldn't be happening. That's it. This was a dream. He would wake up, and all of this would go away.

The she-creature was smiling again. "Of course you are, my dear," it said.

Wait, it...now The Shade knew this was a dream. The she-creature had fangs. And its eyes — they had changed. They were black, like a pair of marbles.

"Not telling the brilliant director what to do or anything, but you might not want to film this," it said.

"Right. Got it," said the guy, and he put his phone away.

The she-creature came closer, shoving The Shade's head to the side. He tried to protest, but it was still pressing his throat. He wasn't sure any words would have come out anyway.

"Now, just relax," it said. Its voice was calm as if they had just met on the street and were talking about the weather. "This will be over very quickly."

He felt a stabbing pain in his neck and heard himself utter an "Ohhh."

With his last bit of consciousness, he heard the tall skinny guy say, "Just an adjustment, Lyria, just an adjustment." And then his world went black.

***

Sergeant Mack McKenzie had an amusing thought. "If they

really want to get these dirtballs to confess," he said to himself, "They oughta make 'em sit out at this desk for a few hours." He laughed. "But then again, they outlawed torture, didn't they?"

Mack was the desk sergeant at the Sudbury Street Station of the Boston Police Department. He knew that most street cops would give their left nut to get this assignment.

"What, you get to sit on your ass all night? And you get paid for it?? No traipsing around when it's minus five out? No worrying about some turd with an itchy trigger finger taking target practice on you out on the street? Where do I sign up for that?"

Yeah, little did they know.

Even Mack himself was pretty jacked up when the call came down. And Gloria? She could hardly contain herself.

But none of them knew how excruciatingly boring this was. He joined the BPD wanting to be a cop. A real cop. Clean up the city and all that. Now, he was...what was he? A doorman? A concierge? Christ, even his buddies didn't include him in street talk anymore.

Most nights, a whole lot of nothing happened at Sudbury Street. Occasionally some of the guys—the "real" cops—would pass through to process an arrest. Or some rich guy from Beacon Hill would stop by to complain about their Mercedes getting a ticket. Yep, he had to admit, he missed the streets. Even with the danger, with the scrutiny that came with every action, he missed it. Gloria would kill him, but he was going to see about getting reassigned.

He was lost in these thoughts when a guy pushed through the doors and walked slowly up to the desk. Mack was still a cop, and he did an instant assessment. Regular looking schmoe. Average height and weight, mussed up brown hair, wearing khakis and a lightweight grey sweatshirt—danger potential: extremely low.

"Yes sir, can I help you?" he asked, looking down from his perch behind the desk.

The guy had kind of a vacant stare, which put Mack on alert. "My name is Mason Williams," he said. "I also call myself The

Shade. I have been molesting women in this area for a long time. I have also molested and raped women in other parts of the city."

At first, McKenzie just stared at the guy. They'd get this every now and then. Some schmuck with low self-esteem or some such crap would come in and confess to a high profile crime. A guy had been pulling women off the streets in the vicinity for a while now, and the sexual assaults had been garnering a high profile. The likelihood of the same guy walking into a police station and confessing was about the same as winning the lottery. But this guy called himself The Shade. Mack seemed to remember that the perp was saying something about *shade* to his victims. This guy seemed as meek as a mouse, but Mack undid the clasp on his holster just the same.

"Okay, Mr...Williams, is it? When did you commit these acts?"

"I attempted my most recent one this evening. It didn't work out that well. Here, let me show you."

The guy reached into his pocket, causing Mack to pull out his gun behind the desk. Williams had a phone. He pushed a few buttons, then held the display up. McKenzie watched, transfixed, and started reaching for the phone to call a detective.

"I used this," said the perp. He held up a six-inch butcher knife.

"Code 99 to the front desk! Immediately!"

Williams stood without moving, still holding the knife when a team of cops streamed in from the backroom and tackled him to the ground.

Mack McKenzie's next thought was, *Well, maybe the front desk isn't so boring after all.*

CHAPTER FOUR

"So, what did you see with this guy?" I asked Lyria.

We were laying in bed. I was catching my breath from our first go 'round of the night. Lyria wasn't even breathing hard.

"Really?" she said. "That's what you want to talk about? Not 'Oooh baby, that was great,' 'Can't wait to do it again,' or maybe just a 'Thank you?'"

"The 'Thank you' is implied. You should know that by now."

This brought a slight smile to her beautiful face.

"No, I was really curious to know what makes a guy like that tick. What makes him do these terrible things?"

Okay, so our conversations were different from most couples, I get that. Some people might be discussing money problems, kids, living arrangements, the weather. There was nothing so mundane with my girlfriend. See, she was converted to a vampire during World War II as part of a Nazi plot to kill some Russian generals.

I know you're probably thinking, "Oh. Why didn't you just say so?" Trust me, if I hadn't seen the evidence with my own farsighted eyes, I too would be questioning my sanity for making such a statement.

Turns out, though, that it was all true, and due to a sequence of events that had occurred the previous fall, I was now said vampire's lover and part-time caretaker.

Hey, who said love was perfect, right?

I actually considered myself quite fortunate. Aside from her nutritional requirements, Lyria was what I considered the perfect woman. She was tall, gorgeous, and shapely—basically, the kind of woman who normally wouldn't give me a second look. I was hardly a catch in the eyes of most of the women I had encountered in my time. I looked—well, like a financial analyst. I was tall and skinny with unruly brown hair and thick glasses. Yet there we were, Lyria and I. Our personalities seemed to mesh quite well.

I tried not to remember that we had originally hooked up because time was running out on Lyria's original caretaker, a dude named Radu. I had met Radu and would say he was somewhere north of ninety. Lyria was on the lookout for a replacement when she walked by me while I was out for an evening stroll one foggy night. Just so happens, two druggies with the charming monikers Snake and Vape tried to relieve me of my valuables at gunpoint that same night. Lyria saved me and later told me that I looked like a good candidate to take Radu's place, as I appeared to be a lonely guy without many social connections.

Can't imagine what made her think that.

Anyway, after we skirted an encounter with the police, Lyria and I settled into a more steady relationship. I took care of her worldly concerns, but I still kept my job at Beacon Hill Associates. I live in an expensive brownstone condo on Beacon Hill courtesy of my old man, who badly wanted me to succeed in investment banking. He thought that setting me up in this pad would help pave the way to the upper echelon at BHA, with the only costs to me being the continuation of his lifelong criticism of everything I do and my pride.

When Lyria and I heard about this guy molesting women in the Beacon Hill area, we knew we had a perfect candidate. See, Lyria was not an evil person at heart. When she needed to feed, she focused on evildoers or people the world could easily do without. Turned out, when Lyria fed—sorry, there's no better way to describe it—she made some sort of mental connection with the subject. She could "see" their life history and what drove their behavior. Meanwhile, the other party could only see what she allowed of her thoughts. Rather than putting them out of their—and our—misery, she adjusted their thinking.

Wherever possible, we recorded the criminal act. We stocked up on these disposable phones, which I truly thought only existed in the movies. Drawing in a creep like the Beacon Hill molester was easy for a woman like Lyria. We figured with her out strolling the streets by herself at night, it was only a matter of time. Then the Mason Williams's of the world headed to the nearest precinct and turned themselves in. The perp was off the street, Lyria took care of her needs, and nobody was any the wiser. I honestly never conceived of the notion that I'd be a part of a crime-fighting duo. Now I fancied myself as kind of a nerd Batman.

"I'd say it was a number of things that caused Mr. Williams to go off track," said Lyria.

I sat up in bed and encouraged her to continue.

"Seems he was neglected as a child and encountered some abusive behavior. But his own conduct didn't become so abhorrent until he took a spill off a bicycle and sustained a head injury."

"No kidding? That caused him to become a molester?"

"Not at first. He spent some of his formative years just experimenting with sexual deviance—I'll spare you the details. But as an adult, he was frustrated in his relationships with females. By the time this all came together, the only way he could get any satisfaction was by exerting power over women. Hence the molestations—and rapes, by the way. I don't think we'll see any more of these terrible acts from Mr. Mason Williams."

I was looking at her in wonder. It occurred to me that I knew very little about what Lyria was capable of. "Was it difficult to stop?"

She gave me a look that said she knew what I was asking, and did I really want to go there?

"I'm sorry, but you have to understand I'm curious. When you started with Williams, I said something like 'just an adjustment.' We had agreed that when we found an evildoer, we would try to adjust their thinking. Like you did with Shrek—er, Darren Dobson—last year. You know, rather than—"

"Yes, I know, Conner."

"So was it? Difficult to stop, I mean?"

She thought for a moment, looking at me the whole time. "Yes."

I just nodded, hoping she would go on.

"The first thing I saw were the attacks," she said. "His victims. He saw them as objects and got such enjoyment out of exerting his power. Frankly, it infuriated me, and I could see no reason to let this monster live. Then I saw more of his life. And also...." She hesitated.

"Yeah?" I asked softly.

"If you must know, it's *always* difficult to stop, as you say. The hunger I feel is much more intense than what you experience when you need to eat. When I was first converted, I was insatiable. There would have been no chance I could contain myself the way I can now. It took...years of practice."

She looked away. I moved over and took her in my arms. It was a rare sign of vulnerability. I had to keep reminding myself that she was forced into this life. She didn't ask for it.

"I'm sorry," I said. "I didn't mean to make you feel bad."

"No, I understand your curiosity. It's not like there's any textbooks about this."

I smiled. "No, that's true. So you gave his thinking an 'adjustment.' But there's still the head injury, right?"

"I tried to help him with that, as well."

"Really? You can do that?"

"It's not quite as certain. I have to give him some of my blood in our...exchange. And it only works some of the time. But certain qualities of my cursed blood can have a curative effect on physical ailments. Might have something to do with why I don't...age."

I figured I needed to lighten the mood. I sat back and put my hands behind my head.

"Yeah, it's not easy for me either. You know, being involved with an older woman." In truth, Lyria looked about the same age as me.

"Is that a fact?" she said, rolling over toward me and reaching down. "Well, why don't we just see who's the first to beg for mercy tonight?"

"Ohhh. I'm pretty sure that will be me. Just saying...."

***

I was not the least bit surprised when I woke up the next morning, and Lyria was gone. She frequently departed after I'd fallen off to sleep. We had her set up in a secure, daylight-proof, enclosed room in an industrial area where few would care to tread.

You see, my girlfriend sleeps during the day—in a coffin. Her room is really a vault that only opens from the inside.

Not exactly Hallmark Card material, is it?

I made my way to the office, feeling pretty good. Whenever I was with Lyria, it tended to lift my spirits. Plus, it was comforting knowing that we had taken care of the Beacon Hill molester and that no more women would become his victims.

At the same time, I was a bit reticent. My relationship with Lyria was fulfilling in so many ways. But the connection we shared was, to put it mildly, unique. And it seemed like I was always waiting for the other shoe to drop, for something to go horribly wrong that I couldn't possibly have foreseen. The love of my life was a creature I never dreamed was a reality outside of novels and horror films. To the best of my knowledge, she was the only one of her kind. There were no Internet message boards I could visit to discuss my issues with other people in like situations. There *was* nobody else in a like situation. Trust me, it's a very isolating feeling.

I was on guard that morning as I started pounding away on my current projects. I couldn't put my finger on why, but the atmosphere in the office felt different. It seemed more like a funeral home than a normally vibrant work environment in a fast-moving industry.

I passed off my feeling as an offshoot of my unusual love life.

The team headed down to the cafeteria for coffee around mid-morning. The company was pretty liberal in allowing our break times. Investment banking was a high-pressure world, and the higher-ups probably figured that if they didn't let us blow off some steam periodically, they'd be carting off a good percentage of their associates on stretchers. Besides, being hopped up on caffeine had to be good for productivity, didn't it?

The caf was crowded as usual. We were sitting at a round table, and nobody was saying much, everyone just contemplating their beverages. But again, something seemed out of kilter.

"Hey, wait a minute," said Boof. "Where's Stillwell?"

I looked around and was a little ashamed of just now noticing that Chauncey Stillwell wasn't with us. But Larry Berman was there. It was highly unusual for the twins to be apart for any length of time.

Boof continued. "I thought something felt out of whack. Berman's here, but no Stillwell? I figured the only time you two pried apart from each other was when you were getting it on with the missus."

Vicky let out a pshhhh sound. Razor and I looked at each other, tight-faced, trying not to laugh at Larry.

"That is right, isn't it, Larry?" asked Boof. "I mean, Stillwell's not around when you and the wife are steaming up the windows. Is he?"

Berman blushed, looking at Vicky. She looked like she wanted to laugh as well but just returned his gaze with a combination of pity and understanding.

"If you must know, Chauncey is working his network," said Berman.

The humor we were feeling evaporated. Whenever something big was happening at BHA, Stillwell was our conduit. He had connections throughout the organization, and we relied on him to give us the dope on a timely basis. I was doubly nervous because of the unexplained angst I had been feeling. And it wasn't like Chauncey could be checking on something *good*. Like, everybody's getting a raise today, hoorah! He usually brought us bad news—a reorganization, a layoff, or somebody getting canned.

The team was quiet for the rest of our break. We were about ready to head back upstairs when Chauncey came bounding over to our table, looking like he was going to explode if he didn't unload his news. He rushed to a seat—next to Berman, of course.

His face was flushed and his breath coming in gasps. "You won't believe this," he said, then had to pause.

"Easy, Chauncey," said Razor. "Just take a deep breath and tell us." Even the normally stoic Razor Rojas looked a little shaken.

"Right. Shrek...I mean Darren Dobson...our boss...."

Vicky put her hand on his in an effort to calm him down. "We know who he is," she said. "What about him?"

"They...they let him go. Shrek got fired."

***

We robotically returned to the cube farm in total silence. I seriously needed a moment to myself to digest this news. A year earlier, our boss getting the axe would have had me break-dancing out in the aisle. But I knew something my associates didn't.

The previous fall, when my relationship with Lyria was just budding, she found out that Mr. Dobson had taken a liking to ripping me a new one on an almost daily basis. She had "paid him a visit" and given him one of her adjustments so he would stop tormenting me. The result was a "kinder, gentler" Shrek, who was suddenly understanding and helpful where he was previously demanding and abusive. I told her at the time that, while I appreciated the thought, she really had to let me fight my own battles. Having an ogre for a boss was not all that unusual in big business, and learning to deal with them was part of the development process for a young executive.

I later came to find out that my dear old dad had a part in Dobson's apparent hatred for me. I originally thought Shrek came down on me because I was a spoiled rich kid whose daddy set him up with a plum job and primo living quarters. But my father, who used to be a partner at BHA, had actually *asked* Dobson to "lay the lumber" in an effort to toughen me up.

Ain't parental love just grand?

But I had to wonder whether the personality change inflicted upon Darren Dobson had cost him his job. Investment banking is a dog-eat-dog industry, and the higher-ups didn't really care if some peon got their feelings hurt as long as the business kept raking in the dough. Maybe the new "touchy feely" version of Shrek wasn't to their liking. Fear can be a great motivator, and

I had to admit that we, the financial analysts, were perhaps not as attentive to every minute detail of our work as we were when trying to avoid having Shrek ridicule our ineptitude in front of others.

I was sitting at my desk staring at my monitor but not actually doing anything as these thoughts swirled through my head. Boof came in and plopped down in my visitor's chair.

"Hey, I figured you'd be happy about the news," he said, looking at my morose expression.

"Well, you figured wrong."

"Buddy, you can't be fooled by Shrek suddenly becoming Mr. Rogers. That could have been a temporary thing, you know. Maybe he was just setting us up for disappointment. One day, he probably would have shown up as his old nasty self. The guy used to do a dance on your face almost every day. But now, what, you're actually *missing* him? Get with it man, this is a good day for all of us."

"Boof, it's a little hard to explain how I'm feeling right now."

"Oh yeah? Give it a shot. I'm trying to become more sensitive in my dealings with others."

"That sounds like a blurb from your dating website. What happened? Did you fail that personality test or something?"

"I wouldn't say I failed it. But some lady called me and asked if I would take it again. Like they put it into their system, and it didn't compute. She asked me that. Like, *how sensitive are you in dealing with others*? What a load. I told her I don't work in one of those touchy feely industries. I start worrying about other people's feelings; I'll end up cruising the help wanted ads with Shrek."

I actually smiled a little. "What was her response to that?"

"We went back and forth on it a little, then she hung up. She sounded somewhat frustrated. I felt like saying, 'You're frustrated?' What the heck do you think I'm doing on this website? You think I'd be on here if I was spending my time fending off all my girlfriends? So, c'mon, give me a try. I promise to be so sensitive, *you'll* probably want to go out with me."

I laughed a little. "Thanks for the offer, Boof, but I really have to work this out on my own."

"Yeah, you're probably right. I gotta work on this whole sensitivity business. Maybe you should go talk to Vicky. Or even better, Stillwell."

I laughed again. As annoying as Boof could be, he was good for an occasional chuckle.

He got up to leave but stopped in my doorway. "You know, I just had a terrible thought."

"Uh, oh. What's that?"

"As bad as Shrek could be, what if they send up somebody *worse*? I'd better go spiff up my resume."

CHAPTER FIVE

She saw him in her dreams.

He was perfect, her little bundle of energy, running toward her, out-of-control, as usual. His angelic face was smooth and flushed with exertion. They dressed him like his father, mostly because the boy insisted. He was wearing jeans, sneakers, and a pint-sized flannel shirt, exactly what Daddy was sporting.

He called out, "Mommy!" and closed the distance. All was right with her world, as long as he was like this. She felt warmth and joy as she crouched down, awaiting his arrival, her arms stretched out.

Then something happened.

He stopped—he couldn't run anymore. Something was holding him back.

At first, she couldn't see what it was. She got up and walked forward. As she got closer, she saw tubes running out of his arm. The tubes were attached to a machine and a bag of some sort hanging overhead. He was lying down, calling for her.

"Mom, I don't like this. I don't want this. Mom...."

She was running but not getting any closer. "I'm coming."

The man in the white coat was there, that doctor, leaning over the boy with a knife. "Don't worry. This won't hurt a bit."

"Mom, stop him. Don't let him. MOM!!"

"Don't!" she screamed. "Get away from him, you bastard!"

She kept moving forward. They kept moving away.

Stop!" she yelled. "STOP...!"

She woke up shrieking. Her husband was there, holding her down by her arms. She struggled against him.

"We have to go to him. We have to help him...."

Someone else was there — her mother-in-law. She remembered they were staying at his parents' house.

Her husband held her while her mother-in-law came close, holding a hypodermic.

"Go ahead, Mom," said the man she'd married. The man who supposedly loved her.

"No...NO!"

She felt the pinch. Her breathing slowed.

"Please," she said to her husband. "Please don't let them...."

"It's all right," he said softly, holding her.

Her last sensation was the wetness of his tears, mixing with hers on her cheek.

CHAPTER SIX

I got home earlier than normal that night. No Shrek around. No boss. Even with his newly found "Shrek-Lite" personality, he was still a presence. It wasn't like anyone in the analysis group had been screwing off or anything after Dobson changed his ways, even though life in the office was much easier. But there was also no mass migration out in the early evening while he was still there. We were all still a little wary, thinking that Shrek playing possum and being ready to eviscerate us at the first provocation was still a possibility.

I was in my kitchen pondering which excuse for a dinner would be my choice. I had never learned to cook—I know. What spoiled rich kid does, right? So my usual subsistence trended toward frozen dinners, chunky soup, and Hot Pockets. If a dietician ever went through my food supply, she'd probably have a stroke right on the spot.

My options were too depressing to consider, and besides, I realized that I didn't have any appetite. I sat at my kitchen table, and my thought pattern immediately headed for Lyria territory. My first thought was that she never had to debate about what to eat. *More like who than what*, said my inner dialog voice, which, I fully realized, was not always my friend.

Not going there, I retorted. My self-doubts frequently clouded out all rational thought.

Being romantically involved with Lyria was not *Ozzie and Harriet*. It was about as far from a normal relationship as one could possibly imagine. She had killed since we'd been involved. A few times, it was to protect me, and once to protect my sister Carly. She had taken out Carly's abusive boyfriend Brent, who, Lyria said, was planning to kill Carly in a drunken rage that night.

Lyria didn't try to hide who she was. The previous fall, we'd encountered a bunch of thugs in the Boston Common. Lyria whisked me out of trouble but later admitted that she would have very much liked to remove the homeboys from their membership in the living. Unbeknownst to me at the time, she had been keeping a living blood bank captive so she could feed at all times. One of her captives was a Boston police detective, the estimable Grace Garvey. Now, since we had taken to teaming up on finding evildoers upon whom she could impose a "mental adjustment" while feeding, Lyria no longer had the need for a captive, ongoing blood supply.

At least not that you're aware of, said my inner voice buddy.

I wondered how I got myself in this predicament. I was never a guy who lived on the edge. I never got in any kind of serious trouble growing up, not even the kind of hooliganism typical for a teenage boy. Prior to encountering Lyria, my most serious injury was a paper cut.

To her credit, Lyria had tried to end our relationship when she realized I was not the type of desolate loner she was seeking to replace Radu as her caretaker. Hey, you have to take compliments where you can get them, right? Once she met my family, she was ready to relieve me of my vampire-land duties for good. But we teamed up again to fake her death, alleviating the heat from a police investigation and a vendetta being lugged around by a modern-day Nazi blockhead named Mikolaj Babka.

Now my thoughts were spinning from this revelation about Darren Dobson. As much as I loved Lyria, I was not comfortable affecting people's lives like this.

I hadn't realized it, but my head was now resting on my arms on top of the table. Seeing no chance of regaining any desire to eat, I headed to the living room to assume my all too familiar prone position on the couch, using throw pillows to cover my head and block out the elements of my new reality.

Before I could reach my own version of denial Nirvana, the doorbell rang, causing my heart to skip a beat. Ever since I had been visited by the police a few times, I was a little jumpy about someone coming to my door. Detective Garvey and her boss, one Don Halberton, considered me a suspect in Lyria-related disappearances, even after meeting me and realizing I was possibly the least likely kidnapper/murderer in the history of criminal justice.

I looked out my peephole and, although my visitor wasn't anybody looking to haul me in, I still gasped a little.

***

It was my brother Caden. The fact that he was on my doorstep was not surprising, but his appearance was.

Where I was the bookworm of the family, Caden was the athlete. He was shorter than I was but twice as muscular. He normally kept his dirty blond hair in a buzz cut, and he was always clean shaven—a prototype "all-American" athlete. My dad had pushed me into the investment banking business because I had the aptitude for numbers, and Caden didn't. Not that Caden wasn't a worker—he had taken a few business courses and was currently working his way up the ladder at a big insurance company. He and his wife Lisa lived in a house out in the burbs near Mom and Dad, and they had a four-year-old son named Jason.

But the guy at my front door looked pale and uncharacteristically stooped over. His hair was longer than normal and a bit unkempt. In addition, he actually had a beard going on. He was dressed in a shabby pair of jeans and a wrinkled T-shirt.

I swung the door open. "Hey, Caden."

"Conner."

"C'mon in. You feeling okay? You don't look too good."

"Yeah. I just had to get out of the house for a while. Mom and Dad were driving me a little nuts."

"Mom and Dad? What were you doing over there?"

"Oh, well, Lisa and I had to kind of…move in temporarily. With Jason, of course."

"Okay. Get in here and sit down. Something must be seriously wrong if you moved in with Mom and Dad. Even temporarily."

My brother moved silently to the sofa and sat down. I settled on the other end. My fear factor was rising fast in my chest.

"Tell me the truth, bro. What the hell's going on?"

Then, something happened that I hadn't seen in a long time. Maybe ever. My rock of a brother put his face in his hands and started bawling.

I honestly didn't know what to do. Caden was two years older than me, so although I'm sure he must have cried some as an infant and toddler, I had never witnessed it. And while we had the normal "ball busting" kind of relationship shared by brothers close in age, I had quietly always looked up to Caden. Seeing him break down like this was unnerving.

My throat was dry, and my voice raspy, but I managed to croak out a, "Tell me what's wrong."

Caden put his hands down but continued sobbing. "It's Jason," he said.

I felt my breath catch. "What happened?" I gasped.

"He's sick. Very sick...."

With that, the floodgates truly opened. Caden leaned forward and cried so hard he was panting for breath. I moved over and patted him on the back. I knew the gesture wasn't much, but consoling people with emotional outbursts was definitely not in my wheelhouse.

"Hey, it'll be okay," I said weakly.

"No. No, it won't."

"What is it? Tell me what happened."

Caden took a deep breath and tried to compose himself. "At first, he had a couple of nosebleeds. Then his appetite started going south. And he was complaining about pain, in his joints and all. So we took him to the doctor, of course. They did a blood test. That was real pleasant, lemme tell you. Ever seen a four-year-old stuck with a needle? Anyway, we took him home and waited for the results. We figured maybe he had the flu or something, you know? A day later, the doctor calls. I started worrying right away. It's never good when the doctor himself calls. He says he needs us to come back to the office to discuss the blood test. Now I'm really freaking out. But I had to stay calm, at least outwardly, for Lisa's sake. When I told her, I thought she was gonna buy it right there. She got hysterical and wanted me to call the doctor back and demand he tell us what was going on."

My brother paused, trying to fend off another breakdown.

"We dropped Jason off at Mom's and headed to the doctor's office. The guy starts spouting off numbers like we were supposed to understand. They must not teach communication in medical school. I'm holding onto Lisa. She looks like she wants to go for the guy's throat. I finally just said to the guy, 'Look, what does this all mean? What is wrong with our son?' The doctor looks down at his chart as if the answer is on there somewhere. He looks back up and says the words no parent wants to hear. He thinks childhood leukemia is indicated."

I was having trouble breathing, but I said, "Leukemia? Are... are they sure?"

Caden was crying again. "They're sure now. They biopsied some of his bone marrow. Had to scrape it out of his hip. I hope I never have to see anything like that again. Then a spinal tap, looking for leukemia cells in his spinal fluid. He has it. It's called acute lymphoblastic leukemia—A-L-L for short. His white blood cell count is all out of whack. It's the most serious form of leukemia. I...." Caden was crying uncontrollably. "I don't know if he's going to make it."

"My god," I said. "What are they going to do? What kind of treatment will they...?"

"I know. It's difficult to think about what he's going to go through. Long-term chemo. Could take up to two years. But the fact that they found cells in his spinal fluid...."

I waited for Caden's crying to ease. While I'm obviously not a doctor, I could tell that the prognosis was not good. I was devastated by this news—my nephew and I were very close. Soon I was crying too, as my arm found its way around Caden's shoulder.

"Caden, I'm so...so sorry."

"We moved in with Mom and Dad. I'm sorry to drop this on

you so suddenly. We didn't want to say anything until...until we were sure. Mom and Dad have been great. And Carly. They want to start the treatments right away. I still have to work, y'know? I've taken a lot of time off lately, and the company's been great and all, but...."

"Yeah, I understand. Obviously, if there's any way I can help...."

"Thanks, bro."

"I know it's a stupid question, but how is Lisa?"

Caden paused. "Not good," he said finally.

I waited while he made an effort to compose himself.

"That day in the doctor's office...when we...found out, she lost it. Went at the doctor, and he had to give her a shot. We... we're keeping her under sedation at Mom's. She wakes up... she's hysterical. Jason is...he's her everything. He's going to stay in the hospital, at least for the initial phase of the treatments."

There was a pause, then Caden looked up and glanced around the condo.

"So, what do you have for booze in this place?"

***

I only had a bottle of scotch that I kept for company. I wasn't much of a drinker, but we both downed a couple of shots. Caden was in no condition to drive, so he sacked out on my couch.

I thought about Lyria. Caden had met her before, so it wouldn't be a surprise for her to be there. I wasn't sure how she got in sometimes. Even if my place was locked up tight, she somehow managed to appear, usually at my bedside. But Caden was essentially passed out, so I figured it wasn't anything to worry about. I headed upstairs, feeling woozy from the booze.

As I stumbled up the stairs, I thought, *Was it just this morning that I was feeling good but waiting for the shoe to drop?* It seemed like an eternity ago. But my instincts were correct. In my situation, it was just a matter of time before something would come along to disrupt my positive vibes.

Before I blacked out, my last conscious thoughts were that the shoe had dropped with a thud and a sick concept that more bad news was almost sure to follow.

CHAPTER SEVEN

Mikolaj Babka expected a hero's welcome. Or at least an acknowledgment of a job well done.

His travel was always perilous. Interpol had a profile on him, and he carried falsified documents. The problem was his appearance. For someone of such short stature, Mikolaj stood out in a crowd. He had a stocky build, with buckteeth, a bald head with frizzy remnants of his hair, and eyes that seemed to go off in different directions. People generally tended to shift away from him as he moved about. He knew that he would be unable to deny who he was if he were matched up to the international police force's picture of him. Nobody else looked like Mikolaj Babka.

He had become adept at disguising himself. There was nothing he could do about his height, but he wore sunglasses and a hairpiece, occasionally augmented by a false mustache or beard.

After witnessing the demise of the creature known as Lyria, Mikolaj sent word back to his superiors. She had been responsible for the deaths of many original members of the SS TV, or *Totenkopfverbande*, a sect of Hitler's dreaded SS during World War II. What these fools in law enforcement didn't know was that the SS TV was still in existence and had made substantial headway toward renewing its rightful place as a major influence in world affairs. Although most of the public thought the SS TV was neutralized after the war, survivors continued to meet in Great Britain for years hence. They became British citizens, and their offspring assumed important positions in the political hierarchy and in the military. Their meetings remained secretive, but the objective of restoring Aryan order to the world was still very much alive.

Mikolaj was a foot soldier for the modern SS TV, and he had been tasked to track the mysterious Lyria and seek an opportunity to avenge her crimes against his predecessors. The fact that her very existence came about because of the SS TV's own human experimentation had no bearing. She was an enemy of the cause, and she had to be eliminated. The fear must be maintained, even if it meant going up against someone who was not truly human.

Mikolaj had tracked Lyria for an eternity, and now, she was no more. He'd completed his undercover journey, and he received word to report back to the organization's secret headquarters in London.

Mikolaj knew the drill. He would meet up with a liaison and would be taken to the headquarters. Even he didn't know where it was, but he half expected to be let in on the secret. Perhaps instead of a solitary contact person, they would send a limousine to meet him. After all, was he not now a hero of the cause?

He was disappointed, however, when he arrived at the meeting place, and there was nobody there. The contact point was a nondescript corner of an intersection in a low-income neighborhood. Although he knew the location was appropriate — people in this area tended to mind their own business and take no note of a stranger — he couldn't help but feel let down. Not only was he not met by a limo, but apparently, his liaison would make him wait out in public. He felt uncomfortable standing on the corner. Even in a place where people kept to themselves, Mikolaj felt like he would be noticed. The weather was warm, but he wore an overcoat and his disguise elements nonetheless. He hugged a nearby building, a rundown remnant of a former pawn shop.

As the wait stretched on, his discomfort grew into anger. Suddenly his arm felt like it was gripped in a vice, and Mikolaj became aware of a dark physical presence towering over him to his left. He knew not to look directly at the man, but he could tell that, whoever he was, he was above average height with a slender but powerful physique, and he was dressed in all black. As Mikolaj turned slightly, the vise on his arm tightened, and he had to keep himself from crying out.

"Don't look," the man hissed. "Were you able to get your prescription filled?"

Mikolaj recognized the coded question, but he had been taken off guard and had to think about the correct response. His hesitance caused an even tighter grip on his arm.

"Were you, friend?"

"Yes," said Mikolaj after a moment. "Yes, Doctor Vogel's instructions were quite clear."

"Very good, friend, let us return home."

A black sedan with darkened windows appeared from out of nowhere and stopped in front of them. The liaison brute propelled Mikolaj toward the back door. He still hadn't seen the man's face, and the liaison intended to keep it that way. Mikolaj was shoved into the back seat, and the car sped off. The driver had a black collar pulled up high and was wearing a black cap. All Mikolaj could see was a small opening above the nape with a thick mane of yellow blond hair.

He got up the gumption to protest his treatment, but when he went to turn to the liaison, the man grabbed his shoulders and turned him away. Before Mikolaj knew what was happening, he was plunged into darkness. A hood of some kind was pulled over his head and quickly secured around his neck. It had a small opening so he could breathe through his mouth, but it was tight to his face so he couldn't see anything through the hole.

"It is an outrage for you to treat me like this," he choked out. "I am a loyal soldier — "

"Be silent," said the man.

Mikolaj heard what sounded like duct tape and felt tight pressure around his head. The man was covering up his ears so he would recognize neither sight nor sound during their journey. To make his captivity complete, the liaison effortlessly pulled Mikolaj's arms behind him and clamped his wrists in handcuffs.

He felt himself shoved over in the seat and was belted in place. There was no further effort at communication. Mikolaj Babka, a hero to the cause, sat bound up like a pig on the way to slaughter, unable to see, hear, or move for the duration of their passage.

***

Mikolaj couldn't tell how long he was in the car. The deprivation of his senses effectively eliminated his sense of time. He was roughly pulled from the vehicle, the tight grip on his arm returning. He sensed they were indoors—a parking garage of some sort? There was a slight odor of gasoline, and he couldn't feel any movement of air.

His equilibrium was suddenly off. They must have been in an elevator, going down. It was unnerving, but Mikolaj remained silent.

They were walking again. His handcuffs were being removed. The hood and the duct tape were ripped from his head. His captors shoved him to the floor. He was completely disoriented as he took in his surroundings. It was dark as he stood. He was in a room, but it looked like the walls were painted black. His vision was fogged, but he could make out a table in front of him. There were three men sitting behind the table. At least he presumed they were men—they all had black hoods covering their heads. Behind them was a symbol Mikolaj knew all too well—the skull and bones symbol of the SS TV. Must have been some sort of fluorescent paint as it glowed in the dark. Mikolaj had the same symbol tattooed on his hand.

He turned around and saw two massive men, also hooded, standing on either side of the entrance to the room. His captors? The door was closed, and Mikolaj suddenly had to fight off a feeling of claustrophobic panic.

"Welcome, brother," said one of the men.

Hearing a voice for the first time since his captivity began broke Mikolaj out of his delirium, and anger at his treatment once again boiled up.

"*Welcome*, you say? And how is it that I am treated like an outsider? Like an enemy to the cause? I contacted the council to tell you of a great victory, the demise of a long-time enemy. I inform you that our ancestors have been avenged, that a supernatural creature has been eliminated, and yet I am bound and blinded like a dog to be presented to its owners—"

The man in the middle interrupted. "You understand, brother, that precautions must be maintained. That secrecy is of the utmost importance."

Mikolaj remembered the tenuousness of his position. He didn't even know who these men were who sat in judgment of him. When he became an active member of the modern day *Totenkopfverbande*, there were other foot soldiers who were his friends, his close associates. But the leadership remained shrouded in secrecy to this day. His associates were off in parts unknown, carrying out missions to further the cause. But, truth be told, Mikolaj could disappear tomorrow, and nobody would miss him. Or even be aware of his absence.

His voice was now calm. "Understood, Master. At any rate, my mission has been accomplished."

"You have done well, brother. But there is more to be done."

Mikolaj felt dread build up in his chest. Is that why he had been summoned? They were going to give him *another* assignment? So soon after he had spent a good part of his existence chasing after an earthly demon?

"More...Master?" he stammered.

"You have proven yourself to be uncommonly adept at dealing with matters of this supernatural nature, as you put it," said the man in the middle. The two other hooded bodies said nothing and were barely moving.

"Master, I was able to track this...*creature*...and bring about her demise. I spent years of my life...I have proven my loyalty...."

"Brother," the man in the middle began hesitantly. "I know I need not remind you that you have been well compensated for your efforts. That your bank account has been filled over the years, even when there were no updates on your progress for long periods of time. The cause is under siege. Every soldier must go above and beyond their normal level of devotion. The blood is becoming more impure with every generation. These efforts you read about...these National Socialist Movements...they are weak. Similar to our forbearers who were the strong ones in the dedication to ethnic purity, we must lead. There are others who will follow, but we must have the strength to survive and thrive. As it is, we must meet in an underground room for fear of reprisal. If we cannot bring about change, the *Totenkopfverbande* will be no more. Our cause will be lost."

"Yes, Master. But what can I do? I mean, what *more* can I do to—?"

"Have you heard talk of the Other?"

Mikolaj stopped breathing. His first thought was to bolt from the room, try to escape. But when he looked behind him, the two mammoth men who brought him here were still standing in front of the only door.

"Master...you cannot be asking me to.... This is but a story, an urban legend, as they say these days."

The man in the middle spoke as if Mikolaj had said nothing.

"You will find the final resting place of the Other. That is your assignment."

"Sir, *please*. Even if the stories are true, this being has done nothing to be avenged. It would not serve the cause to—"

"You misunderstand, brother. Your objective this time is not to seek revenge. You will find the Other. You will end decades of captivity. You will engender positive feelings, even gratitude."

"Do you mean...?"

"We do not seek the Other for vengeance. We will use the Other as a weapon."

CHAPTER EIGHT

Chavez considered himself the baddest dude in the city. That would have been good enough for most. But Chavez was just getting started. He wouldn't rest until he was known by everyone as the baddest dude in the state. *Hell, why not the country*, he asked himself with a sneer.

He had started out as a two-bit weed dealer out on the street. Now he was so feared, he was almost a legend who only went by one name. When the word Chavez was spoken, usually in hushed tones, people knew who you were talking about. And they knew that to pull any antics in dealing with him or someone in his org meant certain painful and gruesome death.

Now that Massachusetts had legalized weed—what the *infierno* were they thinking?—Chavez had moved on to much bigger and better things. He was already the top distributor of cocaine and all of its derivatives. But once the opioid crisis had taken hold, Chavez knew that he had found his calling.

The people getting hooked on these drugs weren't street punks looking to get away from the misery of their lives. They were rich suburbanites who were prescribed painkillers for their latest plastic surgeries and couldn't kick the habit. They would need stronger versions of their oxycodone before long, and Chavez would be there to provide. First, it was fentanyl, then cheese, black stuff, China white. Whatever they needed or wanted, Chavez would be there. Sure, he could still do coke business: bennies, meth, eve, roofies—whatever. But opioids were where it was at. The news was all about people dropping dead from overdoses, but that wasn't his problem. It was simple supply and demand like they taught rich college kids in Boston. There was demand, and he was there to fulfill the supply.

It had taken Chavez some time to consolidate the market — time and a lot of blood. He'd identified the other big players in the city, and one by one, they came to realize that their choices were two. Do business with and through Chavez, or face their own death and that of their families. It wasn't long before the dealers started *wanting* to work with him. They would even ask permission to do business, which Chavez would grant as long as he got his cut. Of course, these apes would try to mess with him — at least at first. Until they started to suffer the consequences.

Chavez still lived in the city — he wanted to be close to his action. He kept a place near Beacon Hill. Not an overly pretentious place since he didn't want to draw more attention than he already did. The local cops and Feds knew about Chavez, but he was a professional. Much as they all wanted to take him down, they could never build a case against him. Everyone who dealt with Chavez was far more afraid of him and his crew than they were of anyone with a badge.

Chavez got home late, passing by the near army guarding his place. They were invisible to passersby, but his building, the parking garage, and the lobby were impenetrable. He walked silently past the doorman, who, of course, also worked for Chavez. The man nodded silently, the kind of respect Chavez craved. He always took the stairs — elevators were just traps waiting to happen.

He entered his lair and immediately sensed something was wrong. In his business, having a sixth sense for danger wasn't paranoia. It was survival. It was...he couldn't place the source of his anxiety. The *air* felt different. His bodyguard was outside, but Chavez pulled the 9 mm, 14 shot Glock pistol from his waist holster and crept slowly through the rooms of his apartment. Nobody there.

He relaxed a little and went to search his room last — no sign of anything amiss in the bedroom. Bathroom was clean. Maybe he *was* a little paranoid, but that was probably a good thing.

He opened his closet door and froze. What he saw caused a delay in what should have been his immediate response to raise his weapon. Then the one and only Chavez, the baddest dude in the city, did something he hadn't done since he was a child.

He let out a high-pitched scream.

He didn't have time to be ashamed. His own noise echoing in his ears would be the last sound the dreaded Chavez would ever hear.

CHAPTER NINE

My mind was in a fog when I woke up the next day. I tried to tell myself that the previous night had only been a dream, but the realization set in quickly that it was all real.

Jason. My nephew. My brother's son. The last time I had seen him, his biggest problem was getting Legos to fit together. Now he would have to fight for his life.

Childhood leukemia. I knew virtually nothing about it, except that the mere utterance of those two words brought about sheer terror among parents.

And uncles.

I made my way downstairs, my head throbbing a bit from last night's alcohol. My compadres in college used to call a guy who couldn't hold his booze a "rookie." By that measure, I was a short-season, single-A rookie punk right out of high school.

I looked in the living room and wasn't all that surprised to see that Caden had gone. My place represented a temporary reprisal, a way to get away for a while. But then he had to get back to our parent's house.

Back to his wife.

I had to think about what day it was, then I realized much to my dismay, that it was Friday and I had to go to work.

Drat.

So I hauled my sorry ass up to the shower and managed to get myself clothed and ready to go. A thought struck me, and I stopped at the door, went back, and sat down on the couch. I took out my phone and dialed.

"Hi, Conner." My sister Carly sounded like she'd been crying.

"Hey. How's everything at the house this morning?"

"About the same. Mom and Caden are in with Lisa. She came out of sedation this morning, screaming, but they don't want to keep giving her shots. They're trying to talk to her, calm her down."

"Yeah. Caden was here last night. He was a wreck, but I guess that's to be expected. What's Dad doing?"

"Oh, you know him. Ever since they confirmed the diagnosis, he's been on the phone to his contacts in the medical field. Calling in all his favors, as he puts it. Wanting to be sure the doctors are covering every angle and that Jason gets the best care available."

I actually took a little bit of comfort hearing that my father was throwing his weight around. Since he retired from a senior position at BHA—yes, my current employer—it seemed like he relished every opportunity to prove that he was still important, still a player.

"Conner?"

"Yeah?"

"I don't know how much Caden told you, but…."

I held my breath. More bad news? "What?"

"According to one of Dad's doctor friends, the prognosis is not good. This type of leukemia is very aggressive. He felt like he owed it to Dad to be completely honest. You know, some of the doctors feel like they have to put up a positive façade, just for the sake of the kid…and the parents. But this guy was being square. He's not even sure the chemo will knock it out."

***

I hung up with Carly and walked to the office. The fact that I lived within walking distance and didn't have to put up with a murderous Boston commute every day was a source of jealousy and even animus from many people at my company, including, most notably, my former boss Darren Dobson. My father setting me up in a Beacon Hill condo that no analyst could ever dream of affording on their own, was just further proof to some suspicious types that I was nothing but a poor little rich kid living off Daddy's influence. I'd be lying if I said that I myself wasn't dogged by such thoughts.

I fought off the urge to fall into my familiar abyss of self-pity by focusing my thoughts on my nephew and what he had lying ahead of him. I was trying to convince myself that the treatment would work and everything would be okay. But in the back of my mind, I wondered if that was really true. Caden had said Jason's leukemia was the most severe form. And Carly confirmed that and then some. I tried to put these thoughts out of my head and focus on my current projects.

I considered bowing out of the morning coffee break but decided that it might do me some good to get out of my cube for a bit. We got to the cafeteria early and seized our usual table. The crew was kibitzing about who our next boss would be, but I wasn't in a very talkative mood.

"Hey, what're you so down about?" asked Boof. "You should be the happiest guy down here. At least there's a possibility that our new boss won't have a hard on for you on day one."

The twins both let out a brief expulsion of air as if they'd rehearsed it. Razor just smiled, while Vicky sported a disapproving look.

"I...just have a lot on my mind this morning," I said. I hadn't told anyone about Jason. I come from a New England family, and they are typically closed-mouthed about family matters.

Chauncey Stillwell piped in. "Maybe Conner will be our next boss."

Boof spit out his coffee while the others stared agape at Stillwell.

"I mean, it makes sense, doesn't it?" said Chauncey. "We all know Charles David still has a lot of pull here. Rumor has it that he got Darren Dobson his job."

"Yeah," said Larry Berman, as if he'd ever disagree with his twin. "Maybe Shrek was just keeping the seat warm until Charles's boy got his sea legs. Makes sense." Berman and Stillwell nodded consecutively.

"What about that, Conner?" Now even Razor was getting in on the fun. "Should we start being extra nice to you?"

"Yeah," said Boof. "Don't forget about all the women I've set you up with."

I looked at Boof, incredulous. "You've never set me up with *any* women."

"Okay, but it wasn't for the lack of trying. I've spent the better part of the last two years dragging you into all these nightclubs. It was like having an anchor around my neck, y'know? It's not my fault that you couldn't make it work. There were plenty of opportunities. No offense, but if social awkwardness were electricity, you could light up the city, buddy."

"How could anybody take offense at that? And I'm sorry, but when does the 'being extra nice to me' start?"

"Do you really think that could happen, Conner?" asked Vicki. "Do you think they could give you FA?"

She was trying to look serious, but even Vicki had a twinkle in her eye. As if this chop-busting episode was too good to resist.

"That's about as likely as Boof applying for the seminary," I said. I turned to Boof. "And in what universe were you *dragging* me to nightclubs? The way I remember it, you practically begged me to hit the clubs with you every Friday night."

"Well, it's all a part of my strategy," said Boof. "Having you alongside me can only up my odds. I mean, compared to you, I look like Hugh f'ing Hefner out there."

Everybody had a good chuckle at that, and then break was over. As we were walking back, Boof said, "Hey, speaking of which, today's Friday. How's about we head out for drinks tonight?"

Everyone shuffled their feet and mumbled excuses.

"C'mon. It'll be the first time since Shrek got the axe. Berman, Vicki, you guys hardly ever go out with us anymore. Think of it as slumming. It doesn't have to be a wild night. We can hit that upholstered morgue known as The Hill."

I hated to admit it, but with everything that had happened recently, going out for drinks didn't sound bad to me. We all shrugged, and it looked like the group outing was on.

***

The Hill was only modestly busy that evening, reminding me

of Boof's upholstered morgue comment. It was a classy place where people generally went for a quiet drink. The walls had upscale paneling, and there was a mahogany bar with an impressive assortment of booze bottles and a mirrored background. Dim lighting and music playing softly in the background added to the similarity to a morgue. Or maybe a funeral home. A small dance floor was currently unoccupied. There was a smattering of customers, mostly couples talking quietly at tables around the perimeter of the bar. About as far from a pickup joint as one could imagine, much to Boof Parson's dismay. But The Hill would always represent a special place in the history of yours truly.

It was where I met Lyria and where our relationship had begun. I surprised myself by wondering if that was necessarily a good thing.

As Boof had referenced earlier, Larry Berman and Vicki Temerlin rarely graced us with their presence on our nights out. Berman was married and usually had to get home to the wife. And on most occasions, Vicki would rather have a tooth extracted than go out socially with the sophomoric nerds with whom she had to spend most of her waking hours. But tonight the gang was all there and, after the first round of drinks arrived, the main topic of conversation was Darren Dobson and his potential replacement.

"I think they'll look internally," said Chauncey Stillwell. Everybody listened, as Chauncey had a lot of sources and a good feel for BHA politics. "Maybe somebody like Perkins from underwriting. Supposedly they're looking to move him up the ladder."

"Perkins?" said Boof with a sneer. "The guy couldn't lead his way out of a paper bag. Two weeks in, we'd be praying for Shrek to make a comeback."

"Maybe they'll appoint a woman," said Vicki. Everybody stopped and looked at her. "I mean, let's face it, BHA is not the most diverse company around. The company photos look like a white male society group. People are paying attention to these things nowadays. They might attract more clients—and investments—by showing that they're at least trying to put women in more senior positions."

Razor Rojas laughed. "Hey, why do you boys look so scared all of a sudden? Here's another thought to make your night. Maybe they'll promote a minority. A Hispanic, perhaps?"

Razor and Vicki clinked glasses. "Here's to the diversification of Beacon Hill Associates," said Vicki, and the two of them laughed.

We all joined in. I thought, *Hey, the company could do a lot worse than to appoint the steady hand and eidetic memory of Razor Rojas.* And, while Vicki probably didn't have enough seniority to get promoted, maybe the company would benefit from a woman's perspective. Men tended to think with their gonads and didn't always make the best decisions.

Anyway, the rest of the evening was great—everyone was loose, laughing and having fun. It took my mind off Jason.

And Lyria.

It was time to call it a night.

"Hey, it's been real," said Boof. "But next time, maybe we can go someplace where the men don't outnumber the women five to one? Talk about a lack of diversity."

We walked outside, and everyone else headed for the parking garage while I took off on foot towards home. My mind was at ease, and I figured I didn't have to get swallowed up by my woes, at least until I walked in my front door. It didn't even faze me when I registered tires screeching nearby. It was Boston, after all, home of the worst drivers in all of mankind.

I was walking west on Irving Street, but when I got to the corner of Revere, I first saw the headlights and then realized they were heading straight for me. I froze for an instant, and that was all it took. The car was jumping the curb, and there was no way to avoid it. All I could do was scrunch myself into a ball and brace for the impact.

I felt a thud on my shoulder, and I was being propelled through the air. I wasn't able to breathe as I heard the car crash into a street light. Tires screeched again as the driver backed up and sped away. *Was that it?* I wondered. *Am I dead?*

It seemed like I was watching the whole scene from afar. I

was on my back on the sidewalk. When I looked up, Lyria was standing over me. She looked completely calm, almost bored.

"Didn't your mother ever teach you to look both ways when you're crossing the street?" she asked.

CHAPTER TEN

We walked home together.

"Looks like you saved my skin again. Thanks."

"No worries, Mr. David. I know it's always a risk when you go out in public."

I had to smile. "That guy was out of control. Probably some drunk headed home from the bars." Lyria didn't respond. "If I didn't know better, I'd think he tried to hit me on purpose."

Lyria took my hand but still said nothing. She felt warm.

"Your hand is warm. Have you been — ?"

"You know, I came by last night, but I saw your brother on the couch," she interrupted. "So, I figured I'd leave you two alone."

I knew when Lyria changed the course of the conversation suddenly like that, the subject was closed. I also knew the only time her skin felt warm was after she fed. And since we hadn't played Batwoman and Robin chasing down any bad guys of late, I couldn't help but wonder about the source of her "nutrition." But sometimes, there were questions that simply couldn't be asked. Besides, she had just saved my life, so I didn't feel like I was in a position to press the issue.

We got to my condo and sat together on the couch. I looked at her, and it struck me yet again what a wondrous creature she was — her flawless facial features and high cheekbones, her long brown hair flowing over her shoulders. She was wearing a purple print dress that clung to her body. My heart lurched as she crossed her legs toward me. I temporarily forgot about the vampirism and all and sat in amazement that I was there, in my home, with such a perfect woman.

"Now, was I mistaken, or did I detect a scent of alcohol here last night?" she asked with a slight smile.

"Yeah, Caden and I had a few pops. Lyria, Caden, came over to tell me that Jason is very sick."

"Oh, no." She shifted even closer to me. "Tell me about it."

I related the whole story about finding out that Jason had leukemia and about my conversation with Carly that the prognosis was not good. Lyria nodded, taking in all the details. On top of everything else, she was a great listener.

"How awful," she said. "How is Lisa doing? And your mother?"

Lyria had met my family the previous fall. To put it mildly, she was a big hit with everyone, including Jason. I tried not to take it personally that my family was incredulous that such an ideal female had taken up with me.

"Lisa and Caden are staying with Mom. Lisa has been kept under sedation since learning of the diagnosis."

"I'm so sorry, Conner."

"Thanks," I said, and ran my fingers through her hair. She put her head on my shoulder, and we sat cuddled together. I felt so close to her at that moment that it felt like nothing else mattered. But as usual, my comfort was quickly disrupted by a disturbing thought.

"Did you see who almost hit me tonight?"

She looked up. "Is that really what you want to talk about?"

"Well, I assumed it was just some drunk. But was it? Did you see the driver?"

Lyria sat up and sighed. "Yes, Conner. I saw the driver."

"Did you recognize him? I assume it was a 'him.' Was it anyone you knew?"

She hesitated. "Yes. I recognized him."

I felt my chest tighten. "Who…who was it?"

Lyria took a deep breath. "It was your boss. It was Darren Dobson."

***

I had trouble breathing. "Dobson?" I gasped.

Lyria was looking at me with sympathetic eyes. "Well, you knew there was some bad feeling there."

"Lyria, I didn't have a chance to tell you…Dobson got fired. He's not my boss anymore."

She nodded somberly.

"I was wondering— You gave him that adjustment last year, and it seemed like his bad feelings went away. He was never anything but nice to me after that. But it felt like his nice-guy persona might have cost him his job. Does the impact last? Does it ever reverse itself? What if we cost him—?"

She took my hand. "Conner, calm down. Everyone is different, the way these adjustments work. They can be temporary, or they can last forever. It varies. And you shouldn't worry about causing him to get fired. The man was a bully from day one. I saw it when we were…connected. He had no qualms about playing dirty to get ahead. A total narcissist. He caused many people to quit or move on. Your company can only be better by ridding itself of such an unscrupulous individual."

"But something must have happened. Tonight…couldn't have been an accident. The guy tried to kill me. He did it on purpose."

"Yes. I might have to visit him again."

"No, please don't. Lyria, I have to be honest. I've been on a guilt trip since finding out about Dobson getting canned. About affecting his life like this."

"I assure you, my only intention was protecting you."

"I know. I know." I took her hand again. "This is all…still new to me."

"I understand. You know, Conner…if there's ever a time when you want me out of your life, all you have to do is say so. I will disappear, and you will never see me again."

She was looking at me with a hint of sadness as she said this. Despite everything, I honestly couldn't imagine my life without her. I had to remind myself that Lyria didn't ask for what happened to her. And she was with me. She needed me, and I needed her.

I hugged her.

"No. Don't think that. This is my problem, not yours. I know you've done all this for me. I'll just have to find a way to deal. And look both ways when I cross the street from now on."

She smiled, her radiance beaming. "I've heard of this technique...to help you *deal*, as you say."

She undid my zipper. I gasped.

"Oh, God. Yeah. Think I might have heard something about that...."

***

We were in bed later that night. Despite all my worries, I felt content and was just about to drift off to sleep. But of course, my subconscious mind couldn't allow such a peaceful end to such a hectic day.

"Lyria?"

"Hmm."

"Do you remember telling me that your blood can cure some illnesses and injuries?"

"No, Conner."

"It was after Mason Williams. You said you might have helped him with his head injury."

"I remember telling you. I'm saying no to what you're about to ask."

"How do you know what I'm about to ask?"

"I just know."

"Is it even possible that you could help Jason?"

"No."

"But are you sure?"

She leaned up on one elbow. "Conner, listen to me. The answer is no. And I'm asking you to please accept that as my final answer. I'll do whatever I can to support your family as they deal with this, but I *can't* do what you're suggesting. Now please try to get some sleep. You've had a difficult day."

Yeah, which included finding out my nephew was dying and my former boss trying to ensure that I would join him.

"Okay. I'm sorry. I was just thinking."

"You do too much of that. Good night."

***

On Monday morning, I was settling into my routine in the office. It seemed quiet in the cube farm. It honestly felt like there was a big void without Shrek around. You wouldn't think that fear and hatred were feelings that one would miss, but in some way, it felt—I don't know—*wrong* to be calmly working away without worrying about the next volcanic eruption from my boss.

About an hour into my morning, I sensed something else different about the work environment. At first, I couldn't place what it was, but then I realized I was actually *smelling* something unusual. Of all my senses that were on high alert at all times, my sense of smell didn't usually come in to play.

I wandered out of my cube, looking like Deputy Dog searching out a clue. Whatever the smell was, it seemed to be emanating from the next row, and when I turned the corner, sure enough, Boof was out sniffing the air as well.

"What is that smell?" I asked.

"I don't know. But there's something familiar about it that I can't quite place."

We walked up and down the aisle a few times. Razor and Vicky were ignoring us as best they could while concentrating on their work.

What a novel concept.

Boof and I narrowed it down to the twins. We looked in on Larry Berman, and he looked up from whatever he was doing. It seemed like he knew something—he looked a little embarrassed.

"Hey, Larry, what smells different?" I asked.

"Hey, it's not me, okay?"

"Yeah, okay, but what…?"

The realization hit us at the same time. It had to be Chauncey.

We looked in the next cube. Stillwell was pretending he didn't see us and continued hammering away on his keyboard.

"I got it!" said Boof. "It's Axe. Stillwell, are you actually wearing cologne? Axe, no less?"

Chauncey finally acknowledged our presence, looking up from his desktop. His face was turning all shades of red.

"Well…um…. I mean…yes. Yes, I'm trying something

different, is all. Sorry if I might have been a little heavy handed."

"Hey, it's okay, buddy," said Boof. "Are you trying to become a player? I get it, but you know it doesn't work the way it does in those ads. Where you just splash some on, and suddenly babes in bikinis are tripping over each other trying to get to your door. Trust me. I've tried."

"No, nothing like that," said Stillwell. "With all the talk about dating recently, I thought it was time to…step up my game some."

"Cool," said Boof. "It's a step in the right direction for you to actually think you *have* a game."

Vicky materialized next to us. "Be nice, Edwin," she said. Vicky had the unique ability to get Boof to shut up. "I think it's sweet, Chauncey. Is there anyone in particular that you're interested in?"

Stillwell sported an embarrassed smile and blushed again.

"There is, Chaunc?" I asked. "You're not just casting your reel? Who is it, do you mind me asking?"

"Well, I really don't want to say…."

"You might as well tell them, Chauncey," said Berman, who had joined the gang in the doorway. "They're going to find out eventually anyway."

"Sure. You're right. Well…okay. It's…Jenna Hughes."

"From accounting?" asked Boof. "Whoa, slow your roll, dog. You're setting your sights way too high. You gotta start slow. Get yourself some experience first. A class one doll like Jenna will eat you alive if you don't know what you're doing."

"I think she's lovely," said Vicky. "Have you spoken to her yet?"

"Of course he hasn't," said Boof. "You think he woulda sprung for a bottle of Axe if she had already shot him down? They don't exactly give that stuff away, you know."

"Ahem."

We turned around in unison, and you could hear the intake of breath from everyone. Boof actually whimpered out loud.

Chud Johnson's imposing figure was standing at the end of the aisle, looking down on us. Chud was a partner at BHA.

He was an African American man who was built like a Sherman tank. His head was completely bald, and his shoulders and chest were barely contained by his expensive-looking tan suit. He was even a bit taller than me.

I dare say there was no more feared person in the entire organization. Chud had skyrocketed through the ranks with a combination of a brilliant mind, a keen sense for business, and a natural ability to physically intimidate. Rumor had it that he had been kicked off the football team at Harvard for being "too mean." We had become used to being cowed by Darren Dobson. This guy made Shrek look like Honey Boo Boo.

I had once asked Chauncey Stillwell, who knew the inside dope on just about everyone in the company, if "Chud" was Mr. Johnson's real name.

"Nobody's had the guts to ask," was his reply.

"What's going on here?" His thunderous low-pitched voice vibrated in my chest.

"Oh, I was just…checking on a detail with my colleagues, Mr. Johnson," said Boof. "Excuse me." He high tailed it back to his cube.

We all made to slink away, but Chud stopped us in our tracks.

"Is this how you're going about your business without Darren Dobson around?"

Nobody knew what to say, so we didn't say anything.

"You're David, right?"

My heart just about stopped as the big boss honed in on me.

"Y-yes, sir."

"How do you think your father would feel if he saw you chit-chatting during business hours?"

"Uh, not…not very good. Sir."

"Then maybe you'd all better get back to work."

Needing no further impetus, we all walked slash ran back to our offices.

Chud made one additional pronouncement even though there was nobody left in the aisle. He correctly assumed we would all hear.

"I expect there will be no drop-off in productivity. And I'll be stopping by periodically to make sure of it."

CHAPTER ELEVEN

Mikolaj had to travel again, which meant disguising himself once more.

He knew he didn't have a choice but to obey the orders of his superiors. In the modern-day SS TV, there was a very fine line between a loyal and valuable soldier and a former asset who had outlived his usefulness and had to be eliminated.

Much as he felt dismay at the assignment, Mikolaj understood why it was given to him. He did, after all, avenge the massacre of his predecessors by seeing to the death of the she-creature Lyria. From Mik's perspective, it was a display of tireless perseverance and facing down enormous odds to successfully complete his mission. Now his masters wanted to find the Other and use it as a weapon for the cause. Who else could be given such an assignment? If Mikolaj were in his master's position, he would have made the exact same choice.

But Mikolaj also knew there was an underlying reason for being sent on such a metaphysical wild goose chase. He was expendable.

It was a dangerous mission. Even if he succeeded, it could well mean his own death. If he failed, he had no doubt the organization to which he had dedicated his life would keep the whole episode under wraps by having him snuffed out without a second thought.

His only hope was to succeed. Surely if he were to bring such an unmatched weapon to the fore, he would be regarded as a hero to the cause. But a nagging thought reminded him that he had presumed such a status before.

With his disguise in place and his false documents in hand, Mikolaj was able to secure a flight out of London. Yes, he thought begrudgingly. His superiors had made the right choice. For virtually anyone else, this assignment would have made the veritable needle in a haystack look like child's play. Nobody else on the planet would have any idea where to even begin looking.

But Mikolaj knew where to start.

He knew *exactly* where to start.

***

Mik didn't care for the Henri Coanda Airpost in Bucharest.

Despite the fact that most Americans he had interacted with thought of Romania as a place still stuck in the dark ages, most of Bucharest was modern. A great deal of the city had been rebuilt after the war. The airport was a shining example of a state-of-the-art metropolis, with wide, bright hallways lined with the latest popular shops and huge atria in each of the four separate buildings.

In fact, it was this wide-open architecture that bothered Mikolaj. He preferred the older airports where it was easier for somebody like him to traverse without being noticed. He made it a point to move quickly but without seeming to be running. People always noticed someone running.

He was close to the exit when someone spoke in his direction. "Draga."

Mikolaj stopped in his tracks and turned slowly, and saw the large man coming toward him. The man was casually dressed — jeans and a lightweight, dark colored jacket. He had a huge bald head and a scruffy beard. His Slavic looks blended in perfectly with his surroundings.

"Naspa, it is good to see you again," said Mikolaj.

They had to use nicknames in case they were being tracked. The large man's real name was Waclaw, and he had assisted Mik in the pursuit of the she-creature in the United States.

"I trust your travel has been pleasant," said Waclaw.

"Very much so."

Waclaw took Mikolaj's small carry on bag. He had learned long ago to travel light. Without another word, they headed toward the parking garage.

Mik had found Waclaw to be a nearly perfect assistant. Yes, he had to part with a portion of his pay from the SS TV, but it was well worth it. Waclaw provided great physical strength and an intimidating presence, qualities that Mikolaj lacked. Plus, the big man did as he was told and asked no questions. He was either a quiet man by nature or simply sensed that Mik didn't have the time or the inclination to chatter about non-business related matters.

They got settled in Waclaw's car, a nondescript sedan. Waclaw naturally took the driver's seat.

"What is our destination, Draga?" Typical Waclaw. Not asking about their mission, just essentially a "where to?"

"Rahova," said Mik. "If my guess is correct, the one we seek will have returned to his roots."

***

The Rahova area was perhaps the best place to experience the contrast of pre and post-war architecture in Bucharest. Where it was once a low-income neighborhood, it had been built up over the years, with wide roadways surrounded by tall apartment buildings and a stretch of offices and storefronts. There was even a streetcar running through the downtown area. Yet, a tourist wouldn't have to look far to see a crumbling façade, still leftover from when the communists had laid waste to a large portion of the city.

Off the beaten path, there were dense strips of residential streets, with tree-lined sidewalks and lower-middle class housing. Mikolaj had to search his memory to find the house they were looking for. So many of them looked alike. They drove down many streets. Waclaw asked no questions, as usual. The fact was that if they couldn't find the correct residence, Mik's chance of completing his mission was essentially nil.

"Slow down," said Mikolaj. "This street looks somewhat familiar." He looked ahead and gasped. "Keep going by the light blue house. Then circle around the block. We will park down the street where we will not be observed."

Waclaw did as he was told, then looked over at Mik.

"As chance would have it," said Mikolaj, "the one we seek was out in front working in his garden. He used to live with his sister. With any luck, the sister will still be present. We must take them both. We need answers from the man, and he will provide them to ensure his sister's safety. Understand, however…."

Waclaw was expressionless.

"If the sister is no longer there, we will need to do whatever is necessary to garner the man's cooperation."

Waclaw nodded his understanding.

"Come now. Look casual as we approach."

They exited the car and walked slowly up the street. It was a warm day, but the trees along the sidewalk provided shade.

As they neared the target house, Waclaw saw an elderly man kneeled over tending to a small patch of flowers in front of the house. The man was extremely frail, wearing overalls and a wide brimmed hat covering wispy gray hair. It was astounding. Waclaw actually recognized him, and their mission became that much more clear to him.

The two men swiftly closed the distance.

"Let's get him in the house," whispered Mikolaj.

They each took a side. They were right next to him, but he still hadn't looked up.

Mik reached down and took his left arm. Seeing this, Waclaw grabbed his right.

"Excuse me, sir," said Mikolaj. "Perhaps we can be of assistance."

The man's expression was pleasant at first. He looked closely at one man, then the other. His eyes focused on Mikolaj. The old man stared, his eyes growing in recognition and terror. He suddenly stood bolt upright.

"YOU!" gasped Radu.

CHAPTER TWELVE

This was not a day I was looking forward to.

I hate to admit this because it will make me sound like more of a priss than I already do, but sadness and tragedy are virtual strangers in the David household. Serious illnesses, drug problems, financial difficulties, even death — truthfully, we never dealt with any of it, at least not while I was growing up. Sure, both of my grandfathers had passed, but everyone said it was just their time, and we threw a party.

Jason was scheduled for his first chemotherapy, and the family all wanted to be there for him — and for Caden and Lisa, who my mother had been weaning off the funny juice. Jason was at Mass General's Hospital for Children. Everyone else was driving into town, but your privileged boy here was within walking distance, so I set out from home.

It was a warm summer Saturday morning, close to perfect conditions for my stroll. I went past city hall and the government center on Cambridge Street toward the Charles River. This area always reminded me that Boston has the best medical facilities in the country, and quite possibly the world. If you had to get sick, this was a heckuva good place to do it. I walked past the bustling entrance to Mass General. The facility was so vast, you were as likely to see someone being rushed in for a gunshot wound as you were some rich old lady getting a tummy tuck. I tried like hell not to think about Jason and what he was going to have to go through until the absolute last minute. But I wondered about people with less means, which included about ninety-nine percent of the population. Were their family members getting the same level of treatment? I shuffled that worry to the back of my mind.

I got to Children's Hospital and asked for directions at the information booth. I took the elevator up to the Oncology Ward, walked past a myriad of rooms, and saw a lot of very sick children. One little girl self-propelled her wheelchair by me. She had no hair, a huge bandage wrapped around her head, and a medication bag hanging from a holder leading to an IV running into her arm. But what caught me was her expression. She was determined to get wherever she was going on her own power, as if to say, "take that" to her illness.

There were parents and relatives piled outside doorways with expressions of various degrees of pain and agony. It occurred to me that the hospital could do some very effective fundraising just by taking people on tours of this ward. It was enough to make anyone with even a semblance of a soul take out their checkbook and ask, "How much do you want?"

Honestly, the atmosphere was freaking me out a bit. Like I said, this was not an environment that held any familiarity for me. But, I sucked in my breath and continued my search for Jason's room.

I paused at the door before entering. I knew everyone was going to try to look strong for Jason's sake. Again, not exactly my forte.

In contrast to the grim setting in the hallway, Jason's room had an almost party atmosphere. It was a small single room, yellow in color, but with the antiseptic air typical of a hospital. My mother and father, Caden and Lisa, and Carly were there and were all doing their best to maintain Jason's spirit. They were watching a video monitor mounted on the wall.

"Hey, there he is!" exalted my brother, and everyone laughed.

"Did you see him, Jase?" asked Carly, and I heard Jason say, "Yeah!"

"Hello, everyone. Hope I'm not interrupting," I said.

"Look who's here!" said my mother.

I got my first look at Jason, and I'll be honest, it took a lot of inner strength to match everyone's positive spirits. I could only remember my nephew as a typical rambunctious four-year-old boy, running around, creating havoc, and getting into trouble. But he was lying in his hospital bed wearing a gown and covered with a blanket up to his waist. His eyes were sunken and baggy, and his skin color was pale. And he looked drawn, as if there was less meat on his bones than usual, even though he had always been on the thin side. He had two IV's running into his left arm, and the arm was taped to a small board, apparently in an effort to keep it straight.

"Uncle Conner!" yelled Jason with as much strength as he could muster.

Everyone continued with the uplifting attitudes, although I began to sense the strain behind it.

Caden got up and joshingly took a boxing stance. "Hey, bro, hauling up the rear as usual." We play wrestled a bit.

Lisa was seated next to Jason's bed. She stood up and came over to me with a smile. "Hi, Conner," she said, but her voice caught. We hugged until she had regained control.

My mother said, "Good to see you, Conner. Glad you didn't dress for our benefit," and everyone laughed. My lack of fashion sense was legendary in our family.

Even my father, whose mien toward me was usually akin to someone having a tooth pulled, acted glad to see me. "We didn't tear you out of the office on a Saturday, now did we?" he asked with a smile.

Carly kept it simple. "Hey, Conner."

I made my way over to the right side of Jason's bed and took his right hand, the one unencumbered by any tubing. "How you holding up there, buddy?" I asked.

"Okay. We're watching *Finding Nemo*. Can you stay for the rest?"

"You bet, I wouldn't miss it. You haven't seen this before, have you?"

That generated a laugh. Jason had probably seen this movie a hundred times.

Even Jason sported a bit of a smile. "Well, yes. Maybe a couple of times. But it's coming to a good part."

"Okay, cool."

I continued to hold Jason's hand while we watched the movie. My family hooped and hollered at their favorite scenes, everyone having the film practically memorized. Jason seemed to truly enjoy the company.

I took the opportunity to search the faces of family members in detail.

Despite the attempt to generate positive energy, Caden looked the same as the last time I saw him, pale and gaunt. Lisa, on the other hand, was barely recognizable. She was a beautiful blonde woman with smooth features and a slim, perfectly proportioned body. It seemed that she never had a hair out of place, leading me to refer to her as "Barbie" while she and Caden were dating.

"How's Barbie doing?" I would ask Caden. When that stopped being effective, I started calling Caden "Ken."

But the woman sitting by her son's bedside was wearing an oversized shift. She had her long blonde hair pulled back behind her, was not sporting any makeup that I could see, and had the puffy-eyed, flushed face of someone who had been crying for a long time.

I met my father's eyes. He was standing behind Jason's bed on the left side, wearing slacks and a cardigan sweater. Dad was a guy who was always upright with perfect posture, but his shoulders were slightly slumped, and he gave the impression of holding onto the bed to keep from falling down. He smiled slightly, but I could see the hurt in his eyes.

My mother was perfectly put together as usual, but she avoided looking at me. I could tell that everyone was on the edge of breaking down.

Carly sidled up next to me and took my right hand in hers. She didn't have to say anything. We had always been close, and we understood each other's unspoken pain.

The movie ended with exclamations of how great it was.

Just then, a serious-looking nurse came in and said everyone except Caden and Lisa had to leave, so Mom, Dad, Carly, and I went out and sat in a waiting area with clowns painted on the wall.

"Did they say how long the first treatment was going to be?" I asked my father.

"Two hours," he said. "Maybe three. Going forward, the treatment time will depend on the results."

I nodded. Now that we were out of Jason's sight, the pretense of frivolity was gone. We sat grim-faced, knowing we were in for a long wait.

***

The time truly crept by. Dad sat upright, barely moving. Mom sat at his side, weeping softly. They held hands.

Despite the trauma of the situation, it was actually gratifying for me to see the "kinder gentler" version of Charles David. While growing up, the signs of affection from my father were few and very far between. And I don't ever remember he and my mother being outwardly touchy feely towards each other. The inner workings of my mind reminded me that they did have three children together, so....

Nope. Cut that one off at the pass. Not going there.

Carly and I sat together and made feeble attempts at small talk. The subject stream naturally came around to Lyria.

"So," she said, her sweet smile emerging. "How are things with Lyria? You two still seeing each other?"

For a moment, at least, our tension was gone. Everything seemed back to normal. My sister was busting my chops about my girlfriend. Dad was pretending not to listen, but I was pretty sure he was taking it all in. All okay in David land.

"Yes, Nosy Nellie. Any reason why we wouldn't be?"

I already knew the answer to that. Every member of my family was stunned into submission when I showed up with such a transcendent beauty as Lyria. I'm sure they all assumed it was just a matter of time before she came to her senses and the whole thing flamed out. Of course, they were also unaware of our "extenuating circumstances."

"No, just haven't seen her again since her debut in the David household," said Carly. "Hey, maybe we can all—"

"No."

"You don't even know what I was going to say."

"Yes, I do. And the answer is no."

"Oh, you're going to try to maintain this dark, brooding loner persona? The one with the mysterious girlfriend, who is several notches too high on the looks scale?"

I had to laugh. I even thought I detected a slight smile on Dad. "Something like that, yeah," I said.

"You know that can't last. We all know you too well," said Carly.

Just as the mood was starting to lighten up a bit, the nurse approached, and we all stiffened.

"The treatment is over," she said. "You can all go back in, but just very briefly to say goodbye. It's important for him to get some rest. Here, you'll have to wear these." She handed us surgical masks. "The risk of infection on chemotherapy is very high. Remember, just goodbye and out."

***

We all put our brave faces on again and headed into the room. The atmosphere couldn't have been more different than when I first arrived. Caden and Lisa were sitting on opposite sides of the bed, each holding a hand. Jason looked half asleep and even more pale than he had earlier. Caden was doing his best to hold in his emotions, but Lisa was sobbing.

Mom and Dad went over first. My father leaned over, his hand caressing Jason's head. Even with the mask on, I could see the pained expression on Dad's face. "Okay, Jason," he said. "Grandma and I are going to let you rest, but we'll see you bright and early tomorrow, okay? We love you."

Jason's voice was barely above a whisper. "Ok. Love you too."

My mother was now crying outright. She did what she could to manage a hug. "Love you, baby."

Carly forced a smile. "I'll see you tomorrow, too, Jase. You be good for the nurses tonight, okay?"

"Okay, Aunt Carly."

"Any particular movie you'd like to see tomorrow?"

Jason thought for a second. *"Finding Nemo,"* he said, and we all managed a laugh.

Then it was my turn. I nudged my brother aside and took Jason's right hand. "Have a good night, Jason. We'll all see you tomorrow."

"Okay, Uncle Conner."

"And you know, you're going to have to get better soon, so we can play some more football."

Jason and I had taken to playing one-on-one football on the side lawn of my parents' house. One of us would throw the ball to the other, and he would then try to get by the thrower for a touchdown. We started out playing tackle, but non-athletic me pleaded to go to "two-hand touch" before someone — likely me — got hurt.

Jason brightened up and seemed delighted at the prospect. "Okay! Shouldn't be that hard now that we don't play tackle anymore."

I ignored the hurt to my pride and joined everybody else in laughing.

We all headed for the door. I heard Caden say, "Sure you'll be okay, honey?"

"Of course, go ahead," said Lisa.

"Conner, can you wait outside? Do you have any free time tonight? I thought maybe we could go for a drink," asked Caden.

Wow, things really had changed with me having a girlfriend. My brother asking if I had any free time? Previously, Caden, and all my family members, for that matter, would have just assumed I'd be free on a Saturday evening.

"Sure thing, bro. Anything you need."

"Great. I'll meet you in the hall in a couple of minutes."

We said our goodbyes in the hallway. Everybody hugged and agreed to meet back there again on Sunday morning.

"Maybe I should go with you guys," said Carly.

"No, that's okay, Carl. You go ahead home with Mom and Dad. Sometimes a guy just needs to be with his brother."

My sister didn't seem like she totally accepted that, but she went with our parents nonetheless. Caden came out a few minutes later.

I put my arm around his shoulder. "How you hanging in, bro?"

He started sobbing. "It's worse than we thought."

My breath caught in my chest. "Wh...what did they tell you?"

He inhaled. "He's going to have to stay here for the duration. Could be months. Maybe even years. They're going to give him the strongest form of chemo available to try to kill the leukemia cells. That increases the chance of infection, so he'll have to stay in isolation. He needs a transfusion every other day because of the lack of healthy blood cells."

I felt like my face was ash white. "What are the IVs he has in now for?"

"One's an antibiotic. The other one is for nausea. The prognosis...." Caden paused to gather himself. "It's not good. Even after chemo, they may have to use radiation. Or a stem cell transplant...maybe something experimental. The insurance won't cover it, but Dad says he'll pay. I don't know...how we're going to get through this. Lisa.... I'm not sure Lisa can...."

My brother couldn't continue.

"Let's go have that drink," I said.

***

The emotions of the day came flooding back that night as I told Lyria about Jason.

I was pretty buzzed. The combination of reliving the emotional devastation of having a sick child with my brother and my microscopic tolerance level left me in a state of high inebriation. Of course, we only intended for our outing to be a brief respite for Caden, but we started feeling comfortable in a small pub on Charles Street. Caden's emotions were flowing, and suddenly one drink turned into a half dozen.

Or so.

My brother fancied himself as very much the "strong, silent type," and most times, he fit the bill pretty well. First, he was indeed physically very strong, always a good athlete, and a guy not too many people teased about having means growing up. Such qualities were, of course, completely foreign to yours truly, causing some in the family to wonder whether Mom had gotten too friendly with a mailman or something before we were born, while Dad was out conquering the world.

Second, I don't ever remember Caden complaining. About anything.

He had his normal share of spills and falls growing up, not to mention the usual number of injuries related to his participation in sports. But he would just brush them off as minor inconveniences. Sprained knee? Ah, I'll be ready to play the next game. Gashed elbow from falling off his skateboard? Okay, stitch it up, and I'll take that turn a little more slowly tomorrow. Limb practically hanging off his body? Push it back in there; I've got a hot date tonight.

And so on.

But Jason being sick was trauma on a whole new level. My brother had put an emphasis on being strong around the family, especially Mom and Dad, who were also struggling to hold it together. So, after we got seated at the bar and had a couple of pops, these pent-up feelings started flooding out. In a way, I was flattered that he felt comfortable enough around me to let loose.

The pub was a standard Boston watering hole. I couldn't even tell you what it was called. It had wood paneling throughout, and the floor was stained with beer spills. It was average sized, with a bunch of unoccupied tables and a full bar. The place was close to the old Boston Garden and the new TD Garden, so the owner had plastered pictures of sports figures imbibing all over the walls.

We started out talking about the diagnosis, and I did my best to be encouraging, citing examples of people who thrived after not being given much of a chance.

"Remember Maribel Adams?" I asked. "She had that liver disease. Her skin always looked yellow? Her doctors said she wouldn't make it through high school. She ended up going to medical school herself. Probably thinking she couldn't do any worse than the clowns who had written her off."

Caden sat sullen, but the Maribel story did seem to help a bit.

"But these doctors…they're like the best in the world. What

are the chances they're all wrong?" He held his head in his hands and started sobbing. "And Lisa," he said. "I'm not sure she's going to make it. We always talked about having kids. It's important for some women — some couples — but it seemed like it was her reason for living. And when Jason came along, he was her whole world. She was doting on him so much, I started getting worried, you know?"

I smiled. "Worried about what?" I asked, even though I knew the answer.

"That he was going to grow up a mamma's boy. Or a candy ass. We both know it's a tough world. And growing up with money will only take you so far."

I said, "Yeah." My main function there was to listen.

"I was always trying to make up for that. Roughhousing with him."

"I noticed. I think you were the one who suggested me playing tackle football with him. Thanks a bunch."

This generated a bit of a smile. "Yeah, I appreciate that. Anyway, whenever Jason would come home with some cuts or bruises from what we were doing, Lisa would throw a nutty. God forbid, but if he ever got seriously hurt, I think she would have taken me out."

A couple of hours — and several drinks — later, we left the bar. We stood outside and hugged.

"Thanks, bro," said Caden.

"No problem."

He headed back to the hospital. He and Lisa were going to become permanent residents while this ordeal was playing out.

And I headed back home, noting for the first time that night had fallen. It was dark outside.

***

Lyria was there when I opened the door.

"How is Jason?" she asked right away.

I hadn't remembered telling her I was going to see my nephew, but it was possible I had. It was also possible that my girlfriend kept me under surveillance, and it occurred to me not to complain. She had, after all, just prevented me from becoming roadkill at the hands of my former boss.

"He…had his first chemo treatment today. It…doesn't look good."

At that point, I broke down, fueled by the built-up heartbreak for my nephew, and, to be honest, the alcohol. We settled in our familiar positions on the couch, my head on her shoulder and her arm around me, stroking my scalp.

I related the day to her with an occasional pause for a sobbing fit. I know that I probably didn't seem very masculine at the time, but my booze-addled brain wasn't making that connection.

"Oh, Conner, I'm so sorry," she said. "How is everybody holding up?"

"We're all trying to be strong around Jason, but it's tearing us up. I went out for drinks with Caden afterward. He's a wreck. I've never seen him so emotional."

"You should be careful. You know you're not much of a drinker."

She had a sympathetic look on her beautiful face, but I couldn't help but smile a bit at the jibe.

"Come on," she said, standing up and taking my hand. "I think we'd better get you to bed."

***

I laid down and was unconscious almost instantly.

I awoke a while later, I couldn't tell you how long. It was still dark, and Lyria was lying next to me under the covers. As an indication of how bad off I was, it took me a moment to realize she was naked. And warm.

"Uh…I must have dozed off. Sorry, you're…," I sputtered.

"I thought we might need to save some time. Assuming, of course, that you're interested."

"Interested? Oh. Yeah. Of course. I mean, always…."

"Now, Conner. You've been through an emotional wringer today. If you'd rather just sleep, that would be okay."

"No!" I said, a little too loudly. "No, I'm good." I put my hands around her back. "I'm great, as a matter of fact."

She moved over, and we started kissing.

"Lyria. I can't help but notice that you're…warm. I mean, did you…?"

She reached down for me.

"Is that really what you want to talk about?" she purred.

"Oh, God! No. Never mind."

***

We were snuggled close to each other afterward. Most of the fog had cleared from my brain.

"That was…you are…amazing," was all I could muster.

"Why thank you, kind sir. I thought you could use a… distraction."

I laughed. "Yes, you certainly succeeded."

We stayed still, wrapped around each other, and I felt myself drifting back to sleep.

At the last second, my subconscious mind kicked into gear. "Are you sure, Lyria?"

She said nothing.

"Are you sure there's no way you could help my nephew?"

After a pause, she spoke softly. "Go to sleep, dear Conner. You need your rest."

CHAPTER THIRTEEN

Mikolaj and Waclaw rushed the old man through the front door before he could make a ruckus. What happened next was exactly what Mik was hoping for.

A woman, who looked even older than Radu, came walking in slowly from another room. She looked shocked at the strangers intruding in her home. She didn't know who they were, but Mikolaj certainly knew who she was.

Radu's sister.

"Oana," said Radu. "Go back to your room. Don't worry. Just go."

Mikolaj had a grip on Radu's arm, preventing him from moving. He nodded at Waclaw.

The big man immediately moved to Oana, took her by the arm, and led her over to a worn-looking sofa on the far wall of the living room.

"Sit down!" ordered Mikolaj.

The old woman looked at Radu for guidance. "Just do as they say." She sat.

"Very good advice," said Mik. "Advice that you should follow as well. As long as you do as you're told, no harm will come to you. Or your sister."

Radu's eyes widened. "What...what do you want?"

Mikolaj pushed the old man into an old brown, cushioned chair. He looked around at the sparse furnishings in the living room.

"Ah, such a shame. Working in dedicated service to your mistress for so many years, and this is all you have to show for it?"

The home was neat but showing its age. The living room was about ten by ten, with the couch and chair being the only furniture. There was no television or any form of outside entertainment. The walls were a faded tan, and paint was peeling close to the ceiling. There was a simple area rug covering most of the floor, and Mikolaj would have guessed that Oana had made it herself.

"Mistress?" said Oana. "What is he talking about, Radu?"

Radu looked at Mikolaj with terror in his eyes. He shook his head as if pleading for his captor to say no more.

Mikolaj smiled. "Do you mean your dear brother hasn't told you what he's been doing all this time he's been away from home?"

Oana was heavyset, wearing a body-length muumuu. Her gray hair was cut short around a heavily wrinkled oval face, showing confusion and concern.

"He's been in government service overseas," she said with conviction. "In America, as a matter of fact."

Couldn't be better, thought Mik. The woman was not only convinced that her brother was doing some top-secret mission for Romania, she was outright proud.

"Government service?" he said with a smile. He looked down at Radu, who was now close to panic.

"I ask you again...what, do you want?"

Mikolaj thought for a moment, then said, "My friend Waclaw will keep your sister company for a moment. Why don't you and I have a private discussion? Perhaps in the kitchen."

Mik grabbed Radu's arm again and hauled him to his feet. They made their way to a small kitchen adjacent to the living room. There was a tiny wooden table with two chairs sporting old cushions.

"Sit," said Mikolaj. Radu fell into his chair, and Mik once again assessed his surroundings. "A very comfortable abode, Radu. My compliments."

The stove was clean with only a teapot on one burner to

show that someone actually lived there. There were no dishes on the counters, and a white towel was draped over the sink faucet.

"You and your sister keep a very neat home. Hoping to quietly live out your days? Hoping nobody finds out how you have really made a living over the past decades?"

Radu looked like he wanted to cry. Or get sick.

"And you've even managed to keep the truth from your sister. Again, my compliments. However, does it occur to you at all that fate would not allow your sins to go unpunished?"

"Sins?"

"Oh, come now, old man. For how many years did you support the she-demon? You mean to tell me that it never bothered you how many lives were taken? How many families destroyed by the loss of their loved ones? Now, I know you personally may have never harmed anyone, but there is still blood on your hands. All those years, those decades caring for a creature that could only survive at the expense of others. Have you actually convinced yourself of your innocence?"

Radu's face paled as he looked down at his shoes, but the old man said nothing.

"Perhaps you have," said Mikolaj. "It is remarkable, is it not, the degree to which people can delude themselves?"

When Radu finally was able to muster speech, he whispered. Mik had to move closer to hear.

"She...she told me she only...dealt with evildoers."

"Ah, so not only have you denied your part in the evil deeds, but you fooled yourself into thinking you were part of something good? Something positive?"

Radu continued looking down but said nothing.

Mikolaj laughed with a sneer.

"Well done, my old friend. I suppose it was necessary to maintain this façade when you returned to your sister. A righteous woman, I'm sure. She would certainly have no part of taking in a mass murderer, even if he was her brother."

Radu looked up, showing the first signs of anger, redness rising in his wrinkled face.

"Yes, but to the moment at hand," said Mikolaj. "You will

take Waclaw and me to the burial place of the Other."

Radu's anger quickly dissipated, his eyes widening in a look of sheer terror. "The...the Other? What are you referring to?"

Again, Mikolaj laughed. "Come now, my old friend. You may be able to put that deceit over on your sister. She undoubtedly loves you very much and still thinks you can do no wrong. I, however, know better."

"I...I—"

"Let there be no mistake about my meaning. You will take us to the burial place. Your sister will accompany us. The alternative would be for me to first inform Oana about your true...career calling, shall we say? Then, you will watch as we slowly put her to death in a most unpleasant way. You see, my friend in the other room? Waclaw? He actually enjoys hurting people. You sneer, but who are you to judge, really? Oh, and the memory of your sister will be your final vision before we end your time on this earth as well. And, as unpleasant as Oana's death will be, yours will make it look easy and painless."

Radu looked like he was ready to fall over on the floor. Mikolaj was suddenly worried he would kill the old man with his words, and his only lead would be gone. He patted Radu's shoulder.

"On the other hand, if all goes according to plan, you and your sister will be returned here to live out the balance of your lives peacefully, and I assure you you will never see us again. The balance will be considered paid, so to speak, for your lifetime of immorality."

Radu sat silently, thinking.

"So, I assume we can expect your full cooperation?"

Radu looked up to the ceiling as if praying. Then his eyes focused on Mikolaj, and he nodded silently.

Mikolaj laughed and patted him on the shoulder once more. "Very good, my old friend. Shall we go?"

CHAPTER FOURTEEN

Monday mornings should be outlawed.

After another day with Jason and family at the hospital on Sunday, I was emotionally drained. About the last thing I wanted to do was put in an effort to make myself presentable and head into the office. But I did it anyway, feeling dead from the neck up during my walk. I knew I had to keep up appearances in case Chud Johnson decided to make another unannounced visit.

I hadn't gone more than a block when I felt someone grab me from behind, and before I had a clue what was happening, I was being dragged down an alley, flung around, and slammed up against the wall of a building. My surprise turned to a sickening feeling in my stomach when I looked into the enraged eyes of Darren Dobson.

I was wearing a polo shirt, and Dobson had a firm grip of my sleeves and was pinning me back. He looked like a deranged version of his old self. His normally buzz-cut hair had grown out, and it looked oily and uncombed. His face was unshaven and red with rage. He was wearing a worn looking jacket despite it being mid-summer.

Dobson was always a bull of a man who took pleasure in physically intimidating his coworkers and staff. He looked thinner than I remembered, but he was still plenty strong enough to keep me in place without much resistance on my part. I was taller than him, but Dobson knew that in a physical confrontation, I was less than useless.

"Mr. Dobson?" I gasped. "What are you — ?"

"You just shut up and listen, David," he hissed. It was early morning, but I smelled stale booze on his breath. "She's with you, isn't she?"

My heart sank, but I said, "She? Who? Mr. Dobson, if you can just let me go, I'll be glad to talk to you — "

His grip tightened, his thumbs getting uncomfortably close to my windpipe. I thought about Lyria, but it was daylight, so I was on my own in this one.

"I said, shut up! I had it all. I was on my way up the corporate ladder. I was making money hand over foot. My home, my life. Now, all I can think about is her. I didn't just change, you know. It was *her*, I know it was. Now I have dreams — do you understand, David? She's in them. I can see her. I can see when it happened. And I've lost everything."

I could barely find my voice, but I tried reasoning with my former boss again. "Mr. Dobson, let's go get some coffee. Maybe we can — "

"COFFEE?" He pulled me toward him and rammed me against the wall even harder. I began to see stars. "Is that your answer, David? Coffee? After what you've done to me?"

"Mr. Dobson, I didn't do anything."

"DON'T LIE TO ME! I know it was you behind this...this *thing* that happened to me. She did this for you, didn't she? What, you didn't like being treated bad? Daddy not around to protect you? You might be interested to know, David, that your dear old dad asked me to go tough on you. He wanted to be sure his little wimp was ready for the big bad world. But you sent her to me instead, didn't you? Always someone else to fight your battles for you. *She* did this to me. She ruined my life. And she's with you, isn't she? I know you have something to do with this. I can see it when I see her. And I can see it in your eyes right now. It's the truth, isn't it? It was really *you* who ruined my life."

I didn't have a good answer for him. Although I didn't ask Lyria to give Darren Dobson "an adjustment," as she put it, what he was saying was enough of the truth that I couldn't even issue a bold-faced denial. I didn't know what Dobson intended to do, but in the back of my mind, I knew I really did deserve it.

A siren sounded off in the distance. My hope soared that someone had seen him drag me into the alley and called the cops. Dobson looked toward the mouth of the alley with the expression of a trapped rat.

"This isn't over, David. This isn't over between you and me."

With that, Darren Dobson tossed me like a rag doll, and I went ass over teacups toward the back of the alley. By the time I gathered my wits about me, Dobson was gone.

***

Thankfully, it was quiet in the office that morning. In addition to my Monday morning blues, I was now a little bruised up thanks to my esteemed former boss playing Toss Across with my torso.

I tried to focus on my work, but before very long, I found myself head-down on my arms crossed on my desk. My desk phone started ringing, nearly giving me heart failure.

It was Caden, and he was sobbing.

"Hey, Conner."

I felt terror build up inside me, fearing the worst. "Caden, what's wrong? What's happening?"

"Jason...he...took a turn for the worse."

"Oh, no...what happened?"

"The chemo is doing a number on him. He couldn't eat anything after you all left last night. He was vomiting everything right back up. Then he got a nosebleed that took forever to stop. Now the doctors don't know if he's even strong enough to continue with his treatments."

"But, what will...won't...the disease just continue progressing if they don't keep up with the chemo?"

"Yes. That's where we're stuck right now. I don't...I don't know what to do...."

I tried to remain calm even though my stomach was churning, and I felt dizzy. "Okay, well, they have to keep up the treatments. Aren't there any meds they can give him to offset the side effects?"

"Yeah, but those meds all have side effects of their own. He's so weak...I don't know how much longer he can hold on. We're headed back to the hospital in a little while. Lisa…we had to give her another tranq last night, so she's still a little drowsy. Hey, I know you're busy, but is there any way you could make it over to the hospital? I might…need some help with Lisa."

"No problem. I'll head right over, and I'll see you there."

It actually *was* a little bit of a problem. BHA was a top-notch investment banking firm, but they weren't exactly known to be genteel with associates dealing with personal issues. If you lost a leg, they expected you to hop in and keep up with your workload.

I was thankful that Shrek Dobson wasn't ruling the roost anymore, although I wished he'd found a more fitting new vocation than bouncing his former peons off of walls. And the specter of another visit from Chud loomed large in my thoughts.

Since Larry Berman was the senior member of the financial analysis group, I went over to tell him I had to go. I was thankful that, for once, Chauncey Stillwell wasn't in his office.

"Larry, can I see you in Dobson's office for a sec?"

The walls had ears in an office cube setting. Telling Larry something at his desk would be like putting it on the front page of the company newsletter.

Larry gave me a look but said, "Yeah, sure." We went in Shrek's office and closed the door. "What's going on?"

"Listen, I have a personal issue I have to deal with, so I'm going to have to bail out for the rest of the day." I really didn't want to get into details about Jason and was thankful that Larry, unlike his "twin" Chauncey, was discreet enough not to pry.

"Oh, okay."

He looked a little taken aback. This just wasn't done at our company, but he knew this was an FYI more than anything. He wasn't, after all, the boss of the department. At least not yet.

He leaned over close. "Everything okay? You're not sick, or anything, are you?"

I hesitated. "No, I'm fine. It's…a family issue. Larry, I know it has to be pretty serious to leave, but trust me, it is. Pretty close to life or death."

My expression told him everything he needed to know.

"Okay, then go. If anyone comes around, I'll…cover for you."

We were both undoubtedly thinking about Chud.

"Hey, thanks, Larry. I'll call you later."

With that, I quietly made my way back to my cube, picked up a few things, and headed out.

***

The hospital staff wouldn't let us in Jason's room when we got there. Mom and Dad were already in the waiting area, and Carly arrived shortly after me. Caden and Lisa were with Jason.

It was the polar opposite of the joviality we were showcasing for Jason's benefit on Saturday. We sat quietly, Mom holding back tears hand-in-hand with Dad, Carly on my left. Time stretched on, and it felt like we were there forever before hearing anything.

Eventually, a nurse came over. She had a grim look about her. "You can go in now, but only for a minute. It's important for him to get his rest."

We put our masks on and entered the room. Jason looked to be asleep, Caden on his right, Lisa holding his hand on his left. Both parents were sobbing quietly.

We didn't want to disturb the boy, so Caden and Lisa came over, and we shared a rare group hug. Everyone was emotional, but Caden implored us to go home and promised he would phone if anything changed. Lisa looked on the verge of collapse, and Mom held her tight.

"Lisa, honey, why don't you come home with us?" asked my mother. "Caden will stay here. He'll keep you up to speed."

"No, I can't...I have to...have to stay—"

"No, it's a good idea, Lis," said Caden. "I'll let you know when he wakes up. There's no sense torturing yourself. Go with Mom. Let her take care of you."

"Yes, come home," said Mom. "I'll fix you some soup. You can get some rest and come back in the morning."

After some additional coaxing—even my father piped in briefly—Lisa agreed. She went to Jason, kissed him lightly on the head, turned, and left the room. The rest of us slowly followed after saying our goodbyes to Caden. I took one last look at my nephew. It was hard to believe how much worse he looked than two days previous when we were joshing around and watching

Finding Nemo. He was lying in the bed, so still and pale, that he looked barely alive.

That was the image of my nephew that I took home with me that night.

***

I walked around my condo like a zombie for the better part of the day. I couldn't bring myself to go back to the office, hoping beyond hope that I didn't leave Larry Berman in an awkward spot explaining my absence. Nine days out of ten, senior management paid the analysis group no never-mind. As long as our reports were being delivered on time, they left us alone. But, I thought, it would be just my luck of late to have Chud Johnson come back and make sure nobody was screwing off with Shrek no longer around.

The stress must have drained me because the next thing I knew, I was in bed, waking up to Lyria sitting on my mattress, stroking my hair.

"Somebody's a tired boy tonight. Tough day at the office?"

I stirred and looked up at her. As usual, she looked wondrous with her flawless visage, high cheekbones, and supermodel body. She was wearing a short purple dress that hugged her amazing figure. Keep in mind that I was taking care of all her mortal business needs, I still had no idea where she got her clothes. It must have been someplace special. Everything she wore fit her perfectly.

I took her hand, noticing once again that it was warm.

"Where do you get your clothes?" I asked.

She looked bemused. "My clothes?"

"Yeah. I mean, I pay all your bills, but I've never paid for any clothes. I was just wondering—"

"Don't you think it's better for us to have just a little mystery in our relationship?" she asked.

I spit out a laugh. "Trust me, there's always going to be mystery in our relationship."

"Might I suggest, Mr. David, that instead of worrying about where I get my clothes, you might be more interested in getting me out of them?" She leaned down and kissed me deeply. She sat back up. "Help me with that zipper in the back, will you please?"

I hesitated.

She looked down at me, bemused. "Something wrong?" she asked.

I just looked at her.

"Do you not want to get me out of my dress? This is a first."

I sat up. "Look, I want to talk. Is that okay?"

Her face didn't change one iota. "Talk? Sure, we can talk." She didn't say anymore, as if waiting for me to start. Problem was, I wasn't sure where to start.

"Why are you warm?" I asked after a moment.

"Oh, is this inquisition night? First, my clothes, now why am I warm?"

"Come on, Lyria. You know what I'm asking. I haven't seen you...feed since that Mason Williams guy. And yet here you are, warm as all get out. Have you been...feeding? You must have been. I thought we agreed that we would take down the evildoers, as you put it, together. That I would be around to make sure you only give them an adjustment. That you don't...."

"Yes?"

"You know. Go too far. Call it whatever you want. Take them out...kill them."

If this line of questioning was upsetting her, you would never know it from her expression. She remained perfectly calm, as always.

"Okay," she said. "Fair enough question. Yes, Conner. Yes, I've been feeding. Without you."

I sat, looking at her. My "new reality," as I liked to think of it, was roiling around in my brain. I had kept my relationship with Lyria going by choice, even after finding out who she was—*what* she was. She had offered to leave and never come back multiple times, but I pleaded with her not to. Part of the reason was that she was a victim, not inherently evil. She had been forced into this life, this...existence. I couldn't deny that she had saved my skin on more than one occasion, but I also couldn't deny her nature. She subsisted by feeding on others. Was I naïve to think she could simply provide these miscreants with an adjustment and be happy?

"Any particular reason?" I asked.

She thought for a moment. "Maybe I didn't like exposing you to danger. The people we're talking about are not exactly angels, you know. Maybe I couldn't stand the thought of something happening to you because of me."

"With you around? I've never been worried in any of the incidents that we worked on together."

"Maybe you should have been."

"I don't feel like you're telling me the whole story. There's more to it, isn't there?"

She looked away but said nothing.

I took her hand. "Lyria, you have to understand. There are times I struggle with this...with our relationship. I care for you a lot. But if I feel like you're hiding something, my mind...my imagination goes crazy wondering what's really going on. Please, I'm asking you to please be honest with me."

"I'm sure you think that's what you want, dear. But the truth is, there are some things better left unsaid. That you are better off not knowing."

We sat silently for what seemed like an eternity.

Finally, I said, "Darren Dobson paid me a visit today."

She looked at me. "Paid you a visit? How?" She was probably remembering that his last "visit" consisted of taking aim at me with his car.

"Uh, well, he was a tad more subtle this time. Guess he figured running me down was too...impersonal. So he dragged me down an alley, accused me of ruining his life—also made reference to you, by the way—then he heard some sirens, tossed me aside like I weighed nothing, and split. He assured me he'd be back, too."

"Oh, Conner, I'm so sorry. Were you hurt?"

"Not really. Other than my pride, that is. So, I was meaning to ask you again about these adjustments you've been giving out. How they affect people in the long run and such. But, I have a feeling you're going to tell me that's another subject that I'm 'better off not knowing' about. Right?"

"As I told you before, they affect different people differently, Conner. Some have a more lasting impact, and so on. Others need to be reinforced occasionally."

"No, please. If you're even thinking about revisiting Mr. Dobson, please don't. Although he didn't hurt me physically, his accusation about ruining his life had a disturbing ring of truth to it."

"I only did what I did to protect you."

"Oh, I know. And a part of me appreciates that. But I have to be honest, Lyria. I'm freaking out a little bit about all this. About affecting people's lives. And now you're off feeding on your own. I assume you're not giving out adjustments. It's weighing on my mind, is all. You understand, don't you?"

"Of course, dear," she said, stroking my hair again. "What can I do to make you feel better?"

I thought for a moment. "Be more honest with me. The *not knowing* is the worst. When I have to use my imagination, I come up with scenarios that give me nightmares."

She looked away and appeared to be thinking about what to tell me. "Yes, Conner. I've been feeding on my own, as you say. The truth is that when we work together and make adjustments to these evildoers, like Mason Williams, for instance, it's...not enough to sustain me."

"Sustain you? Do you mean...?"

"Yes. There are times when I have to...kill."

I sat in stunned silence. When it seemed like we were actually doing some good, like getting a dirtbag like Williams off the street, preventing him from attacking other women, I actually felt some satisfaction. But there was always a nagging thought in the back of my mind that it was too good to be true. And I was right. She was only taking in a small amount of blood during these sessions. It was through her mental connection with the victim that she was changing their mindset. But it was not enough to sustain her. Dear God.

I hadn't realized it, but she was looking at me again. Probably wondering how bad of a freak out I was feeling at the moment.

"So, who...who have you...?"

"I think it's better that you do not know the particulars, Conner. They are evildoers. Hard cases, if you will. Very dangerous. The world is much better off without them."

I rested my head back down on my pillow. Lyria was still looking at me with what I could only infer was a combination of concern and pity.

"This is my reality, Conner. It is who I am. If I could change the way I have to live, I would. But I can't. So I...try to make the best of it."

I still said nothing.

"I've always told you that if you want me to...move on, I will. No hard feelings. I understand that this...lifestyle, this existence, is difficult for others to understand, to accept."

Finally, I sat up. "Lyria, I do love you."

She sported a pained smile.

"Can I come to terms with all this? The...killing? I honestly don't know. But I would certainly feel better if I thought we were doing more good on top of everything else."

"More good? How do you mean?" she asked, but I had a feeling she knew what I was getting at.

"Help my nephew."

She expulsed air and stood up. "I already told you I can't do that."

"I know, but you're not sure of that, are you? You said it yourself, everybody is different. You may have helped Mason Williams with his head injury. Doesn't my nephew at least deserve as much of a chance as a rapist?"

"He's better off being treated at the hospital. They're performing wonders these days, and you have him at the best facility around."

"It's not working, Lyria. I went to see him today, and he looked worse than just a couple of days ago. I'm...not sure how much longer he's going to live. Trust me, it's as desperate a situation as you could imagine. If there's even a chance, you could make a difference...."

"No, Conner."

"That's it? Just no? With all the trouble we've caused? All the killing? Ruining Darren Dobson's life? We have a chance to help a little boy live, my brother's son, and you won't even consider it?"

She sat back down on the bed. "Conner, listen to me. You don't understand what you're asking. You don't understand what is involved. You don't understand why I can't help him... help Jason."

"No? Then explain it to me. Help me understand."

She looked at me silently. After a moment, she took my hand. "I'll explain it to you. You deserve that much."

***

"Children are different in many ways in my world, Conner. First and foremost, I vowed never to feed on a child after I was...changed. For moral reasons, more than anything else. I understand that there are certainly some evil children in the world, but they must be given a chance to amend their ways as they grow into adulthood. Perhaps even more important, it is not possible to simply provide an adjustment, as I did for Darren Dobson and Mason Williams. Or to give back some of my blood in an effort to help with an ailment, as with your nephew."

"But why, Lyria?"

She hesitated again.

"Please," I said.

After a moment, she started speaking again, facing away from me on the bed. "Feeding on a child brings about a euphoria that I cannot truly describe. I'm not able to give you a reason. Maybe it is because their blood and their spirit are pure. Again, I don't know. But I do know that once one...starts, they cannot stop. Until...until the child is completely drained."

I couldn't come up with anything to say to that. I could see that revealing this was painful for Lyria, but I didn't really understand why.

Yet.

Lyria continued. "And if I were to give the child my cursed blood as a replacement...."

"Yes?"

"That child would be...transformed. As was I."

I sat quietly, letting that sink in.

"Even worse," she said.

"Worse?"

"Yes. Again, perhaps due to the lack of impurities in their body, a child who has been changed would be extremely powerful, more so than even me. And you already know that, when Aurel converted me, he made sure that my power, my strength, was vast, exceeding his. And a child who has not yet learned the ways of the world would be unconstrained in the use of this superior power. The evil overcomes them more easily because their own personality is usually not strong enough to provide a counterbalance. They would be beyond anybody's control."

After what seemed like an eternity, I reached over and took her warm hand again.

"I'm sorry," I said. "I didn't mean for you to get upset."

She smiled down at me. "That's all right, my dear Conner. Sometimes I forget what an...awkward situation I have put you in."

We hugged without speaking for a few moments. Then a lightning bolt struck me and, before I could stop, I blurted out a question.

"Lyria, how do you know all this...about children, I mean?"

She pulled back from our embrace and looked deep into my eyes.

"Do you mean...?" I sputtered.

"Yes, Conner. I know about converting a child because...I have done it before."

***

I was sure it was not in Lyria's plans to tell me this story tonight. My guess was she hadn't planned to tell anybody.

Ever.

We headed downstairs. I had a feeling I would need tea. I threw some clothes on, made my tea in the kitchen—I didn't even think to offer Lyria tea anymore—and we settled on the couch.

As if reading my mind—she couldn't do that too, could she?—Lyria said, "This is not a story I have related to anyone else. I'm sure you will understand why."

CHAPTER FIFTEEN

I must begin this history with my tale of how I came to meet Radu, as he is an integral part of the story. You remember Radu, don't you?

After my creation in 1940, my country Romania was war-torn for decades. The butcher Ion Antonescu had aligned himself with the Nazi Axis. As you know, my father was a leader of the resistance against Antonescu's reign. He was a prime target of the Iron Guard, the ultra-nationalist group born of violence, whose charter was to maintain terror to keep the opposition at bay.

After I came to be, I took residence in Bucharest. Although the city is currently the cultural, industrial, and financial center of Romania, and is often referred to as "Little Paris" because of its elegant architecture and the sophistication of its elite, in the forties, it was the epicenter of conflict and geopolitical struggle.

As the capital of an Axis country, Bucharest suffered heavy casualties and destruction of its distinguished and historic buildings due to Allied bombing. Late in the war, my country switched its allegiance to the Allies, but this brought on additional bombing from the Germans. In fact, some of the crumbling structures remain to this day, a result of the war and a devastating earthquake in 1977.

Ah, but back to the tale. The Iron Guard was formally known as The Legion of the Archangel Michael, and its members came to be known as Legionnaires, not to be mistaken for the group that supports veterans in the United States. Antonescu and the Nazis used the Legionnaires as their enforcers during their occupation of Romania. They became so powerful that they were recognized as their own political party under their wartime leader Horia Sima.

Even Anonescu himself became wary of the Legionnaire's influence. In 1941, Sima demanded that the entire government abide by the "legionary spirit," and that all major offices be held by Legionnaires. He said that all economic policies must be coordinated with Germany. Antonescu feared their influence and rejected their demands. The leader was also alarmed at the indiscriminate killings taking place at the hands of Legionnaire death squads.

Antonescu moved in, attempting to destroy the Legionnaires militarily, and a three-day civil war ensued. He was supported by his own army and the Germans. Even so, there was a faction of the Axis that supported Sima and the Legionnaires. That faction was the Schutzstaffel or the SS. As we've come to find out, there are members of this butcher organization still active today.

At any rate, the government forces won out, but some Legionnaire members were given sanctuary in Germany. After the war, a coalition government was formed in Romania, and Communists played a leading role. In 1947, under a then-secret agreement between displaced Legionnaires in Germany and Austria and the Romanian Communist Party, all Legionnaires were allowed to return to Romania, in exchange for which, the Legionnaires would work as thugs to terrorize the anti-Communist opposition in support of the emerging Communist dictatorship aimed at taking over the country.

It was difficult for me to watch the ravages of these wars and conflicts taking place in my home country. Although I was raised on a farm in nearby Iasi, I adapted to the more urban environment quite quickly. At the time, Bucharest offered sanctuary and, as you might imagine....

"Yes?" I said.

A...steady and plentiful supply of evildoers on whom to... feed.

***

While the ravages of war are well documented, it would shock most sane people to see the butchery that one group of humans can bring upon another, as I witnessed in Bucharest during the reign of the Legionnaires. Under the leadership of a sadist named Zelea Gyr, the group would indiscriminately savage anyone with an inkling of opposing the Communist regime. Anti-Semitism was still prominent despite the end of the war and the freeing of prisoners held in concentration camps.

Gyr set up shop in a former meat packing plant. Its dark, gray brick walls were as bleak as the horror taking place inside. Even before the war, the vicinity around the building had the smell of death. Jewish civilians would be snatched off the streets and brought to the slaughterhouse. They would be hung from meat hooks, mutilated, and killed in a vicious parody of kosher meat processing. Indeed, Gyr insisted that the innocents be labeled with placards as "kosher meat," as they were waiting to meet their gruesome fate. Some of the victims were skinned while they were still alive, their screams heard for many blocks around the repugnant building.

The Legion was based on the outskirts of Bucharest in a building known as the Green House. It was located in Rahova, home to many middle-class Romanians who lived in fear of the Legionnaire death squads, whether they were part of the anti-Communist regime or not.

As I'm sure you can imagine, resistance groups formed in opposition to the totalitarianists. They came to be known as the Haiduks, or folk heroes. They would hide out in the Carpathian Mountains and use guerrilla tactics in raids against the Green House, intended to take down leaders of the Legionnaires. The raids had an impact but also had the effect of bringing about more killing of innocents. The Legionnaires would indiscriminately break into and search homes in Rahova. If even a single weapon was found, the entire family would be taken to the dreaded slaughterhouse.

Unknown to many of their neighbors in Rahova — and indeed to Radu's own beloved wife — Radu Fieraru and his sister Oana were leaders of the Haiduk resistance.

***

Radu believed he had found his calling in construction. He had always loved to build things, and his mechanical aptitude stretched far beyond that of others. In the aftermath of the war and the bombing which took place in Romania, his services were always in demand.

His hometown of Rahova had many residences that were badly damaged or leveled. The situation in Bucharest was even more dire, with entire neighborhoods reduced to rubble. It was not uncommon for Radu to be away from his home overnight, or even several consecutive nights, for professional reasons. Although the building and architectural jobs paid substantially more, he actually preferred residential construction because those jobs wouldn't take him away from his idyllic home life.

Radu lived with his sister in a quiet tree-lined area of Rahova. The war had left the neighborhood untouched for the most part, and he and Oana kept their small house in pristine condition.

When he was in his teens, Radu came across Mihaela while doing construction on a street adjacent to his own. He was helping others repair damage to a wall when the occupants came outside to watch. She was with her mother, who was scrutinizing every aspect of the job, but Mihaela's focus was honed in on Radu. Radu glanced in her direction and did a double take after noticing the young girl. She was petite, with long brown hair and huge brown eyes. She wore a simple dress that was old, yet she somehow made it seem elegant. He found himself staring, observing her every move. When he looked at her face, he noticed that she was returning his gaze, and she smiled at him. He was on top of a ladder and had to keep himself from falling to the ground. She saw his near stumble, and she laughed. Radu felt himself go crimson with embarrassment.

When the crew was finished, they started packing up their supplies. Radu hoped among hope that the girl would come back out so he could prove to her that he was more than just a clumsy oaf who almost fell off his ladder. Most of his coworkers headed off, but Radu delayed as long as he could. He had just about given up hope and was walking away from the job site.

"Would you like something to drink?"

He nearly fell again as he turned around. She was standing in the walk, extending a glass to him, with a smile that made his knees go weak.

"Are you sure you should be working on ladders?" she asked.

At first, he was too stunned to speak, but he laughed. How could he not?

With that brief meeting, he already knew this was the girl he would marry.

***

They lived in his house, with Oana. His sister and his wife got along splendidly. They became as close as sisters. He thought of his life as nearly perfect. He would work during the day and come home to his loving wife at night. When they had spare time, they would work on his house or their gardens. Radu, Mihaela, and Oana were inseparable. Mihaela and Oana would prepare meals, and they would eat dinner together, share their stories from the previous day, and laugh at the absurdities of the world.

Radu and Mihaela would retire, worn out from the work filled days, but never too tired for each other. Before long, their daughter was born, and they named her Crina, which means "lily flower."

It seemed like the ideal existence. Radu's work would often require him to be away overnight, and sometimes Oana would accompany him. They had told his wife that Oana was performing administrative tasks for the construction company and was needed on job sites. Mihaela thought they were working in Bucharest, restoring destroyed buildings. Often that was the case, but on other occasions, Radu and Oana were meeting with gangs of insurgents holed up in the Carpathians. They would form raid teams of ten to twenty people and strike the Green House or other Legionnaire targets.

Their most pressing objective was to disrupt operations in the slaughterhouse. The atrocities taking place had become legendary, but the building was heavily guarded. Often they would strike members of the Legion as they were rounding up victims, but they knew this was having limited impact. Romanian nationals were still being butchered in the meat packing plant, and the Haiduks were powerless to stop it. Their failure weighed on Radu, as he was now a leader among the Haiduks. He sent word through his channels that the group would have to amass as many members as possible for one ultimate strike against the site of the butchery. As the time for the assembly neared, he spent as much time as possible with Mihaela and Crina, knowing the chances were quite good that he would not survive the ambush.

"Look how she favors you," said his wife.

Crina was nearly a year old and starting to walk. Radu and Mihaela were sitting on the floor in the front room of their home. They were about ten feet apart, sending the child to walk and stumble between the two of them. The problem was, she would always head back to Radu. When Mihaela sent her towards her father, she would nearly run to him. But when he sent her on the return trip, she would get about halfway, turn around, fall down, get back up, and head back to Radu. He would have to carry her back so Mihaela would have a turn. Michaela tried to look hurt, but they would both end up laughing.

"She's definitely her father's daughter," she said.

Radu's love for his wife and daughter made his role as a Haiduk even more important to him. He did not want his child growing up fearing for her life every time she left the house. He wanted her to grow up in a Romania free of the sadistic Legionnaires.

The time for the Haiduk assembly arrived. Radu and Oana readied to leave.

"We will be in Bucharest overnight." He felt pangs of guilt for lying to his wife but knew it was necessary. She must know nothing of his alternate life. He hugged her extra close and long.

She seemed to sense something out of the ordinary. "Is everything satisfactory with your job?" she asked. "You seem more tense than usual."

He looked at her and came close to blurting out the truth. But finally, he said, "Yes, my darling. It is just that…I find it more and more difficult to leave you and Crina. I will miss you so."

She smiled the smile that always made everything seem all

right. "I know, my love," she said. "But we will be here waiting for you."

Crina had crawled/walked to him and was clutching at his pant leg. He picked her up and again held her long and tight. Finally, he had to leave, and he handed his daughter to his wife, causing the child to wail and reach out to him. His wife laughed, but he could only manage to say, "Come on, Oana." They left to the sound of his beloved child still crying in protest of his leaving.

What Radu did not know at that moment was that he would never see his wife or daughter alive again.

***

The Haiduks were badly overmatched in their resistance against the Legionnaires. They had no set location, fewer arms, and, most importantly, a diminishing number of fighters.

At the start, Radu knew every member by name. But as their ranks were thinned, mostly through losses suffered in combat, the group had to start accepting new members. Radu felt uncomfortable that they were laying out plans for their latest assault, with some members being virtual strangers.

As it turned out, his suspicions were justified.

He huddled with a ten-member team deep in the Carpathians. They felt secure in the pure wilderness, nothing but trees surrounding them. The moss-covered ground even absorbed the sound of their voices. It was pitch black, and they needed to build a fire for light. The men formed a circle. Even in the middle of nowhere, they were used to communicating in hushed voices, so everyone gathered close to hear. Oana settled herself behind Radu. She was only there to provide support but understood that she could never actually take part in combat, much as she wanted to.

The team looked to Radu for leadership. He had trusted associates by his side, Marcu to his left, Vasile on his right. The three of them had grown up together, and Radu knew he could trust them with his life. The rest of the group, however, were unknown to him. But it could not be helped. They needed numbers. Otherwise, they were doomed to failure. And certain death.

"We cannot assault the meat packing plant head on. It would be suicide," said Radu. "Our focus will be to thin the ranks of the support personnel. We will accomplish this with a two-phase approach. Marcu and a team of three will act as snipers near the entrance to the building. Vasile and the others will snipe at or around the Green House. We must strike quickly and move on, as they will send troops to hunt us down, and they will easily outnumber us. Oana and I will follow suspected Legionnaires back to their residences. We will take action against them at a future time."

A member of the group spat in disgust.

"Who are you?" asked Radu.

"I am Marius. Yours is the plan of a sheep. Our people are being butchered in this meat plant, and you propose nothing to stop the pig Gyr. He is the leader. We must cut off the pig head to stop the killing."

Radu felt his anger rise. This dissension was predictable. The Haiduk were an informal group with no military hierarchy holding them together. Radu had no training or formal declaration of his position as a leader. He was essentially taking charge because he had been a member of the resistance for the longest time and had Marcu and Vasile as support. Before he could reply, his attention was drawn to the man stationed next to Marius. The man was acting nervous and twitchy. As the rest were on one knee, this man was squatting as if positioning himself to flee.

"You," said Radu to the nervous man. "What is your name?"

The man's fear level seemed to grow with the attention. "I…I am Sandu."

"Sandu, eh? And where are you from, Sandu? I don't recognize you. How long have you been a warrior?"

Sandu now stood up straight. Radu clutched at his rifle, but before he could act, the man bolted from their circle and quickly disappeared into the woods. Radu suddenly heard a shuffling sound from behind him.

"GET DOWN!" he yelled. "TAKE COVER!"

He pulled Oana close from behind him, and they pinned themselves to the ground as the first shots rang out. Radu was clearly their target, but his fast action avoided the rain of bullets.

His friends Marcu and Vasile were not so lucky. Ultimately, their proximity to Radu was their downfall as bullets intended for their leader tore through their bodies. They fell to the ground, killed instantly.

Radu, Marius, and other members returned fire, but they were shooting blindly into the woods. After another volley of shots, the firing ceased. Radu held Oana down until he was certain the ambush was over.

His sister looked up at him, a look of sheer panic in her eyes. "Radu, we have been infiltrated."

He looked at his sister, the realization dawning on him.

She grabbed his shirt. "They may have identified us. They may know where we live!"

Radu's breath caught in his chest. "Mihaela," he gasped.

***

He started running, leaving Oana behind. It never entered his mind that he could still be in danger from the assault team that had killed his friends, Marcu and Vasile. He had no time to grieve their loss. All he could think of was Mihaela.

And Crina.

He could hear gunshots all around as he approached his hometown. Was the covert assault part of a larger plan to weaken or eliminate the Haiduks?

Ignoring the sounds of gunfire, he plunged into Rahova, his only thought to get to his wife and child. He feared the worse, but when he ran down his quiet, tree-lined street and broke through the front door of his house, what he saw was more horrible than anything he could imagine.

His wife hung from a ceiling support that he himself had installed. The end of a large hook stuck out of her chest. The front of her simple plaid dress was crimson. Her eyes were open, and she seemingly was accusing him, as if to say, "Where were you? Why did you not protect me?"

He ran to her with a guttural moan. Then his nightmare became worse. Behind Mihaela, hanging from the same hook, was Crina, his beloved, his world. He clutched at his wife's legs, and when the blow came from behind, knocking his consciousness out of him, his last thought was a wish that death would take him as well.

***

I watched much of the horror that took place in the slaughterhouse. I was outside waiting for opportunities to thin the horde of sadistic butchers who thought nothing of inflicting the most horrific punishment imaginable on people whose only crime was wanting their freedom and a chance to live out their lives peacefully and productively. I wasn't kidding myself that I was making much of a difference—their ranks were too numerous. But when I did feed, it was invariably on a member of the Legion.

I was lurking near the entrance to the slaughterhouse when two heavily armed Legionnaires appeared, hauling a man who looked to be on the edge of consciousness. Each soldier had one of his arms and were dragging him toward the entrance. The captive appeared to be sobbing and muttering something I could not hear under his breath.

I heard one of his captors taunt the man. "Don't worry about your wife and daughter, pig," he said. "Soon, you will be joining them, and you will know what they experienced."

This comment sent the captive man into a rage. He broke free from the grip of the man who spoke and lunged for his throat. The three men went down in a heap, with the captive man choking the Legion guard on the bottom. The other soldier broke free and pointed his rifle at the prisoner.

"Let him go, pig. Last warning!"

But the captive man did no such thing. He tightened his chokehold on the Legionnaire. "Go ahead and shoot," he said, maintaining his control, the guard weakening underneath him. "I have nothing more to live for, and I can only hope your bullet will pass through me and kill your friend as well."

The standing guard hesitated, then appeared to make up his mind. He aimed his rifle carefully and tensed up. I came up behind him and quickly snapped his neck, and he fell lifelessly to my feet.

The prisoner looked up at me in disbelief. While he was distracted, the other guard found the strength to pull a knife from his belt. He drew it back and aimed for the prisoner's neck. He was ready to plunge it in, but I grabbed the captive and pulled him up and away from the Legionnaire. I tossed him out of harm's way, and he fell to the ground. The soldier got to his feet and looked at me with a combination of fear and rage, his eyes wide, his jaw in a grimace. He emitted a guttural howl and came at me with the knife raised over his head.

I grabbed the knife hand and squeezed tightly. The Legionnaire howled, and the weapon went clattering to the ground. I held his wrist with one hand and pulled his head to one side with the other. I bit into his neck, the man moaned, and before long, he was drained, and I threw his body aside.

I walked over to the former captive. He was still prone and clearly feeling the effects of the blow to the head that had enabled his capture.

It took a great amount of effort, but he raised his head and looked at me.

"What...what manner of being are you? Are you...human?"

I helped him to his feet. "Come," I said. "We must move quickly before other soldiers appear."

I put him over my shoulder and moved at hyper speed to a nearby alcove formed by a bombed-out building, where I knew we would be safe. Conner, you know the impact that moving so fast has on a mortal. The movement and his injuries left the former prisoner disoriented. I took the opportunity to introduce myself to him in the best way I knew how.

I bit into his throat, not with the intent of feeding but rather to establish a connection. I will admit that I had been seeking a mortal "partner" at this time. Someone who would be my eyes and ears during daylight hours, someone who could provide an extra layer of security while I was sleeping, and someone who could take care of any business needs to which I was unable to attend. I know I don't need to say anymore, Conner.

When Radu had stated he no longer had any reason to live, he seemed like a candidate, but I obviously needed to know more about him. Our connection succeeded on that front. It seemed all he had left was his sister, and she probably thought he was dead. Indeed, any remaining resistance fighters would make the same assumption.

More importantly, however, he saw my history, which I have related to you. I completely understand that it stretches the boundaries of reality, changes one's fundamental understanding of the world. When he came to, he looked at me with wonder in his eyes, but no fear. I had also "related" my desire to enlist him as my mortal partner and assistant. Understand that I was not going to force this alternative on him. For it to be a viable relationship, it had to be voluntary. But he had seen with his own eyes that I intended to use my power for good. And he had seen in my thoughts that while the nature of my conversion was evil, I, by my character, was not.

"I must leave this area," I said. "Find a new place to...exist. Will you accompany me?"

He hesitated for a moment, then looked into my eyes. He was sad yet had a look of determination, perhaps savoring the death of the Legionnaire henchmen who had killed his wife and daughter.

"Yes," he said.

Chapter Sixteen

I have to admit, I had been wondering about how Lyria had met Radu, and okay, yes, there was some jealousy there. For all intents and purposes, Lyria had…seduced me. Yes, I know it's hard to believe. It's hard for me to believe too, trust me.

The seduction wasn't very difficult given, as Carly puts it, the "Looks Scale Differential." Ah, leave it to family to keep your ego in check. I was well aware that Lyria was several notches above me on the scale. And I previously found out that her intention was for me to take Radu's place as her mortal caretaker. She saw me out walking around by myself on a foggy night and assumed I was some lonely guy with no wife or girlfriend or family who could take on that role without severing any earthly bonds.

When you think about it, it's a wonder I even have an ego.

She had second thoughts after meeting my family, although the balance of her characterization of me was pretty much spot on. We ended up reaching a compromise, where I would continue most aspects of my mortal life while attending to her worldly needs.

The rest, as they say, is history.

But I couldn't help but wonder whether she had plied Radu in the same way. Although I didn't yet know the rest of the story, I felt a little better, knowing that at least the *way* they had met was completely different.

"Penny for your thoughts," she said, bringing me out of my reverie.

I thought for a minute, then decided to be honest with her. "I have to admit, I had always wondered whether Radu was just your mortal assistant or whether he had achieved 'boy toy' status."

She laughed. "No, Conner. You're my only boy toy."

I beamed with a little pride.

"At least for the moment," she said, bursting my bubble. "I'm kidding, dear. So, on to the rest of the story?"

I was hooked. "Yes, please."

***

I needed to move on because stories were starting to circulate in Bucharest. As discreet as I endeavor to be, the legends invariably start of a being who lives by drinking the blood of others. Before I came into existence, there was Aurel, who had lived for hundreds of years. Much of the lore of the current day most probably was based on our existence.

At any rate, moving around periodically was necessary, and it was much easier with a human counterpart. We decided it was best to stay in densely populated areas where it was easier to avoid notice. We headed to Timisoara, the third most populous city in Romania. Like most regions in my home country, Timisoara was born out of conflict, and many of the causes were still unsettled when we arrived.

Timisoara is located in the far eastern region of Romania, near the borders of Hungary and what is now Serbia. The city has a history of control being determined by armed conflict. Over the years, influence has been spread between Romanians, Germans, Serbs, and Hungarians. The architecture of the city was largely destroyed during the war, as Romania ended up being bombed by both the Allies and the Axis. Gothic structures were in ruins when we arrived, so it was not difficult to find a secluded area where we could reside.

After the war, Romania came under the Soviet sphere of influence, and yes, factions of the Legionnaires were present in Timisoara as well. The city had a large Catholic population. The Orthodox Cathedral was and is the tallest building in the city and dominated the landscape. The Church's influence on the people grated on the Soviet authorities, who demanded unbridled loyalty to the state. The Legionnaires were the perfect group to enforce such loyalty.

The dictator in charge of Timisoara was Yazov, and while he made an effort to appear benevolent, his real objective was to stifle and ultimately eradicate the Catholic influence in the city. Attendance at the great Orthodox church dwindled as rumors swirled that members of the Legion were taking Catholics captive and torturing them. Or worse.

We got situated on the outskirts of the city in the upper floor of a three-story apartment building that had escaped the bombing. Understand, Conner, that for the first time in my new existence, I had to accommodate a human. Previously I could simply locate in an abandoned basement or even underneath the rubble of a bombed out building, my only concern being solitude and the likelihood of being found, even by accident. But now, with Radu, we had to have an actual place to live. He had scouted the city, and we found our new home to be secluded enough to not be bothered by day-to-day foot traffic, yet provide enough accommodations to sustain Radu as my human "counterpart." It was just three rooms, but we reinforced one to keep me safe. There were not many other residents of the building, and the few that were there didn't interact with anyone they didn't know. We moved my sarcophagus there in the pitch black of night. The building had once had a colorful façade, but most of the paint had been scraped off, leaving a plain gray color. There were rows of townhomes surrounding the building, some of which had been obliterated. Many of the units were unoccupied, and it was clear that a large portion of the population had fled and not come back.

As a financial person, I'm sure you're wondering how we funded our living quarters and such necessities as food now that there was a human involved. I don't want to cause any more unease for you, but we obtained the resources we needed through my...victims. That is all I will say for now. Leave it be said that we never lacked for the financial backing we needed.

The Legion henchmen working for Yazov maintained a reign of terror in and around the city. A strict curfew was put in place, and any civilian on the streets after dark was suspected to be up to no good.

It was the winter months when we first settled in. Temperatures were moderate in southwest Romania, and the city teemed with foot traffic during the day. Builders were beginning the onerous task of removing the remainders of destroyed structures, and rebuilding proceeded slowly. Most trade was taking place in temporary arrangements. Where lines of stores once stood near downtown, a series of tents were now in place, with vendors hawking food and clothing. People who had dared not leave their homes during the war now flocked to buy bread and delicacies like fish and beef that had been scarce for so long. But at night, it was rare to see anyone but soldiers loyal to Yazov.

The Legion was frequently seen around places of commerce. They would demand a share of the proprietor's meager earnings for themselves and a share for Yazov. Anyone who resisted was dragged into the street and beaten. After a time, any remaining resistance waned.

Early in our stay in Timisoara, my relationship with Radu grew stronger. Shortly after we arrived, I awoke at darkness and found him in tears.

"My wife. My daughter," he said sobbing. "How could I have left them? I thought my world was fighting the Legion. But in reality, they were my world. Protecting them should have been my top priority. My only priority."

I thought back to my father and all that he sacrificed to protect me. Even though I was no longer mortal, Conner, I truly felt pangs of human sorrow. I did my best to comfort my new partner, taking him in my arms.

"You couldn't have known, Radu. You couldn't be with them every second of every day. And you couldn't have known that your group had been infiltrated. You were doing what you thought was needed to keep your family healthy, to give them a safe environment. You mustn't blame yourself."

"Will we continue, Miss?" He had taken to calling me Miss, a practice that continued to the very end.

"Continue?"

"Yes. Will we continue to fight against the evils of the Legion? To free Romania from their butchery? Will that be your...focus?"

I looked at him as the tears continued to roll down his face. I know you only saw Radu as an old man, Conner. But in his youth, he was quite handsome. He was tall, though not as tall as you. His features were Slavic, with a sharp nose and chin. He had a stubble of beard—appearance had not been his priority since leaving Bucharest. He wore a simple plaid flannel shirt and heavy burlap pants, an outfit that I would come to deem as his uniform over time.

"I will do what I can. You have my word."

He stood, moving away from me. "You are cold. Do you need to—?"

Just then, about the most unexpected occurrence possible came to pass. We heard a knocking on our door.

Radu's eyes grew wide. After a moment, I said, "Answer it."

He opened the door. It was a girl, perhaps seven, wearing a tattered overall dress with a plain white shirt. Her brown hair was pulled back in a ponytail and flowed down to her waist. She was dirty, but her expression was vibrant, with bright eyes and flawless porcelain skin. Her lips were full but cracked. When she smiled, her teeth were imperfect, yet the effect was magnetic as if you couldn't help but be drawn to her.

"I am Angelika," she said, flashing a brilliant smile. "I live downstairs. I saw you come in the other night, sir."

Radu stood agape, staring at the child as if he couldn't bring himself to fashion a response. The child seemed not to notice his reaction. I imagined it was one she got on a regular basis.

"I go to market for my mother, most of the time on Sunday," she said. "She works at the mill, and sometimes she is too tired to go. My father...no longer lives with us. But the markets are better now. They have bread. And sometimes, beef. We didn't have any meat for the longest time. I was thinking...tomorrow is Sunday, and I could bring something back for you if you like. Would you like me to do that, Mister...."

"Radu, I am Radu...and this is...."

"Lyria," I said. "My name is Lyria."

Angelika came bouncing into the apartment, feeling more comfortable now that introductions had been made.

"So nice to meet you," she said. She shook Radu's hand, and I leaned down to accept a brief hug. "Nobody has lived in this building for so long. It used to be full, but many people have fled. My mother and I...we stayed. Mother said she had a good job, and she wasn't going to be forced to move. We only go out during the day. Mother says the soldiers don't like us going out at night. But I usually go to the market early — you get the best choices then."

We didn't have much in the way of furnishings in the front room of our apartment. It had plain gray walls with peeling paint. We had a small wooden table with two metal chairs. There was no sofa or comfortable chairs. Nonetheless, Angelika pulled out one of the metal seats and hoisted up, making herself right at home. Radu and I looked at each other and couldn't help but smile.

"This is nice," she said. "I hope you will stay for a while. Sometimes people come here, but they never stay very long. Where do you come from?" She addressed the question to Radu, clearly favoring him with her attention.

He, in turn, was very taken with our young visitor. "Bucharest," he said. "We come from Bucharest."

Angelika's face lit up even more. "How exciting! I have read about Bucharest. I...I don't go to school. I started, but Mother felt it wasn't safe. But, I'm learning English by listening to the radio! I mostly stay home by myself when Mother is working, but she sometimes gets me books to read. Some of them are in English, and I mostly understand. I don't know where she gets them, but she taught me to read, and sometimes I read about other places and imagine us living there. It must be so much fun. I have read that there are stores there. And libraries. With so many books. Is that true? Were there real libraries in Bucharest?"

At this point, I was a mere spectator in this conversation. So, I just stood back, although I still felt myself smiling.

"Yes," said Radu. "Many books. And schools. And shops. It is...." Radu stopped with a pained expression. "...a wonderful place to grow up."

"I would love to go there sometime." Angelika bounded out of her chair. "Well, I'd best get back downstairs—Mother will start to worry. Let me know if you'd like for me to bring something back for you from the market." She smiled with a twinkle in her eyes. "I leave early, so if you sleep late, you may miss out." She laughed, causing Radu to laugh in turn. I couldn't help but be amazed at how she had lifted his spirit.

"Perhaps I may accompany you," he said. "With your mother's permission, of course. So that I can see what the markets have to offer."

Angelika beamed. "That would be wonderful! I'm sure she won't mind. She says she gets nervous about me going by myself." She shook her head, the notion apparently absurd to her. "Come down when you're ready," she said, heading for the door. She turned and smiled again. "Remember, I leave early! Goodbye!" She bounded down the steps.

Radu was almost in shock as he closed the door.

"Quite the child, eh?" I asked, smiling at him.

"She is. It's as if…."

"What?"

"Crina. She reminds me so much of Crina. How Crina would look and act. If she had…."

I put my arm around him. "She reminds you of your daughter?"

"Yes. I know Crina was much younger. But this child's face… her expressions…they are so similar."

"And she is clearly taken with you as well. Perhaps losing her father…."

Radu stared off into space, then his attention shifted suddenly to me. "I'm sorry, Miss. I offered to go with her tomorrow, but I must stay with you."

"No, Radu," I smiled. "My room is secure. Go with Angelika tomorrow. I think it will be good. For both of you."

***

Radu and Angelika became close. It was clear they were filling voids in each other's lives. The girl's mother was Florin, a simple, hard-working woman who welcomed having someone to keep Angelika company during the day. Radu accompanied her on their trips to the market. They would read together during the day, always downstairs in Angelika's apartment. They would do chores together, repairing furniture, cleaning the apartment, and playing games outdoors. Radu explained away my absence during daylight.

"I told her you were working," he said. "She didn't ask for any details. I think she likes having my full attention." He blushed.

Radu had taken her to a nearby field one day. He had a ball, and they kicked it to each other. He had played soccer when he was younger and endeavored to teach the child.

"She was a natural," he related to me later.

They continued going to the field daily. Soon, they attracted the attention of some other children, and they had enough to play games. They set up goal spaces with old logs or bricks, and if the ball was kicked between the markers, it was a goal. The kids had been cooped up for so long, they were thrilled to have such a chance to run around and play.

Radu would tell me about their games in the evening. "Angelika dominates the game," he said, with as bright a smile as I had seen. "She is faster than everyone, even the older boys. And she has boundless energy. The amazing thing is, none of the other children mind. If someone falls, she is the first one to help them up. She is constantly yelling encouragement and helping teach the younger kids. Everybody loves her! And Miss...."

"Yes? What else?"

"Angelika...she asked me...." Radu was choking back tears.

I sat next to him. "What? What did she ask?"

"She asked if it was all right by me if she were to...call me, Father."

It seemed for Radu, and for me, to be close to an idyllic existence. But it all changed one evening in late spring.

***

I awoke and emerged from the security of my room. I was used to Radu not being there—he was usually off doing something with Angelika. But my first sight that evening made me stop in my tracks.

Radu was sprawled on the floor, blood covering the front of his shirt and pants. Angelika sat, holding his head in her lap, dabbing a towel on cuts and bruises. She had some of his blood on the front of her clothes as well.

Radu looked up at me with glassy eyes. The girl had either not noticed me coming out of my room or didn't care. Her attention was honed in on him.

"There, Father," she said. "Just lie still and let me care for you." She brushed his hair back with her hand and held the bloody towel to a laceration on his forehead.

"What happened?" I asked.

Radu was semi-conscious, but he had the girl's full attention. "Angelika, what happened?"

She looked up as if noticing me for the first time. The usual glow in her eyes was missing—she looked to be almost in shock.

"We were playing soccer. In the meadow...where we usually play. A bunch of other children had joined us. We stopped play while Father gave some pointers in the middle of the field. Nobody saw the two soldiers. They were wearing all green. They came up from behind Father, and one of them hit him with his rifle. He went down, and the other children fled. The men shouted down at him, 'Why do you have time to play games? Why are you not working? Or joining the cause, serving Yazov?' One of the men kicked him in his ribs. I ran to him, I said 'No, leave him alone!' but one of the men held me back. When Father saw the man grab me, he yelled, 'Leave her!' and lunged for the man. He was weakened, and the soldier stepped to the side easily. The men took turns, kicking him and hitting him with their rifles. When I tried to stop them, they merely shoved me aside. When they were through, one of them leaned down and shouted directly into Father's face. 'Don't let us catch you out here again, pig. We shall not go so easy next time.' I managed to get Father back up here."

That night, the two guards were searching for anyone violating the curfew. They approached the mouth of an alley between two industrial buildings a block away from our apartment. I wore a black nightdress and emerged from the dark.

"Are you busy working?" I asked.

The soldiers looked shocked by my appearance, but their surprise soon turned to leers.

"What have we here?" said one of the soldiers. He walked over close to me. "Are you not aware of the curfew? How do you find yourself out alone at night?"

The other man walked behind me.

"I was alone, and I was wanting some company," I said. "So, are you busy working, or would you accompany me to my apartment?"

The man in front took my waist, and the man behind grabbed my shoulders.

"We will see you back home, my pretty one. We will be sure you don't violate curfew again."

The Legion headquarters were close to downtown. The following morning, those arriving early were greeted by the two guards' bodies hanging upside down from the door frame, what little blood left in their bodies dripping onto the ground.

***

The Legion's response to the murders was immediate. And harsh.

They went door to door, indiscriminately beating and torturing. Most people knew no details of the killings, and in some cases, it cost them their lives. Bodies were left out in the streets, a warning to others of their fate if they didn't cooperate. The soldiers understood that what had happened to the guards was related to a man they had encountered earlier that day. They also assumed they were looking for a non-human, a demon, if you will. What kind of creature drained the blood from a body?

You must understand, Conner, that stories of blood-drinking spirits have existed throughout history. The fact that much of the lore centered around Transylvania leads me to believe that the origin of Aurel, my maker, is at the center of these stories. There was the Strigoi from Aurel's time, evil spirits said to have risen from their graves and who gained vitality from drinking the blood of others. The fear caused by these legends was so powerful that it had caused many instances of mass hysteria and public executions of people believed to be possessed of such spirits. The guards, these Legionnaires, they were hunting for such a being. Anyone who was under suspicion was not killed in the traditional manner but indeed burned, sometimes while still alive. The soldiers believed this was the only way to ensure the being could not come back to haunt them from the grave.

I arose that night to the sounds of the Legion's reign of terror. Gunfire, screaming, and explosions filled the air. I came to the front room and saw Radu unconscious on the floor. His battered face was swollen and barely recognizable. His clothes still stained with blood. I looked outside and could barely see beyond our building because of the smoke. Fires raged from nearby neighborhoods, and people were running aimlessly on the street.

Radu had risen and was at my side looking at the carnage. "My god. Angelika...." He stumbled to the door and headed for the stairs.

"Radu, wait!" I yelled, but it was no use.

I followed him down. He was banging on Angelika and Florin's door on the first floor, but there was no response. He turned the knob and found the door unlocked. We heard a whimper from a bedroom and found Florin curled up in a corner. She was so small in her fetal position that she was barely noticeable from the entrance to the room. Radu ran to her. She was bleeding from her scalp, the blood running down her gray burlap dress.

"Florin. What has happened? Where...where is Angelika?" asked Radu. He held her head, but she made no effort to rise.

"They took her," she said, so weakly that we could barely hear.

Radu's eyes grew in terror. "Took her?? You mean...the soldiers?"

"Yes." The girl's mother was staring blankly off into space. "Some of the other families...the other children...they told them that you were her friend. We were across the street. They must have thought we lived there, but we were only trying to stay with somebody…one of the other families. They were looking for Angelika. They said she was a witch. A demon. They accused her of killing the two men. They took her. I ran at them, but one of the men hit me with his rifle, and I went down in the street. When I woke up, she was gone."

"My god," said Radu, and he ran out.

I stopped him before he could get very far. "Wait," I said. "Go back upstairs. I will bring the child back."

"No…I must—"

"You cannot go alone. It will be suicide." I held him firmly by his shoulders. "Go back upstairs."

Finally, he yielded and went into the building. I made my way toward the Legion headquarters. The gray single-story building faced out into the center of town, where a small patch of grass held a pillar made of wood. A handful of soldiers surrounded the pillar, and as I got closer, I realized there was something hanging off the arm. It was the child, Angelika. Her tiny body was limp, and she was held by a noose tied firmly under her arms. The intent of the soldiers became clear. They had arranged a pile of wood below her feet. One of the soldiers had a torch. He held it up.

"This child is a witch and a demon and must be cast from this earth to join her beloved Satan in the bowels of Hell."

He lit the fire underneath Angelika, and I knew I must act fast. I grabbed one of the Legionnaire men from the periphery and held him in a nearby alley. It happened so fast that the man looked at me with shock in his eyes, and his terror grew slowly.

"What…what do you want?" he stammered.

"It is quite simple," I said. "I need you to scream."

I bit into his throat, but instead of drinking, I tore away the flesh. Sure enough, the man began to scream loudly.

I left him on the ground and circled back out the other end of the alley to the square. Sure enough, the soldiers had rushed to find their friend. The fire was licking at Angelika's feet, and legs and the child had stirred from unconsciousness and was howling in terror and pain. I quickly freed her from her bonds and rushed her away from the town square before the soldiers knew what was happening. She met my eyes briefly before she lost consciousness again. I carried her limp body back to our home building.

***

I found Radu sitting in the first floor apartment. He rushed forward when he saw I had the child.

"Is she...is she...?"

"She is alive but just barely," I said. "What of Florin?"

"She...she died."

I laid the child on the floor. She had been beaten about the head and face, and her legs had been burned by the fire, the bottom of her simple cloth dress singed. She opened her eyes briefly and saw Radu holding her.

"Father," she said. "They asked me...about you...but I told them nothing." She closed her eyes.

Radu clutched her broken body tightly. "My god...my child...." He looked at me with wide eyes. "Please, Miss...is there nothing you can do for her? Please...."

I thought for a moment. "I will try. I will give her some of my blood. It may help with her injuries, but it is not certain...you must understand that."

"Yes. I understand, please."

"Give her to me."

He held her out to me. I took her in my arms, and she opened her eyes.

"Lie back, my child. I will see if I can help you."

Her mouth edged upward in a tiny smile before closing her eyes again.

I looked at Radu. His face was set with a look of wonder and fear.

I leaned down and bit into her neck. Our minds connected immediately, but I could tell already that this was different. Different from anyone before. I intended to take in some of her blood and then provide her with mine.

Lyria, she said to me silently. *It is so perfect, so much like Heaven.*

Yes, I answered. *It is. I have never...felt like this...this euphoria... this rapture. It is as if....*

We were meant to be? Yes, I feel it too. Yes, I must....
Angelika.
Lyria.
I cannot. I must not—
No, please...don't stop.
It will be too late.
I can feel us coming together. It is bright, the light...it is wonderful.
My Lyria...my mother....

"Lyria. LYRIA!"

Radu was shouting, shaking me. I awoke with the child's body completely limp. I realized that I had drained her—she was gone. I went back to her neck and reversed the process, letting my blood flow into her. I kept going until I could give no more. I fell back, weak, completely spent. I looked up at Radu. He was staring at Angelika lying on the floor with a look of fear, of terror.

I managed to raise my head. The child's body was convulsing. She raised her head, her look feral, her mouth gaping open. She faced the ceiling and howled with pain in a man's voice, so loud that Radu covered his ears. Angelika was growling, turning over, shaking, rising up on her hands and knees. Her eyes were suddenly bright, and she showed her fangs, resembling a wolf, a predator.

The child was suddenly standing, although I hadn't seen her get up. Radu fell over onto his back, his eyes never leaving the child. She moved, looking down at her own body. Her cuts, bruises, and burns were gone. She looked down at me and smiled, her eyes black pupils, her fangs hanging over her bottom teeth.

"Thank you, Mother," she said to me.

I was too weak to respond as my head fell back onto the floor. Angelika looked at Radu. He cowered, his arms rising to cover his neck.

"I'm hungry," said Angelika, and then she was gone.

***

Radu carried me up the stairs. He went to put me in my coffin.

"No," I protested. "We must go after her. Angelika. There's no telling what she'll do."

"You're in no condition, Miss. Tomorrow night we will find

her. You must rest, regain your strength."

It was not yet light out, but I knew he was right. As soon as he closed the lid, I fell into the same deep sleep as normally happened during the day.

I awoke feeling stronger, but I knew what had to happen for me to get back to normal. I needed to feed.

Radu was nowhere to be found, so I made my way out to the street. If anything, the conditions in our neighborhood were worse than the night before. There were no civilians, nothing but wreckage and trash strewn about the streets. Fires were burning in several buildings, no doubt the result of the continuing reign of terror by the Legion. There were gunshots and faint sounds of screaming off in the distance. The air had a heaviness about it with the acrid smell of smoke and, undeniably, the scent of death.

I moved closer to downtown and finally saw what I needed to see. A three-story office building had apparently been commandeered by the Legion, a single soldier standing guard out front. He looked from side-to-side as if expecting to be attacked at any moment. The man was wearing his green uniform and holding his rifle out in front of him.

In a nearby alley, I picked up some heavy debris and flung it out into the street. The man came rushing over, stopped at the mouth of the alley, and peered into the darkness. He crept forward slowly, till soon, he was in total darkness. Even in my weakened state, the Legionnaire never heard me come up from behind him.

***

I returned to the apartment building, worried about Radu. He was back in his room, sitting on the floor up against his bed. His mouth hung open, and he looked at me with exhausted, glassy eyes.

"I was up all last night and through the day today looking for Angelika," he said. "I roamed the streets looking for any sign of her. I got to the large apartment building on Domasneanu Street. It is low-income housing—small, very basic residences. I walked past and was grabbed from behind. I feared it was the Legion and that I was doomed. I was thrown to the ground. I looked up, and it was Angelika. She had blood running down her chin. 'Are you searching for me, Father?' she asked me. I gasped at her appearance, but I said, 'Yes, come back with me, child. We will help you.' She threw her head back and laughed. She still sounded like herself...her human self. But she picked me up as if I weighed nothing and held me against the wall. She said, 'Listen to me, Father. I am not the one who needs help. If you and Mother leave me be, all will be well between us. But understand, this is your only warning.' With that, she tossed me back to the pavement, and when I looked up, she was gone."

I picked him up and put him on his bed. "You need to rest," I said.

"No, Miss, it's even worse. I heard moaning coming from the building. I went inside the front door. Several apartment doors were open. I walked down the hall. In the first abode, there was a man dead on the floor, his throat ripped open. There was blood everywhere. I went inside. A woman and two children were in the bedroom, dead as well, but there was no blood. They had puncture wounds on their necks. Their eyes were still open, looking upward. I ran out into the hall. A woman and a child were dead in the apartment across the hall. A man appeared with a rifle, pointing it at me. 'GET OUT!' he yelled. His eyes were wide, insane looking. I didn't dare venture any further. I don't know how many she...."

"It is as I feared," I said, almost to myself.

"How can this have come to pass, Miss? You are able to control...to feed only on evildoers—the Legion, the criminals. It seems that Angelika has completely changed as if no part of her remains."

"I was an adult when I was changed," I said. "I was able to retain enough of myself to control my cravings. A child is different. Our spirit is evil. It is meant to be evil. It is clear that it has taken hold of her. As a child, the essence of who she is...who she was...was not strong enough to resist. She will not be able to control herself."

Radu gasped. He moved to get up from his bed. "My god. We must find her! We must stop her!"

I held his shoulders. "You must get rested. We can only stop her if we work together. I have a plan, but we must both be at our strongest to make it work."

"A plan? But how, Miss? Isn't she...?"

"Yes, she is probably more powerful than me. But understand, in order to stop her, we must...."

Radu hesitated. "Yes, I understand."

"In order to do so, however, we must first find out where she sleeps."

***

The following night, the city of Timisoara was in a lockdown, and for once, it had nothing to do with the Russians or the Legion. The streets were still strewn with wreckage and some fires still burned. The air was filled with smoke. But most notable was the lack of any human presence. The neighborhood was completely deserted. Some houses had red crosses painted on the front, with no lights inside. There was no sign of any Legionnaire soldiers.

I made my way toward downtown, where I had rescued Angelika such a short time ago. The stanchion had been torn down, and I wondered whether she had been back here. I checked the Legion headquarters. The front door was closed, and there were no guards. I sensed a level of activity nearby and followed my instincts to the Orthodox Church, its pointy steeple reaching up to the sky. The building had a light brown façade and faced out to a grassy field extending between two residential buildings.

I went to the front door. It was unlocked, so I went inside. It seemed that the majority of the population of Timisoara was present. The pews were filled with people of all castes. Well dressed families in suits and dresses were crammed into pews next to peasants wearing simple cloth overalls and torn frocks. People stood in the center aisle and outside the pews along the walls. Considering how everyone was tightly packed in, there was astonishingly little noise, mostly just children crying.

The interior of the church was stunning, draped in gold with murals of saints facing out from the walls. A checkered floor led to the altar, where a short, balding priest was waving his arms behind a gold dais. A massive statue of Jesus hanging from a cross was behind the priest, and I couldn't help but feel that his eyes were boring in on me.

"God, by your name, save me and by your might, defend my cause," bellowed the priest.

The masses came to life, answering in unison, "God, hear my prayer. Harken to the words of my mouth."

"Turn back the evil that besets our community. Strike terror, Lord, into the beast now laying waste your vineyard. Let your mighty hand cast this devil away from your servants."

"Amen," thundered the crowd.

I continued my search, wandering to Union Square with its odd combination of neoclassic and Communist inspired architecture. I found myself in Elisabetin, one of the city's more well-to-do areas. Unlike most of Timisoara, which had multistory apartment buildings and rows of townhouses, Elisabetin contained mostly gothic mansions with huge fenced-in yards.

I felt myself drawn to one home in particular. It looked like a castle, with a gray front and three pointed arches facing the street. When I got closer, I heard moans coming from inside. The door was unlocked, but there was no sign that it had been forced open. The mansion had a huge tiled atrium, with a wide marble staircase leading to a circular hallway on the second floor. A man and woman lay dead on the floor next to each other to the left of the stairs. Their necks had been broken, and their heads were twisted unnaturally, facing each other. I heard a child scream from upstairs. When I got there, one of the bedroom doors was open, and I peered inside.

Angelika was at the neck of a girl, perhaps five years old. The girl was wearing a pink nightdress, but her arms were hanging lifelessly in Angelika's lap. Some blood dribbled down her neck onto the floor as Angelika jerked up and down. I noticed a boy under her right foot wearing a blue nightshirt. He was struggling to breathe, being held in place.

Angelika gurgled and looked up, her eyes meeting mine. Blood was flowing down the front of her cloth dress, but her head went back in a moan of ecstasy. She looked at me.

"Hello, Mother," she said. "The children are so different, so incredibly delicious. I have never tasted such sweetness. Much tastier than any adults. Then, I guess you already know that, don't you?" She laughed, sounding like a little girl, but with blood staining her teeth and fangs.

"Angelika," I said. "Let the boy go."

"Oh, I'm being rude, aren't I? Would you like him? That is the least I can do for you after saving my life. Besides, I have fed quite enough for tonight. Certainly, Mother. Here."

She lifted her foot, and the boy gasped for air. He tried to stand but fell over. He looked at his sister's lifeless body and started screaming.

"MAMMA! PAPPA! HELP ME! HELP ME PLEASE...."

Angelika stood up, dropping the girl's body to the floor, ignoring the boy's screams.

"Well, I must be going, Mother. Enjoy your treat. But it's getting close to morning, so don't delay too much." She disappeared.

I picked the boy up and sped him to the church entrance. He was nearly catatonic from watching his sister die and the effects of moving so fast. I knelt in front of him. "Go inside. Someone will take care of you."

I moved quickly back to the house, hoping to pick up Angelika's scent. I was able to follow her path even though the smoke and mist were heavy in the air. It was indeed nearing the time of daylight, so I didn't have a lot of time to spare. I found myself in a large graveyard with headstones and markers in a wide variety of shapes and sizes. The grounds extended beyond a small hill, and as I proceeded, I noticed one of the graves had been dug up, a skeleton with remains of rotting flesh lying nearby, and the door to the empty wood coffin was open.

"I know. I was desperate. It got light so quickly last night," said Angelika. She had appeared next to me. "I'm going to do better tonight. Come, I'll show you." She took my hand and frolicked off, looking again like a normal little girl wanting to show her favorite dollhouse to a visitor.

We were facing a giant cement mausoleum with pillars leading to a building with a single heavy wooden door. The name

Propescu was etched above the entrance.

"Come inside."

Angelika pushed the door open. The room was small, with plain cement walls and a built-in sarcophagus on each side. Angelika had propped two corpses up in a sitting position against the back wall, a man and a woman. They must have been deceased fairly recently. Other than their pallor and lifeless eyes, they could have been any couple sitting down for a picnic.

"Mother, this is Mr. and Mrs. Propescu," said Angelika with a bloody smile. "They've been gracious enough to share their home with us." The child giggled. "Much more privacy, don't you think? You're welcome to join me. We can even share one bed if you like. Or we can each have our own, whichever you prefer. Mr. and Mrs. Propescu won't mind a bit." More giggles.

I said, "Thank you, child, but I must get back to your father. He was not well when I left him."

"Ah yes, Father," she said. Her eyes lit up. "Perhaps we can bring him over as well. We can live as a family—wouldn't that be wonderful?"

I didn't answer.

"Oh, I can see that would be painful for you. That's all right. I will take care of that tomorrow night."

Her statement hung in the air.

"Well, good night, Mother."

The crypt on the right had a heavy cement lid that would have taken several mortal men to move. She pushed it aside and laid down in the coffin. She then reached up and pulled the lid back over her.

"Hmm, heavy door," she said before closing herself in.

At that moment, I knew what had to be done.

And that Radu would be the one who would have to do it.

***

I crammed the Propescu couple into the other crypt, closed the lid, and sped back to the apartment. It was late, and the sun was threatening to rise at any moment. But I had to have a quick word with Radu before I went to sleep.

After we spoke, his complexion looked gray, and his eyes

were looking down. It was clear that having to perform the task we both knew was necessary was taking a toll on him.

"I will take care of it, Miss," he said. "You'd best get under cover."

I went to my room. Radu understood that he would have to act during the day when Angelika was asleep. And he would need help. He would have to pay handsomely for that help. Simply pulling her out to expose her to light was too risky. Since her coffin was indoors, they would have to carry her out of the mausoleum. If she were to awake before they got her out the door, they would all die a horrible death. No, the solution had to be different. And permanent.

I awoke the next night and found Radu prone on his bed, a wet towel covering his eyes.

"Radu? Are you all right?"

He removed the towel, revealing red, watery eyes. "Yes," he said. He started sobbing.

"Tell me what happened. Were you able to...?"

He inhaled deeply. "Yes, Miss. The task is done."

I waited for him to continue.

"I did as you suggested. First, I went to the caretaker of the land...the graveyard. I asked him about the owner of the mausoleum. He put me in touch with the Propescus' sons. I went to their residence. They were planning to leave Timisoara. Their parents had been killed in a crash of some sort—they didn't provide any details. When I told them I wanted to buy the structure and flashed the money, they were thrilled. They were never planning on coming back here anyway...."

"Go on," I said

"I went to a nearby construction site. There are so many, with the damage to the city from the war. I told the man in charge what I needed. He, of course, first took me to be insane with such a request. I held out a fistful of cash, and he started taking me seriously. I said, 'I will, of course, pay for the supplies and will double this fee once the job is complete.' He was still hesitant, so I held out more cash. It was done. We went with the truck we needed to the cemetery. I paid off the groundskeeper to go get a drink—to get several drinks. That was a much easier conversation. We backed the truck up to the mausoleum. The construction supervisor had brought along enough of his men to accomplish the task. I started to panic, as the hour was getting late. 'IT MUST BE DONE BEFORE SUNDOWN,' I yelled. The men, who already doubted my sanity, looked at me strangely but picked up their pace. They filled the interior to the ceiling—with cement from the truck. It hardened in place. I had them remove the wooden door and seal the entrance. All that is left...."

He was sobbing again. I held his shoulders.

"All that is left is a huge block of concrete. Even Angelika, with her strength, could never emerge. She is trapped. For all eternity."

I held Radu as he cried. Even though his pseudo daughter was now a monster, it still affected him deeply to have sealed her in her grave until the end of time.

"I think we must move again," I said.

He looked up at me. "Yes?"

"Yes, there has been too much death here. And now there will be people hunting for...the children of the night, responsible for so many killings."

"Where...will we go?"

"Perhaps London?"

He hesitated but nodded his agreement. It was clear we couldn't stay in Timisoara. And we both understood that anywhere in Romania would carry similar risks. We had to go someplace new. Someplace where the legends, the lore, had yet to grow.

Indeed, Conner, the stories of creatures surviving by drinking the blood of others, were now rampant throughout my home country. In fact, some such accounts centered on an adult female and a child. It was assumed they were working together and that the adult was the leader. Without knowing anything about my identity, they would come to call me the She-Devil, and yes, even vampire.

The child would simply be known as The Other.

CHAPTER SEVENTEEN

So that was it. Lyria may or may not have the ability to help my nephew, but she was afraid of accidentally unleashing another monster. Like Angelika.

I trudged back to the office that morning, feeling the effects of the lack of sleep, but still on alert in case Mr. Dobson decided to pay me another visit. There was no sign of Shrek, and I settled into my work routine, thinking how my job made it seem so natural to compartmentalize my life. When I started digging into my current projects, I was at least temporarily able to block out the seeming inevitability that my nephew was going to die. I realized that I had been holding out hope in the back of my mind that Lyria would be able to help him, that she would somehow produce some not-of-this-world magic to do what the doctors apparently couldn't and keep Jason alive. Now that possibility was out the window. But I was working, and I had to devote my energy and attention to my job.

After a few minutes, Larry Berman came in. "All okay yesterday," he said. "Well, at least there was no sign of you-know-who."

He left that comment hanging in the air.

"Did anything else happen?"

"We came to realize that you provide a buffer with Boof."

"A buffer?"

"Yeah, as in, when you're not here, he has to unload his somewhat deranged combination of lies, fantasies, and untruths on someone else."

Chauncey Stillwell poked his head into the doorway. "And it was Monday, so we had to hear about his weekend," he said with a sour expression.

"Oh, hey guys, I'm sorry about that," I said, but I felt a little smile coming on.

"Seriously," said Chauncey. "We probably never appreciated having you around more than yesterday when you were gone."

"Boof asked where you were," said Berman. "I told him you had to take some personal time, and he looked crestfallen. He went in and tried talking to Razor, but he was ignoring him. After a while, he came out and looked in at Vicky, but he just kept going. She must have given him one of her, 'Don't even think about it,' looks."

"That's when he hit me up," said Chauncey. "I tried to look busy, but you know, subtlety has no effect on Boof."

I actually laughed a little.

"Apparently, he'd been corresponding with a girl he met through this new dating service," Chauncey continued. "I was like, oh no, he's not going to tell me about his date, is he? I thought about how Razor got rid of him and kept on working away. But he persisted. Seems they were really hitting it off, texting back and forth. So they agreed to meet on Saturday night. He was waiting for her at the front desk of a restaurant. A tall attractive blonde woman came in, walked right by him, and asked if an Edwin had been seated yet. He said, 'I'm Edwin! You must be Laura.' He said she looked like she wanted to upchuck right on the spot. She was towering over him. 'You're Edwin?' He says, 'Yeah.' Then she stormed right out of the place, saying, 'You must have shrunk overnight,' on the way out. I finally looked up from my desk. I said, 'Okay, Boof, how did you describe yourself to her?' He was like, 'So I mighta snuck in a few inches on my application. So what? Everybody lies on those things anyway.' I said, 'Didn't it occur to you that she was going to see you eventually?' He says, 'Yeah, well, I was hoping that by then I would win her over with my personality.' I just hung my head."

"Yeah, so he moved on to me thinking he'd get a more

sympathetic audience," said Larry. "Turns out, he went to the bar in the same place trying to drown his sorrows. He put a fifty dollar bill on the bar, intending to drink it up. He strikes up a conversation with another girl, said he thought things were going pretty well, so he excuses himself to go to the men's room. He's splashing water, combing his hair, making himself more presentable. Gets back to the bar, the girl had swiped his fifty and disappeared."

We all laughed.

"Bottom line, Conner," said Chauncey. "We're all glad you're back, and...we appreciate you."

The twins left, and a little later, sure enough, Boof came bombing in.

"Hey," I said. "Heard you had a tough weekend."

"What? No, my weekend was great. Why?"

"Well, let's see. I heard that one woman evacuated when her tall, dark, and handsome date turned out to be short, pudgy, and needy."

"Oh, yeah. I'll tell you, some people have no sense of humor."

"Then, there was the one about the girl who ditched you and filched a fifty."

"Yeah, but we talked for almost half an hour. Hey, I've paid more for that much time, know what I mean?"

"Uh, yeah. So, how does that translate as *great*?"

"You know, I didn't tell the twins the whole story. The way I see it, whatever I'm doing on this dating site is working. I scored me up a Grade A Primo babe, right?"

"She ran out as soon as she saw you."

"Yeah, but I'm trending in the right direction is what I'm saying. Now I just have to hope the next one isn't so shallow that she can't overlook a few physical shortcomings."

"A few?"

"You know what I mean. And the other girl seemed real interested for a minute there."

"Boof, she was interested in your fifty."

"I think my mistake was heading to the can when I did. Think I disrupted my momentum."

"Yeah, we'll go with that."

"Anyway, where were you? You think it's okay to just skip out now that Shrek is gone? Hmm. Not a bad thought. Maybe we should head out to a happy hour this Friday. Get in on the ground floor?"

"Uh, that would be a no."

I looked down at my desk. Boof could tell that I didn't really want to talk about my absence.

"Hey, everything okay, buddy?" he asked. "You didn't have to go get a penicillin shot or anything, did you?"

I guffawed. "No, Boof, nothing like that. I...had to take care of something personal is all."

"Oh, hey, that's cool. You don't want to talk about it, huh? One time I got a call from my neighbor. He said someone was heaving all my stuff out the window of my apartment. I high tailed it out of here, even with Shrek around. Good thing too. It was a girl I'd been seeing, and I got there just as my fifty-six inch TV was about to bite the dust."

I laughed. "You're kidding. What was she so mad about?"

"Who knows? Could have been any one of a number of things."

"Yeah, well, we'd better get back to work. We don't want Chud catching us screwing off again."

"Ah, I figure he won't come back around for a while. Let the fear factor sink in a little. Lemme know if you change your mind about happy hour."

Strangely enough, these little discussions with Boof, twisted though they may have been, did tend to lift my spirits some. But I wasn't able to dig into any of my projects before my next visitor appeared.

"Hi, Conner. Everything okay?" asked Vicky.

I thought, *Boy, disappear for an afternoon, and it's like the world came to a stop.*

I felt an annoyance coming about, but then I looked up at Vicky. She was wearing a silky looking top and a knee-length skirt, with her pretty blonde hair flowing about her shoulders.

Pretty hard to get mad.

Her expression was inviting and caring, and I knew I had to be careful not to share too much. Resisting an attractive woman was not exactly my strong suit.

"Hey, Vick." As I said that, a thought struck me. "Do you think for our coffee break we might go to the espresso place across the street?" I asked. *Way to go, Conner. Good luck not spilling your guts once you're out of the office and alone with her.*

Vicky's face lit up. "Oh, I would really like that. Sometimes I feel like I'm in cube prison in this place." We both laughed.

A little later, we left a few minutes before the actual break time to avoid having to ask any other members of the group to join us just to be polite. The coffee shop was a small non-descript place built into a row of stores on the first floor of the office high-rise across the street. The owners probably paid handsomely for the site — Boston real estate is off-the-scale expensive. But whatever they paid, it was worth it. It wasn't unusual to see a line out the door first thing in the morning, as all the stressed-out executives working nearby sought out their initial caffeine fix. Even now, at the ten o'clock traditional break time, the place was packed.

"Hmm," said Vicky. "Looks like a lot of people want to have a temporary reprieve from cube prison."

I laughed. "Yeah."

The café was narrow but deep. There was a counter straight ahead with tables lining the walls and stools set up along the front windows. As usual, with these modern coffee shops, the aroma was overwhelming.

We got in the back of the line and waited.

"Boy, they don't give you much of a chance with that smell, do they?" I asked.

"I know," said Vicky. "It makes you want to camp out here and get buzzed on coffee all day long."

I looked around. Most of the table occupants were men, and I couldn't help but notice them checking Vicky out as we moved by. Hard to blame them, really. She looked fabulous, but she was either oblivious to the attention she was garnering, or she was just used to it. My guess was the latter — what a terrific woman.

Whoa, Conner boy. Remember, we have to resist getting carried away here.

We got our coffees and found a place at the barstools up front.

"Seems like taking an afternoon off is like a national emergency at BHA," I said.

Vicky laughed. "I know. Everyone was curious slash wanting to nose in on your business. I didn't mean to pry, Conner. I just wanted to make sure everything was okay."

"Oh no, not at all. The twins were actually the first ones to hit me up. I think Chauncey, in particular, was wanting a juicy bit of gossip. Sometimes I think he needs a steady supply to trade for all the rumors he brings back to us."

She laughed. "I know. I feel bad that I can't give him more. That I lead such a boring life," she said.

I thought, *Ah, a boring life.* "That actually sounds good to me right now."

"What?"

"A boring life."

She adopted a serious air. She was sitting on her stool facing me, her legs crossed with her skirt hiked up over her knee. I had to resist the urge to gawk.

"I don't mean to invade your privacy, but do you want to tell me what's going on?"

Everything came flooding back to me all at once. I obviously couldn't tell her about my girlfriend, the vampire. There was nobody I could talk to about that. That issue had to stay firmly pent up inside. Now the whole deal with Jason.

I almost lost it right on the spot. To say I had been through an emotional wringer in the last few months would be an understatement. But I couldn't break down in front of Vicky. I just couldn't.

I think she could tell I was fighting back tears. She put her hand on my shoulder.

"Hey, it's just you and me right now," she said. "As friends. Forget about the office."

I did my best to keep it together. "My nephew. My brother's son. He's...sick. Leukemia. The worst kind. I...I don't think he's...going to make it."

"Oh, Conner. I'm so sorry." Vicky stroked my shoulder.

"I haven't spoken to anyone about this. Outside of my family, of course."

She waited for me to continue. On top of everything else, she was a good listener.

"It all came on so suddenly. One day he was healthy, running around creating havoc. He got sick, but nobody thought much of it, you know? Kids get sick. But they brought him in for tests, and they confirmed it was leukemia. He's in the Children's Hospital part of Mass General. They're doing chemo, but if anything, that's just making him weaker. My brother doesn't think he can last much longer. I...don't know what to do."

"My god. How awful. How is his mother holding up?"

"Not good. She and Caden are staying at my parents' house. They're keeping Lisa sedated most of the time. I wish I could help...."

I stopped myself before saying too much.

"There's only so much you can do, Conner. Be there for your family. Support your brother. But you can't make him better by yourself. I know it's a helpless feeling. But he's getting the best care possible."

I thought, *Yeah, but you see, my girlfriend is a vampire, and her cursed blood may have some curative powers.*

Unless my objective was to have Vicky think the stress had sent me over the edge, I'd better not go there.

"I know. You're right. I'm sorry, Vicky. I didn't mean to lay this all on you. I had been keeping the stress pent up for so long—"

My phone rang. Normally I would ignore it, but I looked at Vicky and shrugged.

"You'd better get that," she said.

I answered. Exchanged a few words. Hung up. Vicky was looking at me.

"That was my sister. They're bringing Jason home. Tonight."

***

He had said he wanted to go to Grandma's. At first, the doctors wouldn't even consider it. But they apparently changed their minds when they determined the chemotherapy was ineffective. It sounded a lot like they were granting Jason a last wish.

And here was the kicker. He had also asked to see Lyria.

When I had unveiled Lyria to my family in the fall, with much fanfare, I might add, Lyria and Jason had gotten along swimmingly. Jason was being a bit bratty, and my girlfriend took him in the other room and kept him entertained, playing…well, catch the finger, using Lyria's *real* finger. I still get a little queasy thinking about it.

Since that time, whenever Lyria had been included in family get-togethers, Jason would immediately gravitate to her. To my knowledge, they hadn't played catch the finger again, but Jason clearly loved her. I guess it was safe to say that the entire male population was attracted to Lyria, regardless of age.

That afternoon, after spilling my guts to Vicky, my thoughts were everywhere but on work. My beloved nephew. Was this real? It didn't seem possible. He was a healthy, rambunctious boy not so long ago. Now his doctors were letting him go home because their treatments weren't working. It all seemed so surreal.

Lyria. She was clearly one of the most desirable women I had ever encountered, but talk about baggage. It was in a whole category by itself. My coffee-talk with Vicky had given me a brief sense of what having a regular, non-vampire girlfriend would be like. Not Vicky herself, although she certainly had a lot going for her. She was beautiful, smart, funny, and caring. But working so closely together was a serious impediment. Nobody really knew anything about Vicky's personal life — she kept the details closely guarded. All she revealed at coffee was that her life was boring. And I was probably kidding myself if I thought she would even consider going out with me, even if we didn't work together.

But being with her was so different than being with Lyria. It felt warm and carefree. None of the dark clouds following me around. No constant sense of impending disaster. Little things were important, too, like being together during daylight.

Was that really so much to freaking ask??

I had intentionally focused on some mindless analytical

work to fill my afternoon, knowing that my brain was engaged elsewhere. Before I knew it, it was time to go home. I knew I was going to my mom's that night, so I didn't want to delay. I cleaned up my desk some and headed out. But before leaving, I stopped in Vicky's cube. She was still hammering away on one of her projects.

"Hey, Vick," I said quietly. "Thanks again for this morning. And again, sorry for getting so heavy."

She smiled up at me. "Don't be silly. Glad I could be there for you. Please give my best to your family. And let me know how… everything goes."

"I will."

I headed for home. There was the normal hustle-bustle out on the street, so it came as a total surprise when I got grabbed from behind.

"Leaving kind of early tonight, eh, David?" said Darren Dobson.

He had taken hold of my arms and pinned them behind me as he pulled me back into yet another alley off the main street and slammed me into the wall. He looked even worse than he had in our last encounter. His normally full face was drawn, his skin pale. His hair had grown out even more and was unruly, giving him the look of a crazy homeless man.

"Is that what you do now that I'm not there to babysit you anymore? Huh? Skip out and enjoy the good life?"

"Mr. Dobson, you can't keep doing this. This isn't helping either one of us."

It was as if I hadn't said anything at all. He pushed his face within an inch of mine.

"Tell me something, David. She's still with you, isn't she?"

"She? Who?" I stammered, even though I knew full well who he was talking about.

"You know who." Dobson got closer, and I could smell the stale booze again. "Don't play dumb with me, boy. She's still around. I know she is. I can feel her. Who is she to you? You can't be screwing her—she's too good looking for a little weasel like you. Tell me the truth. You're not leaving here until I know."

"Mr. Dobson, I don't know what you're talking about."

He tightened his grip. "So that's the game you're playing, is it? Well, we'll just see how long you can keep that up."

He cocked his fist back, and I scrunched my eyes, bracing myself for the blow. I heard an, "Unng" sound, and Dobson released his grip. Then another familiar voice.

"Now, Mr. Dobson," said Razor Rojas. "We mustn't get so upset. Somebody could get hurt."

He was holding Dobson's fist in one hand and hammer-locked his other arm behind him. The older man was firmly in his control.

Dobson had a wildly crazy look about him. "Rojas? Is that you? You stay out of this. You don't know what's going on here. Don't get involved. Let me go."

"If I let you go, will you promise to be calm? Maybe we can go to the coffee shop across the street and talk about what's bothering you. How does that sound?"

Shrek's face contortions eased. "All right, Rojas. Yes, just release me, and we'll talk."

Razor maneuvered himself between me and our former boss and released his grip.

Dobson immediately sprinted out of the alley. He stopped and turned toward me. "This isn't over, David. I'll be back." Then he was gone.

***

"Thanks, Razor."

"No worries. I was just leaving when I saw him drag you back in the alley," said the big man. The way he had physically handled Dobson reminded me of how strong this guy was. It was easy to forget in the office setting, and I mostly saw him behind a desk. But I doubted that Dobson could have come out on top of a confrontation with Razor even in his best days.

"What's up with Dobson?" he asked. "He looked pretty rough. And he seems to want to take all his problems out on you."

Again, I had to be guarded in how much I could say. "Yeah, well, he always kind of had it in for me. I guess whatever happened to him before he got fired has manifested itself in even more hatred for me."

Razor nodded. "Sure you'll be okay?"

"Yeah. I'm pretty sure you scared Shrek off. And hey, thanks again."

Razor headed for the parking garage. As I turned to continue my walk home, he called out.

"Conner?" We walked back towards each other. He spoke quietly. "Who is the 'she' Dobson was talking about?"

I was a little ashamed that I had underestimated Razor. I assessed him before answering. He was a little shorter than me but twice as wide. His shoulders strained the seams of the brown sport coat he was wearing. His dark hair was cut short and appropriate for business. And of course, there was the ever-present five o'clock shadow. He had gained a few pounds around the midriff since I first met him—chalk that one up to sitting for a living. But mentally, he was as sharp as anyone in the office, if not more so. He didn't talk much, but we all knew that not much got by Razor Rojas.

A part of me wanted to tell him all about Lyria. If there was anybody in whom I could confide, it was him. He wouldn't be judgmental. He might think I had lost it, but he wouldn't say so and wouldn't suggest that the team attempt a group intervention to get me some help. And I knew I could trust him not to say anything to anyone. But still, I held back. This part of my life seemed destined to be my own internal struggle.

"It's...kind of a long story," I said finally. I sensed he knew that I was conflicted.

He nodded. "Well, if you ever want to talk about it...," he smiled, "you know where to find me."

We both laughed.

***

Our arrival couldn't have been much more different than the last time we were there to meet the family the previous fall. That was the great unveiling, the family's chance to get a look at this supposed hot girlfriend that nobody thought good ole Conner could ever procure. We had pulled up in an Uber, and the family greeting took place out front with everything short of a drum and bugle corps. It was like my family members had to shake Lyria's hand, probably to make sure she was real more than anything else. The whole occasion went off about as well as could be expected, with the possible exception of me almost losing consciousness when I saw Lyria and Jason playing catch the finger.

This time, we let ourselves in the huge front door. Don't know why, but ever since I moved to Boston, I felt a little bit honored when I came back here and realized my key still worked. My parents may not agree with everything about my lifestyle, but at least they hadn't changed the locks.

There was nobody in the front hallway, so we quietly entered the living room. We were very conscious of not making noise, wondering whether either Jason or Lisa was sleeping.

The air was somber—seemed nobody wanted to make any noise. The living room could have doubled as a grand ballroom. It was so big. Most of the space was wasted, as the furniture was all scrunched up near the center of the room. It felt like Mom and Dad had arranged the decor that way, so people had plenty of room to walk the exterior and admire the artwork, sconces, and other elaborate wall hangings.

The gang was all there. Mom and Dad were sitting on one sofa. Carly, Caden, and Lisa were on another, with everyone facing each other. But the center of attention was my nephew. He was in a wheelchair between the two groups, situated at the end so everyone could see him. Lisa was holding his hand from her end of the couch. Nobody even noticed us until we got close. Lisa looked up.

"Hey, look who's here, Jase," she said with as much enthusiasm as she could muster.

Jason saw me first. "Oh, hi, Uncle Conner."

"Hey, big buddy," I said. "How you feeling?"

I already knew the truth. He was wrapped in a hospital robe, looking way too small for the wheelchair. His short brown hair was mussed, and his face was pale and thin, with dark circles under his eyes. His eyelids were droopy, and I wondered what kind of meds they had him on.

"Okay, I guess," he said.

"Hey, there's someone else here who wants to see you."

He strained to look around. "Leera!"

He bound up out of the chair and rushed over. I looked at my family, and they all looked excited to see that he was still capable of exerting such an effort.

Lyria scooped him up into an embrace with a radiant smile. "Hey, how's my favorite guy?" she asked. Everybody laughed, and I didn't even take the "favorite guy" comment as a slight.

"I'm good," he said. "Lemme show you the trains Grandpa bought me!" He pointed to the backside of Mom and Dad's couch.

"Oh, awesome! Let's see!" said Lyria, and I had to laugh.

Everyone had scootched forward in their seats. The gloomy mood of a few seconds ago was forgotten. Jason had come to life when he saw Lyria. He was acting like himself again, probably for the first time in weeks.

"Well, I guess we know who moves the needle here," said my mother. But she said it with a huge smile.

Dad just laughed. "Yes, guess so," he said.

Lisa had stood up so she could watch. She had her hands over her mouth. Caden and Carly got up to walk around.

"Wow, look at this," said Lyria. "Is this all yours?"

She put Jason down, and he ran over. The train set was like something you see in a toy store or at Disneyland. Dad had clearly spared no expense. There were multiple tracks with different trains. There was what looked like a city in the middle and a miniature version of Gillette Stadium. There were little trees, a wind turbine, and a racecar track on the interior. The whole set looked like it cost more than my Beacon Hill condo.

Lyria sat down on the floor near where the trains were lined up. "Now, I'm not up on my trains," she said. "Tell me all about these."

Jason's face lit up. "They're all different ages. This is one of the old ones. It ran on a steam engine. This is a diesel freight train from the '70s. And this one...." He picked up a modern looking engine car with a New England Patriots logo. "...is the Patriots Express train!"

"Oh, that is so cool," said Lyria.

I looked up, and there was laughter all around. There was pure joy in everybody's expression, even my father's, who in my experience only looked this happy when he bought out a company by low-balling the competition.

Jason and Lyria continued going through every detail of the elaborate setup. We all eventually sat back down, as it looked like this was going to go on for a while. Caden had his arm around Lisa, who was weeping happily into his chest.

"Incredible," said my brother. "We honestly didn't know if he'd ever get that energetic again." His face reddened, and he started to sob. "Thanks, bro."

I said, "Hey, don't thank me." Everybody laughed again.

"She's remarkable," said Carly. "Although I still can't quite figure out—"

"I know, I know," I interrupted. "What she's doing with me, right?" More laughter and I didn't mind one bit that it was at my expense. Then we heard Jason say possibly the least expected words of all.

"Mom, I'm hungry."

***

"He hasn't been eating at all," said my father.

The caravan had moved to the kitchen, where Mom had whipped up some microwave chicken nuggets. Jason was sitting at a round wooden table set up in an alcove of the huge room. He had insisted that Lyria sit next to him as he continued raving about his trains in intricate detail.

"The first diesel train didn't come around until 1958, even though diesel engines were invented in the 1890s."

Everyone was standing around, watching in awe.

"He's better at history than I ever was," said Caden.

Mom had asked us several times if we wanted something to eat, but we gracefully declined.

Everything was going so well that what happened next took everyone aback.

Lyria apparently saw it coming. She held a napkin up under Jason's chin right before he vomited up everything he had eaten.

Lisa gasped and ran forward. "Oh, I'm so sorry. Jason?"

"Oh, don't worry about anything," said Lyria, calm as ever.

"I'm sorry, Leera," said Jason weakly.

Caden came over and took the mess from Lyria. She gathered up the boy in her arms. "That's all right, big boy. We've probably had too much excitement today, right?" Jason slumped in her arms.

"Here," said Lisa, tears running down her face. "Let's get you to bed." She took Jason. He looked almost lifeless—such a sudden change from just a few moments earlier.

"I'll help you," said Carly, and they headed to the room where Caden and Lisa were staying. My father was holding my mother, who had her face in his chest.

Just like that, the gleeful mood was over.

***

Back at my place later that night, Lyria and I were sitting together on my couch, neither of us saying anything. We came together in an embrace. I was struggling to hold my emotions in check, even though I felt devastated by once again seeing the severity of Jason's illness. I don't know why I was bothering with the act. Any notion I had about Lyria thinking of me as a manly man had long ago been quashed.

"They had to take him back to the hospital," I said finally.

Lyria made a "Hmmm" noise.

"He's in room 309."

She said nothing.

"You know. In case you wanted to stop by and see him some time. It's obvious how much he loves seeing you."

"Hmmm."

More silence.

I must have dozed off. I woke up with a start, not sure of where I was. It was still dark outside, but my equilibrium must have been thrown off because I was alone.

Lyria was gone.

***

The room was dark. And silent, except for the soft breathing. She stepped over to the bed, still hesitating.

She leaned over. The figure was so slight. He was engulfed in the generic hospital gown and the antiseptic white bedding. His breathing was shallow, and it almost felt like it was going to stop at any moment. He was on his side, facing her. She gently took his shoulder and shifted him onto his back. His tiny eyes blinked open. It took him some time to come to.

"Leera?"

"Yes, honey. It's me." She kept her voice as quiet as possible.

He rubbed his eyes. "You're really here. I thought I was dreaming."

"I'm here, my dear child. I'm…going to see if I can help you."

"Help me? Oh…okay. It's just that I feel so sick…so tired. Are Mommy and Daddy here?"

"Your daddy is outside, dear. Mommy is at your grandma's. I need you to lay back. And relax. Just like you are going back to sleep. Okay?"

"Yes. Sure. Okay, Leera. Thank you for coming to see me."

"You're welcome, my child."

She stroked what was left of his hair, and before long, his breathing was steady again as he drifted off.

"All right, my child. It's you and me. For better or worse."

The boy moaned softly as she bit. The blood started flowing, and the euphoria flooded through her. They spoke to each other silently.

Lyria. You are Lyria.

Yes, child.

I have been saying Leera. I…understand. I can see. This is so wonderful. I have never, never felt so….

I know. It is wonderful.

Can you see me? The way I see you?

Yes.

It is…like we're the same person. Like I am you. And you are me.

Yes.

Please…don't ever let this end. Please tell me it will always be like this. You…and me….

It will. We'll always be as one.

What is that light? Are Mommy and Daddy in there? I feel like I should go to them.

The light?

Yes. I'm going there now. I...have to go.

No.

Goodbye, Lyria.

NO!

She separated. An alarm was flashing on the equipment above the boy. No. NO!

She lifted him up, his arms hanging limply. Through the window. Outdoors. They were on a rooftop, the hospital off in the distance.

"Dear Lord," she said.

She leaned over again. She would bring him back.

Even if it meant draining the last bit of life out of herself.

CHAPTER EIGHTEEN

The cemetery had a look of neglect. Grass and weeds grew to lengths covering the field, as well as the bottoms of trees and many gravestones. A gentle summer wind was blowing, and the flora swayed back and forth.

Many of the stones themselves had been chipped away with age. Some had been uprooted and were strewn about, nowhere near their intended namesakes.

It was dusk, just as Mikolaj had planned. He knew they had to get there in the dark. *All the better,* he thought. *We're less likely to be seen.* Although this graveyard looked like it hadn't been visited by anyone in quite some time.

Completion of this mission would surely satisfy his superiors. It should, in fact, make him a legend in the cause. He would have faced down the supernatural twice and come out on top. If he was indeed able to bring such an unstoppable weapon to the fore, and if the leaders were able to use her to their advantage, his name would be held in reverence. The fools who had written the cause off as a bunch of fanatics living on the fringe would learn otherwise. And it would all be due to the efforts of Mikolaj Babka.

He had left Waclaw back in Rahova, watching the old lady Oana. He didn't want her slowing down the process, and the situation was easier to control this way. Radu knew that with the push of a button, his assistant would snuff out the woman's life without hesitation. Mikolaj had the advantage. His sister was all

Radu had left. She was his sole reason to live.

They were making their way through the old cemetery, Radu leading the way. The old man had said little in their travels—he seemed to have accepted the inevitability of his position. But now he stopped in his tracks and turned to Mikolaj.

"I must ask you to reconsider," he said, his voice weak. The trek seemed to have sapped what little bit of strength he had left. His ragged and weathered face looked more pale and drawn than when Mik had first seen him, happily out tending his garden.

"It seems rather late in the game to be reconsidering, old man. We have come all this way, and now you want to turn back?"

"You...don't know what it is you are asking. You don't understand the danger that could be unleashed."

"Ah, but I do. If my understanding of the legends is correct, it will be unlike anything else in the world. And whoever wields this power will reign supreme."

Radu held up his hands, pleading. "This burial...it took place in the '40s. There couldn't possibly be anything left—any life."

"You let me worry about that, my friend. You just show me the location of the burial place."

"Even if she *is* alive, your hopes of controlling her, of using her for your cause, is insane. Can't you see that?"

"*Continue on,* old man. Don't force me to get in touch with my associate." Mik pulled out his phone to emphasize his point.

Radu looked as if all hope had been lost. He hesitated, and Mik wondered whether he was weighing his sister's life against what he was being forced to do. Mik actually found himself holding his breath. They were so close.

After a moment, Radu turned away, and they continued, the old man walking slowly across a seemingly endless field of battered old graves.

Finally, he stopped in front of a structure. It looked to be a solid cube of cement rising about ten feet out of the ground. The facing looked like it once had a name across the front, but it had been eroded to the point where it was unreadable. The cube had been overrun by weeds and ivy, covering its entire surface. Honestly, Mik thought, unless one was specifically looking for the old mausoleum, it would have been easy to bypass the structure entirely.

Radu stood silently, looking at the cube, his arms hanging limp at his sides.

"This is it? This is where she is buried?" asked Mikolaj.

The old man answered with a barely perceptible nod.

Mik moved forward and tore away some of the fauna on the façade. There looked to have been a doorway on the front, but it was now just a solid wall of concrete.

"You filled the entire interior? Sealed her in cement for eternity?"

Another nod.

Mikolaj smiled at his captor. "Cold-hearted, old man. Perhaps I haven't given you enough credit. My understanding is that you were close with this girl, were you not?"

Radu's sunken face actually reddened. "I was not close with what she had become."

"I see. Where in the cube was the sarcophagus?"

Radu hesitated. "It was on the north side."

Mik nodded. "Well, it looks like we have our work cut out for us. We will have to bring back some tools."

"I have done what you have asked. I have shown you her location. Might I be released now? Might...my sister be freed?"

Mikolaj laughed. "Do you take me for a fool, old man? You will stay with me until I'm sure this is really the place. Besides...," more laughter. "I'm sure the two of you will have much to talk about. Much to catch up on."

***

They returned to town. Mikolaj had looked up a place where they could rent a utility vehicle and the necessary equipment. If the proprietor thought it odd that this strange looking little man and his taller, ancient friend were transacting this late in the day, he didn't say so. Or, more importantly, ask any questions.

Their vehicle was the equivalent of an ATV, which was needed to traverse the rough terrain of the old cemetery. It had a bed in the rear with their equipment, which rattled around as they went over bumps and clumps of weeds and overgrowth.

Mik was driving, with Radu on the passenger side, using what little strength he had left to hold on to the dashboard to keep from falling out the open side. It was now late evening, and the only light was coming from their headlights, the terrain around them pitch black.

"You may stay seated," said Mikolaj. "I wouldn't want you over-taxing yourself. I think I know how to operate this thing."

The little man extracted a jackhammer from the back of the vehicle. Radu had to admit to himself that he was impressed with Mikolaj's physical strength for a man so small in stature. He doubted he himself could have even lifted the large tool.

While he was lost in his thoughts, the jackhammer came to life with a roar. Radu felt the vibrations down to his core. Mikolaj jammed the instrument up against the north wall of the cube, and soon chunks of cement were falling to the ground. Before very long, the outline of the coffin was visible. Mikolaj stopped and looked at the structure, his eyes shining in anticipation.

"We're almost there, old man," he yelled over the racket. "Are you preparing for your reunion? Haha."

He lifted the jackhammer even higher and continued eating away at the wall and the outside of the sarcophagus. His squat body was blocking Radu's view, but suddenly the din from the tool stopped, the noise continuing to ring in Radu's ears.

He heard Mikolaj gasp and ran over to look. Radu stopped breathing when he saw what the little man had unearthed.

They were looking at Angelika from the side. She looked like she was asleep, wearing the same simple cloth dress as when the old man had last seen her. They could see no signs of breathing, but the body was intact even after so many decades.

Mikolaj approached slowly and reached out to touch her arm, causing Radu to gasp.

"Her skin feels...cold. Like ice," he said almost to himself.

The little man managed to get his arms under the girl and lifted her out. He placed her on the ground, and both men stood staring down at her. She opened her eyes and inhaled, causing Radu and Mikolaj to jump back. She grimaced, baring her fangs, and moved her eyes from side to side. Mikolaj had overcome his initial fear and beamed down at her.

"Greetings, child. I am Mikolaj, and I have freed you from your long imprisonment."

Angelika tried to sit up, and Mikolaj bolted forward to help her. She flexed her arms and continued to search her surroundings. Her eyes focused on Radu.

"Father? Is that you? You look so much older."

Her little girl's voice was raspy. Still, Radu said nothing, his eyes wide, his breathing shallow. A realization seemed to dawn in the girl's eyes.

"How long have I been here?" she asked in accented English.

Mikolaj was still crouching next to her. "You have been entombed for over seventy years, child," he said. Angelika stared into his face. "It is I, Mikolaj, who is responsible for your freedom."

"Seventy years," she said, looking at the ground.

All was still for what seemed like an eternity. Mikolaj blinked and missed her springing up from her sitting position. She held her arms out wide, beckoning to Radu. The old man was still, his eyes and mouth wide. He moved forward slowly, went down on one knee. They embraced.

"Tell me, Father," she hissed in Romanian. "Tell me what I have missed."

Mik watched as she bit into the old man's neck. Radu moaned, and his body went slack. She lifted her head, blood running down her chin.

"It was you, Father?" she asked. Radu came to but said nothing. "It was *you* who entombed me? Do you know, soon after I awoke so long ago, I realized I couldn't move, so I screamed. After much time, I went to sleep. I have been sleeping ever since."

She held Radu's shoulders and tightened her grip, causing the old man to whimper.

"You. My father. I trusted you. And you have grown old." Angelika pulled his head to the side. "I trust you have had a nice, comfortable life."

Radu said, "No. Angelika NO…!"

The girl plunged back into his neck, and he fell to the ground.

Her tiny form jerked up and down with a slurping sound. Mikolaj sat, watching silently.

Her head rose from Radu's lifeless form, and she looked off in the distance. "So, Mother had a part in this too...."

She turned and looked at Mikolaj. The little man clutched his chest as her tiny face broke into a grin, blood dripping from her fangs.

He struggled to find his voice. "I...I kept the old man here. I...thought you might need to feed."

"How very thoughtful," she said.

Before Mik knew what was happening, she was holding him down, her bloodied face above his. He struggled to move, but her strength pinned him in place.

"No," he gasped, "I helped you. I set you free...."

"I have found that often what people say is not the truth," she said with a smile that sent shivers down Mikolaj's spine. "So, what is your truth?"

She leaned down. Mik felt a jolt of pain through his entire body. He tried to move but realized he couldn't.

After what seemed like an eternity, she pulled her head back. More blood was around her mouth. Mik gasped, filling his lungs with air. It took a moment for the realization to come about that he was still alive.

Angelika threw her head back and laughed. The sound was like any other seven-year-old girl, perhaps out playing hopscotch. But Mik knew better.

"You intended for me to join your cause?" More laughter. "After seventy years, there are still Nazis? The same people who destroyed my country? Ruined my life? No, I know it was the Legionnaires who were the butchers in my time. But I read much when I was home with my mother. The only reason the Legionnaires were there was because of the Russians ruling Romania. And the Russians were there because of the Nazis. Did you think that would escape me?"

Mikolaj stared up at her but said nothing.

The little girl grabbed his shirt and brought his face up close to hers.

"At any rate, I have let you live. I will need you to assist me. You see, you think my mother, Lyria, is dead. But that is not so. Seems you have been...what's the word in English? Duped? Yes, I think that is correct. She is still alive. My father told me all about it. Hee hee. Yes, I will need you to help me with my travel plans."

"T...travel plans? But where will you—?"

"*We*, my friend. The question is, where will WE go. To the United States, of course. We will go to the United States."

CHAPTER NINETEEN

Carol David sat quietly in her huge, ornately decorated living room, thinking about the uselessness of it all.

All this money. All these possessions. And what do they mean? Nothing, that's what. None of it can save our grandson. Our beloved little boy who brought such joy to our lives.

Carol knew long ago that she was married to a man for whom work came first. If she was looking for someone who would hang out with her after he retired, Charles David was definitely not that man. Some of her friends had taken up joint activities to spend more time with their husbands after their work lives were over — tennis lessons, book clubs, ballroom dancing. She actually laughed when she pictured Charles engaging in any of those activities.

Heaven knows her husband had been a great provider. They lived the lifestyle of the rich and famous because of his success in investment banking. But as a spouse, or when it came to sharing feelings or providing emotional support, Charles was a lost cause. Even now, he spent the great majority of his days doing who-knows-what in his home office. That is, when he wasn't out kibitzing with his other rich male friends at the country club or on the golf course.

Carol had always buried herself in the care of their children. For so many years, that was all she had. She nearly panicked when the boys came of age and moved on with their lives. The only thing that kept her from going insane was Carly still living with them. And she doted on the girl's every need to the point where it was driving Carly crazy. But Carol thought her daughter understood.

Then Jason came along, and all her fears were put to rest, at least for a while. Now Jason was sick. And one didn't need a medical degree to see from the reaction of all these *brilliant* doctors that the prognosis was not good.

Carol thought many times that if she had to give up all the family's wealth to save her grandson, she would do it in a heartbeat.

Her train of thought was interrupted by the sound of the door to the bedroom where Lisa was staying opening up, making her jump a little. Her daughter-in-law was sedated, and Carol didn't expect to hear anything from her for a while.

She looked over. Lisa was still beautiful with her long blonde hair, but she was all skin and bones from the stress of their ordeal. She was walking forward slowly, holding her phone to her ear, a look of shock and distress crumpling her normally perfect features.

"What?" Lisa said. She listened to the phone. "MISSING?" she screamed.

Then Lisa David, the mother of Carol David's only grandchild, fainted, dropping to the floor with a thud, her phone clattering across the tiles.

***

The next morning, all my worries about work, Chud Johnson, family, relationships, and vampires seemed petty compared to what I had witnessed with Jason the previous evening. One minute, with enthusiasm, apparently elicited by Lyria, he seemed like a normal high-spirited boy bragging on his train set. The next minute, he was vomiting and returning to the hospital. I felt bad that I was even thinking about myself, but the whole ordeal was really doing a number on my psyche, which was fairly fragile to begin with.

I was doing my best impression of an investment banking associate who cared about his job when my phone rang. I started a little and realized this was what my life had come to, jumping in fright and expecting catastrophic news every time my phone pealed.

It was Carly, and my premonition came true.

"Conner," she said, her tone causing me to grip the phone tighter.

"Yeah?"

"Jason is missing."

My breath caught in my chest, and I couldn't even muster a response.

"Are you still there?"

I gasped my response. "Yeah. What...what do you mean missing?"

Carly sounded like she was crying. "I mean, the nurse went into his room to check on him last night, and he wasn't there."

The silence between us felt like an elephant sitting on my chest.

"Do...do they have any idea what happened?"

It took her a minute to respond. "It looks like someone took him out the window in his room. It's one of those windows that's not even supposed to open, but the bottom pane was gone. Caden was in the waiting room at the time. He heard the nurse scream and went running in. When he saw the window open, he thought somehow Jason had gotten it open and fell. There's a rooftop just below the window, but there was nothing there. Caden went running out in the street, calling his name. Finally, the police got there. He went back to the hospital and had to be sedated. Mom had to give Lisa a shot at home when she got the call."

"Oh, dear God."

"Dad is with Mom now. She had to take a pill too. The police are at the house. There's a search underway, but they said all they can do is wait for some kind of call for ransom. They think he's been kidnapped by somebody who wants money from Dad."

My breathing was shallow, and I thought I might pass out. Or throw up. Or both.

"They need you to come home. To Mom and Dad's house. Can...can you do that?"

I hesitated. "Yes. Yes, I'll be there."

***

I had the duration of my Uber ride to my parents' house to think through what had happened. It had to have something to do with Lyria. It just had to. A critically ill four-year-old taken out a window? Not likely, even if someone did find out that his grandfather was rich.

She'd left me on my couch last night after I had fallen asleep. Not that that was unusual, but had my begging finally make her go see if she could help Jason? She would have had to take some of his blood and replace it with her own. But she was worried that she wouldn't be able to stop. Children were different, she'd told me—she'd *warned* me—whether it was because they were more innocent or hadn't amassed all the diseases adults collect throughout their lives. Who knows why? But when she attempted to help the little girl back in Romania—Angelika—she'd found that she was overcome by the euphoria and couldn't stop in time. She drained her completely. And she had to give Angelika all cursed blood to keep her alive. And Angelika had…turned.

My god, what if that had happened to Jason? What if Jason was now…?

I had to stop thinking about it. I couldn't even fathom that possibility.

But what else could have happened? My nagging brain refused to let it go. Jason *was* the grandson of a wealthy local businessman who was well known in the community. Maybe this was a real kidnapping.

But would criminals target a boy as sick as Jason? If he died in their custody, they could be up on murder charges.

I was still wrestling with these thoughts as we pulled up to my parents' house. Somehow, the three-story mansion seemed a lot smaller. There was a strange car in the driveway parked in front of a police cruiser with its lights flashing. I imagined the unmarked car belonged to detectives.

I stopped short, and my heart almost seized in my chest. Boston police would have jurisdiction in this case, and the lead detective in charge of missing persons would be none other than Don Halberton. Just the previous fall, we had created a faux death for Lyria to ease the pressure from Don, as well as those numbnuts Nazi wannabes Mikolaj Babka and his buddy Waclaw. If Don was on this case, then he would know....

Oh, dear Lord.

I proceeded forward slowly. And what about Grace Garvey? She was the detective assigned to some suspicious disappearances that tied back to Lyria. And me.

I had to keep myself from hyperventilating as I came to the door. My self-doubts were flooding through my mind. I was a lousy liar, and looking innocent under these circumstances was well above my pay grade as an actor.

I opened the door, and my worst fears were all realized— every last one of them.

They had set up a temporary HQ in the large atrium, with tables, chairs, and telephones. Dad was sitting off to the side in a folding chair, deep in a conversation with the estimable Don Halberton, sitting next to him in close proximity. When I walked in, Don stopped talking, and our eyes met. His look was searing through my very soul, and I saw him clench his jaw. That did nothing for my efforts to fight off the urge to panic right on the spot.

I stood in place, unable to move and suddenly having to pee in the worst way possible. Don resumed his talk with Dad, his eyes never leaving mine. Someone grabbed my arm, and I nearly melted down.

"Hey, Conner. Grace Garvey. Do you remember me?"

As if I was going to forget someone like Grace Garvey. She had the unique ability to get me aroused and terrified all at the same time. When I could breathe again, I said, "Yes...Detective Garvey. Good to see you again."

"Hey, it's *Grace*, remember?"

What I did remember was that *Grace* was gifted at putting a person at ease with her looks and conversational tone. I could imagine real criminals actually wanting to confess to her.

And she looked great, even in cop garb. She was medium height with classic features, and her blonde hair pulled back in a ponytail. She was wearing jeans and a blue police windbreaker. It was still warm out, so I wondered if she was wearing a bulletproof vest or whether that was too many gangster movies talking. Her eyes were penetrating before she even asked me a question, and I *really* had to pee.

A couple of uniformed cops were talking on the phones nearby, so Grace said, "Why don't we go somewhere more quiet so we can talk? You lead the way."

I looked around the rest of the house for the first time. There was no sign of my mother or Lisa, and I presumed they were still sedated. Caden was speaking with another uniform on the living room couch. When he saw me, we rushed forward and embraced.

"Hey, bro," he said. He had been holding it together but started sobbing. "Sorry to keep pulling you out of work."

Now I was crying too. "No problem. How you holding up? How's Lisa?"

He shook his head. "Not too good. We had to give her something even stronger. Mom's in her room with her."

I nodded. Grace was standing nearby. I said, "Uh, well, I'm going to go speak with Detective Garvey."

"Sure. Sure thing." Caden sat back down.

"Uh, Detective? I really, really need to visit a restroom before we get started. Is that okay?"

I felt like a kindergartener having to hold up one or two fingers.

"Of course," she said, cheerful as all get out. "Take your time. I'll meet you in the dining room."

***

I was able to compose myself a bit during my pit stop. I, of course, denied having any knowledge about what happened to Jason. But Grace was in top form, asking, cajoling, and flirting along the way. A part of me wanted to completely spill my guts. Man, she was good.

But I thought if I told her that my vampire girlfriend may be responsible for my nephew's disappearance, I might get carted off in a straitjacket. And heaven forbid I would have to refer to Don Halberton as a corroborating witness.

"You think this may be related to your father?"

"I don't know. I mean, it could be."

I thought, *Way to project a confident, self-assured man, Conner.*

"Does he have any enemies that you know of?"

"I couldn't name them if that's what you mean. But my father worked in investment banking, and he was known as something of a…a shark, you know?"

"Not exactly. What does that mean?"

"Well, like if BHA — uh, Beacon Hill Associates — was looking to buy a company — "

"Wait a minute. Your dad worked at Beacon Hill Associates? Isn't that where you work?"

I thought I was uneasy before, now this comes along. "Yes. Yes, it is."

"Aha," she said, her eyes boring into mine. "Go on."

"So, if they were looking to buy a company and the other party wasn't going along, he was known to play hardball."

Grace leaned forward. She seemed to be really interested in this line of conversation. Now, on top of everything else, I was nervous about centering attention on my father when I was pretty sure his business dealings had nothing to do with this.

"And how would he go about that? Playing hardball."

"They could up the ante, you know, offer more money. Or go to the shareholders. Like if a company's stock was selling at thirty dollars a share and was stagnant, not growing, he could go in at forty dollars, and if they refused, he would contact the shareholders and say, hey, guess what? Management just turned down forty dollars a share, and hope they would pressure the company to accept the deal. Something like that."

"Wow. Sounds like you're really tuned in to these backroom dealings. Pretty impressive." She smiled, and I wondered if she could actually hear my heart thundering in my chest. "Do you think someone your father had business dealings with could have taken your nephew? Like in retribution?"

"Honestly, that's kind of a long shot. I mean, it's not like a lot of people knew that Jason was sick. Or in the hospital. Hey, what if someone in the hospital could have done it?"

"How do you mean?"

"Well, say somebody saw the family when we were in there. Said, hey, they look like they have money. And decided to kidnap Jason?"

My hopes were soaring that she would buy off on that scenario. That's it. Try pinning the whole thing on some faceless person we encountered while we were at the hospital.

"Interesting, but not too likely," said Grace, dashing my hopes.

"No?"

"No. Kidnapping is a very complex crime, especially when it involves a sick child. The person would have to plan it out pretty carefully. They'd have to have a place to accommodate him and keep him alive long enough to collect the ransom. And since we haven't received any ransom demands yet...."

"I see."

"Any other ideas?" she asked.

I was conscious of not meeting her eyes, but I couldn't help myself. "No, not really."

Her gaze stayed on me for a beat or two, and I felt like I might be sick.

"Okay." She handed me her card. "Let me know if you think of anything else."

"Yes...sure. I will."

Smooth, boy.

Grace walked back out to the atrium. I followed, but I saw Dad talking to Caden in the living room and headed in that direction.

This whole ordeal was clearly taking a toll on my father. He was wearing a brown blazer and black slacks, and as usual, there wasn't a hair out of place. But his normal posture was upright and erect, shoulders back. He and I were both tall, but he was muscular through the shoulders and chest, where I looked like a stiff breeze could take me out. I was aware of my dad using his height and physique to intimidate others physically, having been on the short end of many such interactions. Now he looked more pale than normal, and he actually seemed to be slouching a bit.

He looked thin, although that could have just been that he was next to Caden, who was built like a Mack truck.

"The detectives seem to be focusing on my former business dealings," said my dad. He looked at me closely, wondering, I'm sure, whether I had tossed him under the bus since I had in-depth knowledge of his career and work in the same field.

I said, "Do you really think that's it? I mean, who would have known that Jason was sick?"

That seemed to allay his fears.

"I don't know. I think it's a long shot. I said I thought it was probably some hospital employee who saw us while we were visiting Jason."

"I said the same thing to Detective Garvey."

See? We're a team now.

Caden dropped down on the sofa. "I feel so useless," he said. "I should at least be out on the street. Trying to find him."

I sat and put my arm around his shoulders. "Hey, don't think that, bro. The chances of finding him yourself are non-existent. The best thing we can do right now is wait for them to make contact. And take care of Lisa."

Dad sat on the other side of him and put his arm around Caden as well, in a rare show of physical affection. My brother sobbed as the three of us sat huddled up.

"Conner?"

The male voice startled me, and I looked up at Don Halberton at the entrance to the room. My anxiety level, which had been approaching normal again, spiked right back up. Don was one of those straight by-the-book kinds of cops, and he looked the part — his hair cut short, clean-shaven, wearing simple slacks and a sport coat. But his eyes were ablaze.

I patted Caden on the back and walked over.

"Let's step outside for a minute," said Don.

Breathe, Conner. Breathe.

We walked out the front door. The night was warm, and there was a gentle breeze. I thought, *How can anybody have so many problems on a beautiful night like this?*

When we were out of earshot of anyone else, Don stopped in

front of me. He was close, invading my personal space. I was a couple of inches taller than him, but I could feel his breath when he spoke.

"She's still alive, isn't she?"

His face was stern. I wondered how he and Grace Garvey could manage not to blink for such extended periods of time.

I knew to ask, "Who?" would be folly. Don was a witness when we pretended to put Lyria to death. The only thing I had going for me was that Don thought I had kept Lyria from having him as a snack before making her go away. But apparently, those gratitude points had been used up.

I didn't know what to say, so I said nothing. Which pretty much confirmed what Don was thinking anyway.

He moved even closer. "Did she do this? Did she take the kid?"

"Look, Detective—"

"Don't give me any crap either," he hissed. It sounded extra intense coming from someone with a normally calm and professional appearance. It was like getting cursed out by Captain America. "It can't be a coincidence that people around you keep disappearing. I let you off the hook before because I couldn't explain what I saw. And when I thought she was dead, I figured that had solved the problem. What did you do, fake her death to ease the pressure?"

Saying nothing seemed to be the best alternative available to me once more—other than fainting, that is. But again, Halberton took my silence as confirmation of what he was asking.

"Look, David, I called in some favors to keep this out of the press. I convinced my reporter friends that it was just a paperwork screw-up, that the boy was back with his family. If he is still alive, I want him back," he said.

"I—"

He grabbed my arm and squeezed. "No bullshit. Get him back, or I swear, I'll find a way to charge you in his disappearance. And all the other cases from last year as well. They're still open, and the only commonality between them is you. I'll arrest you, and I'll make it stick. Maybe your daddy will hire a high priced lawyer, and maybe he'll get you off. But I assume you don't want those charges hanging over your head for the rest of your life. You think a top notch organization like Beacon Hill Associates is going to keep a suspected kidnapper and murderer on their payroll?"

I couldn't think of anything to say. And besides, I had stopped breathing.

He released my arm, and I felt the blood start flowing back to my extremities.

"I expect to hear from you. Soon."

Don stormed back into the house, and I stood in place, resisting the urge to crumble to the ground and cry.

CHAPTER TWENTY

Something wasn't right.

She awoke as she had thousands of nights before. It wasn't like waking up out of sleep, like a mortal. It was more like coming out of a coma. There were no dreams, no stirring in the middle of the night, no getting up for water or to use the bathroom. It was like being dead and then being alive. Which was impossible. For mortals, but not for her.

Tonight was different. She sensed it right away. Then she remembered. It all came back to her, and she knew it was real, and the evidence was right beside her.

Tonight was different because, for the first time since she started her new existence, she wasn't alone in her coffin. Jason was curled up in her arms, his tiny body lying on her chest, his head on her shoulder.

My god, she thought. *I have done it again.*

She had tried to explain to Conner that she wouldn't be able to stop. It was just like *her*—just like Angelika. Jason had been dead, and she had to bring him back the only way she knew how, the only way possible. Now he was with her, still in the sleeping death that only her kind understood.

There was something else. She was weakened. It had taken a lot to bring the boy back. Everyone was different, and he had been farther gone than Angelika. It had taken virtually all of her strength, her power.

Her blood.

It had worked, but she couldn't remember anything after. She had absolutely no idea how she had gotten back here. With him.

It took all her remaining strength to push the lid open. Jason stirred. She lay still as he opened his eyes. He lifted his head and looked at her. It was his first night, and it took a moment for him to get oriented. Finally, he smiled, a little boy smile with no reticence, just pure and simple, except for the fangs. She had learned to hide them from mortals, but that was one of her tricks, one he hadn't as yet learned.

"Hello, Mother," he said.

***

"How…how did we get back here?" she asked.

He was sitting up, still next to her in the coffin. "I carried you back," he said. "You should see how strong I am. I tried to wake you up, but you were really sleeping. I saw this place when we were…together. I knew we had to come back here. I understood a lot about what was happening. Then…there was the light. I wanted to go there so bad. And it seemed like I did. It was warm there. Peaceful. Then we were on the roof. When I woke up, I could see so much more. And hear so much more. I felt strong again—I was so weak before. I knew you had helped me. Thank you so much, Mother."

"Jason, I…I'm so sorry. I didn't intend for this to happen. I only wanted to help…with your illness."

He beamed, his eyes bright. The room was enclosed with no windows and just a single bulb hanging inert in the ceiling, with a vault door that only opened from the inside. She'd had a similar setup in another building, but she had to move when she and Conner had faked her death. Unless that bulb was on, the room was always pitch-black dark. But she and Jason could see each other clearly.

"Oh, I know. Like I said, I understand a lot. You explained it to me. But you shouldn't feel bad. I think I was going to go into the light anyway before you came to see me. Now I feel great. I don't feel sick any more. But…."

"But what?"

"I hunger, Mother."

"I...I know. We will take care of that. I need some more rest. And then we will...go out."

"Oh, don't worry. I know what to do. You stay here and rest. I'll be back later. I'll share with you, okay? Then you'll feel better."

The child jumped out of the coffin and bound for the heavy vault door, looking again like a boy with unlimited energy.

"Jason, no. Wait!" she yelled, but he pulled the door open with little effort, and then he was gone.

***

I was frantic in the Uber on the way home. The half-hour trip seemed to take forever. I was hoping above hope that Lyria would be there waiting for me, but, of course, she was not.

What had happened? Had she finally given in and gone to Jason? After all my nagging? And if she did, why was he missing? She was only going to take a little of his blood and replace it with her own, to see if that could help the boy where the doctors seemingly couldn't. Had she realized how desperate the situation was after seeing him last night? A normal boy one second and vomiting up the remnants of his life the next? And he had clearly shown his love for Lyria. Did that change her mind?

And the fact that he was missing...did that mean that she failed to stop in time again? As she had with Angelika? That would mean that Jason was either dead or....

Or worse.

Lyria had told me the risks. She told me that she didn't know if she could stop once she started. That feeding on kids gave her an unearthly euphoria, which couldn't be resisted. She said that children were more likely to be pure evil. That their personalities were not as well formed as adults, so their own personas were overcome by the evil spirit originating in her blood. Their own fledgling personalities would be subsumed. Dear Lord. What if that happened to Jason?

I felt like I was going to be sick. There was one possible way to get in touch with Lyria. I had given her a phone, and she accepted it with the understanding that it was only to be used in emergencies. Well, if this wasn't an emergency, I didn't know what was. My nephew was missing, and suddenly I had a cop having wet dreams about sending me to the hoosegow.

I pulled out my phone and dialed. No answer. My imagination, which was already in overdrive conjuring up nightmare after nightmare, started in again. Why would she not answer? It was after dark. She should be awake. Was she with Jason?

Were they...feeding? Together?

I tried one more time — same result.

I felt the need to lie down and not on the couch. I somehow managed to get up my stairs and flopped down on my bed. How many times since I met Lyria had I gone to sleep hoping beyond hope that I would wake up the next day, and the whole deal would turn out to be a bad dream? That was one of my final thoughts, as my subconscious apparently determined that I'd had all I could handle, and I fell into a deep, rich sleep.

***

I was on a date with Vicky — that much was clear. Since I'd had a taste of relative normalcy when we went for coffee, a more conventional relationship had become my overriding desire. Most guys had fantasies about stewardesses or sex with a stranger in a laundromat. Mine were tending more toward Ward Cleaver territory.

We were in a restaurant, Vicky and I, holding hands, sweet-talking each other, the whole nine yards. The waitress sauntered over to take our orders. At first, she was an attractive blonde woman, on the tall side, but with really no distinguishing features. I looked down at my menu, but when I looked up to give her my choice, it was Lyria. She said, "Have you decided, sir?" and I could see her fangs. I looked over at Vicky, and she was staring up at Lyria, frozen in fright. Neither of us could speak, so Lyria said, "Tell you what, I'll just bring you the house special." She had a large platter with a cover, and she dropped it down on the table. Vicky and I stared — we didn't want to open the top. Lyria said, "Oh, come on now. The chef cooked this up, especially for you."

She lifted the lid, and Jason was curled up in a fetal position on the platter. We gasped, but then he lifted his head. "Hey, Uncle Conner," he said. He smiled, and he had fangs too. He stood up slowly, Vicky and I unable to move. Jason grabbed our collars and pulled us close. "Isn't this a great place? Everything I've ever had here has been really good." He angled his way toward my neck, his mouth opening wide, his fangs coming close....

"Aaaaargh. NO!" I heard myself yell, waking out of the dream.

My room seemed darker than normal. I was still waiting for my heartbeat to slow down. But something seemed off. I couldn't pinpoint it, but the air felt different. My eyes were open, but it was pitch black. I couldn't see a thing. I inhaled sharply as I noticed my door was closed. I always left it open. Okay, I'm a big baby, what can I say? I couldn't worry about that—I was frozen in place. The horrible realization came to me that I was not alone. Someone else was in the room. And, there went the heartbeat again. I had a thought about bolting for the door but found that I couldn't move.

"Lyria?" A whisper was all I could muster. Even though I called her name, I knew it wasn't her. My head swiveled to my right, toward my closet. Isn't that where most kids imagine the monsters hanging out? I couldn't see anything, and I didn't detect any movement. When I turned my head back, a girl was standing next to my bed.

I shouted a guttural noise. My heart felt about ready to completely give way. She had pale white skin with straggly dark blonde hair falling past her shoulders, wearing what looked like a simple cloth dress with an almost burlap consistency. She was still, looking at me curiously like I was an art exhibit at a museum.

"Hello, Conner," she said. She smiled, and sure enough, there were the fangs. They made her otherwise little-girl smile look wolfish, and I fought off the urge to pass out right on the spot.

"Who...who are you?" I gasped, although I was pretty sure I already knew the answer.

She giggled again, just like a normal child. But the sound sent additional shivers down my spine.

"I'm Angelika. I think you and I have some mutual friends."

"Mutual...who?" I was still unable to assemble a complete sentence.

"Well, there's Lyria for one. Did you even know you just called out her name? Hee hee. Lyria was kind of my adopted mom. Then we...parted ways. Anyway, another friend of yours is downstairs. He's very anxious to see you. Come on. Let's go down and say hi."

She turned and held out her hand, beckoning me to follow. I hesitated.

"Oh, come on, Conner," she said. "Do you think I bite or something?" More little-girl giggles, her hand awaiting mine.

Not seeing much of a choice, I stood on shaky legs and took her hand. She felt warm.

"There, that wasn't so hard, was it?" I towered over Angelika, but I knew that meant nothing.

We walked down the stairway, still hand-in-hand. We turned into the living room, and I saw a familiar figure sitting on my couch. He was staring straight ahead off into space, not acknowledging our presence.

"M...Mikolaj?" My voice was still a mere whisper. I figured if I didn't wet myself now, I probably never would.

Angelika jumped up and squealed. "Isn't it great to see old friends? I knew you two would be glad to get together."

She led me over to the couch. Mikolaj was still silently staring.

"What...what do you want?" I asked.

"See? That's the question, isn't it?" The little girl smiled and laughed like she was talking about going to the park. She hugged me around the waist. "Oh, it's so good to meet you finally. I've heard so much about you. Why don't you sit down next to Mik, and we'll talk all about it."

I stammered, "Uh, no...that's all right."

"Sit down," she said, suddenly gripping my waist and tossing me to the couch. "That's better," she said, smiling. She was standing close in front of both of us. Her cloth dress hung to her knees. Her legs were pencil thin, but the shoes she wore looked new.

"You like my shoes? Mikolaj bought them for me. I think we'll want to do some clothes shopping too. Isn't that right, Mik?"

"Yes," he said. The little oddball still hadn't moved an inch.

"So, I have a lot of questions," said Angelika. She gave me a sweet, fangy smile. "See, I've been...away for a long time. Mik brought me up to speed on what he knows. My father too. Did you know my daddy? Radu?"

A tiny nod was all I could manage.

"Oh, that's nice. It's like we're all a family. But I have a feeling there's a lot my dad and Mik didn't know. You know, about what's happened more recently. They both thought about you a lot, Conner." Her smile and stare intensified on me, and I'm pretty sure I wasn't breathing at all.

"I...I don't know anything."

She laughed. "Oh, come on now. I'm sure that's not true. I'll tell you what, though, rather than ask a lot of questions—I think Mik might get bored—I'll find out what I need to know. Don't you think that would be better? Besides...." She sidled up close to me and whispered, "I don't think people always tell the truth." More giggles.

She kneeled on my thighs and pinned my shoulders to the back of the couch. Her fangs were bared as she leaned in.

"No...please...."

"Relax, Conner. I just want to see what's going on. It will bring us...closer together.

At first, it felt like a dull ache, then pain through every fiber of my being. I couldn't move or breathe. I saw Angelika's life. It was all I could see as if I was in some virtual reality world. It seemed to go on forever. Then I was looking at Angelika, still perched on top of me. She had drawn back, a drop of blood dripping down her chin.

She smiled, her teeth covered in blood. Her eyes widened. "You really think that's what happened? To your nephew? To Jason?" She stood up and spoke to me and the catatonic Mikolaj Babka. "I think we've just had a change of plans."

I barely managed my question. "Plans? What plans?"

If Angelika answered me, I didn't hear it as I seized that very moment's opportunity to pass out.

***

Larry, the Loser, felt lucky that nobody else knew about his favorite spot.

His friends all vied for positions under bridges and in homeless shelters. Those were all well and good, but Larry knew that when you were camped under a bridge, you were a target for law enforcement and thieves. And the homeless shelter spots were conditional. As in, you can have a bed, but you have to meet with a social worker.

Screw that, he thought.

His place was a nice side doorway to an office building. The door was never used after hours, so he could comfortably set up there as soon as it got dark and rest undisturbed for hours. Not only that, but *his* doorway was in an alley, so it was generally pretty quiet. And it was sideways to the harbor. Boston's icy winter winds generally came whipping in off the water, but Larry was protected in his alley, in his doorway.

Larry the Loser. He remembered when he acquired that nickname. Like many of his homeless brethren, he once had a bright future. His parents never had much, but they emphasized staying in school and finding an honest job when he was ready. He had his high school degree but had no interest in college. He wanted to go to a trade school. Be an electrician or a plumber. So after high school, he was ready to go, but he knew he would have to pay the tuition himself. So he worked a manual labor job in construction. He loved it so much, he was convinced he should bag the trade school and just do construction for a living. In addition to steady work—there was always a big job being done somewhere around town—he built a camaraderie with his co-workers. He got an affordable apartment in South Boston, and life was good.

The back injury changed everything. It seemed like no big deal when it first happened. He and his buddies were lugging bags of cement into the ground floor of an apartment building. He had carried several in already, but when he bent over to pick up another bag, his back seized on him. He went home that day and tried to rest, but the pain became overwhelming. His doctor prescribed a muscle relaxant and painkillers. Before he knew it, he became reliant on the painkillers. Then he was missing work. And when he did report, he couldn't do his share. He started hearing whispers from his former friends. After missing an entire week, he caught wind of his coworkers referring to him as Larry the Loser. His dependency got worse. He lost his job and couldn't find another one. He eventually lost his apartment and started living on the streets. Now, he was firmly entrenched as one of Boston's homeless population, scrounging to eat and find a place to sleep. He knew his story wasn't unique, but that was little consolation to Larry. He had hopes of getting his life back on track, but for now, he was satisfied to have his alley doorway, where he would be safe, quiet, and warm for one more night.

Larry settled in with his worldly possessions, consisting of his raggedy clothes, shoes that were a size too small that he had dug out of a donations dumpster, and a blanket he had stolen from the last shelter where he had spent a night. And he had grabbed a newspaper out of a waste receptacle that day. Newspapers made great pillows. Who knew?

He was in his doorway, half asleep, a distant streetlight casting a small shadow on the building wall across the way. He started. Was there somebody over there? Larry squinted and looked again. Nobody. He passed it off as a combination of his semi-conscious state and the tricky shadows from that streetlight. He dozed again.

"Hi."

Larry gasped, and now all his senses were on alert. There was always a chance of getting rolled on the streets, even in his wonderful doorway so far off the beaten path. You were especially vulnerable if you had shoes. Shoes were a big deal among the homeless.

He looked for the source of the voice. It had sounded like a child. Who would let their child roam around an area like this in the middle of the night? The voice sounded like it came from his right, toward the back of the alley. He clutched his precious blanket to his chest and sat forward.

Again there was nobody there, and Larry thought he had

imagined the child's voice. He sat back and almost screamed out loud when he saw a boy standing to the left of his door entrance. He looked to be four or maybe five years old. He was wearing a hospital gown, no shoes. It gave him a ghostly appearance. He had an angelic face, with a child's unmarked skin and unruly brown hair. But he was completely out of place in this dark alley, and he seemed to have appeared out of nowhere. But what unnerved Larry the most were the child's eyes. He was regarding Larry with what the homeless man thought was a combination of curiosity and...hunger.

"My name is Jason. What's your name?" he asked. He sounded like a normal little boy, which for some reason, made Larry tense up even more.

"L...Larry. My name is Larry."

The boy smiled. Now Larry thought his imagination was really getting the better of him. He thought the boy had fangs where his canine teeth should be.

"Hi, Larry." The boy regarded his doorway. "What are you doing laying in this doorway? Do you live here?"

"No, I just...stay here once in a while." Larry could feel his heart pounding in his chest. The boy stepped closer.

"Oh, kind of like camping out, huh? Sometimes my daddy and I would sleep in a tent out on the lawn. That was fun. You should get a tent. It's a lot easier to sleep in a tent."

He moved even closer. Larry held his blanket tightly to his chest.

"Where...where is your daddy? What are you doing out here? Are you by yourself?"

The boy smiled again. My god. He did have fangs. Larry felt like he might faint.

"Can I tell you a secret, Larry?" He kneeled down, his face now inches from the man who was going to be a master plumber. Or electrician.

Larry couldn't breathe. "A...secret?" he gasped. "What secret?"

The boy grabbed Larry's shoulder, pinning him back against his door. His grip was so powerful, Larry couldn't move any part of his body. How could a child be so strong? The man's eyes were fixated on this boy — this monster.

"My parents don't know where I am tonight. But I'm hungry, Larry. And you...really smell good. That's my secret. Don't tell anyone. Okay?"

Larry let out one final groan as Jason bit into his neck. But the sound was weak, and Larry the Loser's last conscious thought was that in his own very secluded doorway, nobody was going to hear him.

***

She woke with a start as somebody slammed the vault door shut. She wasn't used to being there when it was dark. But, being honest with herself, she was too weak to move.

Jason jumped up next to her on the edge of the coffin. It was still pitch black in the room.

"Here, Mother," he said. "Tip your head up a little. That's it."

He put his hand under her head and gently lifted. He looked like he was pondering what to do next.

"Oh, I know," he said, sounding like just a normal *little mortal* boy.

He held his hand up in front of his face. "This is where they used to put the IV's." Jason tore his wrist open with his teeth and hurriedly put it up to her lips. She started to protest, but the blood was surging into her like a life force.

"Drink, Mother. That's it. You'll feel better. Don't worry, I'll go back out and get us some more later."

CHAPTER TWENTY-ONE

I came to still lying prostrate on the couch. There was no sign of Angelika or Mikolaj. I realized it was daylight, although I had no concept of time. Where was Angelika sleeping?

Fortunately for me, it was summer, and the sun came up early. I looked at the clock on my table, and it was still early enough for me to get my kiester to work. I felt comforted by the daylight. *So this is what my life has come to*, I thought. *I am now officially afraid of the dark.*

I sat up and still felt dizzy, probably from blood loss. *So, what am I supposed to do now?* I wondered to myself. *Just mosey on back to my job as if nothing had happened? As if I hadn't been bit by a child-demon vampire, who only let me live because of some* plan *she was cooking up?*

My only alternative was to call in sick and head back to Mom and Dad's. But that place was crawling with cops, most of whom wanted to question me about Jason's disappearance. And Don Halberton might still be there. Seemed like he was itching to charge me with everything short of the Lindbergh kidnapping. No, I'd best skip that scene.

Lacking viable alternatives, I did my best to impersonate a viable, functioning human being and headed toward the office. I made sure to assess the landscape at every street corner. Sure, it was light out, but there was always my esteemed former boss to consider. I had no idea what kind of mental breakdowns were affecting his thoughts these days.

I made it to the office Shrek-free and started working, my thoughts never straying too far from my laundry list of crises. Fortunately, midweek was not a prime time to catch up socially, like on a Monday. There was little in the way of interaction in the cube farm, just a lot of clickety-clacking away on computers and the occasional moan, a signature of dedicating one's waking hours to the bedrudgery that was our current career. I was suddenly very grateful to Don Halberton for not letting the press run with the story of a missing child. I was sure my well-meaning co-workers would be burying me with sympathy and offers of help, none of which I was equipped to handle. I wondered, though, how long Don's ruse would hold up. Heaven knows, seeing Jason's visage splashed across local newscasts and papers might be all it would take to send me completely over the edge.

I begged out of morning coffee. I was going to do likewise with lunch, but a little voice in my head told me to act as normal as possible to avoid raising suspicions among my peers.

I went to the cafeteria with the team even though I had zero appetite. The group dynamics were about the same as usual. Boof was trying to engage us in an in-depth discussion of the pros and cons of online dating. The twins were attempting to talk business, although Chauncey, in particular, was semi-tuned into Boof's diatribe. It made me wonder briefly whether Stillwell had ever dabbled in that confusing world, or whether he had made any progress in pursuing his office crush. Razor was listening with his typical bemused smile. Vicky looked like she was trying to figure out how to act like she didn't know us, even though she was sitting at the same table. She was also glancing in my direction, and I guessed she was concerned about Jason and how I was holding up.

"Okay, so I might have fudged my appearance a little bit," said Boof. "So what? Doesn't everybody do that sometimes? Puff up their resume, so to speak? Isn't the idea to get to know the person? I'm probably doing these women a favor. They might pass me by because of some shallow criteria about height, but maybe once they get to know me, they'll realize how little that matters."

Stillwell and Berman made sheeshing noises at the same time. Vicky was holding her head in her hands. Razor just smiled.

Undeterred, Boof continued. "Besides, these companies make it too easy to overlook a person. 'Just swipe left if you're not interested.' That means you only have a second or two to make an impression. Right, Vick? I mean, let's be honest. What kind of chance do I have with those criteria?"

Although nobody wanted to come right out and agree, I detected a couple of subtle head nods.

I broke in. "How about we change the subject, huh? Larry. You and Chauncey working on anything interesting these days?"

"Well—" Larry Berman started up.

Boof interrupted. "All I'm saying is that okay, I puff up the appearance criteria some. But that gives me a chance to show off my personality. See? It's a win-win situation."

Awkward silence.

"So, what were you saying, Larry?" I asked.

Berman and Stillwell went on for a few minutes on their current projects, and thankfully, the lunch break was over, and we all headed back upstairs.

Vicky hung back with me, out of earshot of the others.

"Don't take this personally, but you don't look too good today. How are you holding up?"

I imagined that my myriad of problems and loss of blood wasn't doing much for my complexion.

"Oh, okay, I guess. Worried about Jason."

"Any change? Is he any better?"

That drop to the floor and cry urge came rushing back.

"Uh, no. No change."

She stopped, and we were facing each other.

"Well, as I said the other day, let me know if there's anything I can do to help. *Anything at all.*"

Her emphasis on the last sentence gave me pause. Suddenly I was aware we were alone in the hallway looking into each other's eyes. If I didn't know better, I'd say we were having a moment.

We started walking again. "Sure," I said. "Thanks, Vicky. I really appreciate it."

***

Upon further reflection, I passed our moment off to my imagination, overreacting in search of something — anything — positive to happen to me. There was no way a woman like Vicky could be interested in me. And even if she was, I couldn't involve her in the train wreck my life had become.

I started thinking about Lyria. It seemed like a long time since I had seen her. It felt like another lifetime when I was unaware of who and what she was. My biggest worry then was why such an amazing woman appeared to be pursuing a relationship with me. I, of course, didn't know at the time that she really wanted a caretaker. But our bond had grown since then.

Hadn't it?

It all came flooding back to me. I had to find Lyria. And Jason. I had to keep Don Halberton from changing my permanent residence to the local clink.

And what about Angelika? She knew everything I knew at this point. What was she planning to do? Were my friends and family in any danger from her?

I forced myself to get my breathing under control. After work, I rushed home. I needed some time to collect my thoughts.

Sure, I said to myself. *Take your time, Conner. There is a whole hour and a half of daylight left.*

***

It was less of a surprise this time that she wasn't alone. She awoke, feeling somewhat recovered, although still far from full strength.

Jason stirred next to her. Again, it took a moment for him to get his bearings.

"Mother," he said with bright eyes. "Are you feeling better?"

She smiled. It was hard not to. She lifted the coffin lid.

"Yes," she said. "Thanks to you. I appreciate your helping me, but…."

He jumped up out, a bundle of energy. "But what, Mother? Do you want to go out together tonight? That would be fun."

"Jason. I'm sorry about what happened. I didn't mean for any of this to come about."

"That's what you said last night, Mother. Don't you worry, though. I don't think I would have lasted much longer if you didn't help me. Then I was able to help you. See? It worked for both of us. Do you think we could go back to my grandma's house tonight? I'm sure Mommy and Daddy are still worried. I can let them know I'm okay. Wouldn't that be a good idea?"

"Jason, you're...different now. Do you understand that?"

"Oh yeah. I know. I saw the whole thing. How it started with Aurel. He was trying to help his mommy, right? That's how he got...changed. I get it. We have to feed, right? Like I did last night. On Larry."

She got out of the coffin and knelt in front of the boy. "Yes, dear. We have to feed. But we can still do some good. I will show you. Let's go out together, you and I. Tonight. I know exactly where we can start."

"We must focus on evildoers."

"What's that?"

She thought for a moment. "Bad men."

"Oh, I understand. So, how will we know when somebody is bad?"

"We watch them. We can do so without them seeing us. I have been watching this one for some time now. He is evil. He lives for hurting others. But we have to be careful that no one else sees us. Do you understand?"

"I understand, Mother."

She looked down at the boy. She could see the hunger she knew so well. It had been difficult enough for her to control herself when she was changed. Would she be able to instill the necessary discipline in a four-year-old?

They were facing a single family home on the outskirts of the city. The street and the front of the home were dark. The house was two stories, but she knew the basement was the center of the evil that was taking place. The façade was in disrepair, and the grass out front had grown out-of-control. But none of that mattered. His reign of terror was about to end.

***

It had started out so simply for Horace. His crimes were so

minor they were beneath the notice of the Boston police. Those guys always had bigger fish to fry.

Part of Horace's problem had always been his height. He was shorter than a normal man. He grew up feeling like everybody was taller than he was. Even when he had a "growth spurt" in his teens, his so-called spurt was practically inconsequential compared to other boys his age.

But Horace also was well aware that height was not his only problem. He had a dumpy build and a funny-looking overbite. He was always made fun of, even by his own parents. After his father left, his mother was all he had. But it was plain to see what a disappointment Horace was to her. It got to the point where his mother couldn't stand looking at him anymore, so she put him in the closet and left him there for long periods of time. He missed a lot of school, but that never bothered him. School for Horace was just another place to get bullied, mocked, and ignored.

Especially by girls.

When he started understanding that his situation was never going to get better, that his life was going to be one miserable turn after another, he felt like laws didn't apply to him. He had always been given a raw deal, so he would do what he had to in order to satisfy his needs.

He started out peeking in neighbor's windows. He knew where the cute girls in his neighborhood lived, and it wasn't too hard to figure out where their bedrooms were. On weekends, the lights would go out in the parents' room, but Horace knew teenage girls would stay up later, usually talking on the phone with their other cute friends. Then he would hone in.

It never ceased to amaze him how brazenly these girls would act with their window shades up. He guessed they figured they were in the safety of their homes, so what could happen?

When merely looking wasn't doing it for him anymore, he started taking his activities to the next level. He got himself a black mask and dressed all in black, and progressed to break-ins. Then assault. He realized that he—dumpy, funny-looking Horace—actually had the power. He moved around a lot, staying far from home. He never got caught because they didn't know how smart he was.

He got to the point where the roaming became tiresome. His mother had died and left him the house. He worked enough to pay the bills, but he wanted something — someone — he didn't have to leave home for.

It took him a couple of years of saving as much as he could and working by himself to build up his basement. He was fortunate that, while the house certainly didn't look like much, it was isolated from his neighbors by space and overgrown trees and vegetation. Heck, the people who lived around him never paid any attention to him anyway.

When he was finally ready, he made his first acquisition. It was a girl from the streets. A girl nobody would be looking for.

A girl nobody would miss.

Horace thought her cell in the basement was probably an improvement over wherever she was living before. But when he would go down for a "visit," she would beg endlessly for him not to hurt her and to set her free. She promised she would never tell anyone what he had done.

But Horace knew that was a lie. He could never let her out alive. He had the power.

He decided she needed company and that he needed some variety. So he brought another one down. He didn't want to know their names. To him, they were objects.

He was so smart. He knew there would be multiple "guests" and had built the appropriate accommodations. They would each have their own cell.

His new guest was meek, seemingly accepting her fate, although she cried a lot. But Horace had soundproofed the walls, so nobody outside could hear.

Even when they screamed.

His third acquisition was the best one yet. Yes, she was a streetwalker like the other two. But she had a certain something that the other girls lacked.

Call it class. Or maybe it was just the way she carried herself like she knew deep inside that she was too good to be walking the streets. Maybe she was simply doing it to make ends meet until another, more socially acceptable alternative came along. Whatever.

It was so easy. The girls came along willingly as long as he offered to pay generously for their time. Heading to a guy's basement was probably mild compared to what some other men made them do. By the time they realized this was more than some common trick for some oddball-looking guy, it was too late. He forced them into their cell at gunpoint, and the game was over.

Horace was pretty pleased with himself as he headed home from work. It was a glorious summer night with a warm, gentle breeze. He headed to the dark entrance to his house, thinking about which of his acquisitions he would choose tonight.

Ah, to be faced with such important decisions.

He stepped into his dank living room with dusty old furniture and an area rug that had been there since he was a kid. He didn't care how it looked. He never had any legitimate company. He didn't even own a television.

"Hello, Horace."

It was a female voice, but it still caused Horace to gasp. Had he and his treasures been discovered?

His eyes adjusted to the dark, and he was immobilized by what he could make out. It was a woman and a child. They were standing stationary in the shadows, holding hands.

From what Horace could tell, the woman was stunning, tall with an amazing body. She was wearing a pink print dress. Her brown hair was flowing over her shoulders and framed a beautiful face with high cheekbones. She looked like a model from the cover of *Cosmopolitan* — she couldn't possibly be a cop.

The boy looked to be four or five years old, wearing a simple plaid shirt, jeans, and sneakers. He was staring at Horace with a curious look. There was something else there as well. It almost looked like...hunger.

"Who...who are you? What...do you want?"

Neither said anything at first. Then the boy spoke.

"There are others here, Mother," he said. "I can smell them."

"Yes, I know, dear. We'll deal with them in a moment," said the woman.

She released the boy's hand and stepped forward. Horace inhaled sharply and, for a reason he couldn't quite pinpoint, stepped back.

"You've had company for some time now, haven't you, Horace?" she asked. "Thinking nobody could hear. Did you soundproof the house yourself? Well, you might have done a good enough job, but I still heard one of your...guests."

The initial shock had passed, and Horace collected his wits about him. He remembered that he had the power. He lifted his shirt and pulled his pistol out of the holster in his waistband. Feeling emboldened, he held the gun upward toward the woman's head. She was much taller than he was.

The boy giggled, unnerving Horace once again.

When he spoke, his voice was shaky. "I...don't know who you are or what you're doing here, but you've made a big mistake."

More giggling from the child. The sound sent shivers down Horace's spine. He glanced over but realized too late that the woman had moved close to him and was holding his gun hand.

"A sad little boy like you shouldn't be playing with guns," she said. She squeezed, and Horace howled, the gun hitting the floor with a thud. He could only watch, unable to speak or, for that matter, make any noise at all as she grabbed his shoulder, and her beautiful face came closer.

"Let's just see what makes you tick, Horace. Shall we?"

Horace felt a searing pain originating in his neck then spreading throughout his entire body. All he could see, all he was aware of was her. He could see what she was. He knew what was happening. She drew back, her face contorted, with bloody fangs and her pupils completely dilated, making her eyes look black.

"I'm afraid this one can't be helped. Come over here." It was clear she was speaking to the boy.

Horace tried to talk. "Please," he gasped. "Please don't—"

"I understand, Horace," said the woman, her face normal again. She was perfectly calm. "I understand that it's not your fault. Sometimes I can help a person like you. But I'm afraid you are too far gone. And I think you've inflicted enough misery on others." She let him go, and he crumpled to the floor.

Horace started to say something else, but what he saw next stopped the words in his throat. The boy was walking toward him, his eyes black, and smiling with sharp fangs. He looked up at the woman. She nodded briefly.

All Horace could muster was "Noooo."

His last vision was the boy closing in, opening his mouth wide. There was the same pain again, but this time there would be no recovery. Everything went black.

***

They watched from across the street as the police swarmed on Horace's house and eventually came out with the girls who had been held captive in the basement. They were holding blankets around their shoulders and were led to an ambulance.

"Wow, those girls were living downstairs?" asked Jason.

"Yes. But they didn't want to be living there. See? Do you understand what a bad person Horace was? And how we can do good? How we can help people?"

The boy beamed. "Yes, I get it." He paused for a moment. "I like how we can see their thoughts. Can they see ours too?"

"They can if we let them," said Lyria.

Jason had his hand under his chin, thinking. "I would like to help someone else tonight. Do you think we could do that?"

***

Darren Dobson stood patiently in the dark alley watching Conner David's townhouse. It was time to stop screwing around. The little rich boy had ruined his life, and he was going to pay.

Darren knew that coming here at night was a risk — that *she* could be with him. But he couldn't chance being seen in the daylight carrying out his task. He planned on getting his life back on track. He had valuable experience in the lucrative world of investment banking. Potential employers would soon be beating his door down to get Darren on their team. And his life at home would return to normal as well.

Once this job was done. Once he could stop obsessing about Conner David.

And her.

Darren had all the time in the world to wait David out. He knew the little shit went for walks on occasion. Darren had seen him. And David was often alone. Without her.

He imagined that she would have to go off by herself at times. That she would have to *feed*, without her boy toy tagging along. The little weasel didn't have the stomach for anything like that.

Yes, eventually, Conner David would emerge. At night. By himself. And the score would be evened between them.

He took a few steps toward the back of the alley and turned toward the darkness. He had checked his weapon several times, but he wanted to check it again, and he didn't want to chance being seen by a passerby.

He took the pistol out of the pocket of his lightweight jacket. It was amazing how easy it was to get the gun. He just had to ask around to some of the street people he encountered regularly. It didn't take him long to hit pay dirt. *Bottom line,* he thought. *If you have the money, anything is available to you.*

The revolver looked cheap like it had been used many times, but Darren didn't care. It had six rounds, and they would all soon be residing in the body of his nemesis. The guy who had tried to ruin his life.

He turned back toward the mouth of the alley and stopped short with a gasp of breath. A little girl was standing silently, looking at him.

How did she come up on him so quietly, he wondered. She was wearing an overall dress and what looked like new shoes, but he couldn't see her face in the shadows. It must be some kid from the neighborhood, he thought. But there was something about how she was so still that sent Darren's heartbeat racing.

"Hello, Mr. Dobson."

She had a little girl's voice, but it sent icicles through his heart. He thought he detected an accent, but he couldn't place it.

And she knew his name. What madness was this?

"Who…who are you? How…do you know my name?"

She stepped forward. Dobson instinctively raised the pistol.

The child giggled. "Now that's not very nice," she said. "Not a very good way to make friends." She was still moving forward.

Darren took corresponding steps back. He took a deep breath and tried to sound braver than he felt. "Now look, kid. I don't know who you are or how you know my name, but you'd better get back to your home. It's probably past your bedtime, and I'm sure your mother is worried about you. Go on. Get. NOW."

The girl kept inching forward. Darren's eyes adjusted, and he could see her curly hair draped over her shoulders. She seemed to be smiling, but he couldn't see her eyes. Was it still too dark? All he could see were black orbs.

"Hee hee. We don't want to talk about *my* bedtime. And as for how I know your name, I think we have a mutual friend. You know Conner David, right? Isn't that who you came here to see tonight?"

With the mentioning of David's name, Dobson sucked in his breath again. He pointed the pistol straight at her. "What...do you want? Stay where you are."

She kept coming forward. Dobson kept moving back. The presence of his weapon seemed to have no impact on her. Did she think he wouldn't shoot a little girl?

She said, "I'm putting a little group together, and I thought you might want to join."

"Group? What kind of group? What are you talking about?" Dobson hated the desperation in his voice. The fear.

"Oh, don't worry." Her singsong tone sounded almost as if she was mocking his discomfort. "It will be a lot of fun. We'll get to spend a lot of time together."

Darren backed up another step and tripped on a piece of garbage. Suddenly he was falling backwards, and he was so high strung he could feel himself pulling the trigger. The blast echoed in the alley, and he was only vaguely aware that he had cried out before thumping down to the ground on his back.

His only thought was, *My God, what if I killed her?* He looked up.

She was still standing, looking down at him, a plume of blood spreading in a circle on her white shirt.

"Look what you've done now, Mr. Dobson. Mik just bought me this shirt. He's going to be very angry with you."

"I...didn't mean to—"

"Oh, I know. Accidents happen. But with the noise and all, we're going to have to get down to business. Here, let's just make sure there are no more little mistakes."

She shot forward and grabbed the gun. He tried to pull his hand back, but he couldn't move it.

"Come on now, Mr. Dobson. May I call you Darren? Let me take that before somebody gets hurt. Hee hee."

She grabbed his wrist with her other hand and squeezed, Dobson, howling in pain.

"That's better. I think I'll hold onto this."

She put the gun in her pocket, and her face was suddenly in front of his. She was smiling. He could see.... *Oh my god....*

"I'll tell you what, Darren. Since we don't have a lot of time, I'm going to explain everything the easy way."

She moved in toward his neck. All Darren Dobson could muster was a very weak, "Noooo."

He felt the pain, and he couldn't move, and it all became clear how this all could have come about.

Darren's final independent thought was that his plans for revenge and redemption were all now a thing of the past.

CHAPTER TWENTY-TWO

My paranoia at an all-time high, I didn't think calling Lyria on the burner phone I had bought for her was a good idea anymore. What if they subpoenaed my phone records as part of the missing child investigation? They did that in real life, right?

My only alternative was one that I truly dreaded. I had to go to Lyria's place. This wasn't like the old pickup line, "My place or yours?" Lyria's place was where she kept her coffin. Where she slept.

I knew where it was because after faking her death in front of Mikolaj and Don Halberton, we had to move her to another spot. It had all been pre-arranged before our charade so that she could get there quickly and hole up away from the impending daylight.

My mind wandered to those TV shows where people are looking for a new house, like one close to the beach, say. They always list their requirements for their realtor at the start of the show.

"Well, we need three bedrooms, two baths, an open concept, and under our budget. Oh, and if we can get an interior room with no windows, big enough for a custom sarcophagus, and that can be fitted with a one-way vault door, that would be great."

The thought kicked me into a laughing fit, which I'm sure was more a result of the pressures associated with my life coming undone than anything else. I could just as well have been crying hysterically.

I got myself under control and started thinking through the

logistics of what I needed to do. Most people would just pop into their car and head out, but for me, that presented a little problem. I didn't have a car.

My overactive self-doubt reared its ugly head. What kind of loser in their twenties doesn't have a vehicle? But, since dear old Dad had set me up with a primo condo within walking distance of the office, the expense of keeping a car in Boston wasn't really practical. I read somewhere that a nearby garage was selling parking condos, where you actually owned your parking space for a tidy sum of money. What a world we live in. I pictured myself in Dad's home office asking him to buy me a parking condo after shelling out the big bucks for my Beacon Hill digs. My biggest concern would have been making sure his office door was open before he kicked me through it.

I thought about an Uber, but my paranoia perked up again about leaving a trail that could be presented as evidence in my trial. I again wondered if I was being too dramatic, but I still couldn't make myself do it. A wild thought came to me about calling one of my office buddies for a ride, but I surely didn't want to involve anyone else in my mess.

Public transportation? Nah. Too many witnesses.

So, it was settled. I was going to walk.

Lyria's lair was in a sparsely populated industrial area south of town. There were many abandoned and vacant buildings around, which had served our needs in a couple of ways. First, we simply didn't want a lot of people around, and second, when I researched the owner of our building, he was all too happy to rent the space to me, no questions asked.

The distance of my walk didn't really bother me, but I was a little worried about strolling through some fairly sketchy areas of Boston in the middle of the night. As I found out the hard way, I presented a nice target for those living on the less conventional side of the law. When street predators saw a tall skinny guy out walking by himself at night, they probably looked up and thanked the Lord for making Christmas come early. So I made my best attempt to look like I belonged out there.

I was conscious of the fact that if I pranced out in my designer jeans and preppy polo shirt, I was just pre-ordaining my status as a mugging victim. So, I dug through my stuff and came up with a black pair of sneakers, black socks, dark colored pants, and a black windbreaker. I must have wanted to be a ninja at some point in my life. I also found a black knit hat. Although it was still warm out, I thought the hat would give me street cred.

Out I went. While I was still in my neighborhood, I practiced my street walk. I thought about how some of the tough-looking guys I had seen in the city moved. Long strides, a little side-to-side action. After a few minutes, I couldn't decide if it made me look tough or just constipated, so I gave it up, put my head down, and pushed forward.

There certainly weren't many people around at this hour and very few vehicles. But as I made my way to cut through the downtown shopping district, I noticed some headlights coming from behind me. I made a couple of turns that I really didn't need to make. Isn't that how spies in the movies would shake their tail? I didn't see the headlights anymore. Huh, must be something to that.

But then, back on Washington Street, the headlights were back. I kept walking as I risked a look around. Sure enough, there was a car inching forward about fifty yards behind me. I thought it was a sedan of some sort, although I couldn't get a make on it.

I really do watch too much TV.

I turned back toward the Common. This time, the headlights followed. I circled around the block back to Washington.

They were still there.

Holy crap. This wasn't my CSI-induced paranoia this time. I was actually being followed.

Continuing to head toward Lyria's was out of the question. I honestly didn't know what to do. Despite being out on a stealth mission at night, I was still a clueless financial analyst stuck in the middle of a shit storm that I had no idea how to address.

So I stood stationary, on a dark sidewalk in downtown Boston, at who-knows-what-time at night. I turned back and looked at the car for what seemed like an eternity but was really just a few seconds. The headlights went out, and I sucked in my breath as I saw someone getting out on the driver's side.

I was not at all surprised to see Don Halberton approach me slowly on the sidewalk. He was wearing the same clothes as when I last encountered him, and I couldn't imagine there was any chance he'd be in a better mood now. I still had the height advantage working for me, but it didn't make me feel any less sick. My father had tried in vain to teach me that being taller than someone else gives you an advantage in interpersonal communications. Problem was, Dad was built thickly through the shoulders and had a naturally intimidating personality. With my skinny build and thick glasses, I was about as intimidating as Mickey Mouse.

"Out late tonight, huh, Conner? Where you headed?" he asked, still moving forward.

I made an attempt to normalize my breathing. I didn't think passing out due to hyperventilation would improve my chances of a positive outcome.

"Uh...just out for a walk. Couldn't sleep. You know how it is."

"Yeah, I know. Seems strange, though, strolling through downtown. Lots of nice walking routes closer to your condo back up on the Hill. What brings you down to this area?"

Don was now standing right in front of me. He wasn't up in my grille like the last time yet, but I sensed that was still an option.

"Ah, just wanted to go someplace different tonight...a little variety."

That sounded lame even to me.

"Okay, let's quit screwing around, shall we?" Don stepped forward, his eyes narrowing. "You're going to meet with *her*, aren't you? I know you don't have a car. And you're too smart to take a cab or an Uber. That's what you kids do nowadays, isn't it? You're all dressed in black. Hoping to blend into the night? I'll ask you one more time. *Where are you headed?*"

"No...nowhere in particular."

"Why don't you give me the address? Or I can take you there. I have a lot of questions I need answered."

The thought of me leading an angry police officer to Lyria's coffin almost made me physically ill. Halberton must have sensed my discomfort.

"You don't look too good, Conner. Tell you what, why don't you get in my car, and I can either drive you to where you were going, or I can take you home."

"Uh no," I said. "That's okay. I mean...I'll be okay."

Don stepped forward again. "Get in the car."

Seeing no alternative, I walked back to his car with him and got in the passenger side.

He got behind the wheel. "Where to?" he asked. To say the tone was not polite would be an understatement.

"I guess you can take me home."

Halberton turned toward me. "You know, Conner, I'm working this case on my own. I can't explain the circumstances to anyone else. If I told them what I saw last fall, they'd think I was ready for an early medical retirement. But there's no doubt in my mind that she's involved in this. It can't be a coincidence that people around you keep disappearing. Right now, I've kept the press at bay, but that won't hold for long. How would you like it if a swarm of reporters was camped outside your swanky little condo waiting to question you in Jason's disappearance? Cause that's where we're headed."

I think I was trembling as I sat looking straight ahead through his windshield.

Don softened his tone. "Look, you don't seem like a bad guy. Heck, maybe you got caught up in something that's over your head. Something that got out of control. And now you don't know how to deal with it. Talk to me. Tell me what's going on. I don't want to arrest you. I want to help you."

He let that hang in the air as we sat, the engine idling away. I have to admit, it was tempting. Explaining Lyria to most people would result in a referral to the family psychiatrist. But Don Halberton had seen her. He shot her with his gun and watched her spit the bullet out. But what would happen then? Would he put out an APB to arrest her on sight? I had to think about Lyria. And Jason. I decided I had to find out about Jason before I said anything else.

And what about Angelika?

"Let me think about it...please. I need a little more time." I was speaking in a virtual whisper.

Don sat back and put the car in gear. "Keep in mind, time is a luxury. And you are fast running out."

***

The room was pitch black, but Lisa still wore a night mask, as if she needed to blot out her reality in addition to any stray light. The drugs were becoming less effective. At first, she could count on a deep, dreamless sleep, a virtual escape from consciousness. Now she was out for a little while, but then she would wake up, and it would all come flooding back.

Jason. Her Jason.

Wasn't it a short time ago they were living together as a happy family? Before this darkness descended? He was a normal little boy, laughing, roughhousing with his father, getting into trouble. Their life was blessed. They had even discussed another child, a brother or sister for him.

Now that seemed like an alternate reality. She thought about Caden and Jason, and even herself for that matter, as if they were other people. Like she had seen their happy times on some TV show.

Call in to vote for your favorite character.

She was awake but had no desire to get up. To move. As long as she was here, by herself in the dark, it couldn't get any worse, right? They couldn't tell her any more bad news.

She had virtually shut down all her senses. And when she heard the voice, she ignored it at first, convinced it was conjured up by her drug-addled imagination.

"Mommy?"

There it was again. It sounded so real. It sounded like Jason. Her heart beat faster. Even if she was imagining it, it provided a feeling of euphoria, as if endorphins were flooding her veins.

She lifted her head, but there was only darkness. Then she remembered the mask. She lifted it off, but she still couldn't see anything, the room completely devoid of light.

"Hi, Mommy."

She stopped breathing as she barely made out a tiny figure, his features dim, but it looked like....

No. She had to be dreaming. Those meds were screwing with her mind.

The apparition came forward. The figure in her dream. She had to be dreaming, but it was okay. She was okay with it.

"Jason?" she gasped.

"Yes, Mommy. I missed you."

She moved to the edge of the bed, but her muscles weren't working correctly, and she tumbled to the floor. She got up on her knees, and Jason was in her arms. The tears started flowing for real as she felt his body. His arms were around her neck. She held him, not wanting to let go, not wanting the dream to end. It felt so real.

"Jason." She was blubbering. She could feel him. Smell him. "You're here. You're really here."

"Yes, Mommy. I'm here."

The embrace made her feel alive again. Her senses were activating. She started to think she wasn't dreaming. She held his waist as she leaned back and looked at her son. She tried to focus through the tears and the darkness.

"You look so...normal. But how...how did you get here? We have to get you back to the hospital."

"No, Mommy. We don't need to go back there anymore. I'm...I'm better now."

She hugged him close again. This was insane. That was it. She had gone insane. It was understandable. This couldn't be real. Jason was kissing her cheek, and she could feel the wetness.

"I...I know this isn't real," she stammered. "But I don't care. I'm okay with being crazy as long as I can have you with me."

Jason held her face and whispered. "You're not crazy, Mommy. I am real. And I'm here. With you. But I have to explain something to you. I've...changed. See, if I just tell you, you probably won't believe me. I know I used to make up stories sometimes."

She laughed. They both laughed, and they were back in their

embrace. When she was holding him, everything seemed to be right in her world.

He lifted his head up. "So, is it okay if I *show* you, Mommy? I'll show you how I got well. It will be better when you can understand everything. Is that all right?"

"Yes, baby. Whatever you want."

He smiled, and they were locked together once more. She didn't ever want it to end.

Lisa felt a pinch in her neck, and her body went numb. She was Jason in his hospital bed. She was one with him. She could see what he saw. His thoughts were hers.

See Mommy, I was about to go into the light.

Lisa didn't hear his voice. She was somehow sharing his thoughts. It brought them so close together. She was Jason, and he was her.

They looked up from their bed and saw Lyria leaning down toward them, her beautiful face coming closer. Her mouth opened with huge, sharp canine teeth.

"For better or for worse, my dear child," she said.

They both saw the light, and Lisa started to understand.

***

The woman and the child had to hurry to get back on time. It was a busy night, but daylight was coming shortly. She was still feeling weak. She had shared the evildoer with Jason and hadn't fully recovered from his conversion.

The air felt different as they entered the abandoned building, and Lyria's senses immediately went on alert. She grabbed Jason and pulled him close as they ascended. They were in the hallway outside her vault-like door, which she always kept slightly ajar. But now, it was wide open.

Someone was inside their room.

"Mother? Is that you?"

She stiffened. It was like a voice from a crypt, one she never thought she would hear again. How was this possible?

"Who is that, Mother?" asked Jason. His eyes were wide, but not with fright. More like excitement.

She did her best to keep the boy behind her, but it was no

use. He went running ahead of her.

"Jason!" she cried out.

She entered the room, and Jason was staring straight ahead, entranced. Lyria did her best to keep the shock off her face.

Angelika.

The child was sitting upright in their coffin, wearing a huge smile, the light from the single bulb shining off her fangs. She was wearing an overall denim dress and a bloodstained white shirt. To add to the shock of her appearance, Mikolaj Babka and Darren Dobson were standing stationary near the head of her sarcophagus, staring straight ahead.

"How did you get here?" was all Lyria could muster.

"Oh, now, is that any way to greet your firstborn child? After all this time? And you. You must be Jason."

The girl leapt out of the coffin and swept Jason up in an embrace. The boy was clearly taken by her and returned the hug.

"I'm your sister," said Angelika. "Didn't Mother tell you about me?"

Jason was beaming with delight. "I...I saw you, but I thought you were...."

"Yes, that was unfortunate. Mother, I'm sure we could have worked out our differences. But you and Father decided you had to...."

She actually looked sad for a moment. Then she was back to smiling brightly.

"Anyway, that was a long time ago. Thanks to Mikolaj — and Father, actually — I got free from your little trap. Tell you what, why don't we...what do they say these days, Mik? Move forward? Hee hee."

Mikolaj continued staring straight ahead.

Angelika held Jason by the shoulders. "I've got big plans for us, though. Tell you what, why don't you wait outside with the boys while I have a little talk with Mother? And don't hurt them, okay? Hee hee. Boys?"

Mikolaj and Darren moved toward Jason. Lyria shouted, "No!" and moved to intervene. But Angelika grabbed her by the waist and sent her hurtling to the corner of the room. She landed with a thud.

Lyria looked up as Mikolaj, Dobson, and Jason left the room. Jason looked over his shoulder at her but kept walking.

Angelika appeared on top of her, pinning her to the floor, holding the collar of her dress. Her face was now inches away.

"I'm surprised, Mother. I knew I was stronger than you, but I really thought you'd put up a better fight. Are you weak from making Jason?"

"Angelika, listen to me...."

"No, I think you'd better listen to me, Mother. I came here intending to take revenge on you. Being encased in concrete for decades was...not very nice. But I didn't realize how good you have it here. Nobody is even aware of us. Then, when I found out you had made me a little brother, I started thinking it over. I mean, you did save me before...carrying out your little plot. And making Jason? What a nice surprise. Ah, but it's almost light out, so I'd better get to the point, right?"

The child came even closer.

"I intend to make this our feeding ground. And without any of the nonsense you worry about. Evildoers only? Do you know how good children taste? Oh, hee hee. I guess you do. Not saying we'll only feed on children, but they will be part of a balanced diet, hee hee hee."

"No...wait—"

"Just listen, Mother. I have what I want. A companion and a safe place to live. Now, you have a couple of choices. You can join us. Wouldn't that be fun? Or, you can try to interfere. And I promise you, Mother...." The child bared her fangs. "That will not be fun. The boys are going to look after me while I'm sleeping. You and your boyfriend can just continue on as you were. You two got pretty wild there, didn't you? Oh, and just to provide more reason for you to stay out of our way, I will make another promise to you." She paused. "I promise that if there is any sign of interference from you, your little boyfriend is the one who will pay the price. And that lovely family of his? My, what beautiful things they have in this country. I saw their home when I was with Conner. I know where they live, and make no mistake,

Mother…I will kill them all. And it will be on your conscience. If you even still have such a thing. Hee hee."

There was another pause, letting her threat sink in.

"Well, I have to go. And you need to get some rest. Why don't you think about it? If you decide you want to join us, we shouldn't be too difficult to find. Goodbye, Mother."

In an instant, she was gone.

"Angelika, wait!" Lyria ran down the stairs and outside, but there was no sign of any of them.

She felt overcome with despair. Jason.

But the child was right. Daylight was coming. And she definitely needed some rest.

CHAPTER TWENTY-THREE

Charles and Carol David were stunned when they saw Lisa that morning.

Neither one of them had slept very much that night. This ordeal — Jason critically ill, then disappearing — had taken a toll on them. Charles considered himself a man of action. When there was a problem, he fixed it. He had resources and an iron will.

But this was different. He couldn't fix this problem. His grandson was gone, and there was absolutely nothing he could do about it.

He looked at his wife as they headed to the kitchen. She looked older, her skin more wrinkled, her posture more slouched than even a few days ago. He reached for her hand.

She gave a start. He was not a physically demonstrative man, far from it. And her thoughts were undoubtedly consumed with worries about Jason.

"Sorry," he said. They both managed a little laugh. "How are you holding up?"

She looked unsure about how to answer. It was also unusual for him to ask about someone else's feelings. Even her. Even his wife.

"Oh, as well as can be expected, I guess." Her voice sounded scratchy, and Charles knew that she had spent most of the night crying.

He impulsively took her in his arms. She was taken aback but melted into him. The crying started for real, his wife convulsing as he held her.

Charles had spent his awake time thinking—about his life, about the way he'd raised his family. There was no question that he was a great provider. They had every material need taken care of. But had he shortchanged everyone nonetheless? His children always considered him cold. And, he had to admit, they actually feared him. When they had a problem, they always went to Mom. They undoubtedly felt that Dad wouldn't understand.

Or even care.

He was a stern disciplinarian, at work and at home. It was the only way to excel in a ruthless business like investment banking, and Charles simply didn't have the ability to turn off his approach when it came time to go home. It was the only way he knew.

Now, his family was in crisis. His wife and his children needed him. Not monetarily, but emotionally.

For the first time in his life, Charles felt ill-equipped to handle a problem.

"I'm sorry, Charles," said his wife, still sobbing.

"No, it's all right," he said. Comforting words were eluding him, so he offered a rare instance of physical comfort. As much as she needed.

They moved in tandem to their kitchen table and sat. She held onto his hand. "I...I just feel so helpless," she said. "Like there's something more I should be doing."

"I know. I feel the same way."

She looked at him—an admission of weakness. A morning full of firsts. She squeezed his hand.

"Let me get you something to eat," she said. "Our diet has been a little off the last couple of days."

He smiled at her with as much warmth as he could muster. But as she got up, Lisa came bounding into the kitchen.

"Well, good morning, everyone. I hope you slept well. I know I did."

Charles and Carol looked at each other, then stared agape at their daughter-in-law, who they'd had to keep sedated for the last two days.

She was barefoot, her blonde hair flowing over a brightly colored sundress. Her face was flush with color, and she looked like she had put makeup around her eyes. She looked like their naturally beautiful daughter-in-law again, for the first time in recent memory.

"Lisa," said Charles as Carol continued to stare. "Are you okay?"

"I'm great, thanks for asking. Oh, but you two look really tired. Tell you what, Carol, you sit back down, and I'll make everyone a nice breakfast."

She started pulling out pots and pans and eggs and bread from the refrigerator. Carol walked over, stopped her frenetic motion, and gathered her in her arms.

"Take it easy, sweetie. You don't have to do that. Maybe you should get some rest."

Lisa gave a hearty laugh. "Rest? My gosh, that's all I've been doing lately. Come on, sit down." She guided Carol back to her chair. "I've been a real burden to you. I'm aware of that. Let me at least try to make it up to you." She started back in on her work. "Charles, what would you like?"

"Oh, uh, anything is fine. Uh, would you excuse me? I have to make a phone call."

"Of course. Carol will keep me company. And I'll have breakfast ready in no time. I really love you guys."

Charles nodded and walked to his study. He pulled out his phone. Caden had decided to get up early and head into Boston to look for Jason.

"Dad? What's up?"

"Caden, you'd better forget about whatever you're doing and get back home."

***

Now I was truly stuck. I had no earthly idea what to do next.

I woke up to my infernal alarm clock after a fitful and all too brief night's sleep. I still had no clue what was going on with Lyria and Jason. And, to further complicate matters, Don Halberton was seemingly a heartbeat away from having me locked up.

Unless, of course, I came clean about Lyria.

On the plus side, Don was the one person to whom I could relate my whole story from the start and who wouldn't want to have me committed right on the spot. He had seen Lyria. He would believe me.

On the other hand, what would happen to her if I did? Don was only trying to clear up the mystery about what had happened to Jason. But would he let her skate on the other missing person cases? I seriously doubted that. He had to at least suspect that she had killed. And, at his core, he was a straight-laced, by-the-book cop. There was no way he was just going to let her go on with her current course.

And, if Jason had been converted to save his life? The implications were too gruesome to consider.

Lacking a better alternative and figuring that being unemployed would make matters materially worse, I headed to the office.

Funny how I used to think of my job as being such a burden. Now it was like a sanctuary for me—a place to escape from the insanity that was my life.

I no sooner settled into my routine when Boof Parsons came bombing into my cube and parked himself in front of my desk. So much for my sanctuary.

"Don't you ever knock?" I asked.

He looked incredulous. "Knock? Hey, this is BHA, not Kensington Palace. Anyway, I'm glad you're here. I came across a woman on my dating app last night and, I gotta tell you, Conner, I think she might be the one."

I was afraid to ask what he meant by that, so I just said, "Hey, that's great, Boof. Have you arranged a first date?"

"Ah, well, here's the thing. I sent her a note, you know, trying to set something up, and, well...." He paused.

"Well, what?"

"Well, she hasn't actually responded. But I know it's gonna work out. I mean, she's really beautiful. And we have a lot in common. It's a can't miss."

"Uh huh. What exactly do you have in common?"

"Well...uh...we're both on the same website, right? So, I

figured out why she didn't respond right away. I re-read my note, and it might have come off as slightly Neanderthal, you know?"

"Yeah, *that* I believe."

"Right. So I was up all last night cooking up a better letter as a follow up. Lemme run this by you. I mean, I think it's good, but I don't want to end up in creepy-guy prison."

Boof whipped out a folded legal-sized yellow page, straightened it out, and started reading.

Dearest Emily,

Sorry about the lame attempt to connect I sent earlier. I should have realized that a classy babe like you would require something more. I think we are destined to get to know each other. After all, we must both be pretty desperate to be on this site to begin with, correct? When I saw your picture, it made me happy. It reminded me of chocolate cake with really gooey icing. I'd like to present myself as a prospective mate. I have a good paying job, above average looks, and don't go in for too much of the kinky stuff. Please respond in kind.

Truly yours, Edwin Parsons.

"So, what do you think?"

"I think I need the address of that creepy-guy prison. You know, in case I want to write."

"Come on, get serious, willya? Do you think this has the right amount of sizzle? Or should I spiff it up some more?"

Thankfully Vicky appeared in my doorway before I had to devise a response. "Conner, could we go over some details on the Sanderson deal?" she asked.

"Oh, yeah, sure. Could you excuse us, Boof?"

"Sanderson?? That's that plastic company, right? Hey, what's more important — the love of my life, or making sure Aunt Harriet has enough disposable forks and knives for her next sewing circle?"

"Boof...."

"Okay, okay. But make sure you get back to me on the note. My...um...manly nature ain't getting any younger if you know what I mean."

Boof stormed out, and Vicky sat down. She was smiling and looking radiant in a light-colored business suit, her blonde hair cascading over her shoulders. I thought, *This is a serious upgrade on the visitor front.*

"Thanks," I said, and we both started to laugh quietly.

"You're welcome. Fortunately, Boof doesn't know that Sanderson closed last week."

"Yeah, thank goodness."

"I overheard him reading his love note and figured you needed to be rescued. Not to mention the poor girl he's going to send that letter to."

I laughed. "Boof might be the first person to get banned from a dating app."

We were both laughing. Then she looked serious. "How is your nephew? Any better?"

My mood came crashing down to earth. "Ah...it's kind of a long story."

She frowned. "That doesn't sound good. Hey, do you have time for lunch today? I really enjoyed getting out of the office the other day. The Syrian sub place up the street is having a special. And I...." Vicky fished around in her pocket and pulled out a little paper square. "...have a coupon!"

She was so ebullient that I had to laugh. "Well, who could say no to that?"

"Great. So what say we sneak out of here at 11:30, before everyone else heads downstairs?"

"Deal."

She smiled and swept out of my office.

Holy smokes. Maybe I wasn't imagining things the other day when Vicky and I had "our moment."

Whoa, Conner boy. This is just two colleagues going to lunch. Don't start making wedding plans just yet.

But for the next couple of hours, my mind swirled with possibilities. It could be just that—an innocent lunch invitation. Certainly, members of my group craved getting out of the office for any reason, real or imagined.

But what if it was something more? What if Vicky Temerlin was actually taking an interest in me? A few days ago, the notion would have seemed absurd. But I wasn't experienced enough in matters of the heart to tell the difference between a potential love interest and a woman simply seeking fresh air.

Not to mention everything I had going on in my life at that moment. There was Lyria, Jason, Angelika, Don Halberton, Darren Dobson, missing persons, vampires, and potential murder charges, just to name a few. Did I really want to involve somebody else in my mess? And what would it be like being in a relationship with someone you worked with in a tight knit group?

I didn't have anything resembling an answer to any of these questions, but I found myself eagerly anticipating our lunch and hoping the time would go by quickly.

***

With Vicky's coupon, the subs were buy one, get one fifty percent off. I sprang for lunch.

What a guy.

"I can't even imagine a woman's reaction when Boof shows up for a first date," said Vicky.

"Yeah, especially when he's described himself as six foot four and resembling Brad Pitt."

We both laughed.

"Seriously, though, it must be awful having to maneuver through the online dating world these days," she said. "I don't even know why Boof does that."

"Well, he's spent at least the last two years since I've known him trying to pick up women in bars, and that hasn't succeeded. I think the anonymity and the opportunity to dummy up your first impression probably appeals to him. You know, since she won't actually be able to see him and all."

Vicky laughed again. I was totally relaxed, and Vicky seemed the same. It's remarkable how different, and great, it felt to get out of the office.

She had a bit of a twinkle in her eyes as she asked, "So Conner, have you ever dabbled in that endeavor?"

"What? Online dating?"

"Yes."

"No. I never even considered it. I'm socially awkward among

people I know. I can't imagine meeting up with a stranger. In public. Talk about a bad first impression."

She laughed. "Oh, I think you do pretty well among people you know."

"You really think so?"

"Absolutely."

"Wow, I'm so glad to hear that, even if you're just being polite. It's much appreciated. Sometimes after work, I replay interactions I've had during the day, and I want to kick myself for sounding so stupid."

"Ha-ha. I'll admit there was a bit of awkwardness when we first started working together, but once the ice melted, you came off pretty well."

I smiled. We were quiet for a moment while I let that sink in. I finally got up the gumption to ask her something I never could have back in the office.

"So, Vick, have *you* ever dabbled in the online dating world?"

She flashed me a flawless smile. "I'm sure there's a lot of curiosity about my social life among you guys, isn't there?"

"Whatever gave you that idea?"

She laughed. "Oh, just the subtle and, in the case of Boof, not so subtle questions that I get sometimes."

"Oh yeah? Like what?"

"Well, if it's Larry Berman, the question would be something along the line of, 'So Vicky, what did you think of that Monday Night Football game last night? What, you didn't see it? Why? What, were you out or something?' Or, 'Hey, have you had a chance to see such-and-such movie yet? It was really good.' But Boof's question would be more like, 'Got any hot dates lined up for the weekend or what?'"

We both laughed at that one.

I said, "I hope he doesn't offend you."

"No, he's been a lot better since last fall. And I understand he doesn't know any better."

I looked at her expectantly.

"I guess you want an answer to your question, huh?"

"Only if you feel comfortable talking about it. And I assure you whatever you say will not be fed into the rumor pipeline."

Another great smile.

"No, Conner. I've never dabbled. I know it's socially acceptable now—my gosh, it seems like everybody meets that way nowadays—but I'm like you. I couldn't deal with the awkwardness. And for a woman, there's always the safety factor."

I nodded.

She continued. "But I have to admit, living in the city by myself and working so many hours, it can get to feel a bit... isolating."

I must have looked surprised.

She said, "Yes. Even for me. What, did you guys cook up any imaginary scenarios of what you thought my life was like?"

"Well...."

"Come on. Spill it. We're being honest with each other here, right?" Big smile.

"Okay, the most likely activities are being flown to Paris on a private supersonic jet for lunch and cruising Boston Harbor on a yacht."

She had a hearty laugh at that one. "Geez, I wish," she said. "I can assure you neither of those has ever happened. My life outside the office is pretty boring, actually. I go to the gym. Meet my high school girlfriend for dinner. Every once in a great while, we might hit a club. But most times, when I need company, I spend the weekend at Mom and Dad's. Not exactly Harlequin Romance territory, huh?"

We both laughed.

"How about you?" she asked. She looked serious all of a sudden.

My mind started swirling with child vampires and potential prison time. And Lyria.

I must have looked grim. Vicky said, "Oh, I don't mean to pry—"

"No, no. I'm sorry. It's only fair that I should share as well. I have a lot going on in my life right now, but I'll be honest, not much of it is good."

"I understand. With your nephew and all, it must be very

hard on your family."

She didn't know the half of it. Nobody knew about Jason disappearing. Or where he might have gone.

"Yeah. Everyone is struggling. They've been keeping my sister-in-law sedated."

"Oh, Conner. I'm so sorry."

Vicky put her hand on mine. I took it, and our eyes met.

I wondered if all this talk about our social lives was a precursor to something. Vicky as much as admitted that she wasn't seeing anyone, and now, here we were holding hands.

I heard myself say, "I wish...it could be different."

She held my gaze. "Maybe it can," she said.

I became aware that I was breathing harder and wondered if she could hear it.

"I...have some issues I have to work through."

She pursed her lips and said, "Sure. Let me know when things change for you."

"I will. I definitely will."

"Well, guess we'd better head back. I don't want anyone thinking you stole me away to Paris."

We laughed, and I found myself happy that the lunch had ended on a positive note.

***

Pitch black. That was the way she liked it. And she could see that he was coming around to her way of thinking. After all, it was natural for them to like the dark.

"This is a good spot," she said. "Now, you remember what we're going to do, right?"

He smiled. She loved his smile. She loved having a companion. A little brother. And he was taken with her too. It was obvious. Someone closer to his age. It was like they were on a camping trip with no parents around. They could have fun.

They could do whatever they wanted.

"Yes, I remember," he said. He was laughing. "We're going to play. To pretend. I like to pretend. Mommy and Daddy didn't understand all the time. They would try to play too, but it wasn't the same. Hee."

"Yes, but you have to be serious, okay? If you're all laughing and smiling, it won't work."

"Okay, I'll get serious."

"All right. Now lay down. Remember, you have to act like you're sick. Or hurt. So you can't be acting like you're having fun."

"I know. I remember how. I was sick for a long time, so I know how to do it."

The boy positioned himself on the ground and had another giggling fit. She tried to be exasperated with him, but his laughter was infectious. Soon she was laughing too.

After a moment, she said, "Okay, we got that out of our systems. Now we have to start pretending."

"Okay."

She leaned over him, a big sister looking after her little brother. "Start moaning or something. Remember, you're sick. Or hurt."

"Right, I know. Okay, how's this? Oooooooh...."

It sounded pretty good, but then he was laughing again. Now she *was* feeling exasperated.

"If you don't do this right, you're going to go hungry for the whole night. Is that what you want?"

"No. Hee hee. You sounded just like Mommy when you said that."

"Come on. When you do this right, you'll see how easy it is."

***

Donna Raimundi was a little annoyed as she headed to the parking garage. She was a nurse working the four to midnight shift at Children's.

Except, of course, that midnight was a loose approximation of when she would really get off work. It was now — she had to check her watch — 1:30 a.m. That actually wasn't bad the way her job had been going of late. The hospital was short of help, to begin with, then a couple of her peers had taken ill. It was a hazard of her profession. They took care of sick kids and, despite what people apparently thought, nurses were not immune to catching whatever was ailing their patients. Donna was one of the lucky ones. She had a strong immune system that held up to the ongoing assault by strange microbes, which took no mercy on her coworkers.

Of course, that also meant she would be the one working when everyone else was home recovering. It hadn't been unusual of late for her to have to pull a double shift. And then some.

But for Donna, her occupation was a labor of love. She wasn't just a caregiver. The children in her ward *needed* her. When she decided to become a nurse, she went all in. Her own personal life was a distant second on her priority list. This had caused her to break off relationships and even ditch a couple of marriage proposals. She didn't have time for any of that. The children in her care came first.

When she started at Children's, it creeped her out to have to walk to her car alone in the middle of the night. After all, this wasn't some suburban hospital surrounded by million dollar homes and perfectly trimmed lawns. Children's was an urban hospital in the middle of a big city. But she faced her fears, and after a while, it became routine.

She was walking on Fruit Street between Mass General and Mass Eye and Ear when she heard the noise. She had walked this route a thousand times before, so she was pretty comfortable. The street was well lit, but there was nobody else around at this hour.

The noise was also familiar. It was one that she heard throughout most of her days. Throughout most of her career.

It sounded like a child in distress.

She started thinking she'd imagined it but then heard it again. It was coming from an area off her beaten path, but her natural instinct was to gravitate toward the noise. It was toward the back of a building, and this area was most assuredly *not* well lit.

Her heart rate was up. As she got closer to the sound, it was darker still.

Another moan. Then a voice.

It sounded like a girl. The voice was faint, but as Donna continued towards it, she could make it out a little better. "It's okay," she said. "I'm here. I'll take care of you."

She was now in total darkness but still moving forward slowly. She called out. "Hello?" She meant it to come out louder, but it was all she could muster.

"Oh, yes, please," said the girl. "We're back here. Please, can you help us?" Another moan.

Donna stepped further into the blackness. She was on alert, her pulse racing, her muscles tight. What would children be doing back here? Regardless, there was a child in need, and she had to help.

As she got closer to the sound, she could make out two figures. It looked like a boy lying on the ground, the girl leaning over him. She looked up, and Donna froze in her tracks. The child's look was not one of distress. It looked more like...hunger.

She came close to turning around and running back to the light, but the girl pleaded. "Please, can you help him?" The boy was not moving.

"What...what happened to him? What's wrong with him?"

"Please, can you look at him? He's not breathing."

Donna's calling overcame her building fear as she knelt down and immediately reached to feel for a pulse in the boy's neck. His skin felt cold.

She gasped as the boy opened his eyes and smiled. His teeth...they looked like....

She felt a sharp pain in her neck. Her body went numb, and she was aware of slumping to the ground. She tried to take in air but stopped when she saw the girl standing over her. She was smiling, with blood dripping from her elongated teeth. Donna knew the blood was hers.

"Hee hee. See how easy it is?" said the girl.

The boy was standing. He was smiling too. He had fangs. What was this? What was happening?

Donna felt warm blood flowing out of her neck.

"Get down there," said the girl. "You're letting it all go to waste."

She tried to say something, to protest. Her job—her life—was dedicated to helping children. If she could only tell these...child demons.

The boy dropped down next to her and started lapping up the fluid on her neck. Then the sharp pain again.

And it all became clear to her. Donna understood now.

But she also knew that understanding would do her no good.

CHAPTER TWENTY-FOUR

I had no doubt that Halberton was still out there watching me, waiting for me to move. It felt suffocating, like being enclosed in a small space. Hard to breathe. I had so much I needed to be doing, and yet I was immobilized, a prisoner in my own home.

I was pacing downstairs most of the evening, my frustration building. I felt like pounding the walls and yelling out loud. But I wasn't a real physical guy. One time, I got super aggravated with Shrek over something, and I threw my stapler against the wall of my cube.

I hurt my shoulder.

Yelling out loud was not really an option, either. I didn't want to disturb the neighbors.

With my alternatives for "Raging Conner" fairly limited, I did the next best thing. I went into the kitchen, made myself some tea, and decided to take my single-attendee brooding party up to my room.

When I walked through my kitchen door, Lyria was standing in the living room. I gasped and dropped my teacup. The scalding fluid burned my foot, and I jumped up with an, "Ouch!"

"Ah, still my smooth and debonair guy," she said. "Glad to see that hasn't changed."

I laughed a little, looked up, and our eyes met. We rushed forward and were in each other's arms. She had dominated my life for months now, and not seeing her for a couple of days felt like an eternity. I was more than a little surprised to realize that

I'd genuinely missed her. And, our embrace felt natural. It felt right.

After a moment, she said, "I think there may be hope for 'Romantic Conner' yet."

I laughed. "I've...really missed you. Are you okay? Angelika. Angelika is here...in Boston. She was here...with Mikolaj. And Jason...what happened with Jason?"

"Easy. Slow down, Mr. David. You're going to give yourself a stroke. Let's go sit down, and I'll tell you everything."

We sat together on the couch. I still had my arm around her shoulder.

"I think I should begin with Jason," she said. She was looking down, avoiding my eyes.

I felt my throat constrict, and when I tried to speak, it came out more like a croak. "Did you...is he?"

"I...went to him that night. In the hospital. After seeing him at your parents' house, I thought there wasn't much time. And I was right. He would have been...gone before morning. So, I decided to risk trying to help him." She was still looking down.

"Oh my god. Are you saying...?"

"Conner, it was as I feared. I lost control, and he was.... Anyway, I was able to bring him back. But it was with my blood. He's...."

I went from being unable to breathe a few minutes earlier to hyperventilating. I drew my arm back and leaned over, trying to keep from passing out. "He's...with you now?" It was all I could manage to say.

"He was," she said.

My head was bent, looking down at my shoes. I was clutching my chest. I looked up at her. She met my eyes.

"He *was*? What do you mean? Where is he now?"

"He's with Angelika."

I thought I might be sick. "With Angelika? Oh dear Lord. Lyria, what...what are we going to do?" I got up and started walking back and forth across the room. "Jason...my nephew. My god, what will I tell Caden? And Lisa?"

"Conner, come sit down. We can't help your nephew if we

don't stay calm."

"Okay...okay." I sat back down, but I still felt like passing out and/or vomiting were viable options.

Lyria looked concerned but was her usual calm self. "First of all, Lisa already knows."

"She...already knows? But...how?"

"Jason had me bring him to her. He made everything clear to her."

"Made everything clear? Do you mean he...?"

"Yes. It allowed her to actually *see* what had happened. Trust me, it's much more effective than merely telling someone verbally."

I took a deep breath. "Yeah. I know. Angelika...she—"

"I know, Conner."

"Okay. Okay. I got it. Jason is...*changed*. And Lisa knows about it. Got it. But, how did he get with Angelika?"

"She saw where I live through you. She knows everything about us. She came that night. Mikolaj and Darren Dobson were with her."

"Darren Dobson," I gasped.

She just nodded. I had to lean over again.

"She...took Jason. I couldn't stop her."

More hyperventilation. Lyria patted me on the back. "I know this is a lot to digest, but we have to face reality if we want to be able to...rescue your nephew."

"Rescue him? But how?"

"First of all, we have to remember what we're up against. Are you hearing me?"

I put forth my best effort into getting myself together. "Yes. Yes, okay."

"Remember what I told you about children? The cursed blood has more of an impact on them. Their personalities aren't developed enough to fight through, so the evil dominates them more easily. Angelika was not an inherently bad person, but now, she is essentially a demon child."

"Will Jason be...that way too?"

"I don't think so. Everybody is different, and the time I spent with him, it seemed like he still had some of his own persona. But, with Angelika's influence…."

I had my elbows on my knees, holding my head in my hands. I was a financial analyst. This couldn't be my life. It just couldn't.

Lyria continued. "Plus, I had to bring both children back from the precipice. They are both very strong, stronger even than me. Bringing Jason back…weakened me. And I'm still not completely recovered."

I was barely able to nod my head.

"Even worse," she said.

"Worse? What could be worse?"

"Angelika told me she intends to make Boston her feeding ground."

"Oh dear God. With Jason?"

She nodded.

I sat immobile for what seemed like hours but was only about a minute.

"Don't forget to breathe, Conner."

I inhaled sharply. I hadn't been breathing. I was like a zombie when I heard myself say, "The police are after me…and you. Over Jason."

"Who is investigating?"

"Detective Don Halberton. Remember him? You…."

"Yes, I remember, Conner. He's outside right now watching your house."

"Right, but he knows about you. He figured you were still alive when Jason disappeared."

We both sat silently for a while. There were a million thoughts swirling around in my head. I couldn't wrap my mind around Jason being…converted.

"You said you had a plan," I blurted out.

"Yes. I have to get Jason away from Angelika. And stop her. There's no telling how many people she will kill. Innocent people. And children."

I thought I might throw up again, but I fought it back. "How… how will you do that?"

She looked at me deeply. "I have to find out where she sleeps.

Then I will need your help. And we may need to get someone else to help us."

"Someone else? Who?"

"Not now, Conner. It's better that you not know."

"It would really be better if I didn't know any of this."

She reached for my hand. "I know. And I'm sorry. For what it's worth, I never intended for any of this to happen."

"Well, it's partly my fault too. I pressured you into helping Jason. You warned me about what might happen, and I kept going. I…I'm sorry, Lyria. I shouldn't have done that."

We were holding each other again. She backed up and looked at me. "I might not be able to come back for a night or two," she said.

"Dare I ask why not?"

"If we are going to stop Angelika, I have to get stronger."

I knew what that meant. "Will you—?"

"Only evildoers, Conner. There are plenty of candidates around."

I inhaled deeply again. "Yeah. I understand."

"Do you want to go upstairs?"

She gave me a hint of a smile on her beautiful face.

"Uh, Lyria, I…. What I mean to say is that with all this going on, I'm not sure how much I…. Or even *if* I can…."

She laughed. "I'll make a deal with you. Why don't we go up and just hold each other for a little while. I have a feeling we both might need it."

"Yeah. Okay. That actually sounds pretty good."

***

The girl and boy were walking down a residential street, holding hands and talking softly as a gentle breeze rippled through the trees arching over the surrounding sidewalks. It was a densely populated neighborhood with apartments squeezed closely together on both sides, but activity was minimal at the early morning hour.

"I'm just saying I feel bad, that's all," said the boy.

"But why. It's better than feeling hungry, isn't it?"

"When I was in the hospital, all the nurses were so nice to

me. She was a nurse too. You saw it, right? How she helped so many children?"

"Jason, look at me." She stopped and took the boy's other hand. "You have to understand. We're superior beings now. We're better than everyone else. These...mortals...they don't matter. Just think of them as a food source. You used to eat chicken and meat, didn't you?"

"Yes."

"Well, that's what these people are to us now. Think about it."

The boy put his head down as they started walking again. "Okay," he said. It seemed like everything was fine as long as he had a sister to share with.

"You'll see how it will be. People will fear us. Then we'll be able to do whatever we want."

Jason smiled.

The pair walked quietly for a short way. Suddenly, Angelika went on alert. "Did you hear that?" she asked.

"Yes, what was it?"

"Just keep walking."

Jason could tell his sister was getting excited. He had come to know her so quickly.

The first voice seemingly came out of the dark, but Jason could see the source as clearly as if they were in bright daylight.

"Hey, lookee here, guys."

Three boys were walking toward them. They were on the sidewalk, but they came out on the street, right in front of Jason and his sister. They were dressed funny, thought Jason. They were all wearing baggy pants and sneakers. Two of the boys had loose shirts with no sleeves. The other boy wasn't wearing a shirt. All three had a lot of tattoos. And they were skinny but muscular.

"Yo, Street, they'ze just a couple a kids," said the boy with no shirt.

"Shut up, Zeen," said the boy in front. "I jes wanna be sure they ain't lost. What're you kids doing out here?"

Neither child answered.

"Hey, yooz deef?"

Nothing.

The boys got closer. The one called Street said, "Maybe let's jes see how they'ze set for funds. An' see if little miss princess here wants to be friends." He laughed. The other boy laughed too, but Zeen stood back.

"Get on the udder side of dem, Irish."

The two boys were so close to the children they were almost touching them. Street saw the girl turn to the boy. He couldn't believe it. She was smiling at him. The boy smiled back. Street's eyes widened, and he gave a gasp as he looked in closer. But by the time he noticed the fangs, it was too late.

***

Don Halberton heard a familiar voice on the radio.

"I'm coming up behind you, so don't jump out and start shooting."

"Grace?"

"Roger that."

"What are you doing here?"

"Relieving you."

"I didn't call for relief."

"I know, but you *need* relief."

"Says who?"

"Says me."

Despite being dog tired and a little aggravated that one of his people was essentially ordering him to be relieved, Halberton couldn't help but smile. That was Grace for you.

He had told Parker Gebelein, his other missing persons detective, that he was going all-in on this Jason David case and that he wouldn't be around the precinct a whole lot until he got it taken care of. Grace must have figured out where he was. And, even though it was God-knows-what-time o'clock, here she was.

Don appreciated the thought, but he had misgivings about leaving Grace alone on this stakeout. She had been captured by *her* last fall and held prisoner.

Or, whatever.

Although she apparently had no memory of the episode, it still concerned him. He thought *she* was dead, but now that he knew she wasn't, what if she decided to take Grace again?

The car pulled up behind him, headlights off. He could vaguely make out her head behind the wheel, her blonde hair pulled back.

"Come sit with me for a minute," he said. She got out of the car and approached his passenger side door, wearing her standard garb—khaki pants and a dark windbreaker. It didn't have POLICE stenciled across the back like in the movies. These days that made you a target. She was wearing it despite the warm temperatures because it covered up her bulletproof vest.

She got in and sat. Even dressed down, Grace was a real looker, but, as her boss, he had to keep such thoughts suppressed. He tried to keep a stern look and evince displeasure that she had disobeyed his order to be left alone.

"So, we having fun yet?" she asked.

Halberton did his best to keep it together, but eventually, he couldn't help but laugh.

"I assume Gebelein told you what I was doing?"

"I don't know what you're talking about. Or who. Who's Gebenstein?"

He laughed again. "I'll deal with him later. What made you think I needed you to come rescue me?"

"Oh, I don't know. Maybe the fact that you've been working this case for going on three days now and haven't had any rest. Or maybe it was envisioning the news coverage showing the senior missing persons detective snoring away in his car when the case breaks. That video would probably get a couple of million hits on YouTube in about twenty seconds."

"Jeez."

"Seriously, boss. Go home and get some rest. I'll watch over Mr. David. And I promise I'll treat him harshly if he steps out of line. I have a rubber hose in my trunk and everything."

Don failed again at playing angry cop and laughed. That's why Grace was so good at interrogation. She effortlessly broke down barriers. Besides, he had to admit that he was so tired his judgment was probably impaired.

"Okay, but you let me know if there's any activity. Call me

immediately."

"Oh, I promise. If someone is hauling off the furniture, I'll ask them to please wait until my supervisor gets here."

"I'm serious, Grace. I don't know how, but this David kid is hip deep in this thing, and I'm not sure how much longer I can keep this out of the press."

"Scout's honor, boss. Now get home, and don't forget to introduce yourself to the missus — you know, in case she's forgotten what you look like."

He guffawed. "I keep saying, I did this to myself."

"I know it was your lucky day. Now scram."

***

Halberton didn't tell Grace Garvey, but there was one stop he wanted to make before he went home and crashed. He didn't have the time or the energy to sustain the inevitable argument that would ensue.

He drove toward downtown, then took side streets to his destination. He didn't want to take the expressway even though it would be quicker. He wanted to get a feel for his surroundings along the way. Most of it was a barren industrial urban landscape, with a combination of office buildings — many of which were vacant — and warehouse type facilities, few of which were in use. He had found over the years that many clues got overlooked when one suffered from tunnel vision and ignored or just missed what could end up being case-breaking evidence because it seemed secondary or even tertiary in nature.

He found the location easily, even though it had been several months since he had been here. No surprise there, he thought. It was the site of the most disturbing episode of his life. One that had altered his understanding of human nature and fundamentally changed his concept of reality.

It was here that he had encountered her — Lyria, the kid had called her — a suspect in several disappearances. He knew as soon as he saw her that there was something different. Indeed, when he made to arrest her — at gunpoint no less — she had acted as if he were telling her she had to change her appointment at the salon. She kept coming closer even though he had his gun pointed right at her. She even smiled, and he saw the fangs. What on earth, he had wondered. He gave her warnings. Then he fired when the warnings did no good. The blood spurted from the middle of her chest, but—how was this even possible? She was still nearing him.

Then she did the most extraordinary thing he had ever seen. She coughed the bullet up and spit it out on the floor. He could still hear the rat-a-tat-a-tat noise it had made. Before he could make sense of that, as if he ever could, she held him up off the floor in one hand. She brought him closer—closer to her mouth. Closer to the fangs. The kid, Conner David, had yelled for her to stop. What was she going to do? Bite him? Drink his blood? This wasn't a horror movie. Or was it?

David threatened to pull the shades off the window. She dropped Don like a used newspaper. The kid pulled down the shades. She screamed and disappeared in a flash. Insanity. But he now knew she hadn't died. She was still around. There was no doubt in Don Halberton's mind that she had been responsible for the missing persons the previous year, including Arnold Shaw, an important local businessman and friend of the mayor. Don had never put any of what he had seen in any report. How could he? They'd have pulled his badge and sent him off for therapy. The cases remained open, although he doubted they would ever find Arnold Shaw or the others.

Now the boy was missing. Jason David. Conner's nephew. There is no such thing as coincidence in law enforcement. The boy was gone, and somehow, she was responsible. He couldn't tell anyone else about how he knew, but he would find out what happened, no matter what it cost him.

No matter what.

He made his way through the garbage strewn alley. There was virtually no light, and he kept his hand on his gun the whole way. He wasn't sure what he expected to find in here, but he had to check it out.

No matter what.

The metal door was still ajar. It looked like it was in the same position as when he had left it, but he couldn't be sure. The interior of the first floor looked the same, vacant and dusty with empty boxes and other trash. He heard the same rustling as he had last year, and he had worked in the city long enough to know what it was.

Rats.

As he made his way up the stairs, he was surprised to realize he had his gun out in front of him. When had he drawn his gun?

He got to the top floor. The door, which had been secured by some flimsy alarm system, was wide open. He entered the hallway. This was where it had occurred, where everything he had learned in his life, all his training, was rendered useless. Where he learned that he could no longer take for granted some of the fundamental tenets of his understanding of life.

His gun still out front. He walked slowly down the hallway. It was dark, and the air smelled musty. As his eyes adjusted, he could make out the gray shade in a heap on the floor, right where Conner had left it. There was a burn mark on the plain wood in front of him. Right where Lyria had disappeared.

He kept moving forward. There were two rooms at the end of the hall, one on each side. He remembered the one on the left had a steel vault door, but it was no longer there. He peered into the other room, where the old man, Radu, had slept. It was empty — the furniture had been removed. He stepped into the room and walked toward a doorway in the back. It was the bathroom where Radu had been kept bound up during the incident. There was nothing in there either. There was a toilet, sink, and shower, but none of them looked like they had been used in a long time.

He went back. His breathing increased as he walked slowly across the hall to the other room. Where the steel vault door had been.

He knew. This must have been *her* room.

There was a faint street light coming through the uncovered window. It wasn't much, but Don appreciated it nonetheless. He had to admit, the place gave him a major case of the creeps. He moved slowly toward the entrance. He stopped, counted to three, and charged through the doorway, gun first.

Nothing. Completely vacant. No furniture, no trash, nothing.

Just a single bulb in the ceiling. Out of curiosity, he flicked on the switch beside the doorway, but the light didn't come on. Don looked around one more time, then headed back to the hall.

"Hello, Detective."

He gasped, crouched into a firing position, and pointed his gun. His heart nearly stopped as he looked toward the back door, down the hallway where he had just been. She emerged from the shadow silently. No footsteps, as if she was gliding forward.

"I think we both know that won't do you any good, but you go ahead and keep it if it makes you feel better," she said, looking down at his gun.

She stopped ten feet away, and he saw her clearly. She was tall, wearing a blue print dress, with brown hair flowing over her shoulders. She could have walked right off the cover of *Elle*, but Don knew that he couldn't be fooled by her beauty.

"Back up!" It was all he could think of to say. She was right. He had no leverage. He might as well have been brandishing a Devil Dog for all the good his gun was going to do.

She looked perfectly calm. "Don't worry. I'm not going to hurt you," she said.

"W…what do you want?"

"Good question. Actually, I want to talk to you."

Don's heart was hammering in his chest, and he could barely form words.

"T…talk?"

"Yes. Perhaps explain some of the things I'm sure have been — is haunting the correct word? Yes, I think there has probably been a lot haunting you for the last few months."

"Why? Why would you want to explain?"

"Another good question. I think if you will hear me out, you'll understand that we might have a common problem. One that we may need to work together to solve. It involves Jason."

Now he couldn't form any words. Or move for that matter.

"Please," she said. "Why don't you put your gun away, try to relax for a moment, and I'll do my best to clarify everything. I'm sure it will make you feel better. No tricks. Promise."

Don sucked in a couple of deep breaths. He realized he didn't have any alternatives. He stood up straight and hesitated, then holstered his weapon.

"Thank you," said Lyria. "Now I'll stay right here while I make a proposition. As I'm sure you can imagine, we have a lot of ground to cover. But I have a way to make everything clear very quickly. You...would have to trust me. Do you think you could do that?"

***

"You want to bite me?" asked Don Halberton. "And I'm supposed to stand here and let you do it?"

"Detective, if I wanted to hurt you...or worse...I would have done it by now. It's difficult to grasp, but we would be sharing our thoughts. You would be able to see what is happening right now and what has happened in the past that led up to this. I'm sure you have a lot of questions in your mind. I'm also sure that this has, in some way, altered your understanding of reality."

Don had to admit that he had used those same exact words thinking about what had happened in the fall. And what was happening now.

"It would clarify a lot for you. However...."

"However?"

"I can't promise that you will like everything you see. In fact, some of it will violate your fundamental tenets as a human being and as a police officer."

"Why would I want to do that? I'm sure that, at least in some cases, there won't be any way to change anything, correct?"

"Correct. But as you will see, if you let me do this, what has happened in the past is nothing compared to what will happen in the future. Unless we work together to stop it."

Don stood silently, thinking. Being honest with himself, he had to admit that he couldn't help but be taken in by her, in no small part because of the way she looked. But he knew that she wasn't just another beautiful woman. That she was something else. Her presence had dominated his thinking in one way or another for months now. If he was to understand...if he had any chance to stem the tide of what was happening around him, did he really have any choice?

"All right. But before you start, let me ask you something."

"Yes?"

"If I refused, would you let me out of here...alive?"

She smiled, but he couldn't help but notice that there was sadness in her eyes.

"Despite what you may think, I'm really not a monster."

He took a deep breath, then nodded.

She came closer, and his heartbeat accelerated. His breathing was heavy. In normal circumstances, a woman like her would bring about an involuntary biological reaction. But now he felt nothing but fear, bordering on raw terror.

She must have noticed. "Relax, Detective. You'll feel pain at first, but it will be brief. And replaced by an almost euphoric state. I will wait after. You will understand, and then we can talk."

He tried unsuccessfully to regulate his breathing. She was holding him, and her head moved toward his neck.

He heard himself emit an "uuugggh" sound. The pain. Now the euphoria. It was real. They were thinking as one. She took him back — back to the very beginning.

***

When he came to, he was on the floor, and she was holding his head in her lap. Her skin felt warm under her clothing. Her beautiful face looking down at him, her expression was...he couldn't quite read it, but it almost seemed like affection. His head felt heavy as if he had just come out of a strong anesthesia.

He made to stand, but she held him in place.

"Easy now," she said. "You've been through a lot. Maybe you should take a moment and collect your thoughts."

"Good suggestion."

"Does everything seem a little bit clearer now?"

"It's...much clearer. I never would have thought it possible. But I saw it with my own eyes."

After another moment, she asked, "Do you feel strong enough to stand?"

"Yes. Yes, I think so."

He didn't get up in a normal sense, but suddenly they were upright, her still holding him. He felt his neck. It felt completely normal. He stared at her with something resembling awe.

She broke the silence. "As you can see, we have a serious problem."

"Yes. Angelika. And...Jason?"

"She's leading him. She is taking full advantage of their closeness in age. She wants him to be her little brother. And he's impressionable enough to go along. He's still...finding his way."

"Dear God. What will we do? What do you need me to do?"

"There are likely to be victims. Probably quite a few. You will be able to tell them apart from other murders."

"How?"

She looked him in the eye. "Their blood will be drained."

"Right. Of course."

"Angelika is smart. She'll probably move around quite a bit. But if you can detect any pattern that might indicate her location—"

"Her location? You mean...?"

"Yes, Detective. If we have any chance of stopping her, we will have to find out where she sleeps."

Don stood immobile, deep in thought.

"I know this is a lot to grasp. I'll understand if you need to take some time, but keep in mind that Angelika—"

"Yes, I know," he said. He thought some more. "Okay," he said finally. "I'll help you, but...."

"But?"

"I'll only do so on one condition."

CHAPTER TWENTY-FIVE

Chuck Rabb knew people found his manner of getting exercise strange, but he really didn't care. From his point of view, his workout habits—and his location—were absolute perfection. He lived in Milton, on the edge of the Blue Hills Reservation. He had an easy commute to his job in Boston and all the wilderness he could handle right next door to his home. The reservation consisted of seven thousand acres and 125 miles of trails. Chuck was average height and build, but he'd seen many of his coworkers develop "butts and guts," as his friends put it, and he thrived to maintain his athletic build. So every morning before leaving for work, Chuck could be found traipsing through the woods—sometimes walking at a brisk pace, sometimes jogging, although he had to admit the jogging portion of his routine was diminishing in proportion.

His job required him to interact with people all day every day, whether in person or via phone. He was a mortgage broker for a large downtown firm, so he spent the great majority of his workday explaining, negotiating, selling, arguing, cajoling, and sometimes even threatening. When he wasn't in the office, he required solitude to maintain his sanity. And when he was walking/running through the Blue Hills in the pre-dawn hours, boy, did he have solitude.

It was still dark this morning as he was trotting toward an uphill portion of the trail he had selected. When he was close enough to make out the incline, he slowed to a walk.

"Wimp," he said out loud to himself.

He was trudging up the hill surrounded by trees, ground undergrowth, and not much else. It was a warm morning, and he was putting a decent amount of sweat into the effort, which was just what he liked. As he neared the crest of the hill, though, something felt off. He couldn't exactly pinpoint the problem, but it was as if the air felt different.

"That's it," he mused out loud again. "You've finally cracked up. You go from complete seclusion to a zoo every day, and it's sent you over the top."

He ignored his instinct and continued on. But a few yards shy of the crest, he heard a rustling in the bushes to his left. He looked over. It was a thick copse of wild shrubbery that he couldn't see through. Was something behind there? An animal, maybe? Most of the animal life on the reservation was harmless. He'd never heard of anyone being attacked by a bear up here, but, he thought, leave it to him to be the first.

He started walking again, but the bushes moved. Even more weird, he heard a noise that sounded like a child giggling. How could a child be up in these woods? At this hour?

He stopped, considered his options, and called out. "Hello?"

More rustling and giggling. It seemed like there might be more than one child laughing.

Chuck's heartbeat accelerated, and he strongly considered bolting back down the hill. But if there was a child — or children — up here, what if they needed help? Although they certainly didn't sound distressed.

Against his better judgment, he walked toward the bushes. "Hello?" he tried again. "Is anyone in there?"

More distinct laughter. Definitely more than one child. Now he heard the sounds of footsteps scurrying away from him.

He steeled himself and grabbed the front of the bushes with both hands, and jerked them apart like he was opening a set of blinds.

He gasped and emitted a guttural moan that he didn't recognize as his own. Then Chuck Rabb fell backward, lost all control, and rolled to the bottom of the hill. He got up and ran toward his home, arms flailing, making throaty noises, thinking his morning exercise, and his sole source of solitude would never be the same.

***

State Police Detective Chick Harris was a no-nonsense kind of guy. He worked out of the Milton Barracks, which had jurisdiction over the entire Blue Hills Reservation. Since the reservation spanned parts of six Massachusetts towns, the state police handled the rare criminal case that originated within its boundary. *Well*, thought Harris, *I've got a case now, and it's a doozy.*

Chick was a reedy African American man, but nobody doubted his physical strength. His hair had gone gray years before, and Chick chalked it up to job-related stress. He considered his current post in Milton a cush job, and he had mixed feelings about the assignment after focusing most of his career on an organized crime taskforce in Boston. He had grown to near legendary status by fearlessly pursuing some of the most violent and dreaded criminals in the history of the city. When he agreed to move to Milton for the last couple of years before retirement, he was treated with reverence by the other officers in the Barracks, even his superiors. Chick wasn't a big talker, but when he did speak, everybody stopped whatever they were doing and listened. He secretly enjoyed such scenes; they reminded him of the old E.F. Hutton ads on TV.

Chick was none too pleased that he had to haul his carcass up a goddamn mountain to get to his crime scene. He was wearing an off-the-rack brown suit and dress shoes, and he looked completely out-of-place in this wilderness. He had grown up in the city, and he admitted to himself that being in the middle of a forest gave him the willies. But he would never admit to such feelings out loud — it would be inconsistent with the aura of invincibility he had earned throughout his career.

He was directed where to go by staties who had been called to the scene earlier that morning. He pulled his unmarked car behind a state police SUV parked with its lights flashing at the bottom of the foot trail leading up the hill. They had taken their cruiser as far into the woods as it could go in an effort to keep other citizens from using that particular path and potentially contaminating the crime scene. Other units and the medical examiner had to park farther away and make their way up the hill on foot.

Just as he was about to do.

The two cops from the SUV were drinking coffee and shooting the breeze when he arrived, but when they saw him, they put their cups down on the hood of the vehicle and did everything short of snapping to attention as he approached.

"I hear it's a bad scene up there," he said, skipping any kind of greeting.

"Yes, sir," said one of the cops. "They haven't started working it yet. They wanted you to see it first."

"How many vic's?"

"Three, sir."

Without another word, Chick began his ascent. About a half mile up, he started getting winded, and he had to acknowledge that maybe he had gotten a bit soft in this nice cushy Barracks assignment, not that he would ever show it in front of anyone else.

As he got closer to a plateau at the top of the hill, he saw a couple of uniforms and two men and a woman in white lab coats staring into a thick bush to the left of the trail. They all sported grim expressions, and Chick quickly discovered why.

The uniforms nodded to him silently, but the two men in coats kept staring forward. The woman said, "Hey, Chick." She was Helen Albergo from the state medical examiner's office, and Chick knew her from way back. She was normally outgoing and always willing to share a pearl of sick humor inherent in her line of work, but now she looked pale and, as Chick read it, a little angry.

"What do we got here, Helen?" he asked.

She pointed to the shrubbery. Chick pulled the bushes open, and even he, the feared and revered Chick Harris drew his breath in sharply.

Three young men, teenagers in all probability, were hanging upside down, their limp arms about a foot off the ground. They were still wearing pants, but they were bare chested their skin ashy grey. Blood streaks from their necks covered their faces. Their eyes were open and their mouths agape as if they were pleading for help.

"Dear Lord," said Chick. He gathered himself and scanned the ground underneath the bodies. No blood.

"Looks like this was done somewhere else," he said, looking around at Helen. She nodded. "We'll have to check the surroundings as we work the scene. If someone dragged them up here, I want to know from which direction. Where's the guy who found them?"

"He's at home, not far from here," said one of the cops. "To put in mildly, he's a bit traumatized."

"Aren't we all?" Chick crouched down, so he was level with the faces. He wished there was a way he could ask them what had happened, but he knew they were going to have to work much harder than that to get any answers.

"Okay," he said finally. "Let's get to it."

***

I was about to leave for work the next morning when someone rang my doorbell.

"This can't be good," I said to myself. Number one, I had damn few visitors, to begin with. And of course, I'm talking about living, breathing, mortal visitors. Number two, the chances of anybody coming by at this hour were ridiculously small.

I tried to be as quiet as I could walking over to the peephole. You know, in case I had to pretend that I wasn't home. I looked out and saw about the last person I expected. I swung my door open.

"Lisa? What...what are you doing here?" She actually looked a lot better than the last time I had seen her right after Jason disappeared. My sister-in-law was a natural beauty with long blonde hair, a perfect angular face, captivating green eyes, and the kind of body that used to keep me awake at night as a teenager. She was wearing a leather jacket, stylish but a bit heavy for this time of year, and slacks with sandals. She looked like she was hitting a local flea market looking for a deal on stolen pocketbooks or something. But I knew that wasn't what she was doing out and about.

"I need to talk to you. Can I come in?"

"Sure. Of course."

Calm down, Conner, I told myself. *She's your sister-in-law, remember?* Yet, despite the fact that we were family, we had spent precious little time alone together. And I was a bit surprised to realize that she had the same effect on me that any other attractive woman would. In other words, my stomach started churning, and I felt that if I tried to say anything, it would come out as complete gibberish.

Lisa marched by me and headed for the sofa. It was clear from her demeanor that whatever was on her mind, she meant business.

"I need to see my son," she said.

If I thought I was tongue-tied before, this little bombshell almost knocked me off my feet. I sat next to her on the couch before I fell on the floor. "Your…. You need to…. What?"

Smooth, Conner boy.

"I know everything. You know that, right? I'm sure Lyria must have told you."

"Uh, yes. She…um…told me."

It seemed so strange to be speaking openly to a member of my family about Lyria. And Jason, for that matter. Someone who, as Lisa put it, knew everything.

"Well, I need to see him. Jason. I need to tell him something."

"Uh, Lisa…you might not quite know *everything*."

"Don't play games with me, Conner. Tonight, after dark, I want you to tell Lyria and Jason that I have a proposition. I think they'll both find it very…appealing."

"A…proposition?"

"Yes. You're looking at me like I'm crazy. Don't worry. The whole family thinks I'm crazy—even Caden. After Jason came to see me the other night, I felt wonderful knowing that he was still alive, even though he had…changed. I didn't tell anyone he had come to see me. It would have been too difficult to explain. Besides, they would probably be *sure* I was crazy if I told them, right?"

She said this with a smile that, for some reason, I found unnerving.

"Right. Of course."

"Well, the next day, I spent a lot of time thinking things through from every angle. I ended up with two options for myself. I could completely freak out about the whole situation — that would be pretty natural, wouldn't it?"

All I could do was nod.

"Right. Or I could simply come to accept it and do everything I can to help my son."

"What about Caden? And Mom and Dad?" My voice was barely louder than a whisper.

"Yes. I think we have to explain it all to them as well."

"Lisa, do you know what you're saying?"

"I know. It's hard to envision. But afterward, I'm sure everyone will agree that we did the right thing. It may not be perfect, but we'll have Jason back, and that's all that's important."

"Dear God."

"Right, but anyway, I told you I had a proposition."

I wasn't sure I wanted to hear it, but I said, "Yes?"

"I had a coffin delivered to your parents' basement."

"You...what?"

"I told you everyone thought I had gone over the edge, right? Well, you should have seen the look on your brother's face when it was delivered. And your mother and father's." Lisa laughed out loud, but it was a shrilly sound, not her normal laugh. Like the laugh of a person who had lost touch with reality.

"Lisa, what are you suggesting?"

"I want them to come live with me — Lyria and Jason. They can share the coffin at your parent's house, where Jason was always so happy. Lyria can take care of him at night, and I will make sure no harm comes to them during the day. I know they have to...feed. But Lyria focuses on evildoers. Perfect. I don't think anyone would complain if they knew we were eliminating some of the scumbags walking around, would they? Those assholes are the real predators. We'll be...providing some balance."

I started hyperventilating again. "Lisa, you don't know what you're saying."

"Conner, when Jason was born, I took a vow to myself that I would dedicate my life to him. I haven't been a perfect person in my life — far from it. But I swore I was going to make up for some of my…transgressions by doing everything for my boy. You see, he's more than just my son. Jason is…a part of me. It's like we coexist. Can you see that? Now, obviously, nobody could foresee all of this happening. But it did happen. So what am I supposed to do? Bail out the first time we face adversity?"

I was speechless.

She continued. "I owe Lyria a debt of gratitude. Jason would have died, and she brought him back to me. It was the only way possible. And I want to spend my life taking care of him. It's what I was meant to do."

"Lisa," I gasped.

"What? Tell me. Tell me how I'm wrong."

I paused before I began to speak.

The night before, I had been worried about disturbing my neighbors. But the balance of the conversation with my sister-in-law resulted in a blood-curdling scream by her, and a few minutes later, a gut-wrenching howl on my part.

The noises no doubt pierced the normal quiet on my street, especially first thing in the morning. I was immediately worried that someone might complain about us disturbing the peace. My concerns were overcome by the feeling that a very bad situation had just become even worse.

***

Don Halberton had called off the surveillance on Conner David, gone home, and grabbed a few hours of much needed sleep. His wife was naturally concerned about him working so many hours, but when she saw him, she almost had a meltdown.

"My god! What happened to you?" she had asked, her eyes boring in on him. "And don't tell me it's just work related either."

Jane had been a stunning beauty when they met in high school, and Don was the envy of all the boys in his class when they started dating. She still had her looks, but time — *and being married to a cop* — had aged her beyond her years. Her lustrous long, light brown hair was cut short. The wrinkles on her face grew more pronounced. And, while she was still physically active, she carried a few extra pounds on her slim torso.

"What do you mean?" he asked, although he knew perfectly well what she meant.

"Let me show you, Detective. I know you probably haven't done this in a while."

Jane dragged him into the bathroom and positioned him in front of a mirror. She was right. He barely recognized himself. His face was gaunt and unshaven, his normally cropped hair was a mess. Some of his colleagues referred to him as a "boy scout" because his appearance was normally downright prim.

This whole ordeal had taken a toll on him; truly since — well, if he was, to be honest with himself, since last fall, when he first encountered her. She was right, Lyria was. It had completely shattered his sense of reality. What kind of person — creature — spat out a bullet after getting shot in the chest? That had tormented him for months.

But now, he knew. *Was knowing the truth better or worse?* he wondered. Don was known as a straight-laced, honest, hard-working, by-the-book cop. However, nothing about this case could be handled by-the-book, and he honestly had no fricking idea, to put it in Grace Garvey parlance, how it was going to turn out.

Jane insisted that he have some dinner before crashing, and he complied, although truthfully, he had no appetite. When he got up the next morning, he was careful not to disturb her. He did what he could with his personal grooming and headed into the precinct, wondering what this day would bring about.

It didn't take long to find out.

Don knew something was amiss as soon as he got to his office. He looked out at the desks of his detectives, and Parker Gebelein's desk was empty. Parker's desk was never empty. He was as much a workaholic as Don himself, and the only time he left the office was when they were working a case together.

Don moseyed out among the empty desks and heard a

din coming from one of the break rooms. He walked over and stuck his head in. Parker and a few other people were standing around watching the television. The screen was showing a press helicopter hovering over a bunch of trees. The location looked familiar, but Don couldn't place it.

Gebelein looked around. "Bad scene down at Blue Hills, boss."

"Oh yeah? What went down?"

"Three teenage boys. Some guy out jogging discovered the bodies. The state police are on scene."

Don felt his breath catch in his chest. Did this have anything to do with…? He took a minute to gather himself before trying to speak.

"Anything on COD?" he asked about the cause of death.

"Not yet, but the report said they found all three hanging upside down from a tree. The press is making it out as some sort of satanic ritual, but not sure if there's anything to that."

Halberton felt the color drain from his cheeks.

"Hey, you okay, boss?" asked Gebelein. "I know you've been putting in a lot of hours on that David kid."

"Yeah. Yeah, I'm fine. Just tired is all." They walked back to their desks. "Anything else while I was out?"

"Nothing really. Thought we had a hot case. A pediatric nurse who works over at Children's, one Donna Raimundi, didn't show up for her shift. She's supposedly super reliable, so the alert went out right away."

Children's….

"So…did she turn up?"

"Yeah, unfortunately, they found the body in a nearby alley. Case went over to homicide. Looks pretty ugly."

"Wh…what do you mean?"

"Well, apparently, there were wounds on her neck, but all the blood had been drained out of her body. There was no blood around the scene, so the homicide dicks think she was killed somewhere else, then moved."

All Don could manage was a nod as he staggered back to his office and shut the door.

"My god," he said to himself. "This is really happening."

He was in a trance, thinking through the implications, when his desk phone rang, giving him a start. He was almost afraid to answer it.

"Halberton."

"Yo, Don, this is Chick Harris with the SP. How you doin' this morning?"

Don did his best to sound like himself. "Hello, Chick. Long time no see. You doing okay?"

"I was 'til I got a call this morning. You been watching TV at all about this Blue Hills mess?"

His heart pounding, he said, "Yeah, real briefly. You got three vics?"

"Yes, here's the thing. We ID'd one of the boys, and it looks like they were from your territory—Roslindale. I wondered if you'd had any MP reports on any of them."

"Not that I'm aware of, Chick. I'll check with my detectives, though. Looks like a pretty bad case."

"As bad as I've seen. Who could've hung them upside down like that? Plus, there was no blood underneath any of the bodies, so it looks like they were moved post mortem. I had Helen Albergo up here, and she told me they were all completely drained. Said she'd have to get 'em on the table to be sure."

Halberton was stunned silent.

"Don, you still there?"

"Oh, yeah. Yeah, Chick. Uh...anything from the jogger who discovered the bodies?"

"That was pretty weird too. Local guy goes running through the Hills almost every day. Said right before he found the vics, he thought he heard the sound of children giggling. But he was pretty traumatized, so not sure what to make of that."

"Children...."

There was a momentary silence, then the state police detective said, "Uh, Don...you wouldn't know anything about these cases, would you?"

It had been a while since Don had worked with Chick Harris. But it came back to him—he didn't miss anything.

"Uh, no Chick, just sounds unusual, that's all. Children at *that* crime scene."

Harris paused but then said, "Yeah, there's a lot that's unusual about this scene."

Don struggled to find his voice. "Okay, well, I'll check to see if anyone reported the boys missing, and I'll let you know."

"Yeah. Keep me up to speed on this one, okay, Don?"

"Sure thing."

He hung up, feeling like Chick Harris was not fooled. Don never was a very good liar.

Bodies piling up. He couldn't talk to anyone about it. He couldn't tell Chick Harris, or anyone else for that matter, what he knew. They'd think he finally went off the deep end. Don had seen it happen to good cops. Real solid guys who nobody suspected were experiencing any kind of trauma. The breakdowns were ugly, the guys eventually losing touch with reality. Everyone would think that had happened to him if he started talking about Lyria. Or child vampires.

He knew he was regarded as a solid guy. People looked to him for steady guidance in difficult times. Young cops, and even some older veterans, looked up to him. Nobody ever questioned his loyalty, his honesty.

His sanity.

He sat at his desk with his door closed for a long time. Alone. Thinking. He found himself putting his head down, resting on his arms.

He had been through a myriad of emotions in his time on the force. He had been happy, sad, infuriated, disgusted, satisfied. But now he was feeling something completely different.

For the first time in his career—in his life—the esteemed Detective Don Halberton felt...helpless.

CHAPTER TWENTY-SIX

After my morning conversation with Lisa, I started to wonder what the hell else could possibly go wrong. Then I stopped myself because I realized that in my singular circumstances, something new could *always* go wrong.

With that little bit of Zen to boost my spirits, I headed to the office. I avoided interacting with anyone and focused on my mindless assortment of work. I thought that was one good thing about being a financial analyst. There was always plenty of mindless work to go around.

I was in the middle of doing something or other when my phone rang. Once again, I felt like the sound portended certain doom, and I held my breath as I picked it up. At first, I didn't say anything, just listened.

"Conner?"

It was about the last person I expected to hear from. "Mom?"

"Is that how you answer the phone? By saying nothing?"

"Uh...sorry, Mom."

I don't think my mother had ever called me at the office before. Certainly not to castigate me for my phone etiquette.

"What's going on?" I asked, again worrying that it was going to be more bad news.

"I wanted to let you know that your father and I are...going away for a while."

"Going away? Where?"

"We're going to go stay in Florida."

ROBERT NORTHAM

My parents had purchased a vacation/retirement home in Naples a few years ago.

"Yeah. Okay. Sounds good. But Mom, do you think…?"

"I know. I know. But it's too difficult sitting around this house all day…waiting for news. Caden and Lisa are going to stay here, with Carly. They…put their house on the market just this morning. I feel like the news is going to be horrible when it comes, and…we need to get away. This whole nightmare has taken a toll on your father and I, and…well, you know how your father is. He keeps everything bottled up inside. And I feel like a change in scenery is what we need. You…you understand, don't you?"

"Of course, Mom. I understand completely."

"Caden will let us know as soon as he knows something. And we can get back here very quickly when…."

She didn't have to say it, but her meaning was clear. When they find Jason's body. For all she knew, he was a kidnap victim off his death bed who couldn't survive any significant time outside of the hospital.

"Sure, Mom. Sure. And I think you're right. You guys do need a change of scenery."

"Yes. Being around here is too painful right now."

Mom sounded like she was starting to cry. And since I'm a complete knucklehead when it comes to dealing with emotions, I couldn't come up with any pearls of wisdom to make her feel better.

"All right, Mom. Let me know when you arrive in Naples, okay?"

"I will. And Conner?"

"Yes, Mom?"

"I…love you."

This morning was full of bombshells. Despite the closeness of our family, such expressions were atypical. I knew it came from the top, as for my father, verbalizing feelings was akin to joining the Young Communists of America.

"Thanks, Mom. I love you too."

It felt almost as weird to say it as to hear it, but it almost seemed like my mother was saying goodbye forever.

She sounded a little better when she said, "I'll speak with you soon." Then she hung up.

***

When I got home that evening, I felt like I was still waiting for the other shoe to drop. I knew it wouldn't get dark for another couple of hours, so I wouldn't be seeing Lyria for a while. I thought I had some time to relax and obsess over the day's events while in my familiar position, sprawled out on my couch with a throw pillow over my face.

Hah! Foolish me.

I didn't even have time to start hyperventilating before my doorbell rang.

I realized how I was intensely jealous of the people in the world for whom the sound of a doorbell or telephone was *not* a traumatic event as I made my way over to my precious peephole.

"Oh dear God," I said, looking out at Don Halberton. He was staring intently at my peephole, and I was immediately mad at myself for not having been quiet enough to pretend I wasn't home. Hell, he'd probably been watching for me anyway, out in his car. Normally nobody gave a hoot where I was; now, my every move was being scrutinized.

I thought Halberton looked different somehow. He normally killed it with the clean-cut honest-hard-working cop look. But at first glance through my eye-on-the-outside-world, he looked a bit more gaunt, a little disheveled, and his eyes gave a sense of being somewhat...unhinged. I guess chasing a vampire around will do strange things to a person.

Lacking any viable alternative or a back door to run out of, I opened up. "Detective."

"We need to talk, Conner."

With that, he barged past me and made himself at home in the living room. He nodded to my easy chair for me, leaving very little doubt about who was in charge.

"I know about Lyria," he said.

"You...wait. What?"

"That's right. I met with her last night at her old apartment.

And we…communicated."

"Do you mean she…?"

"Yes, that's what I mean. Okay, now here's the deal. I know she's been responsible for some of the disappearances I've investigated. I don't like it, but there's no way I can arrest her or follow up in any normal way. Nobody would believe me, and our current situation would get even worse."

I sat nodding like an idiot. To say I was overwhelmed by these sudden disclosures would be an absurd understatement. Was there anybody left who *didn't* know about Lyria?

Don continued. "Bottom line, we need to stop Angelika. And…Jason. They're going on a killing spree, and we need Lyria to help us."

"Us?"

"That's right. You and me. Like it or not, we're in this together. You bear some responsibility for what has gone on."

"Me? But I didn't —"

"Don't play innocent with me. If you had come forward when you first met her and realized what she was doing, some of this — maybe all of this — could have been prevented."

I gulped hard, but words escaped me. Putting up some half-assed denial was useless. What he was saying was correct. I hadn't come forward, as he put it, because of my feelings for Lyria and my fear of being locked up in an asylum.

"Don't worry," he said. "Again, I couldn't possibly follow the normal procedures, much as I might like to, because nobody would believe the circumstances. We need to focus all our attention on Angelika. She has started killing and won't stop until we stop her."

"But how will we? How could we possibly…?"

"Lyria is going to seek her out and follow her. Find out where she and Jason are sleeping during the day. My understanding is they are being guarded by Mikolaj Babka and Darren Dobson."

I managed a nod.

"They are accessories to all the crimes Angelika has committed, so I can arrest them, but they need to be taken out one way or the other."

"And then we—"

"That's right. Once her guardians are out of the way, we have to expose them to daylight."

"But my nephew…Jason…."

"It can't be helped, Conner. I know he didn't ask for this, but he has come under Angelika's influence. Right now, he is just as vicious a killer as she is. And we can't take the chance that he'll mend his ways without her around."

"Dear God."

"I know this is a lot to wrap your mind around, but we may have to move with little to no notice. As soon as we have a location, we'll have to act with the next sunrise. We can't risk something going wrong and those two remaining on the loose. There's no telling how many innocent people would die."

I had to put my head in my hands and lean over. Suddenly, the possibility of fainting was downright appealing. Don said nothing for a few minutes, allowing me to gather my thoughts and maintain consciousness.

Then he adopted a somewhat softer tone and said, "I have to know I can count on you, Conner. Are you in?"

I took a deep breath, but it still took all my strength to respond. Up to now, about the riskiest thing I had done in my life was goose up the deductions on my tax return. Now I was about to star in the pilot episode of *Conner, The Vampire Slayer*.

Finally, I got up the gumption to answer. "Yes, Detective. I'm in." Did I really have a choice?

"Good." He got up and headed for the door. "Oh, and call me Don," he said before walking out.

***

It was way too late for the kids to be outside. Lauren knew that. But her twin girls had just finished soccer practice, and now they were romping on the playground having a great old time, and Mom didn't have the heart to interrupt.

Sometimes she had the feeling they needed to freelance some on their extracurricular activities. Their lives were so regimented. There was school, soccer, meals, and homework. That was it. Lauren felt like they never had time to just be kids, like they were now — running around through the gym set, trying and failing to traverse the monkey bars, alternately hitting the swings, seesaw, slide, and merry-go-round with their new friends.

They had encountered the adorable brother and sister when they first made their way over from the field, and the four of them had hit it off instantly. She had a thought that if only adults could make friends as easily as children, the world would be a better place. Her twins were five, and the new girl looked to be a bit older, but she was doing a great job of leading the fun and trying new activities, and her girls were eating it up.

Nonetheless, it was getting late, and they had better head home before their excursion became an excuse for being too tired to go to school the next day.

Lauren looked around. The crowd from practice was thinning out. It was dark, and it got to the point where the only people left in the park were the four children and her. Where were the parents of these other kids?

They were on the gym set as she made her way over.

"I hate to be the one to break up the fun, but Emma, Mia, we have to get going."

"Oh, Mom, can't we stay a little longer? We're having so much fun," said Emma, the more rebellious of the two.

"I'm sure your friends have to be getting home too. Do you two live around here?" She addressed her question to the girl, the older one.

She hung her head, looking heartbreakingly sad. "You're right. We should go," she said. The girl had a bit of an accent that Lauren couldn't place. Her brother stood silently, but there was something in his look that put Lauren on guard. Was it...hunger?

"Well, who are you here with? Is your mother around?"

The little girl said, "No."

Her motherly instinct overcame a growing uncertainty about the whole situation.

"Would you like me to call your mother?"

"Oh, no, thank you."

"Mom, can they come over for dinner?" asked Emma.

The strange girl seemed to perk up at the question but began brooding again.

Lauren said, "Em, I'm sure that…. What are your names?"

The girl spoke while facing away from her. "I'm Angelika. And this is my brother Jason."

"Right. I'm sure Angelika and Jason's mother will worry about them. Don't you think so, Angelika?"

"Um, no. Nobody will worry about us."

Lauren looked at the two kids. What a weird turn this evening had taken. What was the story on these two? Were they runaways? At any rate, she couldn't very well just leave them here by themselves. She made a quick decision.

"Okay. Why don't you come have dinner with us, and afterward, we'll see about contacting whoever is supposed to be taking care of you. Would that be all right?"

The girl's countenance brightened. "Yes. Thank you. That would be wonderful."

***

There was nothing else for Don to do but wait, so he headed home. He thought about his wife on the way. She had long ago accepted that she wasn't married to any nine to five guy, but since this whole episode with Lyria had taken place, he had taken spousal neglect to a new level. Don totally understood the high divorce rate among members of the force. The job naturally put a lot of stress on personal relationships, and some of the women, and men for that matter, just weren't up to it. Extra-marital affairs were rampant, and while he never doubted Jane's loyalty, he could hardly blame her if she did look for affection elsewhere. He promised himself that he would do something special for her when this was over.

Then he thought, will this *ever* really be over?

He was lost in thought when his phone rang. He was distracted, so he didn't think to look to see who was calling.

"Halberton," he answered through his car.

"Don, Chick Harris."

He instantly regretted answering. He had a sinking feeling about the reason for Chick's call. Don was not by nature a deceptive person, so he tried his best to keep his end of the conversation brief.

"Hey, Chick."

"Just FYI, those boys were completely drained of blood."

Don swallowed hard before responding. "Yeah?"

"Yeah. Does that mean anything to you, by chance?"

"Well…I know it's unusual."

"Unusual. Uh huh. It's near impossible. The worst accidents, the worst fights — hell, even serials who fashion themselves to be some kind of vampire — don't get every drop of blood out of their vics."

Chick mentioning the word vampire caused Don's chest to constrict. "Do you need me to follow up on anything?" It was all he could think of to say.

"Earlier, it seemed like you knew something you weren't telling me. And, as it turns out, one of my dicks ran the MO to see about any similar cases. That guy Horace Goff? The one who was keeping girls locked up in his basement? Lo and behold, his blood was drained as well. Also, some bum…."

Don waited, breathing hard while Chick shuffled through some papers.

"Here it is. One Larry Wilkins found expired in an alley near the hospitals. They almost didn't even check him, but eventually, someone did. Want to guess what they found?"

"No blood?"

"Correct. And, to cap it off, there was a nurse from Children's Hospital found dead in a nearby alley. I'll skip to the chase. She was drained as well. Had you heard about any of those cases, Don?"

Halberton tried hard to show some bravado. "What are you getting at here, Chick?"

"What I'm getting at is, at the very least, the nurse was reported missing, and your team must have been up on the case. And it seems odd that when I told you the boys had no blood in their bodies, you didn't say anything to me this morning. Not to mention these other cases, which you may or may not have known about. But what I'm really getting at is that if we have some serial psycho draining the blood out of bodies, we can't be withholding information from each other because of some half-assed territoriality."

Don paused before responding. "I hope you know me well enough to know I wouldn't do that."

"I thought I did." Chick was starting to sound pissed. "Now, is there anything you want to tell me about these cases?"

Halberton took a deep breath. He couldn't very well tell Chick Harris the truth. "Let me check with my guys, and I'll get back to you."

Now it was Chick with the awkward pause. "Okay," he said finally. "But, Don?"

"Yeah?"

"I don't need to tell you that if this *is* a serial, we don't have much time." Chick hung up.

Don thought out loud, "If you only knew the half of it."

***

The troop of five headed to the front door of the upscale suburban home, Lauren in the lead, having just pulled into the driveway. The lawn was neatly manicured, and the front gardens all spiffed up from their once-a-week visit from the landscaper earlier that day. She looked around at her charges. Emma and Mia were right behind her, the strange new kids following closely. The girl, Angelika, seemed awed looking up at the two-story brick-front house. The boy, Jason, seemed less impressed and a bit hesitant to come in.

Their different reactions gave Lauren even more pause than she already had about inviting these children inside. She knew absolutely nothing about them. And Angelika had said that nobody would be worried about them. If they were runaways, what should she do? Call the police? Have CPS come pick them up? Her husband Tom was travelling, but she thought about calling him as soon as everybody was situated.

She unlocked the front door and swung it open. "Emma, you and Mia get your stuff put away and show Angelika and Jason where to wash up."

Their dog Swede, a boxer Lauren had picked up from an animal shelter a year earlier, came padding forward, happy to see them but stopped suddenly. Mia exclaimed, "Hey, Swede," and started scratching his neck, but the dog remained still. Now he emitted a low growl, his attention honed in on the two newcomers.

Lauren looked around. Jason hadn't moved, but Angelika was staring down at Swede with angry eyes.

"Swede, stop that," said Lauren. She looked at Angelika. "Don't worry honey, he's harmless." But it was yet another factor that felt off about this whole episode. Swede normally loved strangers, regarding them as an opportunity for more affection. Lauren had never seen him act like this before.

"Mia, put him out back while we get dinner ready, will you?" Her daughter tended to the dog.

"Come on in, you guys," said Emma. "We can use our bathroom upstairs."

"Okay!" said Angelika, happy again now that the dog was gone.

They stepped forward, but Jason remained in place.

Lauren wasn't sure what to do. "Jason, honey," she said. "Do you want to come in and have some dinner?"

The boy stood silently, and Lauren realized he hadn't said a word the entire time. She wondered, *Oh dear Lord, is there something wrong with this boy on top of everything else?*

"Yeah, come on, Jason," Angelika said through clenched teeth. The situation was feeling stranger and stranger to Lauren.

"No. I don't think so," said Jason.

Angelika darted to his side and grabbed his arm. "Little brother," she said. Her tone sent a shiver down Lauren's spine. "These nice people want to serve us *dinner*. Now let's go."

Jason thought for a moment, looked up at Lauren, and jerked his arm free of his sister's grasp.

"No!" he yelled, backing away from the front door.

Angelika was in a rage. "What is wrong with you? Get in the house. NOW!"

"No, I won't do it. It's not right," said Jason.

The boy turned, and he was gone. He didn't run off like a normal child in a snit. One second he was on Lauren's front walk, then she saw a slight blur, and the boy disappeared.

She sucked in her breath as Angelika turned toward her.

"I'm sorry, maybe some other time."

The girl gave a slight smile, and now Lauren was questioning her own sanity. She could swear the child had...fangs. Lauren gasped, but before she could look closer, Angelika turned and was gone.

Without thinking any further about this insane evening or making an attempt to analyze what was happening, Lauren stumbled inside her front hallway and slammed the door shut.

CHAPTER TWENTY-SEVEN

She was angry when she caught up to him. Her nostrils were flaring, and she bared her teeth.

"What is wrong with you? Do you know what you did? We were *in* the house, with those delicious little girls. Now it's almost light out, and we have to go home hungry."

He started walking away. "I couldn't. That's all."

She grabbed him again and turned him towards her. "Why not?"

"Because…she…the mother—"

"What about her? She wouldn't have been any trouble. We take care of her first, and she's out of the way."

"It's not that, it's…."

She pulled him close. Her eyes were like black marbles. "What?"

"With her long blonde hair and all, she…."

"Say it," she hissed.

"She reminded me of my mommy. Okay? That's why I couldn't do it." He broke free of her grasp and started walking away.

She hesitated, then rushed up beside him. "Listen to me, brother." She was gentle now. He looked at her, and her features were normal again like an ordinary girl.

"These people, these…mortals…they are inferior. They exist merely to sustain us. We have to stop seeing them as members of our family. They are no longer important like that. We have to sever our earthly bonds so that we may take our proper place as the rulers of these beings."

He started walking again. "I don't know, sister."

"Trust me on this. These people are vile. They would prey on us if they had the chance. That's what the older ones do. You saw those boys, those street hoodlums. If we were mortal, they would have hurt us in ways you cannot even understand. But we are more powerful."

"It was easy with them. But this mother...she was different."

"She was no different. She has served her usefulness to us by producing those daughters. Children, their taste is...I can't even describe it with words. Once you experience them, you will understand."

They walked in silence for a few moments. She stopped and held him by his arms.

"Trust me," she said. "I will do whatever I have to do to make you happy."

He looked into her eyes, and slowly, he smiled.

***

I was thankful when the weekend rolled around. Living on pins and needles every minute of every waking hour was bad enough without having to do it in an office with other people around.

I was dreading getting a call from Don Halberton with every fiber of my being. What on earth would I do if the call came while I was working? It's not like I could simply take a half-day for family leave or some such pedestrian reason.

"Yeah, see, I have to go kill a demonic child vampire and my nephew to save the city of Boston. See ya at noon."

Chud Johnson would probably have me locked away somewhere.

I sat at my kitchen table on Saturday morning, pondering these potential conversations, all of which ranged from patently absurd to outright commitment-worthy. My phone rang, causing me to jump in my seat. I seriously considered not answering, but when I got up the courage to peek at the screen, I saw it was Carly.

"Hey, sis."

"Hey." She sounded really glum.

"How's everything on the home front? I know it can't be good."

"You got that right. It's more like insanity-central around here. Mom and Dad couldn't take it anymore and got out of town. At first, I was kind of mad at them over it, but now I'm more jealous than anything else."

"Is it that bad?"

"It's Lisa. It seems like she's completely lost it. Not that I blame her. First, Jason gets sick. Then he disappears. That's enough to make just about any mother crazy. I don't know how I would handle it. *If* I could handle it."

"I'm with you."

"First, she sends all the cops away. She says, 'Oh, it's okay. My son's not really missing.' And your friend, Detective Halberton, okays it. Tells everyone to go work on something else."

I realized I was gnashing my teeth and forced myself to stop before I broke my own jaw.

Carly continued. "Then she goes and puts a coffin in the basement. That was the last straw for Mom and Dad. I think they envisioned her putting Jason's body down there—you know, assuming…."

"Yeah, I know."

"I mean, I don't want to be Debbie Downer here, but I think we all have to be realistic that it's only a matter of time before his body turns up."

That phrasing struck me as intensely funny, and I had to keep myself from a hysterical laughing fit. I was thanking my lucky stars this conversation was not taking place in person.

"Conner? Are you okay?"

"Uh, yeah. I was just…blocking a burp."

"Ugh. Anyway, I think Dad wanted to hang in, but Mom said something like, 'Listen, Charles, if she's going to bring my grandson's body back and inter him in our basement, I'm not going to hang around and watch.' So, Dad eventually went along for the sake of Mom's sanity."

"What has Caden been doing in all this?"

"At first, he was a crazy man, convinced he was going to find Jason. He was gone for two days, I guess, roaming the streets of Boston, searching. It's a wonder he didn't get picked up for vagrancy. When he came back home, he looked like hell, and he broke down, crying hysterically. He wanted to go back out, but Lisa and Mom talked him out of it. Now he just sits staring off at nothing. It's like he's catatonic most of the day."

"Jeez." The urge to laugh was now completely gone.

"Listen, I called to see if you could cheer me up some, but so far, you're doing a lousy job."

"Sorry, Carl. It's hard for any of us to have positive thoughts right now."

"I know. I know, I'm sorry. Let's talk about something else. Anything else. How's Lyria?"

I thought, *Yeah, like that's going to take my mind off this mess.* But I said, "Good."

"Good? That's it? Just good? You know, Conner...."

"Here we go."

"What?"

"More dating advice, right? If you're going to tell me everything I'm doing wrong, will it suffice to say that it already keeps me up nights? That I know I'm a bonehead and that I'm lucky such a beautiful woman finds a way to tolerate me?"

"Well, that just killed a good ten minutes of lecture material."

We both laughed.

"Thanks, Conner. I needed that. Stop by some time if you can. This big house seems awfully small all of a sudden."

I couldn't very well tell her that I couldn't because I was on-call to go vampire hunting, so I said, "Sure. I'll see what I can do."

***

Don Halberton was sitting alone in the dark in the study of his home. He had to wait until nighttime to make his call. And he had to make sure Jane was asleep. She had retired to their room before he holed up in here, but he crept out into the hallway just the same.

He had to be doubly sure.

She kept the door to their room slightly ajar, a habit developed when they were raising their children. Don stuck his ear in the opening and heard his wife's soft, steady breathing. He stayed for a moment until he was satisfied, then walked silently back to the study and closed the door. He pulled the window curtain aside. Darkness.

It was time.

He pulled his phone out of his pocket and took a deep breath.

He punched in the number from memory. Don hadn't even wanted to add it to his contacts for fear of being discovered somewhere down the road. A thought occurred to him that he was acting like one of the criminals he had come across in his years on the force. But the circumstances were as different as any he could have imagined in his wildest dreams, and desperate times called for desperate measures.

And boy were these ever desperate times.

She answered after one ring. "Detective."

Her voice made him gasp, and he hoped she hadn't heard. *Don't forget who you're dealing with,* he told himself. *Of course, she heard.*

"I have something," he said. Even though he knew his wife was asleep, he kept his voice to just above a whisper.

"Go on."

"A woman in West Roxbury reported that her twin daughters met two strange kids at the park after soccer practice. A girl and a boy. They appeared to be brother and sister. She estimated the girl's age at seven and the boy at around four."

"Yes?"

"The woman said the children identified themselves as Angelika and Jason."

She paused on the other end. "What happened then?"

"The woman's name is Lauren Springer. The twin daughters, Emma and Mia, are her only children. Her husband is out of town. When Mrs. Springer asked about the children's parents, they were evasive and said nobody was going to pick them up. She didn't want to just leave them out in the park, so she invited them to have dinner at their house."

Don thought he heard a sharp intake of breath on the other end.

"When they got to the house, the boy didn't want to go in, and he got into an argument with his sister. The boy ran off. She said it was more like he quote 'vanished,' but Mrs. Springer convinced herself that the darkness was playing tricks on her. The girl turned to her and said, quote, 'I'm sorry, maybe some other time,' then she vanished, apparently after her brother."

She was silent for a moment, then she asked, "Anything else?"

"Yes...the woman said she knew it sounded crazy, but that it looked like the girl had fangs, but she convinced herself that she imagined it because it was dark and she was pretty shaken up. But she felt it was necessary to report it anyway. She called the police, and the report came to me in case the children had been reported missing."

"I see."

"This is in the same general vicinity as Blue Hills. It might narrow our search parameters some."

"It may do more than that."

"What do you mean?"

Don thought he was prepared for just about anything now, but her answer still shook him to his core.

"If Angelika has targeted the twin girls, she may go back and try again."

***

"LETICIA!"

She remembered how scared she was of Chick when she first got hired. The fact that they were both African American got her absolutely nowhere. She was brought on to provide administrative help to the Milton State Police Barracks. Working with cops was not exactly how she had planned her life, but here she was.

At first, Detective Harris was an equal abuser, meaning he treated everyone the same—badly. Of course, it depended on his mood. When he was first assigned to Milton, he looked at the move as a demotion. He had worked on such high profile cases in Boston that he didn't know what to do with himself "out here in the burbs," as he put it. As a result, when Leticia first started working for him, he was insufferable. She came to understand how many barriers he had to cross in his career to get where he was. For a black man to get ahead in the Massachusetts State Police, he had to do extraordinary work. Work that was leaps and bounds ahead of others who were up for promotion. And that was what Chick Harris had done.

In one of his calmer moments, Leticia had told him how proud she was. She knew that his wife had convinced him that moving to Milton was a good thing, a way to put in the necessary years before retirement without worrying about getting gunned down at every street corner in Boston. Eventually, he had learned to accept that outlook, and he came to see Leticia as more than someone to make copies. The other cops in the barracks still feared Chick—you could see it in their eyes. They also knew that Leticia was one of his few confidants, perhaps his only one. As a result, she was treated with a good deal more respect than when she had started.

But that didn't mean that it was all roses around the office. Leticia knew that this triple murder in the Blue Hills had Chick on edge, and now he was bellowing for her.

Fun fun.

She was casual as she entered his office. She had tried to explain to the other staties that you couldn't take it personally when Chick mistreated you. In fact, it probably meant you were in good standing with him.

"Yes, boss?"

Chick looked like he hadn't slept in days, and in fact, she was pretty sure he was wearing the same wrinkled suit as the day before.

"Where are those autopsy reports on the boys? I had them right here in front of me yesterday!"

"I put them in their respective files."

"WHAT? I've got the case file right here, and they're not in there."

"Right. That's the general case file. You had me start up a

file on each boy individually. The coroner issued three separate statements, and the reports are in the named files. Just like you wanted."

To emphasize the point, she pulled one of the individual files off his desk and whipped out the autopsy report. She gently placed it in front of him.

He sat silently, staring at the paper while she kept her place in front of his desk. *This could go one of two ways,* she thought. *He's either going to start acting contrite or explain to me in no uncertain terms how incompetent I am at my job.*

After what seemed like an eternity, he blew out his breath. "Yeah. Sorry," he said.

"No worries. This case is a tough one, huh?"

He actually smiled a bit before answering. "It is. The boys had prints on their skin, but we got no match on any of our databases."

She sat down in front of his desk. "Anything to check for DNA?"

He hesitated, and Leticia knew that if he didn't trust her, he wouldn't divulge anything else.

"That's what's really weird about this. It's bad enough that we find three teenage boys — tough boys with street reps — hanging upside down with almost every drop of blood drained from their bodies. But then Helen Albergo tells me the only sign they even encountered someone else was on their necks."

"Their necks?"

He nodded.

"Was she able to identify it?"

"Yes."

She waited, not sure she was going to hear any more.

"It was saliva."

"S-saliva? Do you mean someone…?"

"Looks that way. We haven't divulged any of this to the press, but they know enough to cook up a story about some kind of satanic ritual."

"My Lord."

"I know. I know. The real kicker is the BPD has at least three other vics with the same MO."

"Drained of blood?"

Chick nodded. He was staring off in the distance.

"What are they saying about those cases?"

"Very little. The missing persons detective is Don Halberton, an old friend of mine. When I called him, he acted as befuddled as I feel right now. But, there was something else...."

"Something else?"

"Yeah. I've known Don a long time. He's normally a straight shooter. A guy you can really trust. The type who has trouble telling an untruth. And I couldn't help but feel that Don knew more than he was telling me. That he was...hiding something." He continued his vacant stare.

"Chick." She was one of the honored few who could address him by his given name. "What are you going to do?"

He sharpened his attention on her suddenly. He hesitated, then said, "I'm gonna do something I never like to do. Something I've only done once or twice in my entire career."

"What's that?"

"I'm gonna start following another cop."

CHAPTER TWENTY-EIGHT

"See? Look how they move. You can feel their life energy. These two are special."

The boy and the girl stood off to the side of the park, out of sight. They watched the barely controlled chaos of the soccer game. With all the kids on the field, their focus was honed in on the two girls.

There were several games going on at the same time and a plethora of parents watching and screaming support. She generally disliked crowds of mortals—they made her nervous. But this gamble was worth it.

She looked down at the boy. He was hungry, she could tell. He stared at the children romping around on the fields. His mouth was slightly open, his fangs visible over his lower lip. He actually emitted a low, guttural moan that no human could have heard. Her strategy was working. She'd felt that if they slept without feeding last night, he would overcome his hesitance with this family. He would no longer be bothered that the woman resembled his own mother.

Hunger was a great motivator.

"We have to wait," she said. "Be patient. Last night, she stayed late with them. Hopefully, she will again tonight. Are you ready? Do you understand now? This is how it is supposed to work. We are superior." She waved her arm in front of her. "This is our sustenance."

He looked at her, scrunching his eyes.

"Sustenance," she repeated. "Our feeding ground. Why should we only subsist on drunks passed out in some alley? We can have our choice. And these...these *taste* so much better. You will see. After tonight, you will no longer be satisfied with your hobos and child molesters." She referred to these mortals as objects, hoping he would see how unimportant they were. And it felt like it was working. By the time the mother and children were alone, he would jump at the chance to participate. He wouldn't hold her back again.

"Who is that?" he asked.

She looked off to her left. A man was lurking in the shadows of the trees. He couldn't look more out of place. He was wearing an overcoat and brimmed hat despite the warm night, and sunglasses despite the dark. He stood abnormally still, completely unlike the parents watching their children. These adults were jumping up and down, cheering, and generating body English with every movement of their child on the field, as if it would help their efforts to compete. But this man just stood. And stared.

"Looks like another one of your perverts enjoying the show," she said. "You see? Most of these humans are foul creatures. And they taste foul. But these two, they haven't lived long enough to have been spoiled. They are innocents, and we will savor them."

***

The boy looked back from the pervert onto the field, at the twins, Emma and Mia. They stood out among the field full of children. They even moved in sync with one another, as if sharing some unspoken communication. He had to admit, his sister was right. His desire grew so strong that he actually trembled with anticipation.

"Patience, little brother," she said. Angelika must have sensed his hunger. His desperation. She was smiling down at him, showing her fangs. He considered himself lucky to have a big sister to guide him through this new existence. She opened up a new outlook for him, one that he wouldn't have gotten from Mother.

From Lyria.

He hadn't thought about her for some time. A part of him

wanted to stay with her and spend time with his human mother. But they would never have let him experience the world of possibilities that his sister had shown him. Perhaps there was what his dad used to call a middle ground when he and Mom were arguing. He didn't really understand what that meant at the time, but now, he thought he did.

"Look, the game is ending," said his sister, bringing him out of his reverie.

The children were gathering on the field, the winning team — Emma and Mia's, of course — congratulating each other and high fiving their opponents. Eventually, the crowd thinned as adults collected their girls and headed home. Emma and Mia were with their mom and other teammates, and parents grouped together.

"This is it," she said. He felt her tense up. "When the three of them leave, we will follow them. This time we won't need an invitation. They will be ours. Are you ready?"

He nodded. His hunger was overcoming his sentiment about the mother. Perhaps Sister was right. Maybe he should regard these mortals as a means of sustenance and nothing more. The thought of feeding on Emma and Mia was overwhelming his senses.

She took his hand. They watched the group, which looked like it was getting ready to disperse. Emma and Mia's mother held up her hands.

"Hey everyone," she spoke loudly to the entire team, her face beaming. "Why don't you all come over to our house, and we'll order pizzas to celebrate tonight's win? And...I think we have enough ice cream in our freezer to provide dessert!"

A cheer rose from the children. Parents discussed the unplanned party, and most agreed to attend. The group headed to the house, which was within walking distance from the park — the perfect place for a post-victory celebration.

Sister squeezed his hand, causing him to wince.

"Curses." He felt her rage build up, knowing their plans were now ruined once again. "That bitch." She turned to face him. Lacking any other outlet, she grabbed him by the shoulders and pushed them inward. He realized how much stronger she was than him and somehow understood it was because she'd had the blood for so much longer. "I was going to be nice to her," she hissed. "But now she will die painfully. Maybe we will let her watch as we feed on her precious twins."

"What...will we do now?" he asked. "Sister, I...hunger...."

She released him and looked off toward the woods. "Your pervert is gone too. His entertainment dried up." She was calming down, her voice more regular. "This is not our night so far, little brother. Come. We will find an alternative. But don't forget about Emma and Mia. They will yet be ours."

***

Don drifted on the periphery of consciousness. He realized in the back of his mind that he had fallen asleep in his home office. Again.

He made his way slowly down the hallway toward their bedroom. Was the hall always this long?

The door was ajar, but when he pushed it open, he stopped and gasped, his heart clutching in his chest.

Jane was prone, her legs extending lifelessly toward him. Someone was on top of her, hunched over like...like a predator feeding on its prey. It was jerking up and down, and he felt more than heard a gulping sound.

He wanted to cry out for his wife, but he couldn't. He couldn't breathe.

He looked at the creature more closely. It was wearing a brightly colored print dress and had long brown hair. His effort at denial eroded, and he knew who it was. What it was.

Lyria finished as Jane spasmed her last breath of life. The vampire looked up at him and smiled, the lifeblood of the woman he loved dripping from her fangs, her eyes like black marbles.

"Just because we're working together, Don," she said. "Don't forget who I am." She reached out her hand. "Come here, darling."

He woke with a start and gasped for air. He was still in his office — his head had been slumped down on his desk. He pushed the chair back and leaned forward on his elbows, his heart thundering in his chest like a lumberjack hacking at a tree. He tried to collect himself, but a thought flashed through his vision.

Jane.

It was only a dream, of course, it was, but still, he had to be sure.

He ran to their door and looked in, his gun in his hand. It wasn't until later that he would realize how futile it was to pull his weapon.

Jane was sleeping peacefully, her breathing regular.

Don was still panting for air as he stood looking at his wife. She was on the right side of the bed as always, but she was facing away from where he normally slept. When they were first married — in happier times — she was always facing toward him. Even when he came home late, she would be on her right side, as if welcoming him home. Welcoming him to their bed.

His immediate thought was that he had a lot of ground to cover to make things better with Jane after this ordeal was over. He walked slowly back to his office, packing his Glock back in his holster. After this ordeal was over. Would it really ever be over? Since his first encounter with *her*, his entire sense of reality had been altered. Forever.

No matter what happened, his outlook on life would never be the same. His dream had sized his situation up nicely. He was working with Lyria to stop the children. The child-monsters.

But his feelings toward *her* went much deeper. He feared her — that much was clear. He couldn't dismiss the possibility that she would do something like what he had dreamt.

But when the dream-Lyria had beckoned him forward, he was horrified that she had killed his wife, yet he couldn't deny that another feeling had presented itself as well. Exhilaration. There was no question that her beauty had taken hold of him, despite knowing who she was — *what* she was.

Don dropped back down in his chair and leaned forward, his head in his hands. He nearly bought it for good when his phone rang. At first, he wondered who would be calling him in the middle of the night. Looking down at his screen, his breath caught in his chest once again.

It was just a number, no identification. But he recognized the number for sure. It was her.

He took a deep breath and swallowed before answering. "Yes?"

She hesitated. "Detective. I have them," she said.

***

Normally, killing time was not a problem for me on Sundays. I would read some, take a nap, occasionally flick on the tube. I might even take a walk, depending on the weather.

But there were no such pedestrian pastimes in my near future. My stomach was way too tied up in knots to take up the latest James Patterson novel or check what was happening on *Game of Thrones*.

I knew Lyria would somehow find out where Angelika and Jason were resting during the day and convey that information to my new partner, Don Halberton. Then, we were on.

I was working through an array of possible excuses I could lay out to Don about why I couldn't participate in becoming a real-life vampire hunter. Chief among them was dealing with Jason.

There was no question that Don had become unbalanced by this whole episode. Something about having your entire sense of reality disrupted. But he couldn't really expect me to *kill* my nephew.

Could he?

I didn't even assume my normal freaking out position on my couch. I was so nervous, I paced back and forth throughout my condo: kitchen, living room, upstairs, downstairs. I was feeling totally claustrophobic and wondered how people confined to an eight by ten cell managed to live their entire lives that way.

You may just have a chance to find that out, Conner boy, said my wonderful sub-conscious voice.

Rather than wear a path out on my rugs, I decided to park it in my kitchen. I had zero appetite and thought that worrying about vampires in one's life made for a heck of a weight-loss therapy. Good luck marketing *that,* though.

I had just settled in when I heard a BANG-BANG-BANG on my front door. I almost cratered right there on my linoleum.

I crept into my foyer, not knowing what to expect. Don

Halberton yelled, "Open up, Conner," from outside, and BANG-BANG-BANGED again.

I thought, *Oh my god, this is happening. This is really happening.*

Out of force of habit, I checked the peephole. Don was out there staring back at me, looking outright certifiable. Again, lacking an alternative — *I have GOT to get a back door* — I opened up, and once again, Don just about steamrolled me heading to my living room.

"It's on, Conner. You ready?"

Don was wearing wrinkled slacks, a buttoned dress shirt, and a windbreaker. Since it was still warm, I assumed the jacket was to cover up his piece. There I go again with the TV cop lingo. He looked like he hadn't shaved in a couple of days, which ran totally contrary to his clean-cut image. His eyes were wild, darting back and forth as if a new danger might emerge from the walls at any second. This ordeal had clearly taken a toll on him.

"What? It's on? What's on?" To say I was near panic status would have summed up my frame of mind nicely. My voice even sounded higher and squeakier than normal.

Don didn't miss a beat. "The operation we discussed." He sat on the edge of my sofa and pulled a paper out of his jacket pocket. It looked like a map.

I was still standing where I had opened the door, unable to budge.

Don looked up at me, not realizing I hadn't moved. "Come on." He sounded impatient. "Sit down. We have to discuss this plan."

"P-plan?"

"Yes. Lyria followed them back to where they're sleeping. Don't play dumb with me here. We've got to move. And fast."

"Detective — uh, I mean, Don — I don't think I'm up to this. Jason is my nephew, and you want me to — "

"I told you before, it can't be helped. They've already killed five people that we know of. And they targeted a family in West Roxbury — a mother and two daughters. They'll keep on killing until we stop them. Nobody else can do it."

I slunk down into my chair next to the couch. "What happened with the family?"

"We think Jason backed out. We don't know why."

"You see? He's not…evil, like Angelika. She has him under her influence. Maybe we can—"

"What? Only take her out? We can't do that. We can't take the chance. We know that he helped her kill three teenagers from Roslindale and, most probably, a nurse from Children's Hospital. Besides…."

"Besides what?"

"I don't want to sound cold-hearted, but Lyria told me he would have died that night anyway. If she hadn't…changed him."

"Wait, Don. Can we at least talk about this?"

"There's no time to talk. This has to be done today. We can't risk them moving; we'd be right back to square one. And more innocent people will die."

Despite my anguish, I knew he was right. And I knew he was correct previously when he said I was at least partially responsible for all this.

I took a deep breath, which did little to allay the pain I was feeling in my chest.

"Okay," I said finally. "What do we do?"

***

I wasn't qualified to say whether the plan Don laid out was a good one or not, so we rushed out and got in his car. It felt a little funny sitting in a vehicle that had been primarily used of late to do surveillance on *me*. I expected the interior to be a lot like Don—neat and organized. But I had to move a couple of fast food bags just to sit down.

"Throw those in the back," said Don.

When I went to do so, I noticed that this new trash would have a lot of company. Garbage, mostly food-related, was stacked up almost to the top of the front seat. After my new partner closed his door, the smell set in. It seemed like he had been living in his vehicle—for quite a while.

I let out a "phew." If Don noticed it, he had no reaction. He looked like he was laser-focused on the task at hand. He pulled away from the curb with screeching tires. I immediately fastened my seatbelt and pulled it tight around my waist.

"Dare I ask where we're going?"

Halberton stared straight ahead. We swung around a turn so fast I let out a small gasp, and I hoped my partner didn't notice.

"Mission Hill," he barked.

I held tight to my door handle, as I wasn't sure the seatbelt would hold up to the centrifugal forces acting outwardly on my inert body. I had a thought that somebody driving this crazily should really get pulled over but then remembered that it was a cop car, so that probably wouldn't happen.

"Mission Hill? In Boston?"

"Do you know of any other Mission Hill?"

"That's a pretty densely populated area. Wasn't she taking a chance that someone would see her?"

Don glanced at me, sporting a half-smile that held no happiness whatsoever. "Not where we're going."

"Where are we going?"

"Her resting place. The Mission Hill Convent."

***

"Convent?" I was so aghast I could barely form words. "You don't mean she.... She couldn't have...." Thoughts of Angelika killing a house full of nuns bolted through my brain.

"No, it's been abandoned for years. It's the perfect place for her. Close enough to all the major population centers of Boston. Desolate enough that nobody will bother her."

We peeled down Huntington Avenue and hung a left on Tremont Street. I was basically keeping my eyes closed but occasionally peeked to see where we were. Don was driving like a man possessed, street obstacles and pedestrians be damned. The fact that we made it to our destination without any fatalities gave me hope that we were being watched over by a higher power.

We came to a skidding halt in front of a dilapidated parking lot surrounded on three sides by very old gothic buildings. I immediately saw what Don meant. Despite being close to a bustling population, this looked more like an old ghost town from the Wild West. The trees and the U-shaped setup of the buildings set it apart from the rest of the area. There wasn't a soul in sight. You couldn't even hear any traffic noise from nearby. I started getting a creepy feeling crawling up my spine.

"This is the Mission Church Complex. Used to be a happening place. These other buildings were the basilica, the rectory, the grammar school, and Saint Alphonsus Hall Auditorium. But the one we're looking for is that one." Don pointed to the three-story brick building on the left of the lot. "That's the old convent. She's down in the basement."

We sat looking at the building before jumping into action. It was narrow, with boarded-up cathedral windows on all sides and a boarded up front door. A chain-link fence surrounded the small property. A small patch of grass and vines grew out-of-control along the left side of the structure.

"Let's go."

My partner jumped out of the driver's seat, flung open the back door, and started rifling through the garbage in the back. I was still seated, transfixed, watching him operate and not fully able to process what it was we were about to do.

He found what he was looking for—a gigantic crowbar. It looked heavy, but Don wielded it like it was a toothpick. He also pulled out a duffle bag, contents unknown.

"Let's go, Conner. We're losing daylight here," he barked.

My nerves were so frayed, I opened my door, undid my seatbelt, and fell out onto the pavement.

Some action hero.

I was able to right myself. "Don, what…what are you doing with the crowbar?"

My first thought was that he was going to use it to crown Mikolaj and/or Darren Dobson if they tried to interfere, but he said, "We may need to pry those boards off. Unless you can think of a better way, we're going to need it. Now let's move."

He lugged his gear to the entrance of the walkway leading to the front door, stopped, dropped the bag, and unzipped it. He pulled something out and handed it to me.

"A gun? What am I supposed to do with a gun?"

"You may need it, in case I'm occupied and either Mikolaj or

Dobson come at me. Or come at you."

"But I've never shot a gun in my life."

"Look. This is a 38-caliber snub nose revolver. Probably the greatest weapon ever devised, and the easiest to use. These days, we have to carry semi-automatic pistols, or we risk getting outgunned on the street. But the revolver never jams. It's perfect. You just aim it and pull the trigger."

"Sure...simple." I was seeing stars dance around in front of my eyes.

"Right, now before we pry these boards off, let's check around back. I'm suspecting they need an easier entrance for the humans to access."

"The humans...."

I somehow avoided passing out, and we headed to the back of the building. Sure enough, there was a small stairway to a door leading directly to the basement. The door looked like it was made of heavy wood and had no windows.

Don pressed his finger to his lips, indicating for me to be quiet. Unless I threw up, I couldn't imagine making any noise anyway. He walked down the steps very slowly and reached for the handle. Suddenly, having a gun in my hand felt very reassuring.

The door was locked, of course, and Don gently put his bag on the ground and pulled out what looked like a ring of keys. It dawned on me that they weren't keys. They were picks. He was going to pick the lock. This guy came prepared for everything.

I was barely breathing as he selected one of the picks and inserted it, jimmying around in the lock. I held the gun up in front of me and didn't even feel stupid doing it. Amazing how fearing for my life could instantly overcome insecurities that took all my adult years to develop.

I heard a click, and Don nodded. He looked at me and whispered, "Ready?" He pulled his own gun out. It was much bigger than mine.

Without waiting for an answer about my readiness, he slowly opened the door. I inhaled in anticipation, but the interior of the basement was pitch black. Don turned on a flashlight. Where did he get that?

We stood looking at a dusty, empty hallway. It seemed like there hadn't been anybody down here in decades. The interior was gloomy and stale smelling. There was also an odor that seemed human in origin, but my mind refused to analyze exactly what it was. Because of the angle of the sun, the doorway only provided a sliver of light—we would have been in complete darkness without my partner's flashlight. There were what looked like four room entrances, two on each side of the hall. The entrances didn't have any doors that we could see, and the interiors were completely dark.

Still looking straight ahead, Don elbowed me and whispered, "C'mon." He moved forward slowly. He was in a crouched position, pointing his gun with one hand and holding the flashlight with the other. Not knowing any better, I assumed the same stance.

Still didn't feel stupid. Remarkable.

I was more numb than scared. Truth be told, if either Mikolaj or Shrek jumped out of one of those rooms, I'm pretty sure I would have died right on the spot. Don had a lot of guts positioning himself in front of me like that. I had a real fear that I was going to get startled and shoot him in the back by mistake.

Halberton's stealth was admirable. Creeping forward without making a sound, he looked a little like a mountain lion stalking his prey. He suddenly jutted forward, causing me to utter an "ah." The beam of the flashlight found nothing in the first room. Don bolted across the hall. Nothing in the second room either.

He looked back at me and gave me a hand signal that I didn't understand. What I did understand was that we were nearing a point of no return. If Angelika, Jason, and the humans weren't in the first two rooms, they had to be in at least one of the other two. My chest felt heavy, and I found myself grinding my teeth. I really didn't want to go any farther, but I sensed that dropping to the floor in a hissy fit wasn't an option.

Don advanced quickly, aiming the flashlight and his gun into the third room. He paused, then shot over to the last room and beamed in. I heard him intake air, and he stood upright. I stayed rooted in place, still in my combat stance.

"The humans aren't here," he said. Speaking out loud after all the tension made it sound like he was announcing it over a megaphone, and I had to resist the urge to shush him to silence. Don casually strode back to the third room.

"Look in here," he said, shining the flashlight.

I mustered up the courage to move from my spot and peered into the room. It was a non-descript, roughly eight by ten enclosure with no windows, just like the first two. But this one had two rusty cots with grayish nylon bedding set up side by side. There were fast food bags strewn about on the floor. A wisecrack floated into my brain along the lines of, "Hmm, kind of reminds you of your car, huh, Don?" But given the circumstances, I thought it best to keep that to myself.

"This is what we came for, though," said Halberton, stepping to the fourth room entrance. I held my breath as I walked over. He raised the light into the interior. At first, it seemed like another empty enclosure, but then we looked to our left.

"Oh, dear Lord," I gasped.

It was set up on some kind of stand in the back of the room. My mind went into immediate denial, but as we stood staring, the truth became real.

There was a coffin resting against the wall.

***

"Watch my back," Don commanded as we stepped slowly into the room. Despite his order, I kept looking forward, my eyes glued to the unholy sleeping place. Don had his flashlight pointed at the sarcophagus, but it was still too dark to make out any details. What I could see looked solid and heavy, with markings on the side. I envisioned Angelika ordering Dobson and Mikolaj around like one of those high maintenance interior designers.

"No, a little to the left...no, that's too far. A little to the right...."

My heart was pounding so hard I wondered if Don could hear it. He was standing in front of the coffin looking down, probably contemplating what he was about to do. It actually made me feel a little better that even the steely-nerved Don Halberton, who seemed so singular in his focus on the task at hand, was perhaps a bit overcome with the circumstances.

I sure as hell knew I was.

"Okay," he said, making me jump. "You hold the light. I'll open this up."

He was speaking softly but out loud. When I answered, it was barely a whisper. "Right. Then what?"

"Then…I'm going to take them one at a time and carry them out into the light."

I knew that was what we were doing here, but it was still a shock to hear him say it. "Don, are you…are you sure?"

"Look, I know it's difficult, with your nephew and all. But we already discussed this. It has to be done. Here." He shoved the flashlight into my hand. "Hold it on the opening."

I did as I was told, but when Don reached down for the lid, I couldn't help but close my eyes tight.

The cover made a god-awful creaking sound as it opened. After focusing on being quiet for so long, the noise sent a shiver down my spine. I thought about the old vampire movies. That's exactly how it used to happen. The coffin would open with a creak, and Bela Lugosi would sit up and say, "Good evening."

But all I heard after the opening sound was a "psshhh" of disgust from my partner. I willed myself to pry my eyes open, mentally preparing to see Angelika and Jason locked in some unnatural embrace.

I beamed the light into the coffin and let out a gush of air. I didn't realize I had been holding my breath. I immediately understood Don's reaction.

There were no kids. The coffin was empty, except for a single sheet of white paper in the middle of the purple velour lining. I dare say such a benign object had never before loomed so ominously.

Don picked it up and read. It was hard to tell in this environment, but I thought I detected the blood draining from his head and face. His features were grim when he handed me the sheet.

I looked and immediately recognized the scrawl of my former

boss, Darren Dobson. But the words he had written were clearly a message from Angelika, and they made my blood run cold.

It said, "You brought this on yourself."

CHAPTER TWENTY-NINE

"What the holy hell is Halberton doing?" Chick Harris wondered aloud to himself. He had picked up the tall skinny kid on Beacon Hill, then driven like a madman to the long abandoned Mission Hill Convent.

These were not the actions of a rational man. While Chick hadn't known Don that long or that well, he trusted his ability to judge the character of a person. A lifetime of dealing with the dregs of society helped develop that skill. Chick could tell instantly whether or not a suspect was "dirty" when an investigation was underway. Proving it in court was a whole other matter, but when he was sure he had the right person, usually he was able to peel back the layers on whatever bullshit cover story they were using, and their alibi would unravel.

He always thought of Don Halberton as a picture of rationality. Tough, but trustworthy to a tee. Chick had seen others of his ilk succumb to the pressures of being a cop in large urban areas. You were asked to devote your life to dealing with the very underbelly of humanity and get paid just enough to eke out a living.

Got a wife and children to support? Tough nuts, work it out on your own. Oh, and by the way, how's that investigation of the mob boss selling kids into slavery coming along?

Chick knew that few people could handle such stress, but Don Halberton had always seemed like a pillar of strength. But here he was breaking into the basement of this boarded-up building. And who was this kid, his accomplice? He looked about as unlikely to be involved in anything illegal as anyone Chick had experienced. Unless it was stealing a book from the library.

The timing lining up with this rash of blood-drained murder victims could be a coincidence, but Chick didn't believe in coincidences. So what was he dealing with here? A rogue cop? Had Halberton gone insane? Could he and this bookworm possibly be involved in some of the most gruesome killings he had ever seen?

One thing Chick knew for sure. He had no other leads on these homicides, so he was going to stay on Don Halberton as long as it took to get some answers.

***

Killing time was the worst, especially in her circumstances. Of course, nobody had been in her circumstances before, so there was not a soul on earth with whom she could commiserate.

She left the house early—she didn't want to answer any questions about where she was going. Probably nobody would miss her anyway; everybody's mind was understandably somewhere else.

So there she was killing time in her car. She knew where she had to go, she knew how to get there and when she had to be there. The only other pastime that came to her mind was a bigger one than it might seem.

She focused on enjoying the daylight.

***

"What…what do you think it means?" I asked Don.

We were walking back to his car, the daylight stinging my eyes after being in the dark for so long. Don seemed completely unaffected, but his normally handsome features were scrunched up from stress. I noticed he looked a lot older than when I had first met him the previous fall.

Can't imagine what had caused that.

"I don't know."

He started double timing it back to his vehicle, and unathletic me had to run as fast as I could to keep up. I envisioned him peeling off, leaving me behind, and my mind wandered to how much cash I had on me in case I had to Uber it home.

But I got to the passenger-side door just in the knick of time before Halberton started the car and floored it into a U-turn. I let out a slight yelp and rushed to get my seatbelt fastened.

I understood that whatever Angelika's note meant, it couldn't be good. Clearly, she had known we had managed to find her sleeping spot and vacated before we could take action. Equally clear was that our finding her had pissed her off, and she meant to exact revenge. What form that revenge would take was not clear at all.

"But, where...where are we going?" I asked while holding onto the edge of the dashboard for dear life.

"Back to your place," Don growled.

"M-my place? What are we going to do there?"

"Wait."

"Wait? Wait for what?"

"Lyria."

"What? We're waiting for Lyria? At my place?"

"That's normally where you meet up with her, isn't it?"

Halberton sped up to avoid stopping at a light, an act that normally would have evoked a terrified scream out of me. I didn't even want to think about how fast we were going in miles-per-hour.

"Why are we waiting for Lyria? What if she doesn't show up? I haven't seen her in a while."

"We need her help. And if she doesn't show, you have to call her."

"Call her?"

It came back to me that Lyria still had that "burner phone" I had bought for her. The fact that Don knew about it as well was a shock. But, I remembered that he and Lyria had "shared their thoughts" and that we had few to no secrets from Don Halberton anymore.

"What...what will we do then?"

Don glanced over at me with a pitiable look that said, "Seriously, how can you be so stupid?"

"We're going to have to do whatever we can to stop Angelika

before she goes on a killing spree."

***

I barely got my door unlocked before Don barged past me and headed for the living room. He parked it on the couch while I paced away the stress of our "Indy 500" style drive over here.

He pulled out his phone and hit a speed dial listing. There were no niceties when he got an answer. "Yeah, Parker," he said. "Whatever you've got going on tonight, forget about it."

And here I thought financial analysts in the investment banking industry were the only ones subject to such workplace abuses.

"I want you to get down to dispatch and stay there. Monitor all the incoming calls."

I assumed he was speaking with Parker Gebelein, one of his detectives, with whom, by the way, I had exchanged some pleasantries the previous fall. Don paused while Parker spoke.

"For how long? Until dawn."

Another pause.

"That's right, you heard me. Listen for any kind of unusual calls."

I imagined Gebelein asking, "What kind of unusual calls?" and I waited with bated breath to hear Halberton's response.

The boss detective sat, thinking for a bit. Then he said, "Homicides. Likely a string of them, possibly in the same vicinity. They might be similar to those boys up in Blue Hill."

Pause. I couldn't imagine how the normally staid Parker Gebelein was reacting. Probably a lot like his normally even more staid boss reacted when he became enlightened by my erstwhile girlfriend.

When he started up again, his voice was raised slightly. "Well, Parker, if we knew where they were going to take place, we'd be out there stopping them, wouldn't we?"

He glanced over at me. I imagined he was wondering whether he really thought anyone could stop Angelika if she went on a killing spree.

"That's right. Call me immediately if anything comes up."

With that, Don hung up. He obviously wasn't too concerned

with the fundamentals of phone etiquette.

"We have a couple of hours of daylight left. I recommend you get some sleep. I'll sack out here."

Don shed his shoes and put his feet up on my couch.

I didn't have the first clue what to say, but what came out was, "Uh...Don...I have to work tomorrow."

He gave me his best "Are you for real?" look and said, "Get some rest. It's going to be a long night."

***

She arose already seething with anger. Jason had never seen her like that before, and honestly, it scared him. He had become convinced that they had nothing to fear but daylight, but the look on his "sister's" face made him think otherwise.

"Come on," she ordered. "We have a lot to do tonight."

"Sister, wh...why are you so mad?"

She turned toward him, baring her fangs. "You know why," she hissed. "Mother has betrayed us to the humans. She followed us last night. No doubt, she told someone where we were sleeping so they could come and end our lives. Don't you understand? She wants us dead."

She grabbed him by the shoulders so tightly he let out a whimper. Her red face was now an inch from his.

"We had to move our sleeping place. Is this how you want to live? Constantly on the run? Always looking over our shoulder to see if she is watching? This cannot continue. We have to punish Mother. Show her that if she continues on this path, it will cost her precious humans."

"What do you mean, her precious humans? What are you going to do?"

She tightened her grip even more.

"Sister, that...that hurts."

"*We* are going to do this tonight, little brother. Not I. WE. Do you understand?"

"Yes...yes, I understand."

Angelika released her grip and threw him to the ground. She moved close and stood over him.

"We must teach Mother a lesson she will not forget. She must have humans involved with her plan. Someone who can come to our place of sleep during daylight. It has to be that boy, Conner. He has to be involved."

"My uncle Conner? No, sister. He would never…he could never cause me harm."

She picked him up off the ground as if he were one of his toys. The ones he used to play with when he was….

She casually dusted him off. Her tone now was softer.

"You're still thinking as if you have mortal family bonds, brother. Those bonds no longer exist, remember? These people are now our enemies. They want to destroy us. But never forget…we are superior. My plan is to show our superiority tonight. Ensure that we are no longer threatened."

"But what…what *is* your plan?"

When she told him, he felt like he was a human boy again. He exhibited an emotion he wasn't sure he was capable of anymore.

He started crying.

***

Chick had felt a void since moving to the Milton Barracks. At first, the transfer seemed like a permanent vacation, a place to finish out his time before he disappeared off into the sunset of retirement. But over time, he'd become aware that boredom was creeping into his life like vines growing over the wall of an Ivy League college. He had to stop kidding himself. After working in the intensity of a place like Boston, facing down real hard-case criminals, mob bosses, gang members, and serial killers, moving to Blue Hills was like being put out to pasture.

And Chick Harris wasn't ready to be put out to pasture. Not even close.

It wasn't his fault that his idiot supervisors couldn't see the value of someone with his street smarts and experience. The guys they put in to replace him might have been aces at pulling over old ladies going five miles-per-hour over the speed limit coming home from church, but they wouldn't know a hardened criminal if one came up and stole their desk right out from under them.

What had happened to him wasn't fair, but life was unfair. The best thing Chick could do was crack a big case and show the brass how wrong they were. The problem with that plan was that there *were* no big cases in the Milton Barracks.

Until now.

This bizarre triple murder was the one he had been waiting for. The vics may not have been innocent, but they were young, and the case had garnered a lot of press. To be sure, Chick didn't care about getting ink, but solving such a high profile crime would serve to show his bosses at the state police that they had made a mistake in sending him off to never-never land. The possibility of a Boston police officer being involved was something only he knew at this point, but if that was so, it ratcheted up the importance of the situation even more.

Chick had his underlings doing the usual grunt work — checking the background of the vics to see if they had any common enemies, canvassing the nearby neighborhoods in case anyone saw or heard anything, digging through evidence collected from the crime scene. His gut told him nothing would come of any of that. He had gotten a weird vibe from Don Halberton from his first phone call, and he felt like the veteran cop knew more than he was letting on. But was it really possible that Don could somehow be involved in such a gruesome crime? Or was he indeed being territorial, hoping to crack the case and ensuring that the BPD would get full credit?

There were more questions than answers at this point, but Halberton's behavior since Chick started watching him was beyond strange. First, there was that whole scene at the Mission Hill Convent with the tall skinny kid. Now, it seemed like they were hanging out at the kid's home on Beacon Hill. Chick had the office check for ownership of the townhouse, and it had come back to a Charles David. He had Leticia do some research, and it turned out this David guy was a former bigwig in the investment banking business, which explained how he could afford this home. But Halberton's partner was way too young to be Charles David. One of his sons, perhaps? Leticia said he had two boys, Caden and Conner. This was probably one of them.

Chick was sitting in his car about a half a block from David's townhouse. He was certainly no stranger to long stakeouts, but he found himself getting edgy. It got dark late in the summer, but night had fallen, and there was no sign of activity.

He would wait, though, as long as it took. He had a feeling in his bones that he would know a lot more about this case after this night was over.

***

Vicky Temerlin needed to clear her head. There were certainly times when living alone was a panacea. Tonight was not one of them.

On weekdays after work, she treasured time to herself, especially on a day filled with business meetings, many of which could properly be classified as glorified gripe sessions. Despite recent advances, investment banking was still a largely male dominated industry, and she frequently found herself being the only female in some of these meetings. She would have to project an air of confidence to keep from being overlooked. Sometimes men who didn't know her well would overtly flirt with her in the middle of a serious discussion. Everything short of playing *footsie* under the table was apparently in play. This would infuriate her, and it took a lot of effort to keep presenting a cool façade. There were days when she would have multiple meetings back-to-back. It was exhausting, and she really wanted nothing more than to hole up in her little apartment near the Fens and dial it down. Just to go back the next day and have the whole scenario play itself out again.

But on this particular Sunday night, it felt like the walls in her tiny flat were closing in on her. She even thought about taking a drive and dropping in on her parents unannounced, but these days their conversations inevitably swung around to the "when are you getting married and giving us grandchildren?" territory. Oh, they wouldn't come right out and ask her that, but their little insinuations were clear.

"I assume you heard about Julia McCorkle?" her mom had asked during her last visit.

Vicky knew what was coming, but she said, "No, Mom."

"Well, she's expecting. Isn't that exciting? And Amber Pellin is going on number two."

Her mom saw every visit as a chance to update her on local "roster changes." The subtlety was not so subtle.

"Think I'll pass," she thought to herself out loud.

The other issue clogging her thoughts these days was Conner David. Vicky had to admit her feelings toward Conner had evolved. At first, she simply saw him as a coworker. But as she came to know the personalities of the financial analysis group better, she realized he had by far the best "friend potential" on the team.

Razor Rojas was a great guy, but getting him to share feelings would make getting blood out of a turnip look easy. All the twins ever talked about was work. And if she spent too much time with Boof Parsons, she was pretty sure she'd end up needing therapy she couldn't afford.

Vicky found it easy to talk to Conner, and she was pretty sure he felt the same way with her. Their forays outside the office felt so...what was the word she was looking for? Natural. That was it; they felt natural.

At lunch, they'd nearly had a breakthrough—hand holding, goo-goo eyes, the works. But he professed to having a lot going on in his personal life. With his nephew dying, that was easy to believe.

So, should she just give up on him? She had never been involved in an office romance before, especially with someone she worked with closely every day. And the rumor mill at the office was brutal.

If they had a relationship, it would have to remain clandestine. But Vicky thought that was possible with Conner. He certainly would never pull a Boof on her and run around bragging about his conquest.

"I definitely need some air," she said to herself.

***

It was still dusk when Vicky headed out, which made her feel better about walking by herself. It was a breezy, balmy day in Boston with a lot of people out enjoying the weather, another positive factor. She usually was very careful about going solo, especially after dark. But the day was still holding onto its final vestiges of summer daylight, the sun streaming through the trees to her west.

Living on the Fenway presented its challenges, but the rent was cheap and the scenery substantial. If you had to describe where you lived to someone unfamiliar with Boston, and you said you lived "on The Fenway, right next to the park," they would invariably exclaim, "You live at Fenway Park? Radical!" or some such pearl of wisdom. But locals understood there was Fenway Park and there was a nearby walking park with grass, trees and ponds, and it was called The Fenway. There were a multitude of apartment dwellings on the perimeter of the urban oasis, and residents commonly referred to their area of the city as The Fens. The Fens made up a substantial proportion of the Back Bay neighborhood, where demand for real estate and housing had skyrocketed in recent years.

The rising prices had incented the city to clean up the park area and step up the safety factor, especially after dark. At a point in the not-so-distant past, a woman strolling by herself through The Fenway at night would be taking a substantial risk. Now it was generally safe, but Vicky understood that you still had to be smart about your surroundings.

She was feeling energetic, and the fresh air was indeed helping to clear her head of her list of issues, like generating a grandchild for her parents and a potential office romance. She was feeling so good, in fact, that she lost track of time and found herself on the far side of Kenmore Square, a good couple of miles from her apartment building. Not only that, but it was getting dark, so she figured she'd better hightail it on home. There were still plenty of people around, so she felt comfortable taking the most direct route through the park.

By the time she reached the north side of The Fens, it was downright pitch black out. Vicky hesitated before starting across Agassiz Road, a walking path through the heart of the greenery.

"Come on," she said to herself. "You got yourself into this, now be brave."

She put her head down and plunged forward. There were lights around most of the path, but some areas were darker than others, and suddenly the robust foot traffic had completely died out. She realized with a shudder that she was in the dark in the middle of the park and, worst of all, totally alone.

Her heartbeat elevated, she stepped up her pace. She had the thought that if some maniac sprang out of the trees, he wouldn't even have to kill her. They'd be cleaning up what was left of her with a mop.

After mindlessly scurrying to the south side of the park, she took a breath of relief when the opening of Agassiz onto Fenway Road was in her sight. Once she got on Fenway, her apartment building was only about a quarter of a mile to the right.

She was just about to make the turn when she heard a noise. She stopped and listened but didn't hear anything more. There were only a few cars whizzing by on Fenway, but she thought maybe one of them had created the sound.

"Great, now you're imagining things. Get a grip, girl."

She started forward just a few yards short of the turn when she heard it again. This time she was sure, and it wasn't any kind of car noise. It sounded almost like...a child whimpering.

A part of her wanted to ignore it and sprint the rest of the way home. But Vicky was emboldened by making it almost the whole way through the park, so she stopped and listened again.

"Mommy...where are you?"

Vicky turned in the direction of the voice, which was coming from behind her on the walking path. She saw a little girl sitting by herself on a bench set back slightly from the pavement. She had just passed that way and wondered how she hadn't noticed the girl. Vicky thought it must have been because she was so worked up and focused on getting home. And as there was virtually no light around her, she would have been easy to miss.

As Vicky crept slowly back towards the bench, she was able to see better. The child had her elbows on her knees, holding her head in her hands, making an up and down sobbing motion, curly blonde hair covering her face. The sight was unsettling, and Vicky had a mind to hurry home and call the police.

The girl looked up. "Mommy? Is that you?"

Vicky continued toward her, despite her heartbeat racing

once again. She couldn't very well leave her here, could she? The child had a strange accent. Had she been abandoned somehow?

She got close and leaned down. "No honey, I'm... not your mommy. Are you lost? Where did your mommy go?"

"I don't know, I just don't know," she sobbed, her head back down.

Vicky crouched down in front of her and reached over, rubbing her shoulders gently. "It's okay, honey. Do you know where you live?"

The girl lurched forward into an embrace. "No, I don't. I...I don't know where to go."

Vicky wrapped her arms around her. "Shhh, It's okay now, I'm here. I'll help you. What's your name?"

The child's head was on Vicky's shoulder.

"Angelika. My name is Angelika."

"Well, that's a beautiful name."

"Didn't Conner tell you about me?"

Vicky's breath caught in her chest. She pulled back, holding the girl's shoulders. "Did you say...Conner?"

Angelika moved her face close. When Vicky tried to move away, the child was suddenly holding her arms in a crushing grip that made her cry out.

"Yes. Conner. Does it surprise you to hear we have a mutual friend?"

She was no longer crying. In fact, Vicky watched agape as the child's face contorted into one of rage and...was it hunger? Her eyes were completely black, and now she was smiling, but in anger—her teeth. Vicky felt a scream building up in her chest, but she couldn't breathe in. Her instinct was to run, but Angelika held her in place.

"Don't be rushing off now, Miss Vicky," said the child-demon still inches from her face.

She knew her name. But how?

"We have a lot to do tonight," she continued. "Conner, such a shame. It's not like he wasn't warned. But now he has to understand that when he does what he's not supposed to, there will be consequences. Aren't we all taught that at an early age?"

Vicky gasped in a breath. "Who are you? How do you...?"

"I know." The child-demon laughed, sounding like a normal little girl. "Many questions. Well, don't you worry, Miss Vicky, you'll get all your answers tonight. The situation will be clearer for everybody. I promise."

"Please...I was only trying to...."

"Oh, I know, pretty one. Your intentions were good. But sometimes we find that we *all* pay consequences. Even when we have done nothing wrong ourselves. Isn't that right?" Another little-girl laugh. "I suppose if it wasn't true, I wouldn't even be here now. You just relax. This will all be over very soon."

Vicky was unable to speak, move, or breathe as the child-demon leaned down toward her neck, fang teeth bared. She was conscious of emitting a guttural grunting sound and nothing else.

CHAPTER THIRTY

"Uncle Conner."

I was dreaming. I must have been.

I was out with Lyria. We were at Grotto, where we had been the previous fall with Carly and her abusive boyfriend, Brent. Then we were in the park. Those thugs came at us again, the ones we had seen last year when we were out walking.

Lyria stood up and held me close, ready to bolt out of there. But she said, "I can't, Conner."

"What? What do you mean you can't?" I asked. My heart was racing. The hoodlums—four of them—were circling around us and closing in. They were hooting, taunting us, just like they had when this had really happened. Lyria looked down at herself. When I looked to see what she was looking at, I saw her belly was swollen.

"You're...pregnant?"

Lyria smiled, ignoring the thugs. "Yes, Conner."

I said, "I need to get you out of here."

I picked Lyria up and started running. We got to the hospital, but when I looked at Lyria, I was carrying Vicky.

"Hurry, Conner," she said.

We were in the delivery room surrounded by doctors and nurses. I was holding Vicky's hand. She screamed in pain. The doctor stood up from behind the sheet covering her outstretched, elevated legs, and he howled. The nurses all screamed—one fainted, one bolted from the room. I couldn't handle anymore, and I dropped to the ground, wishing for unconsciousness.

Whatever it was that Vicky had birthed, it was moving behind the sheet. The doctor tried to hold it, but somehow it flung him to the side. It moved out from behind the sheet, and I could see that it was Jason. Not as a newborn or a baby, but four-year-old Jason. He was naked and covered with blood. He smiled at me with fangs, and blood dripped off his elongated teeth. He walked toward me. I tried to yell for help, but nothing came out.

He reached over and grabbed my arm. Smiling his bloody smile, he said, "Uncle Conner."

"Uncle Conner, wake up."

I was in my room and shook my head, trying to clear the cobwebs. My heart was still pounding from the dream. I realized that Jason was holding my arm, shaking me awake.

I gasped and pulled away. "Jason? Jason, what are you doing here?"

It was dark in my room, but Jason looked just like he did the last time we played football in my parents' yard. He was wearing jeans, sneakers, and one of his favorite T-shirts with a T-Rex on the front.

"I need your help," he said.

I had pulled myself to the far side of the bed, holding my covers up in front of me. Jason must have sensed my fear and stood stationary.

"Please, Uncle Conner."

I knew he had changed, but he was still my nephew. My Jason. And I hadn't seen him since....

"Jason. Jason, you're really here."

I found myself tossing the covers aside, moving back over, and sitting on the side of my bed. Jason came forward into my embrace. We held each other for a long time. I realized Jason was crying. I pulled back, held his shoulders, and looked at him. Tears streamed down his little boy face. He shuddered a breath, and I saw his fangs, but I wasn't scared anymore. Now I felt my own tears.

"Jason, are you okay?"

"I'm okay, Uncle Conner. But I need your help. Can we go

downstairs? Your friend is sleeping on the couch. Maybe he can help too."

"Friend? Oh, Don. Don Halberton. He's a policeman."

"A policeman?" Jason's face lit up. He thought for a second, and the glow diminished. "I don't know how much help he can be, but we have to do something. Soon."

"Do something? Jason, what…what do we have to do?"

"We have to find Angelika. She's really mad. And I think she's going to hurt a lot of people."

I sat staring at my nephew, too stunned to speak.

"Soon!" he said again.

***

I was still fully dressed, so the two of us went charging down the stairs. Don was completely motionless on the couch, and for a horrible second, I wondered whether Jason had….

No, of course not. But from somewhere deep in the back of my mind, a memory bolted forward, and I couldn't tell you the source if my life depended on it. I seemed to recall that people with mental illness slept very soundly. It was probably a generality, but I couldn't help but think about Don Halberton.

In my previous dealings with him, he had always seemed so put-together, even when he was threatening to deprive me of my freedom. But the last couple of times I had seen him, including the better part of that day when we had suddenly become a vampire-slaying duo, Don's appearance was uncharacteristically unkempt—wrinkly clothes, hair askew, unshaven. Clearly, his encounter with Lyria the previous year, and currently chasing down child vampires, had taken a toll. I was sure that merely finding out that there really were vampires was enough to make just about anybody question their own sanity. It certainly had for me.

We approached him slowly. His head was back, supported by a throw pillow, and his breathing was deep. I had a sense that Don hadn't slept very much in the past few days, and now his body was nearly comatose, making up for the lack of rest.

"Wow, he's really sleeping," said Jason.

"Yeah, we better be careful, waking him up." I reached over

and gently jostled his arm. "Don."

He didn't even stir. His breathing was the only sign that he hadn't gone to that big precinct in the sky.

I tried again, a little more firmly. "Don."

He shook his head, opened his eyes, and looked at us. It took a few seconds to get his bearings. His eyes were more focused. He looked at me, scanned my living room, then glanced down at Jason.

"Hello, Mr. Policeman," said the boy, sounding every bit his age.

Don stared. Suddenly he wailed, rolled onto the floor, pulled his gun out of his holster, and sprang into a firing pose on one knee, both hands holding the pistol aimed at my nephew.

All I could think to do was hit the floor. "Don, no...wait!" I yelled.

Jason hadn't moved. He looked at Halberton with what I could only discern was mild curiosity.

"Don't move. STAY WHERE YOU ARE."

"Okay, Mr. Policeman. I won't move. Your name is Don? Hi Don. I'm not going to hurt you. I promise. I came here because I need your help. You and Uncle Conner."

I was still trying to become one with my living room area rug. At the mention of my name, Halberton glanced over at me as if just realizing I was there.

My body stayed stationary in the prone position. I said, "Don, put the gun down, okay? It wouldn't do any good anyway. Jason is here to help. Just listen. Listen to what he has to say."

Halberton had a wild, wide-eyed look about him as his head swiveled between me and my nephew.

"Please, Don," said Jason. "We don't have much time."

The detective kept his gun steady.

"Don, if Jason wanted to hurt us, he could have done it already." I slowly started to stand, no small feat considering the shakiness in my legs. "Please, just listen to him."

He didn't lower his weapon, but the cobwebs must have been clearing in his head. "What is it? What do you want?"

"It's Angelika," said Jason.

I could hear Don's intake of breath at the mention of her name. "Wh-what about... her?"

"She's going to kill some people. Tonight. And I know where she's going."

***

After Jason told us what Angelika was planning, we all raced out to Halberton's car, nary a thought among us as to how exactly we were planning to stop her. Jason and I dove into the back seat and pushed enough garbage aside to get situated. As soon as Don's butt hit vinyl, he started the car up and floored it, screeching away from the curb at top speed.

"Wow, he goes fast," said Jason, as we struggled to get seat-belted in. At that point, I wasn't sure whether the greater threat to our well-being was Angelika or Don's driving.

"Tell me again what she said," Don barked from the front seat.

He took a turn at warp speed, and when we recovered from the inertia, Jason said, "She was going back after that nice family with the twin girls. She was mad about being tracked and having to move our sleeping spot. She wanted to teach you a lesson. You and Mother."

I knew he meant Lyria.

"What were you supposed to do?" I asked.

"She wanted me to...uh...how did she put it? Oh yeah, 'create a distraction' someplace else. She thought you would be looking for her again tonight."

I thought back to Don ordering poor Parker Gebelein to stay up all night monitoring the airwaves for some kind of unusual report that might lead us to Angelika.

"Don, is this the family you were telling me about last night? In West Roxbury?"

"The Springers, yes. I know where they live."

I looked at Jason. "Lyria said you backed out when Angelika wanted to harm that family."

"Yes, the mom, she...reminded me of Mommy. I...didn't want to hurt them."

I reached over and patted his arm. He smiled at me. Fangs

and all, he was still my nephew — still just a little boy.

"Don, what...what if we're too late? I mean...it's already past 2 a.m."

Halberton didn't answer but instead sped up even more. We pulled into an upscale neighborhood with tree-lined streets and expensive homes. Don slowed, checking house numbers. He saw the one we were looking for and pulled into the driveway.

We all sat still — I had no idea what we were supposed to do. Halberton, looking even more frazzled than before, shifted around in his seat and looked behind him at Jason.

"Jason," he said with a calmness that I somehow found unnerving. "If she's here — if Angelika is here — can you...stop her?"

Jason thought for a moment. "I can try. But she's much stronger than I am."

"We'll all have to do whatever it takes to save this family," said Don. He was looking at me, making my blood run cold. Didn't he know I couldn't fight my way out of a paper bag? "Let's go," he said, pulling out his gun, which was probably about as useless as my fighting ability.

We got out of the car. The front of the huge, two-story house was dark. "These people haven't heard about security lighting?" I whispered.

"Hush," hissed Don. "She may have knocked the lights out."

We crept forward toward the front door, Don in the lead, then me, crouching down, and Jason, who was walking upright and looked like by far the calmest of the trio.

Don reached the entrance. He had his pistol in his right hand, his left on the ornate brass doorknob. He glanced around at us. "Ready?"

I could barely breathe, so I didn't say anything.

"Mother?" said Jason, and I looked around at him.

When we turned back around, Lyria was standing to the side of the door, holding Don's wrist, preventing him from trying to turn the knob.

"Wait, Detective, you don't have to do that," she said.

Don gasped and jumped back, stumbled, and fell backward.

I stood agape. Lyria was wearing a stunning print dress. But when she looked at me, I could tell something was different. Something was wrong.

"Lyria? How did you know? H-how did you get here?"

She walked over to me. "Conner, there's no time to explain. This is a ruse. Angelika isn't here. It's all a distraction. We have to get to your parents' house. Right away. It will be light soon, and she'll have to...she'll have to...."

Before Lyria could finish what she wanted to tell me, she collapsed to the ground at my feet.

CHAPTER THIRTY-ONE

"Get in the front seat, Uncle Conner."

I did as I was told, and once again, before even getting the door closed, Don Halberton floored the gas pedal, headed for my parents' house. Jason and Lyria were in the back seat. This time I was glad for the reckless speed.

My god. Angelika at my parents' house. With Caden and Lisa. And Carly. This was how she was going to exact revenge for us tracking her last night by hitting us — by hitting *me* where it hurt the most.

My family.

I heard myself uttering, "Hurry, Don. My god, please hurry."

He didn't acknowledge me in any way, his singular focus on hurtling to our destination without getting us killed.

I didn't know what we were going to do once we got there or what we would find. But I knew we had to get there. Nothing else mattered.

I glanced toward the back. Jason was sitting with Lyria's head in his lap. Her eyes were glassy. I had never seen her so vulnerable before. So weak.

Jason bit into his wrist, and a spurt of blood splashed onto his face. I watched, mesmerized, as he put the wrist to Lyria's mouth.

"Drink, Mother," he said.

She turned her head away. "No." Her voice was so weak I could barely hear it.

"It's okay, Mother, drink." Jason held her head in place with his other hand. "You need it. I…have extra."

Finally, she relented, taking Jason's wrist in her mouth with a chugging, slurping sound. After what seemed like an eternity but was actually only a few seconds, she pulled back.

"That's enough," she said, her voice sounding stronger. "Jason, you'll need your strength too."

She sat up. I looked back at my nephew. The wound on his wrist had already healed.

"Lyria, how…what…?" I stammered.

"Conner." She looked at me with affection. I hadn't realized how long it had been since we were together. "Angelika told Jason she was going back after this family as a ruse, a distraction. She had warned me previously that if I…interfered with her, she would take revenge on you and *your* family. I watched her and you as best I could. When I saw you head down here, I raced after you. I understood what was happening."

"But what…what happened to you? Why are you so weak?"

"I'll explain it all, in time. We're almost there."

I turned back around just as Don was skidding to a halt in front of my parents' house. The façade of the huge structure was completely dark. Unlike the Springers, my folks had a massive lighting system that would probably be visible from outer space. It was all set on a timer, so the fact that the lights were not on was our first sign of trouble. I was conscious of the sun coming up early this time of year. We were running out of time.

Don and I jettisoned ourselves from the car and ran for the front door. I looked back. Jason was holding onto Lyria as they made their way forward. The horrible thought came rushing through my head that, in their weakened state, the two of them were no match for Angelika.

But none of that mattered. We reached the front door.

We were headed in.

***

We were greeted by a thick darkness that I wouldn't have thought possible in this house. My parents spent more on interior lighting than some small countries generated in GDP. I didn't hear anything, which creeped me out even more. Despite being equally sensory-deprived, Halberton moved forward, crouched, holding his gun out in front of him. I turned and could vaguely make out Lyria and Jason.

Lyria suddenly stood upright. "Stop, Conner," she said.

My feet stopped moving, and my heart almost stopped beating all at about the same time. I wanted to ask Lyria a couple of hundred questions, but my stream of thought was disrupted by a little girl's voice.

"Ooh, look who's here. Hee hee. Catch."

Something came crashing forward. I was knocked flat onto my back. Halberton was hit too, and let out an "oomph" sound. At first, I had no idea what had hit me, then I realized with horror that it was a body.

Before I could make sense of any of this, I heard Angelika again, this time right next to me. My eyes had adjusted enough to see her tiny form hovering above Don Halberton.

"Here, let me take care of that before someone gets hurt. Hee hee."

She grabbed Don's pistol. He resisted giving it up, but it was no use. The child effortlessly wrenched his wrist backwards in an unnatural position, causing him to howl in pain and release his grip.

"I can see we're going to be difficult," she said. "What's the saying about there being one in every party?"

With that, she grabbed Don by the hair and slammed his head into the floor. I could see well enough to realize that his body went slack.

Angelika looked at Lyria and Jason in the doorway. "Mother. Brother. I didn't expect to see you tonight. I guess you figured out my little game, huh? I need to work on that. I was going to leave this as a lesson for you. But, perhaps it is for the best. Maybe actually seeing it take place will be more effective. Tee hee."

"Angelika, listen—" said Lyria.

The little girl bared her fangs. "You be quiet, Mother. I warned you about this. I warned you not to interfere."

"Sister, please," cried Jason. "I'll help you again, but...not here. Please not here."

"I'm disappointed in you the most, little brother. We made a good team. But it turns out you are weak. Like her. Tell me, will you be satisfied feeding off drunks in an alley? And perverts holding other mortals hostage? We could have ruled this city, you and I. Now, I'll have to do it myself. Or...perhaps find a substitute. Hee hee. You know, somebody I can trust. Move out of the doorway."

Angelika tossed both Lyria and Jason aside like they were rag dolls. The two skidded on the floor into a wall on the far side of the vestibule. The child slammed the door shut.

I had been so rapt watching the scene that I forgot about the body still on top of me. All I could tell was that it was a female.

"Come on in the living room, Conner," said Angelika. "It will be like a family reunion. You can bring your friend. Guests are allowed."

When I didn't move, Angelika walked over.

"I can see I'll have to do everything myself," she said.

She grabbed me by the hair with one hand and took the limp body around the neck, and dragged us into the pitch-black living room. I was conscious of making some gurgling sounds of resistance, but it did no good.

The child released us.

"Okay, Mik. Hit the light."

A lamp next to the sofa in the middle of the room came on with a click. What I saw was the stuff of nightmares. I almost wished the light hadn't come on.

Mikolaj Babka was expressionless, standing next to the lamp. Darren Dobson stood in the middle of the room, holding a pistol. Caden and Carly were on the sofa, their arms wrapped around each other. They looked at me with bewilderment, as if they were waiting for an explanation. Lisa stood by herself next to the couch. Somehow, she looked completely calm.

I looked down at the body next to me and gasped out loud. "Vicky...!"

Angelika laughed. She sounded like a little girl who had just put a frog down her brother's shirt. "A little something extra for you, Conner. Oh, don't act so surprised. I could see you had feelings for her when we first met. You remember? Our little 'get to know you' session?"

My eyes involuntarily went to Lyria. She showed no emotion. Jason was up trying to come forward, trying to intervene, but Lyria was holding him around the waist, restraining him.

"Conner...what?" uttered Carly from the couch.

"NO TALKING." Angelika's little-girl voice was replaced with a growl. My sister buried her head in my brother's side. Caden was alert but somehow seemed like his senses were dulled. As if he thought this whole scene was a dream, and when it got too ugly, he would simply wake up.

"That's better," said Angelika. Her little girl voice was back. "Now, I know you all think I'm a monster. Hee hee. I guess you're right, but actually, none of this is my fault. You see, I warned Mother that if she interfered with me, Conner and his family would pay. I thought that would be enough, but what can I say? I'm young. Hee hee. And still learning."

"Sister, please," yelled Jason. Lyria continued to hold him.

"You saw it, little brother. Mother tracked us down anyway. It was no fun having to move in the middle of the night, was it? I'm sure somebody came after us during the day. Was it you, Conner? And maybe your friend over there?"

Don was completely still.

I didn't answer.

"What did you think they were going to do, brother? Crawl into our bed and sleep with us? That would have been interesting. Hee hee. No, they meant to do away with us. Pull us out into the sun. Don't you see? Your own dear uncle wanted to kill you. And me. Well, I don't know about you, but I don't want to live like that. Always worrying, always watching. I like it here. And I'm going to stay here. Without interference from any of you."

Vicky emitted a low moan, startling me. I had thought she was....

Angelika laughed. "No, your friend is still with us, Conner. I was going to leave everyone here for you. But things have changed, haven't they? Maybe this is better. Now you get to watch."

The child stopped and put her finger up to her chin in a thinking pose.

"I think I'll let you live, Conner. Let you remember what you're going to see. Maybe that way, you can use your influence to keep Mother from interfering again. Does that sound like a plan, boys?"

Mikolaj and Dobson stood silently.

"They're not much on conversation, but they come in handy. Hee hee. Okay, now, where should we start? How about Miss Carly?"

***

I heard myself say, "Angelika, wait. We…won't track you anymore. We'll leave you alone. I promise."

"Oh now, Conner. If you did it once, you'd do it again. I know that much. And look at it this way — I'll still have your Mom and Dad to use as leverage." She nodded, and Darren Dobson roughly ripped Carly away from Caden and brought her to the monster child. Carly resisted, her eyes wide, but her fright was so total, she didn't make a sound.

"No," said Caden, his voice weak.

"Sister, no," yelled Jason.

Lisa stood completely still next to the couch.

Angelika grabbed Carly by the hair and shoulder, immobilizing her. My sister looked up at the child and fainted, going slack in her arms.

The child laughed. "Maybe that's for the best." She lowered herself toward my sister's neck.

"NO. DON'T."

Caden shoved past Dobson and rushed at Angelika. But the child was too quick. She dropped Carly to the floor, sidestepped his rush, and roughly pinned him to the floor.

"Ah, we have a volunteer," she said. "I love when that happens. But now I have to make an example of you. Hmmm. I think your head would look very nice up on the mantle, don't you?"

Caden said nothing.

"It's not personal, mind you. It's just that—well, my kind will do *anything* to protect our territory. Perhaps you all will understand that after tonight."

Angelika pulled my brother's head up and raised her hand, making her intention clear. I groaned and tried to look away, but I wasn't able to. I couldn't breathe, waiting for her to strike.

"NOOO!" yelled Jason. His voice seemed far off.

Her arm was suspended in the air. Then I realized she was trying to bring it down on Caden's neck, but she couldn't. She tried again, but her arm wouldn't move. A look of confusion overcame her youthful face. She looked up. I looked at her arm and realized she couldn't move because her arm was being held in place.

Lisa was holding Angelika's arm, looking down on the child vampire with a combination of fury and disdain.

"Wh-what...?" Angelika stammered.

How could this be happening? How could Lisa possibly...?

"What *you* have to understand," said my sister-in-law. She grimaced, and I saw her fangs. I felt like my heart had stopped in my chest.

"Is that a wife...and a mother...." She glanced over at Jason. "Will do *anything* to protect her family."

Lisa growled and picked Angelika up by the throat. The shock and terror on the child's face was complete. She tried to speak. "Wait. How...? You can't...."

"Oh, I can," said Lisa, now holding the girl up off the floor. "And your other mistake is that you lost track of time."

The best Angelika could muster was a gurgling sound. She reached up and gouged Lisa's face, but it had no effect, and the wounds healed instantly.

Lisa was a blur rushing over to the bay window, the child struggling to no avail in her grip.

"Mommy, no. DON'T."

Lisa stopped and turned toward her son. "It's okay, baby. I love you more than life itself. Lyria, please...take him."

Lyria held the boy with all her strength and ran toward the door to the basement, Jason screaming in anguish. An instant before they disappeared, my nephew emitted an "NOOO" that belied his age and size. The sound seemed to shake the foundation of the house.

"Now for you, you little bitch," said Lisa. She held Angelika in both hands and leapt forward, smashing through the window and into the daylight.

I heard two blood-curdling screams and saw a blinding flash of light outside.

And then, there was silence.

***

I had watched the scene unfold as if I were hovering above my own body as if I were watching it all on film. Except in the back of my mind, I knew it was real.

I was still on the floor, holding Vicky. Carly was unconscious a few feet away. I hadn't moved until I sensed motion. I looked over as Caden stood up from where Angelika had held him. He suddenly slumped to the floor in a heap, his eyes glazed. He almost looked catatonic, his mouth hanging open.

Mikolaj and Darren Dobson were still the whole time, standing in place like robots awaiting their next command. Dobson had his pistol pointed at the couch even though there was nobody sitting there. But the motion of Caden dropping seemed to bring him out of his trance. He looked around the room as if wondering how he had gotten there. He turned, and much to my dismay, his gaze fell on me. He blinked a few times, but then his eyes became clear, and his focus complete.

He looked down and realized he still had the gun in his hand. His eyes honed back on me. Then his face became contorted with a look of pure hatred, his skin flushing beyond red to an almost purple hue that I didn't think was possible. He grit his teeth in a grin that would have done a scary Halloween pumpkin proud. The pistol came up slowly, and I gasped as it was pointed directly at my head.

I struggled to make any sound, but I managed to emit something that sounded like, "Mr. Dobson, no...please...it's... it's over...."

Dobson tensed, and I knew what was coming. My last act,

believe it or not, was one of bravery as I shoved Vicky to the side, out of harm's way. I scrunched my eyes shut. There was nothing else to do but wait for the impact. *What does it feel like to get shot?* I knew I was about to find out.

The shot was deafening, and I was conscious of emitting a guttural sound. I took a breath and tried to figure out where I'd been hit. It couldn't be in the head, or I wouldn't have been able to think, right? My hands roamed over my body, searching for the wound. I opened my eyes.

Dobson was still standing in front of me, but he had dropped the gun. He looked down in shock as a red bloom spread over his chest. He gazed at me as if accusing me, and he tried to say something. We'd never know what it was, however. Darren Dobson, my former boss and tormentor, dropped to the floor and stopped moving, his lifeless eyes still honed in on yours truly.

I looked over and saw a black man with graying hair and a badly wrinkled tan suit standing in the doorway, his pistol held out in front of him in both hands.

"I'm Detective Chick Harris of the Massachusetts State Police," he said. "Everybody just stay where you are until we figure out exactly what is going on here."

EPILOGUE

The newspaper headline read, "Satanic Cult Responsible for Local Deaths."

My heart was pounding as I read the story a few days later. Don Halberton recovered from his head injury, and he and Detective Harris somehow managed to spin the story into a cult run by Mikolaj Babka and the late Darren Dobson. The paper said they were to blame for the brutal murders of three teenagers from Roslindale, a Children's Hospital nurse, and my sister-in-law, Lisa David. Lisa was killed during a home invasion intended to exact revenge on a former corporate underling of Dobson, who he saw as being responsible for him losing his job.

That would be me.

I didn't think the police were getting any kind of rebuttal from Mr. Babka. When he was led out of my parents' house, he was still in a trance-like state, not saying a word. Apparently, when Angelika made him and Dobson into mindless robots at her disposal, she did a number on their minds that were irreversible.

I had my doubts about whether this storyline would hold water over time, and I had no idea how much, if any, of the real story Don had conveyed to Detective Chick Harris, who struck me as an extremely sharp guy. But I guess the bottom line was that they couldn't very well go public with a child vampire being responsible for the whole shebang. Not and still be allowed to carry a loaded firearm out among the general populace.

Anyway, Lyria and Jason spent the day in the coffin Lisa

had set up down in the basement, and I hadn't seen hide nor hair of them since. I thought they might be waiting until the heat died down but also worried that that was yet another television-generated concept I had cooked up in my brain.

When they heard what had happened, Mom and Dad rushed back home from Florida. They didn't ask a lot of questions. Their main goal was to provide a needed dose of TLC to Carly, and especially Caden.

My sister had the good sense to lose consciousness before the real craziness took place. She was totally on board with the home invasion story.

Caden, however, remained in a catatonic state after the incident. But, I knew he would be in good hands with Mom back in town.

***

I thought back to the morning, Lisa had come to visit me. When I told her what was going on, she had screamed. And when she told me what she wanted to do about it, I had howled. I had actually worried about disturbing my neighbors. That seemed laughable now, considering what had just happened.

Lisa knew that Lyria had converted Jason. She hadn't meant to, of course. She only intended to give him some of her blood to see if it would help with the leukemia. Once she started, though, she couldn't stop. Lyria had warned me this might happen. The same thing happened when Angelika was created. But I kept badgering her. Lisa also knew, however, that Jason likely wouldn't have made it through the night otherwise.

What Lisa didn't know at the time was that Jason had taken up with Angelika. Lyria had explained to me that the cursed blood had a different effect on different people, especially children. Angelika was evil to the core, interested in feeding and gaining power with no remnant of human remorse. When I told Lisa that her son was hanging out with this monster, she let out a scream that to this day was still ringing in my ears. I did my best to comfort her, but after she overcame the initial shock, she sat still on my couch, apparently lost in thought.

After what seemed like an eternity, I said, "Lisa? Um...I'm

sorry, but I have to be getting to work—"

"I know what to do," she interrupted. She shifted on the sofa and looked deeply into my eyes. "I want Lyria to change me as well."

Now I was the one who was shocked. I looked to see if she was serious. There was no doubt.

"NOOO!" I howled. You don't know what you're saying...."

***

Despite my histrionics, Lisa forced me to promise I would ask. At first, Lyria wouldn't even consider it.

"She doesn't know what she's asking, Conner." She was her usual calm self.

"I know, that's what I said."

It became a non-issue—for a while.

But when Angelika's intentions became clear, and the number of potential deaths of innocent people climbed, she relented.

It had happened that night, just before Lyria came out to warn us that Angelika was going to my parents' house. She was in the weakest state I had ever seen. And it was because she had given Lisa every ounce of strength she could without killing herself.

Lyria knew she was no match for the child. As she had explained to me, the cursed blood could be more powerful in children because they start with fewer impurities than an adult. The only chance she had of stopping her was to make Lisa strong.

And count on the element of surprise.

***

To say that Darren Dobson being part of a satanic cult and going after a former associate caused a stir in the BHA office would be a vast understatement.

The members of the financial analysis group came into my office individually—okay, the twins came in together—to express relief that I was okay and condolences about my sister-in-law. They all pried for more details of the incident in their own ways but gave up when they could tell none were forthcoming.

Before Boof left after his visit, though, he sidled up to me sitting at my desk. "I still think it was DSB," he muttered under his breath.

"What?"

"You know—deadly sperm backup. I think that was what sent Dobson over the edge."

I snorted. "You know, Boof, I really don't think he became a member of a satanic cult because he wasn't getting any."

"Hey, think what you want. But I've seen it make guys do crazier things in my time."

With that pearl of wisdom, he went back to his cube, leaving me thankful that at least he didn't list off examples of other nutzo behavior caused by DSB.

When Vicky came in, she showed no signs of remembering anything about being attacked by Angelika. Unlike the other people, though, she wasn't satisfied with mere commiseration from the guest chair in front of my desk.

"Oh, Conner, my god, I'm so sorry for what happened with your family. I hope you're okay."

She looked nothing short of sensational, wearing a skirted business suit with her dark blonde hair pinned in a ponytail. She passed up the guest chair and the desk and walked over right beside my chair.

Even though I'm still something of a dunce when it comes to women, I knew what to do. I stood, and we embraced. I wasn't really sure how long to hold the hug and was thankful when she shifted backward slightly. Then she sat in my guest chair.

"How are your brother and sister?" Tears were forming in her eyes.

"They're holding up. Mom and Dad are back from Florida, so they'll take good care of them."

With that, Vicky reached over and took my hand. "Well, I don't want to take up too much time, but I want you to know…."

She hesitated.

"Yes," I said. "Thanks, Vick. I appreciate it."

She smiled, let go of my hand slowly, and left.

***

The furor had died down some a couple of days later when I got an email that sent shivers down my spine. Chud Johnson had called a meeting for the entire financial analysis group that afternoon in a nearby conference room.

That meeting notice caused me near blackout-level fear for a couple of reasons. One was that Chud was as far above us on the org chart as we were above an amoeba on the evolutionary scale. Another was that I realized I had unwillingly committed a Cardinal sin with my involvement in the whole Darren Dobson affair. Something nobody is supposed to do, especially not a lowly financial analyst.

I had caused the BHA name to be associated with two dreaded words in the investment banking industry. And those words were Bad Publicity.

My initial feeling was the firm wouldn't want to make matters worse by shit-canning the son of a company founder who, after all, was the victim of a violent crime. And after I had survived the first few days, I thought there was truly some merit to that theory.

Then that email notice came about. I had a horrible notion that not only was I going to get axed, but Chud was going to make the execution public. As if to convey the notion to my coworkers, "See what happens when you taint the BHA name?"

The sense of doom was palpable among the team. We skipped lunch that day—I don't think anyone had much of an appetite. Boof said Chud scheduling a meeting with us was like, "A shark calling a meeting with a harp seal."

Time crawled as the meeting time approached. I was so sure I was going to get fired. I actually spend some time organizing my personal belongings so I could make a quick and easy escape afterward.

Nobody was speaking as we got seated in the conference room. A few minutes after the scheduled start of the meeting, Chud Johnson entered the room. His massive physique and bald head give him a natural presence, but today he was even more intimidating. He was wearing an expensive looking black suit, and I couldn't help but think he looked like he was attending a funeral.

Chud remained standing and didn't waste time with any niceties. "I called you here today to make an important announcement."

I felt the vibrations from his booming voice deep in my chest, and I realized I had stopped breathing.

"We're appointing a new director to be in charge of the financial analysis group."

That was it? The meeting was to bring in a new boss? Relief flooded through my body as I realized I might not be getting my walking papers after all.

Chud continued. "I'm proud to point out that this promotion is coming from within."

From within? Someone from the existing analysis group was getting the job? I was pretty sure nobody in the room was breathing at that point.

"The new director is an individual who has proven himself with top quality work and, more importantly, an outstanding work ethic. Please join me in congratulating the head of the financial analysis group, Mister Fernando Rojas. Fernando, we're counting on you to do a great job."

With that bombshell dropped, Chud left.

***

After a moment of stunned silence, the team erupted around Razor—congratulatory handshakes, pats on the back, hugs galore. He seemed to soak it all in, all the while maintaining the same low-key mien we had all come to know.

A couple of thoughts struck me as the celebration continued. One was happiness for Razor. He definitely deserved the promotion. He was smart, hard working, and a quiet leader in his own way. The other was about that day when Chud had caught us all screwing around. Razor was the only one still plugging away at his desk. I wondered how much of an impact that had on Chud's decision. Certainly couldn't have hurt.

"Geez. What do I call you now? Mr. Razor?" asked Boof.

Razor laughed slightly, towering over Boof. Then his face got serious. "I think Mr. Rojas would be better," he said.

Boof adopted what I would call a classic "deer in the headlights" look, and for once in his life, was completely speechless. I had to keep myself from laughing out loud.

Razor smiled. "Hey, ease up, man. I'm just busting on you."

Everybody laughed. But when Razor started talking again, we all stopped to listen.

"There *are* going to be some changes around here, though. I'll go through them with you individually and as a group over the next few days. Now let's all get back to work."

***

I got home a little later than normal that evening. Seemed like nobody wanted to leave before the new boss, so we all walked out together and, after yet another round of congratulatory merriment around Razor, everybody went their own way.

Summer was coming to a close, and it was getting dark earlier, but the temp was still warm. It made for a peaceful but somewhat melancholy walk home. I felt happiness for Razor, and if being honest, that I still had a job. But I was also sad. Sad for Lisa. Sad for Jason. And Caden. I wondered how and *if* my family would manage to heal these gaping wounds.

All these thoughts were swirling through my head as I sank down on the couch. I dozed off, my mind tired out from working overtime. I had no idea how long I had been out, but when I opened my eyes, Lyria was standing in front of me.

"Hey," I said, rubbing my eyes.

"Hey yourself," she said. I knew immediately that something was different. She looked amazing, as always, wearing a flowered print dress. But where she normally would have sat next to me and stroked my face to wake me, she stood, showing no emotion.

"Is…everything okay? Where's Jason?"

"I'm leaving, Conner."

"Leaving? Wait. What do you mean? Can you sit down?"

She hesitated but sat next to me on the sofa, leaving some space between us. I thought I knew what was going on. It probably had to do with what Angelika had said about Vicky.

"Lyria, I'm sorry about what Angelika said…about Vicky. She was just playing mind games with us. Can't you see that?"

She gave me a dazzling smile. "My sweet Conner. Actually, I was happy about what Angelika said."

"Happy?"

"Yes. I think you need to find someone...like Vicky, or someone else. You deserve a chance to live your life. A normal life. Get married, have children. I think you'd make a great father."

"Lyria—"

"I've caused enough damage, Conner. To you. To your family. I wish I could take it all back—make it all better—but unfortunately, I can't."

"But, you didn't cause—"

"Oh, yes. My being with you brought about almost everything bad that has happened. I understand that. And I hope you can understand how sorry I am. I truly never intended for it to turn out this way."

"So you're just...leaving."

"Yes, and Jason is going with me."

"But where will you go?"

"I don't know. Somewhere else. Conner, I have to do this."

"You have to?"

"Yes. I think it's best for you. Besides, I gave my word."

"Gave your word? But...who?"

"When I first...met with Don Halberton and asked for his help in locating and dealing with Angelika, he said he would help, but on one condition. And that condition was that when it was over, I would leave his city, as he called it."

"And you agreed to that?"

"Yes. I was planning on leaving anyway."

"Lyria, I have so much I want to say."

"Come outside with me, Conner."

She took my hand, stood, and we walked out the front door. A warm breeze was blowing as we stood on my walk. Lyria turned, and we kissed, holding each other tight. To any passersby, we probably looked like a normal couple enjoying the last vestiges of summer.

She pulled back, still holding my hands. "I will never forget you, my sweet Conner. Goodbye."

I felt a change in the air pressure around me, almost like a vacuum pulling me forward. Then it stopped. Everything was back to normal.

And Lyria was gone.

***

The man was prone, lying motionless, staring sightlessly at the ceiling in the room where he had grown up. The darkness and silence enveloped him. It was his reality now.

The child emerged as if materializing from the inky black. He walked over and jumped up on the bed, looked down at the man. The man didn't move, didn't look back.

The child lowered his head. As he felt the contact with his skin, the man's body spasmed.

"It's all right, Daddy. I'm here to help you," said the child.

He leaned back down. The man emitted a gasping sound as they were joined. After the boy rubbed the man's neck with his own blood, and the wounds were healed. The man looked. Now he could see.

"Jason," he said. "Jason, my god."

They embraced for what seemed like an eternity. Finally, the man pulled back, still holding his son by his shoulders, tears streaming down his face.

"I understand," said the man.

ACKNOWLEDGEMENTS

I would like to thank the great people at World Castle Publishing, especially Karen Fuller and Maxine Bringenberg, for publishing this book, as well as My Girlfriend the Vampire. I am also eternally indebted to Donna Northam and Nancy Leibundgut for helping me get the manuscript in tiptop shape before I submitted it to my publisher.

Most of all, I need to thank you, the reader, for taking time out of your busy lives to take in my work. I truly hope that I have made your investment in time feel like a worthwhile experience. Please leave a review on Amazon and/or Goodreads, especially if you loved it!!

If you would like to correspond with me, please send an email to bob@bobnortham.com or leave a message on the contact form of my website – www.robertnortham.net.

Thanks again, happy reading!

Hey, it's Robert.

I hope you enjoyed reading **Lyria**, a follow up to **My Girlfriend the Vampire**. Interesting that as a novelist, one would think you have a very defined path on which to tell your story. But I often find that my characters are "telling" me where I should take them, and indeed even how the tale should end. I have a feeling those same personalities will be insisting that this storyline should continue.

Since 'My Girlfriend' was published, probably the question I've been asked most often is something along the lines of, "How did someone with your background come to tell stories about vampires?" Most inquisitors are aware that I spend over 30 years in corporate America, the last fifteen or so as VP of Finance for a Fortune 500 company.

Very good question, and I'd be lying if I said I never wondered that myself. Fact is, I always had the writing bug but never had time for it to come to fruition while working in the hectic big business environment. But I've also always had a keen interest in vampires lurking in the back of my brain. And when I retired, I was finally able to devote enough time to bring the two interests together.

Corporate finance and vampires – ah, a match made in heaven.

After spending almost eight years on the shoreline of New Hampshire, my wife Donna and I have relocated from whence we came – Texas. Our two adult children are getting along just fine and one of our two grandkids just hit double digits. Boy does time go by fast!

Thanks for reading and, if my characters have anything to say about it, we'll speak to you later!

Made in the USA
Columbia, SC
14 November 2020